A
SIMPLE HABANA
MELODY

(from when the world was good)

HARPERCOLLINSPUBLISHERS

A

SIMPLE HABANA

MELODY

(from when the world was good)

a novel

OSCAR HIJUELOS

The author wishes to thank the staff of HarperCollins, Harriet Wasserman and the late Robert Jones, for their generous support. Author also gratefully acknowledges masters Mario Bauza, Marco Rizo and Chico O'Farrill, whose lives and music helped to inspire this book.

HarperCollins books may be purchased for educational, business, or sales promotional use. For information, please write: Special Markets Department, HarperCollins Publishers Inc., 10 East 53rd Street, New York, NY 10022.

FIRST EDITION

Printed on acid-free paper

Library of Congress Cataloging-in-Publication Data is available upon request.

ISBN 0-06-017569-9

02 03 04 05 06 NMSG/RRD 10 9 8 7 6 5 4 3 2 1

I travel my way through galleries of sound
I flow among echoing presences. . . .

OCTAVIO PAZ

What is the use of all this joy and pain?
Sweet peace,
come, oh come to my heart. . . .

GOETHE

"I'm feeling inspired—quick, I need a drink!"

ISRAEL LEVIS,

Habana, 1928

Zarzuela

A form of Spanish opera, it has its origins in those entertain-ments of the sixteenth and seventeenth centuries when traveling musicians and actors would appear in the lodges and palaces of their noble lords in Spain (notably, el palacio de las Zarzuelas, near Madrid) to mount shows that loosely brought together whatever folk songs, gypsy melodies, bits of poetry and prose, dance and stage trickery that could be organized around the con-cept of a simple and capricious plot—usually one of love or of the devastation of war—a simple premise, often tragic, often comedic, for which in time original music would be written, when every entrance, every spoken word, worked toward the presentation of a melody. It had found its greatest heights in the late nineteenth century in Spain and had thrived in Cuba, with the presence of composers like Manuel Fernández Caballero, a Spaniard who had lived in Habana in the 1860s, his work inspiring a generation of zarzuela writers, like Israel Levis himself, who had become a mas-ter of that and many other forms of Cuban song.

HIS RETURN

TO THE

CITY OF MUSIC

Every sea wave was a clanging bell, the wind blowing from the west like a great and sonorous section of one hundred and seven violins; the sun at dusk was a glaring crimson cymbal, and the earth a kettle-drum. On the horizon, beyond the water's edge, a choir had gathered—a million choristers in long silk robes singing from the balconies of a palace, hidden in a maze of distantly humming sea mists, and in the waters below, beneath the currents, a hundred dance halls, and a hundred pianists, and rooms and rooms filled with instruments and musicians at the ready; an overture, as melodic as the picaresque orchestral ruminations of the Italian Alfredo Cassella filling the air, a voice like Caruso's calling down into the world, for the lights of day to be dimmed, a momentary silence prevailing, before the music would once again begin. . . .

IN THE SPRING OF 1947, when Israel Levis, composer of that most famous of rumbas *"Rosas Puras,"* returned to Habana, Cuba, from Europe aboard the SS *Fortuna,* those of his old friends who had not seen him in more than a decade were startled by his appearance. He was not yet sixty, but his hair had turned white and he had grown an unruly beard, so that he resembled a forlorn *guajiro* of the countryside, or the painter Matisse in his later years. Peering out at the world through the distortions of his thick-lensed wire-rim glasses, his eyes seemed lost, as if under water, and he was gaunt, perhaps too frail, his expression careworn, and, in any event, beyond easy recognition—a bit of a joke because during his heyday in the Habana of the 1920s and early 1930s he had been quite tall and broad-shouldered and so corpulent that while walking along the narrow sidewalks of Habana on his way to the music conservatory or to the Teátro Albisu he would have to stand aside, his back pressed flatly against a wall, or duck into a doorway, to allow the ladies with their *parasoles* and beaded purses to pass. So great was his girth and imposing physicality that with his trademark mustache he reminded his friends of the silent-film comedian Oliver Hardy, *"El Gordo"* (of *"El Gordo y el Flaco,"* "The Fat One and the Skinny One"), which had become one of his affectionately intended nicknames, an appellation that he, in his good nature and with his grand reputation, frequenting the bars and restaurants and concert halls of the city, had always taken in stride.

But by the time Israel Levis sailed past the Morro Castle and its lighthouse toward the rosified fortifications of La Punta and the glories of Habana proper, its blanched neoclassical facades as regal as Cartagena's, he had undergone certain transformations, for the events of his recent past had not been in keeping with the comforts and pleasures that his bourgois existence in Paris and fame as a composer and orchestra leader had accustomed him to. With his stooping shoulders and bent back, he seemed to have shrunk to half his original size, and he had lost so much weight during the war that he now floated through the voluminous expanses of his old linen suits. In fact, he, whose idea of a diet had been to forgo a second helping of crème brûlée or strawberry shortcake after a heavy five-course dinner in the Paris Ritz, was now as thin, if not thinner, than Stan Laurel, *El Gordo*'s dim sidekick, and might have been called *"El Flaco"* had the clock been turned back to his glory days, and had the events of his recent years not seemed so tragic, or confounding to his soul.

He had never been a handsome man, even in his best days; he did not have the Spanish good looks of his older brother, Fernando; rather, he considered that his charm had once arisen from his gallant manner, his affability and the attention he paid to others, staring directly into their eyes, save when he felt blinded— or outraged—by the most beautiful of women or the most strikingly handsome of men. In those moments a mixture of envy and admiration entered his heart, for these favored daughters and sons of life, moving through the world with effortless grandeur, embodied the very qualities of beauty that he had always aspired to through his music. Some women were like glorious sarabands, their dark and intense eyes mysterious as the deepest tones of an operatic aria; others more lustily disposed—the cheap women whom he had often cherished in his youth—were like jaunty rumbas, the wild gyrations of the Charleston. And men? Some were as graceful as the tango, or surefooted and capricious in their movement through life as the habanera—while he, lumbrous, awkward and ever careful, had always been the equivalent of a waltz or a simple box step. For many years he knew this to be the truth, as most of his grace lingered within, and he had spent so many hours, as a younger man, in private self-ostracism, wishing he could change this or that on his face or some part of his body, as if it were not enough to attract others through the power of his understated personality and a presence that most found enchanting; how foolish he had been, he now thought, to have wasted so much of his time on such petty concerns.

He left the port city of Vigo in northwestern Spain a week before, the ship stopping off for one morning in the Canary Islands to pick up other passengers. He brought along a single black trunk containing what personal effects he had managed to salvage from his last years in Paris during the German occupation: letters that he treasured—among them his correspondences with Stravinsky and Ravel; a dense cache of notes from his old composer friends in Habana, Ernesto Lecuona and Gonzalo Roig to name but two; and of course those correspondences with his own family in the cities of Habana and Santiago, letters whose nostalgic significance and worth increased as he entered into his period of troubles. It should be mentioned that among the treasures he managed to smuggle away with sympathetic friends, among them the kindly but inept Spanish attaché Señor Ramos, were the letters and postcards he'd received over the years from one Rita Valladares, of Habana, with whom he supposed he'd once been in love—or as close to love as so guarded a man could have been. He would sigh thinking about Valladares, the petite singer affectionately known to many as "La Chiquita"—my beloved—and over how so many years had passed without his ever once saying how deeply he felt about her. Even when he belatedly realized just how much he loved her—after his life in Paris had begun and he had moved on into a too-brief romance with a Parisian named Sarah Rubenstein—not a day passed when he failed to remember their times together. A single photograph of Rita, in a Saturn-shaped hat, the photo no larger than a prayer card, remained tucked in his wallet for those years, its surface cracked, edges tearing, Rita smiling, her eyes emanating life and love, a kind of music, like that of a fandango, entering his heart when he beheld that fading but beautiful image. Even though her letters, filled as they were with tender asides and happy memories of their collaborations in the musical theaters of Habana, often disappointed him with their sometimes hurried tone, and even though she married two other men during those years, he always kept them, taking pains to ensure their safekeeping in the event he survived the war.

And what were those letters often about but the occasional discomforts and exaltations of her life: "Hollywood is crazy, but certain stars like Gary Cooper are very nice"; or: "My last tour was barbaric—my promoters are working me like a slave, my dear boy; my throat is hoarse and I think, on top of it all, I've caught a cold. I'm tired of living out of a suitcase in a hotel.... I miss my children, and Habana. I can't wait until I get home.—Love, Chiquita...."

Why did he treasure those letters so?

In that trunk, aside from a suit and a second pair of shoes that a kindly *gallego* had given him in Madrid, and a pearl white Bible that had been inscribed by Pope Pius XII some years before during a visit to Rome, there were the fragments of several scores that he had been working on when his blissful but increasingly uneasy life was disrupted. For more than a decade he lived in a well-lighted suite on an upper floor of Le Grand Hôtel, and, in his parlor, with high arching windows that faced the sunny boulevards off Opera Square, he kept a Concert Grand Steinway on which he wrote his music. In late 1943, as he entered into his autumnal years, Levis—or *"El Maestro"*—had been in the midst of two projects that he believed would finally take him beyond the category of composer of "popular tunes" and light lyric reviews into a more serious realm. These were the scores of an opera that was to be based on Zola's novel *Germinal* and an impressionistic ballet about *Apollo and Daphne,* two-thirds completed before Levis had been taken away.

9

As he sailed aboard the SS *Fortuna,* Levis could care less about those compositions. They had become the artifacts from a recent past that he'd rather forget. *What were those works but the feeble attempts of a mediocre composer who might have been better off as a piano teacher, anyway?* And while he had been an affable and pleasant enough passenger, gentlemanly and beyond reproach, and obviously of great importance—for he occupied one of the finer cabins on that ship and dined at the captain's table—he was mainly thought of as the elderly Cuban who, indulging himself with a game of whist in the common room with some Spaniards, did not have much to say about his life.

Among his fellow passengers were a contingent of black Americans who had volunteered for the Loyalist cause and were now returning from imprisonment in Spain; an Englishman and his proper family; and many Spaniards, mainly *asturianos* and *gallegos,* heading to Cuba. Levis was cordial to them all. There were the ship's musicians who, knowing that the composer was in their midst, one night greeted his entrance into the dining room with a stirring, string-driven rendition of *"Rosas Puras,"* or "Pretty Roses," as it was known in English. Ever politely, with his large ears brimming red, he had stood before the small stage, motionless, his hands and the weight of his body resting on his eagle-headed cane, listening to their tribute respectfully but without any joy. Bowing and acknowledging their skills (as he had always loved musicians), he sat down to pick at his meal and drink his wine in silence.

His greatest pleasures were taken by the ship's railing, where he sipped some brandy from a flask and watched the horizon of the sea by day or the starry heavens by night, his thoughts—his oft repeated murmurings of *"¡Esta vida es un carajo!"* ("This life is worthless!")—interrupted only when the young Spaniard Antonio Solar, who'd accompanied him on this journey, appeared by his side with a blanket or to escort him to the dining room for dinner or to help the composer to his cabin.

Often he daydreamed, the horizon turning upside down; at once he was seeing his beloved Habana again, the city dense with its winding streets, great mansions, dust and smoke and horses and carriages and Packard automobiles, and with its alleys and courtyards in which the *rumberos* gathered past midnight; Habana as it had been, floating in the sky, he and his musical colleagues rushing to the Campoamor theater, circa 1922, where Pablo Casals or Ignacy Paderewski was appearing. Or he would see himself as a boy standing amid a crowd in the Parque Central listening to a municipal band playing a brassy rendition of Gioacchino Rossini's "William Tell Overture," the epauletted musicians dressed in military regalia, with their plumed and cord-wrapped shakos, brims gleaming in the sun. Or he saw Paris on a lovely spring day with its lilting willow trees and shaded parks; or he was mounting a stage in a grand theater—could have been in Mexico City or Buenos Aires or Paris itself—to lead an orchestra in a recital of his own compositions, the clamorous applause with which he had once been greeted coming back to him, even as so many foam-rimmed waves slapped against the ship's prow, a rush of water like so many voices calling out to him.

Now and then, Levis would tap the deck with his cane, three times, a signal for the diminutive, quite handsome young man Antonio to assist him. Usually he would send him off to refill his flask, otherwise Levis would offer Antonio the crook of his arm so that he could walk more steadily around the deck for his constitutional. Twice a day, after breakfast and after lunch, he made these rounds. Often he wore a white linen suit, a black-brimmed fedora and a black opera cape that was a remnant of his more prosperous and confident past. As he moved slowly along, cane in hand, with tremendous dignity, nodding to his fellow passengers, he seemed in the harshness of his expressions to be castigating his assistant, which was not the case. He had simply forgotten how to express himself without anger, his tone sharp and strident, even if he was only telling Antonio about some pain in his gut, his stomach destroyed by so many medicines (and from drink), or asking for a few aspirins, as he was prone to the most debilitating of headaches and a lethargy of the soul.

Levis did not speak about the war to his assistant; there was no need to because Solar already knew. Antonio had been an orderly in the Madrid hospital ward where Levis, at war's end, spent nearly a year recovering from hepatitis and diphtheria, among other maladies. There he might have perished, in a long and cavernous room of unfortunates, not so much from the illnesses of the body but from a flagging of the spirit and the will to live. Day in and day out for months he drifted through a world of dreams and sleep and memories, a scream or a cry of pain from someone in difficulty often awakening him in the middle of the night. Levis, startled, still clinging to the shreds of some lovely recollection of youth—a walk with his father and brother through a field of wild-flowers outside of Habana in pursuit of a fleck-wing butterfly, a night spent happily in a Habana or Paris brothel, the pleasures of crafting a song, the coolness of the interior of a church knave alongside his beloved mother, Doña Concepción, and younger sister, Anabella, as they knelt before the altar, crossing themselves, the security of God around them, faith strong in the air. . . .

The orderly was twenty-three years old when he had become Levis's attendant in that hospital. Nearly illiterate, good for changing bedsheets and emptying bedpans, Antonio, in his atten- tiveness and kindly nature, had seen the composer through that harsh time. As something of a musician himself, Antonio consid- ered such duties an honor. In the years of his early adolescence, before the Civil War of 1936–39, when he was a farm boy in Galicia with his own musical aspirations, Antonio played the clarinet in a band that had traveled throughout northwestern Spain, performing in village squares and weddings and *fiestas* a lively repertoire of popular dance tunes, among them Levis's own "*Rosas Puras,*" whose famous melody flew from his clarinet countless times, enrapturing even the most aged of priests, grand- mothers and widows.

That Levis had written such a tune, beloved by many, pro- voked in Antonio a steadfast devotion to the old man's care, the orderly regarding Levis with reverence and gratitude, whatever the cantankerousness of the composer's moods, during that stay. Even when Levis shouted "*¡Déjame tranquilo!*" and was a gruff piece of work, brooding, screaming from lousy nightmares, and preferring to rot away, Antonio found ways to lift his spirits, regaling him with sunny tales of life in Galicia before the Civil War and bringing Levis an occasional honey-drenched or cara- melized *dulce.* Antonio was so cheerful a soul that he once came into the ward with his clarinet and, finding an accordionist among the patients, presented a number of tunes to the infirm, the mad,

the hopeless, rendering, on that suffocating afternoon of a blister-
ing heat, an austere but lively version of *"Rosas Puras"* with which
he'd hoped to please the composer. (*"If you only knew how that song
had been both a blessing and a curse to me,"* Levis had thought, while
putting on a grateful face.)

All in all, Antonio Solar had been fascinated by the depths of
the composer's talents and religiosity (for in the ward, on the worst
of his days, he held on to a rosary, whispering prayers) even if, in
that period, Levis often seemed lost to the world.

For his part, Levis liked Antonio from the beginning. Aside
from his joyfulness at the proximity of youth, the purity of Solar's
eyes and the pockmarks on his face reminded Levis of his dear
late friend and lyricist Manny Cortez, with whom he had once
collaborated on many a song and zarzuela—his idealistic friend
who was like a beloved brother to him. Such were his feelings of
attachment and gratitude to the young man that Levis, upon his
repatriation, prevailed upon the Cuban government to pay for
Solar's ship fare to Habana. Lacking plans for the future and without children of his own, Levis hoped, in a small way, to help find
Antonio, who had no liking for the fascist government of Franco,
a new life in his own country—*"Cuba, mi maravillosa Cuba,"* he
often said. Once in Habana, if he so wanted, Antonio could go to
school, learn to read and write, find work and become a proper
caballero; or if he wanted to pursue the often hopeless destiny of a
performer, Levis, through his connections, could procure him a
job as a musician in the city.

"You may stay for as long as you like in my house in Habana,"
he told Antonio one day. "Believe me, you will be treated well." In

good humor, and remembering the pleasures of his youth, Levis added, "And you will find the Cuban women unbelievable."

He patted his young assistant on the shoulder and turned back to the railing, half-smiling, even if when looking out over the water he often trembled with the despair of a man fitful over the inescapable thoughts that haunted his mind. Considering his memories of the war such an affront to all that he believed about himself, the world and God, Levis sometimes thought about throwing himself over the side of that ship into the water. But he still loved life itself and, theologically speaking, he had become something of a coward.

Besides, he believed, simply, that he was returning to Cuba to die in what peace he could find.

Where Levis once lived in a florid and pleasant universe, filled with much wondrous music, especially so during his happiest years in Habana, he, with the unavoidable romanticism of an artist, now had to contend with those "contaminants"—to use a Nazi turn of phrase—that violated even the loveliest of his thoughts. How could he, Israel Levis, composer of so many lighthearted zarzuelas and danzones, even consider the delights of a harmonically pleasing major scale when his very thoughts were continually invaded by the unpleasantries of his recent past? Indeed, even if he had remained a part of this world, he still could not as much as look at the sweetest of children playing on the ship's deck without thinking about the infants and mothers he had seen being herded off to their doom by the "Aryan masters." What difference had his little compositions, or his lofty plans for aesthetic excellence, or his magnificent penis (to speak of the physical), or his life of luxury, or his faith in God—and a good Catholic God, such as the God his beloved mother had prayed to every morning and night—what difference had any of that made to the workings of history? And how was it that the very same Israel Levis, of the ever-burgeoning stomach, who in his younger days had never passed up a tasty morsel, had now lost his cravings for both food and the exertions of creativity that had once so excited him?

He did not like to dwell upon these things—but such torments came to him, anyway, followed him through his days and often put him in such a perturbed frame of mind that even with someone like Antonio he was severe.

"Forgive me," he would say, after barking out some order. "It is my unfortunate manner."

Occasionally, as he watched the sea, he tried hard to think pleasant thoughts. He might utter a telling phrase: "My father, Leocadio, was a physician, you know—and a good one—but his first love was nature." Or, "My late mother believed that the stars were the tears of heaven." One night, as the sun was setting, Levis pointed to the horizon, a great band of orange and red light and fiery clouds crossing endlessly before them, and said, "Mira, las glorias de Dios"—"Look at the glories of God."

"It is beautiful, Don Israel," Antonio answered.

And then Levis said, "Once, long ago, when I was a boy, I was certain that God existed. I saw him in everything—in every flower and plant, in the light of the day itself. And at night, I believed that I could go to sleep protected. I had my good and pure soul, and an angel watching over me. Sometimes, at night, I would look at the sky for hours and feel certain that this wondrous divinity was all around me—even the moon seemed like a manifestation of His being, as if its surface was the face of Jesus Christ. Why, my older brother and I would concoct some wild theories about the moon—that God had hidden all those souls who were waiting for life in our world under its surface, and we concluded that these souls resembled little glowing pearls. *Y fíjate"*—and imagine this— "because we truly believed in heaven when we were little, we always wondered where it might be. Of course my mother always said it was located at *el Camino de Santiago"*—the center of the Milky Way—"and I would look up until my neck ached, hoping to get a clear glimpse of those souls who I believed were pouring through its entrance." And then, with some other thought intruding, he added: "Such, dear Antonio, were the sweet fairy tales of my youth."

In Habana, May 1947

Once the ship came into harbor, Levis was so filled with joy at seeing Habana again—Belén College on a high hill, the elegant Malecón drive, the Prado boulevard stretching into the center of the city toward the Presidential Palace, the many parks and high royal palms—that he nearly wept. Though eager to return to his house in the Vedado section of Habana, he waited for the other passengers to disembark first; a black *portero* with his trunk, Antonio with his own suitcase and clarinet beside him. Slowly descending the gangplank, his cane in hand, he found that the quietude of his thoughts, that revelry of memory and expectation then coming over him, was quickly shattered. There gathered on

the pier to greet Israel Levis was a group of journalists, representatives from the municipal Conservatory, and an *oficial* of the
Chamber of Commerce. Preferring to be left alone, he reluctantly
agreed to pose on the quayside for a photographer from *El Diario
de la Marina* (Levis standing straight up, in his white three-piece
suit, his hands folded over his cane, looking regal, stately, like a
founding father of the republic), the picture making it into the
next morning's edition with the caption "A TREASURED SON OF
CUBA RETURNS." Articles would appear in other Habana papers,
lauding the return of "that grand composer whose famous 'Rosas
Puras' had done so much to bring Cuban music to the world."

Despite his frail condition, he did two brief interviews, rather
impatiently ("Of course I am happy to be back in Cuba!" he testily
declared, "What do you think?"), breaking off the second interview when he caught sight through his quite myopic eyes of his
late older brother Fernando's son, Victor, then about twenty-two,
and behind him his brother's pretty widow, Gloria. She ran up to
him, wrapping her arms around his waist, declaring, "We prayed
and prayed for your return. Thanks be to Saint Lázaro!"—as if
Levis had come back from the dead. And, "*¡Dios mío!* What a
beard!"

In those moments, he had to contend with his nephew's
expression of pure pity and shock, for the last time Israel saw
Victor, back in 1938 in his late brother's house in Santiago, on
the eastern end of the island, the composer seemed buoyantly
immense and jovial, well satisfied with his life in Paris and his
many travels, even if the political situation in Europe was changing in ways that should have made him wary.

During that visit to Santiago those years before, in 1938, he had sat in the parlor of his brother's house, coaxing a hug from his nephew. "Reach into my bag, I've got something for you," the composer told him. There his nephew found *caramelos*—hard candies—and a baseball, and shortly, like any Cuban boy, he ran out into the street to play with his friends, who were soon laughing and shouting with delight. Pleased with himself, Levis quickly downed his glass of orange juice and rum, a lovely diversion in the midst of a sunny day. Elated, he got up to make himself another drink. That's when his thin and majestic older brother, Doctor Fernando Levis, stood by the doorway with a faint smile on his face, and having assessed his younger brother's joy, asked: "My goodness, brother, why do you have to live so far away?"—he meant Paris. "It's obvious that you love being with the family; when are you coming home for good?" And even as he began his answer ("One day, perhaps. . . .") he could hear his mother castigating him from another room: "You know why he hasn't come back to us? It's because now he does just as he pleases! Don't you know that he's famous?"

Now the composer seemed a different man, saddened by a knowledge of things that he could not express, his body nearly weightless, as if he would be swept off by the slightest salt-scented wind. Even his movements were different, for his head was thrust slightly forward, his body, it seemed, struggling to follow behind it, as if the gravity of his very thoughts would cause him to suddenly topple over.

As for his nephew, Victor, a "beautiful" youth (for all that was youthful was beautiful to the composer), the young man had yet to get over the fact that his father had passed away from leukemia the year before. A sad period that also saw the death of his grandmother Doña Concepción, from "natural" causes—worry and grief because of what had happened to her sons. Levis himself learned of these events in Spain, long after they had occurred, and had been inconsolable. *I was so pained and distraught over the deaths of my mother and brother that I wept secretly like a baby.* But at least Victor, so young and with the future before him, could find refuge from his sorrows through his medical studies at the university in Habana, as he wanted, in the family tradition, to become a doctor.

What could he do but wrap his arms around his nephew and feel proud.

"My God," Don Israel said to Victor. "You've grown into a sturdy young man."

Then his nephew planted a kiss on the composer's neck, and Israel, after all he had been through, declared, laughing with the joyfulness of a child, "Oh you shouldn't make such a fuss over me. I'm so happy to see you both."

Disoriented, but pleased to have made the long journey home—finally to home—he had all the same regretted that one of the great loves of his life, Rita Valladares, had not been on hand to greet him. A few weeks before, she had telephoned him in Madrid at the Hotel Velásquez, lamenting the fact that upon his arrival she would be on tour, concertizing in Latin America—Caracas, Buenos Aires, and Rio de Janeiro. "You don't know how much I've missed you, *querido,*" she had said—that missed connection a common occur-rence between them through the years, for their lives, over the past two decades, had never intersected in ways that allowed their romance to blossom. Though he always cited circumstances—his grand professional life with its commitments to tours and long runs of his own work in the capitals of Europe (yes, even in Berlin and

Vienna), the writing of film scores, and countless deadlines—he could blame only the shortsightedness of his own inward-turned personality and his tendency for indecision when it came to matters of love as the reasons for his failures with Rita. And there had been the composer's devotion to his mother (when she was alive), and his inability to state how he really felt about Valladares...and others.

Of course, it was now all too late.

He was not a bitter man, but prone to an ironic view of life, as if it were all useless, as if a man passed his years building upon his accomplishments only to watch everything—his loves, his work, his very world—turn into air in the end. With so much time and energy wasted by wondering how his little destiny might have played out had he been of a different character and disposition, Levis resolved to accept his situation—that of an aging man, plagued by illness, seeking the quiet and unspectacular finale to his days.

Still, he once loved Valladares enough that thoughts of her and music (and much good luck by way, he had sometimes thought, of divine intervention) had sustained him through some very bad times; and if he felt some disappointment that "La Chiquita" had not been waiting for him on the dock, he could not help but to thank God (Please let there be a God) that at the very least they would soon be united again, if not as lovers, as dear and vital friends.

Accompanied by his relatives and a member of the city council, Levis made his way to the Customs House, where his green passport was stamped. With his trunk loaded into the back of a taxi, he and his small entourage then made their way over to Vedado, the streets along their route jostling with life. Tourists, vendors and ordinary citizens jammed the sidewalks. The sight of familiar storefronts and cafés, the splendid architectural flourishes, the arcades and colonnade galleries, balconies and high doorways and windows of the buildings, and the very smells of that city, of flowers, beer, perfume, fried foods and burning fuels a tonic to his soul. And to see the city through Antonio's eyes! For the young man took in everything with a great intensity and pleasure—every pretty, big-rumped woman, sashaying along; every musician standing outside a restaurant, strumming a guitar and singing. His youthful enthusiasm—indeed his handsomeness—was so redolent of what Levis himself had left behind (a sense of a promising future) that he found himself thinking that if he, in his current state of health and solemnity of mind, could not look forward to the myriad pleasures of life, then he would at least have the satisfaction of helping others find their way.

Sitting in the front of the taxi, Levis thought about what he would do for Antonio. The young man was good-looking despite his flawed complexion, and had a broad and expansive smile that, alas, was compromised by a set of rotting teeth. With that in mind the composer made the aside, "Antonio, we must make sure to get you to the dentist soon—you don't want to lose your teeth." And then: "I will of course pay for it." And to his nephew he said, "Whatever you need by way of money you let me know," for he meant to put his modest fortune (backlogged royalties to *"Rosas Puras"* accounting for a large part of it) to good use. To Gloria he said, "I know that my brother, may God bless his soul, took good care of you—you have been provided for, yes? But I extend to you the same offer, and don't think twice about asking for it, as I have learned in my life that money doesn't matter that much."

"But Don Israel," she told him. "You know that we are with you out of love."

He appreciated that remark—those affectionate words flow-ing into him as a kind of sunlight. He told her, barely turning his head, and speaking softly: "You are too kind to me, sister-in-law."

He did not have much to say. He did not care to convey his experiences during the war, not about his year and a half of internment, nor the name of that place, with its idyllic Alpine set-ting where he witnessed enough suffering to last a hundred life-times: *Buchenwald,* his little secret that was not a secret at all. On his arm seven numbers in green ink. In his heart, a rancor and dis-appointment over the way that his pipe dreams about morality, religion and the beauty and importance of music meant nothing; a black cloud of thought, passing through his mind, in such a way as to make him feel that his life as a composer and conductor of orchestras was really the life of a clown, or an impostor, or some-one tricked by fate. It had not been so long ago that Levis believed himself a most fortunate man—even if his romantic vision had been wanting—an individual, blessed by a Catholic God, far beyond the "normal" rules of existence. But he had been cheated, throttled by his own failings, and that feeling, along with the dis-abilities of his physical state, produced in the character of his expression a solemn longing for a better world and a different, rejuvenated self.

An impossibility, he believed, though he yearned for it.

And why was it that even as he felt a great enthusiasm—even

joy—and a nostalgia for his life in Habana, and a true affection for his family and those of his friends that remained, there existed within him a numbness to feeling? This disheartened Levis, for without emotion there would never be music, and without music his life would be a living death.

So it happened that without intending to the composer sank into a deep state of apprehension. Even as Gloria spoke gently about her son's humility, his work ethic and high grades in medical school, and laid out the plans for that afternoon—"Of course, you will take a nap and bathe; and later we will have a wonderful dinner"—he could not imagine the point of his continuing existence. In those moments, as he went driving through the streets of that splendid city, he truly believed that he would never compose another piece of music again—not a tango nor a bolero nor a lyric opera nor another zarzuela, not even another simple Habana melody—as he once often did with effortless control.

His house in Vedado

Such were his thoughts when they finally arrived before the front gate to his house on the calle Olivares, where he had been born and had lived for most of his life in Habana. The house was set behind walls of pinkish stone covered with bougainvillea, honeysuckle scented the air, and immediately as he passed inside he saw the familiar sight of the massive acacia that loomed over the front patio's now wild garden. That house was a familiar yet strange apparition—why, he could nearly hear himself as a child, back before the turn of the century, practicing his scales on the piano, the tinkle of notes coming from a room deep inside; hear the very melody of that song which had so changed his life, "Rosas Puras," on that day in 1928 when he first wrote it.

No sooner had he entered the foyer, with its arabesque tile walls, did the unmistakable aroma of his own past hit him, flowing out from the shadows, for the house's shutters were closed: old wooden medical cabinets; the mildewy bathroom, or "inodoro," as it was called in his day; the very smell of the piano and the cloth flowers that he had always kept in a vase on top of it; a thirty-year-old pencil that he had laid atop the piano a decade before, unmoved beside the vase (he wondered what notes he'd written with it). And of arrested time itself: the hallway with its photographs of family and of high points from his illustrious career; the crucifixes that his mother had put up everywhere, still in their place, the small evidences that his had been a beautiful life hitting him all at once—and he thought, *This is where I will spend the rest of my days.*

It was Gloria who threw open the shutters, flooding the rooms with light; Gloria who led her brother-in-law, Israel Levis, slowly toward the study, which looked out into a courtyard and garden, where he kept his piano, his "old friend."

"Look, Israel, it's waiting for you."

He did not know what to do. Slowly, tentatively, he sat in a chair near that piano, as if, as in years past, he would once again preside over a student's lessons or listen to a young composer's latest efforts. As if friends like Ernesto Lecuona or Gonzalo Roig or Sindo Garay had dropped by and were about to premiere a new composition. As if Rita Valladares herself would pop through that door to go over a song. As if it were 1904 again and Fernando, attempting to study his medical books, would storm into that room, begging that he hold off on his scales: "You are a wonderful musician, but, *por Dios,* brother, I can barely concentrate!" As if on a Sunday morning, his late mother would find him, well into his thirties and quite plump, bending over his shoes to tie their laces, ready as always for their traditional outing to church, her hand stroking his dense neck and saying, despite his age, "My little son, it's time to go." As if he were about to see his physician father pull from the high oak shelves that lined the study one of his beloved volumes on ornithology or flowers, as he prepared for their weekly outings to the countryside, where he would often declare: "God is nature, my son." Or, as if before him, his younger sister, Anabella, quivered in anticipation over the prospect of turning the pages of his piano scores as the young Levis prepared for a recital of Bach and Schumann to be given at a municipal fair in 1904. As if he were looking over at his handsome (and beloved) lyricist Manny Cortez, who, in a snit over some woman, declared, "I've had enough of all this nonsense, let's go out and get drunk." As if he were going to a salon in progress—so many of his composer friends and singers from the Albisu and José Martí theaters gathered by that piano, on a long and fruitful evening of drinking, eating and song.

In those moments, Levis, surprised by such memories, was barely aware of his sister-in-law's voice: "Israel, come, we will get you into your room for a nap."

"Yes, of course," he responded. And then crankily, as she took hold of his arm, he told her: "I can get up by myself, thank you!"

And as quickly he said: "Forgive me, I am rather tired."

But he was not beyond giving Antonio a certain instruction: "My boy, down that hallway, your room is inside the second door." And he led Antonio there and told him: "This was my brother's room when he was a boy." And then looking around, he told everyone: "Don't be worried, I am still very much alive, after all."

HIS FIRST DAYS BACK IN HABANA

During his first days back in Habana, the pattern of his life with its little routines was established. Each morning he rewound the mechanism of an old Swiss clock on his dresser, moved idly through the rooms of his house with a cloth of felt in hand to dust every sur-face. Until about noon, wearing only a robe, a pair of white linen *pantalones* and slippers, he found much to amuse himself in watching his newly hired maid Octavia, who always hummed to herself as she scrubbed the tile floors, or laundered his clothes in a tub on the back patio, the composer taking great solace in observing her pre-cise manner as she hung his undergarments and shirts out to dry on a line. Sometimes he sat in the shade under the trees, as the shifting sunlight went on its rounds, the plants and bushes and flowers around him suddenly ablaze. He was surprised to find himself feel-ing sentimental over the rediscovery of certain objects—things that he had forgotten about—his younger sister Anabella's bisque dolls, set out on an old Spanish trunk in the hall, unchanged and unmov-ing for so many years, the sparkling hems of their dresses, crisp to the touch; an orrery—a wooden-and-bronze-limbed solar system, kept upon a mantel—that his father had once purchased in Holland and prized as a model of God's universe.

"*Here is Mercury, then Venus—and we are here on this Earth, sus-pended around the Sun, in the Heavens. . . .*"

Mainly he dedicated himself to putting his things in order, going over the contents of his *escritorio,* at which, in years past, he often sat refining scores: pencils and fountain pens in their place, a compartment for old watches, another for religious medals, another for tacks and erasers. Fastidiously he would arrange old scores in piles, laying them out on a table: first by key, then by category, then alphabetically—as if anyone would care. He seemed not to mind the pointlessness of such tasks, for it idled away the time.

Slowly he got around to attending to the practical matter of finances. On certain afternoons his Habana agent, José Huertas, would come by to go over old contracts and to sort through payment owed on backlogged royalties, the two of them sitting at a parlor table with pencils and a ledger, a process to which the composer was poorly disposed.

Levis would sleep late. Even as a "gift to the nation of Cuba," he no longer had any pressing matters to which to attend. He passed his afternoon awaiting the mail, and he received many letters that he opened but rarely answered. Letters from old acquaintances, distant family, and concert promoters in Europe and the United States, the latter inquiring if Israel Levis was still composing and conducting orchestras. *No.* A letter from the Spanish Society in New York expressing an interest in his presence at the restaging of one of his old zarzuelas, *La Reina Isabel,* that coming fall. *No.* A carefully written request in Spanish from the *New York Herald Tribune* for an interview about his experience as a repatriated "Jewish" refugee after the war. *No.* A letter from the music department of MGM studios asking if he would have any interest in writing some "incidental music" for a film, *The Gentlemen of Seville. No.* An inquiry from Juilliard in New York, as to whether he might be available to come to the school to teach composition and theory. *No.* Requests from Madrid, from Paris, from Rome. *No.*

In the evenings he often remained at home receiving friends. He had many beautiful reunions: Ernesto and Ernestina Lecuona came to pay their respects, and by and by, he played host to a number of other composers and musicians who, knowing of what had happened to Levis during the war, descended upon him with open arms and promised to help bring the "broken" composer back to his former stride. During a banquet held in his honor at the Centro Gallego, one of the largest social clubs in Cuba, the director of the Teátro Martí offered him a commission to write a light opera, but the gloom that had recently beset his heart was such that he had not been able to compose a thing in years. At best he could only promise to "consider the matter," but alone in his study he would pace about the piano without touching a sin-gle of its humidity-dampened, out-of-tune keys, the days when the rhapsodic chortling of parrots in their cages or the singsong of vendors on the street would serve as a source of inspiration far behind him. And his poor maid—how she tried to cheer him up, setting out fresh-cut flowers in vases atop his piano and offering to accompany Levis on his constitutionals through the city, walks that often took him to the cathedral in the afternoons.

A man who kept his promises, he prevailed upon his connec-tions to find Antonio Solar a job as a stagehand at the Martí. And he did not mind when the young Spaniard made a racket practicing his clarinet, for music still cheered him, as long as he did not play *"Rosas Puras."* He bought four parakeets, whom he doted on as if they were his children, and was amused by their purity of spirit, their innocence. He found the Spaniard a guitar in a shop on the calle O'Reilly ("Maestro Levis, it's been too long a time!" the owner had said), and allowed Solar the use of drums and gourds that Israel had acquired during his years in Habana when he was constantly on the prowl for instruments useful to his own compo-sitions—*agogo bells, claves, tumbadores, guiros, maracas, quijadas.* He even succeeded in persuading Antonio to get his teeth fixed, so that one day, six months hence, the young man came home after an endless series of dental visits cured, "whole." And truly handsome.

A little secret: Levis would never confess, not even to a priest, that over the years he sometimes felt inexplicable curiosities about men, that a welling of untoward feelings in the company of certain men filled him with desire. He had experienced this feeling most greatly with the Italian tenor Beniamino Gigli, who had performed often in Habana in the 1920s, a fellow whose superior physical attributes and Latin beauty made Levis quite nervous. Once, while chatting with Gigli backstage at the Teátro Campoamor, Levis had felt the strongest compulsion to embrace him in an amorous way but put that impulse off in the same manner he repressed himself around women. And sometimes when he and his lyricist Manny Cortez had been out drinking together and the composer was feel-ing such pure affection for their friendship, the same "nervousness" came over him, and he would crave a kiss from his friend, to touch him—to feel his skin, the tenseness of his body. He'd never acted on these feelings, or at least that he could remember—or chose not to remember, if he had. Sometimes in the mornings those years before, when he had been out late drinking with the crowd, he awakened with the oddest sense that he might have mistakenly allowed himself to get carried away and would anxiously await that moment when he would meet Manny again, or one of the more handsome fellows whom he knew from around, checking to see if there was an inkling of revulsion or pity in his friend's eyes, some evidence that he had behaved in an unmanly fashion, the very thought making him tremble and ashamed.

For all the years that had passed, Levis had never gotten used to such temptations. Even in libertine Paris, whenever those sinful and "unnatural" impulses came over him, Levis had despaired.

But with Antonio in his house, as he made his way down the hall at night, knowing that the young and handsome Spaniard was resting in bed, he sometimes had the urge to rap on his door—not to fondle or kiss him in any unseemly way, nothing to do with a desire for the physical, but more out of the loneliness that comes to a man late in his life; and out of a fear of the dark, he told himself.

You see, when I was young I always knew that my family was never far away, just a few steps beyond my door, sleeping peacefully in their rooms, so that even in the midst of my worst dreams—of sinking like a phantasma into a stone wall without being able to escape, of going deaf, of my bed catching on fire—I knew that my family would be my salvation, their love flowing into me—my beloved family just a few steps away, down those beautiful tiled floors, in this house where I once lived when the world was good . . . how empty my bed is now. . . .

He did not make plans. His neighbors next door, a happy family, were always coming by with plates of food and much goodwill. He got along well enough with the father of that household, a fellow named Eduardo who owned a cinema in downtown Habana and was always inviting the composer to see the latest Hollywood movies.

"There's a new Esther Williams film," he'd say, handing Levis some tickets.

"Thank you. Perhaps I will go tomorrow," he'd answer, later sending off Antonio or Victor to the cinema in his stead.

He shaved off his beard one day, leaving his mustache, and was amazed by his thin, age-riddled visage, his eyes soft and searching.

Despite the sadness of his thoughts, he was determined to put a good face on his circumstances. He commenced the routine of making a weekly telephone call to Gloria in Santiago, reporting that all was well. And he always found time to meet with his nephew for the occasional lunch—usually at one of his own haunts, a harborside café—the young man ever busy with his studies. Faced with the delicate matter of his late brother's death, Levis avoided the subject with Victor. He would have liked to say with conviction that his brother had gone off to some heavenly award, for all his years of dedicated and uncompromised service as a doctor and his decency and good nature as a man, but Levis could not bring himself to do so. And it was unnecessary: Victor, despite his sadness over the loss of his father, was a well-adjusted young man, ambitious and steady, and like many other Cubans of that generation, so taken by the promise of the future that the brunt of his energies were dedicated toward gaining admission to an American medical school—hopefully Johns Hopkins. To that end, Levis promised to help his nephew with the finances.

During this period, Rita Valladares telephoned him twice, once from Caracas, then from Montevideo. He could not remember the call from Venezuela, for it had come late at night after he had consumed a great quantity of brandy, but during the second, he had listened to the tone of her cheerful and wondrous voice, hanging on to her every word: "I cannot wait to see you Israel. . . . Once I am back in Habana, we will get together, as we used to. . . ." Then: "Please, Israel, take care of yourself."

"Yes, yes, I will," he answered.

Ghosts

One night, not two weeks after his return to Habana, he awoke because he thought he heard his dead father, Doctor Leocadio Levis, opening the door to his study, but when he called out—"Papá!"—and roused himself out of bed, he discovered that it was Antonio making his way out of the kitchen with a bottle of Hatuey beer. Later, he awakened to the music of a Bach fugue playing on his piano, and though the sound dissipated as he, with great difficulty, made his way into that room, he was convinced that his dear father was somewhere in that house, no doubt with the pallid ghost of Israel's mother by his side.

He asked himself certain questions: How was it that he had outlived his brother and sister? How was it that he had outlived so many others in Europe?

To pass those sometimes sleepless nights, he looked over his late father's books, the smell and texture of the pages, delicious, for they were redolent of his own youth. And he sometimes amused himself with books on spiritism and reincarnation, as he had once been a member of the Theosophical Society, from those days when he believed in fortune-tellers, astrology and destiny.

From time to time, he would summon a lovely memory of his

father. He would remember how his father was sometimes contracted by certain large plantations as a visiting physician, these
trips taking him far away from Habana to the eastern end of the
island, where he would often assist in minor surgeries at the United
Fruit Company hospitals in Preston and Banes. His father relished
those journeys, for he was an amateur naturalist who loved to roam
the forests and gardens of the island's most distant provinces in
search of rare species of flora and fauna, and knew Cuba's riches by
heart—the mangrove-fringed shorelines along the coast, the donax
cane that grew wild along the streams, the royal palms that rose to
stupendous heights everywhere. He was such an enthusiast that he
had filled the large and airy study of their house with books,
imported from England and America and Spain, massive volumes
and small pamphlets on botany and ornithology, the works of
Linnaeus and Darwin, nestled alongside his medical encyclopedias
and reference books.

He traveled by carriage—pulled by two sturdy white horses—
later by a Model T Ford, and sometimes took his sons along with
him. On those boyhood journeys, along the dirt roads of the
island, Israel had relished the sight of those little creatures and
birds—"tan pequeños"—that he, with an hawk's eye, happily spot-
ted in their hiding places: tiny toads; froglets called "little bells,"
or campanillas, in rotting piles of banana leaves; chameleons doz-
ing under the petals of cowlilies. A Urania moth, with its irides-
cent wings, preceding them with a lilting buoyancy, as if, while
bouncing in the air, its job was to lead the doctor and his sons on
their progress along the roads. Above, in the trees, so many
birds—doves and red-winged lizard cuckoos; owls and hawks;
woodpeckers crying out ta ha; crows and little-winged vireos,

lurking in the tangle of vines and creepers that hung down from the thick-rooted flamboyanes and ceibas; cave swallows, *Golon-drinas;* orioles and redwings; or, in a patch of carolina blossoms, gently floating hummingbirds, which his father especially loved—rearing their heads. (And they seemed to love him, too, for sometimes when his father sat by his study desk, a book on respiratory illnesses open before him, or while he examined something under a microscope, in that cool room at the far end of their house which opened to the garden, a pair of pygmy hummingbirds would fly in through the window and alight upon his desk—so gentle was his soul when it came to the little creatures of this world.)

And in that dense forest there were the slender yayajabica trees (*"Suriana marítima,"* his father would say in his precise manner) and majaguas (*Hibiscus tilaceus*). And then the *Erythrina* trees, sprays of carmine buds flourishing around them; then the flowering trees with trunks that seemed like candles dipped in blood (whose name the composer could not remember).

What did his father once say to him about such beauty, those years before?

"All this comes from *Dios.*"

Leocadio had made that pronouncement one morning long ago, with so much certainty that, right then and there, a nearly pagan appreciation for nature came over Israel. In those moments, every flower, plant and leaf seemed to reflect God's love for man. His spirits and angels moved invisibly around the young boy; as if God's own caressing hand could be felt in the sunlight itself.

And he would remember how the music of nature—the bird-

calls, the wind, the rushing of streams, the soporific rains churn-
ing in the woods—enchanted him with its spell. . . .

HIS MUSIC WAS EVERYWHERE

When his maid, Octavia, happened to be listening to radio station CMQ, as a distraction from her chores, chances were that
sooner or later some version of one of his older compositions from
his heyday in the 1920s and '30s would be broadcast over the air,
a rendition perhaps of *"La Habana Mía"* ("My Habana") or *"Qué
Bellas Estrellas"* ("How Beautiful the Stars"), among so many others
of his oeuvre that were still being performed and recorded by the
orchestras and "tropical bands" of the city and north in the States.
And he would tell her as politely as possible, *"Por favor, cambia la
estación"*—"Please, change the station." And while making his way,
as he often did in the afternoons, through the streets of Habana, on
his constitutionals, slowly, slowly, his music often came drifting
out of restaurant, bodega and bar doorways, and from car radios.
And he heard it being performed by lounge pianists and sidewalk
musicians, fellows who wore magic amulets and gold chains, the
notes of his famous *"Rosas Puras"* occasionally mocking him—for
the Israel Levis who had composed so many popular melodies and
had given to the world, as *Variety* put it in 1931, "the infectious
charms of the tropics in a song," no longer existed.

Even at night, when Levis, his body weary and heart forlorn,
lay in his late mother and father's canopied bed, he sometimes
heard certain of his compositions—maybe the melody of a *danzón*
from one of his antique zarzuelas—emanating in the distance from

the veranda of a local social club, and he'd marvel, uneasily, how, as much as he tried, he could not shut out the world.

He had memories of walking into a Paris brothel, circa 1940, the salon Pianola playing a roll version of *"Rosas Puras,"* and he'd recall not only the lividly red nipples of a favorite paramour, Gigi, expanding in his ravenous mouth, nor just the enormous but fleeting pleasures of those nights, but of what a pompous and deluded fool he had been, to assume that he, a Cuban Catholic with a name like Israel Levis, was immune to the terrors descending upon the Jews of Europe. Or that he'd find himself in Vienna in 1933, conducting his symphonic variation of the zarzuela based on the aforementioned song, bowing in his long-tailed tuxedo before a packed house of the culturally elite, among them many Nazis—such cheerful and carefree Cuban music, thanks to him, a favorite in Europe—his head brimming with a false intimation of "immortality." Or that on certain evenings in 1944 in the nicely appointed salon at the inn of Ettersberg, near Weimar, Germany, just a few miles outside of Buchenwald, he, as a privileged inmate of that camp, would sit behind a grand Bosendorfer piano under an enormous chandelier and gilded ceiling, performing Bach and Beethoven pieces for an *obergruppenfuehrer* and his aides and their wives. Or that when one of the commandants requested that the haggard pianist play *"Rosas Puras,"* an admittedly decadent but memorable song that this commandant had much enjoyed during his days in occupied France, at the Opéra Bouffe de Paris, Israel Levis, once the toast of Europe and now a "detainee" at Buchenwald, wanting to live, would smile and nod his head in accord.

What most tormented him was the violation of his belief that goodness would prevail over evil in this world, that the sovereignty of beauty should have magically protected him from the likes of Reinhard Heydrich, expediter of the "final solution" in France.

And he'd twist and turn in his bed, unable to help himself from seeing a clip of the 1935 MGM film short *Rhumba Crazy,* featuring the famous dancer Fred Astaire, stepping to the music of *"Rosas Puras"* across the polished floor of a grand ballroom of an imaginary palace "somewhere in the tropics"; Astaire spinning in circles and taking Ginger Rogers's hands into his own and twirling her around, Astaire singing, ever so happily, his heart filled with love— the image of the dapper bon vivant kicking up his heels and somehow bringing forth a smell of ashes, a cry of murmured, prayerful chants from another time, 1944.

In the Cathedral

Taking a trolley into the center of the city and making his way into Habana Cathedral (and other churches) became a part of his daily routine. He went there to think and to pray, for he felt himself waiting—not for some flash of inspiration that would help him to finish a composition, nor for some meditative insight, nor for that matter a sweet reflection on the Sacrifice of the Lord for the salvation of Man, but for some reassertion of everything that he had once believed. He was waiting for something wondrous that would inspirit new life into his soul—a miracle, as if he would go back to the house on Olivares in the evening and, after having his nightly brandies, rest in bed and dream, a lovely and gentle

dream in which Jesus Himself would come to him, and with a single whispered command remove from his mind the latter history
of his life when he had witnessed so much useless suffering
around him, breathe new life into his flesh, peeling away those sea
green numbers of a diminutive size that had been tattooed onto
his arm and that seemed the indirect emanation of a song.

He would sit for hours in a back pew, under the high ceilings,
surrounded by columns, stunned that he now felt nothing at all.
He could remember when he never failed to walk into a church,
whether in Cuba or Europe, simply out of curiosity and because
he always enjoyed those feelings of familiarity that came over him,
and of nostalgia, no matter his state of mind. Liking most people
who entered such places of worship, he held his greatest affection
for those elderly ladies and gentlemen who seemed to truly
believe in God and never failed to dip their fingers into the Holy
Water font. But he was sometimes annoyed when he visited ca-
thedrals and observed a lack of proper reverence around him—
especially in Europe, where so many tourists and art historians
went into churches simply to "appreciate" and "see" the superficial adornments of Catholicism, their casual attitudes toward the
divine often provoking in Levis a sense of outrage. Even in his
easygoing youth, if someone was in church speaking loudly and
asking about some mundane matter, he would hush them, his face
brimming with outrage. At one time he almost had a superior attitude about his religiosity, which seemed to blossom whenever he
found himself inside a sanctuary, and although he never censored
himself when it came to the enjoyments of the fleshly life, when
the composer of *"Rosas Puras"* entered a church, he became as
pious as anyone could be.

God, after all, as his mother had told him a thousand times, had given him his talents.

Yet, upon his return, he could care less if a group of loud and irreverent tourists stormed into the cathedral making jokes, chew-ing gum and clicking off their cameras—for, in fact, experience at that juncture in his life had taught Levis that the reliquaries, altars and other embellishments of the Church were now meaningless, at least to him.

THE SOUL

Principally, when alone, and feeling doubts (in his old age, in his house on Olivares and while walking in Habana as a younger man), he believed in the soul—sensed it within himself, and in oth-ers. And he always swore by a certain childhood memory that involved the soul and his father's ministrations to the poor, when he and his brother would accompany their father on his rounds into the countryside. Though his father presided over the births of infants, and dispensed medicines among the poor like candies, he was often called to a dying patient's bed only after the re-sources of prayer and the incantatory powers of the *santeros* had failed, when the ingestion of heads of garlic and the burning of candles had proved futile and there was often little that Doctor Levis could do. The sight of an old man, breathing his last, ex-hausted by a lifetime in the cane fields, although inspiring his brother to later pursue the study of medicine ("*Yes, dear good-hearted Fernando....*"), had made a different impression on Israel. He had no stomach for suffering, and the idea that a person might lay dying inside a hut had overwhelmed him, so that he often wanted to run away into the countryside, to reside among the flowers and lianas, with life thriving around him. Often he simply waited outside in the front yard, occasionally climbing a tree or playing with the other children. But one afternoon, when Israel had reached the tender age of twelve, his father called him into a shack so that he might bear witness to an inescapable fact of life.

Doctor Levis had been attending to a mulatto of middle age, who had been suffering from tuberculosis and was breathing his last. Israel had been not three paces from his bed when the man's throat constricted and he gave off what his father called the "death rattle."

Then something unusual happened: In that moment, as the man expired, not only did an expression of tranquillity come over his face, but simultaneously the cane-walled room, with its dirt floor and flickering animal-fat candles, filled with the slightest aroma of strawberries, and a presence, invisible to the eye, radiated peace—this man's soul lingering briefly before flowing out that bohío's door and integrating into the air. The man's family praised God, for they had felt the presence. His widow had screamed in joy (or terror) and fainted. Attending to the widow, his father had looked at each of his son's with bemusement, his scientific bent of mind knowing not what to make of this phenomenon. As he left, he said, "You see, this is what happens—and it all goes by very quickly."

Then he simply picked up his bag, and nodding, said to his sons, "Bueno, vamos pa' casa."

Such was Levis's belief in spirits that he often dreamed about his own soul—a spirit of light, tinged by blue, in a flowing robe, shooting across the night sky, each star resonating with music. . . .

As I used to say to some of my friends after a few drinks, each one of us

possesses a spirit—what it matters to this world I do not know, but it is a
fact, I am convinced of that, I swear to you.

Until the years of his internment in the camp, he had no doubts about his life as a composer. That torment had not only been a slap from God, but had disemboweled and humiliated the grand deity before his very eyes, unraveling over a course of so many dangerous and disheartening days that sweet love of life and those religious convictions that had given an air of nobility to his own vocation. Levis, in fact, had very much preferred life before his notions of God had gone out the window. Not only had Levis missed that feeling of companionship and love that had been given him, but also the sense that he had been guided by—and, as it were, protected by—the Almighty (who, because of his time spent with the Jews, he had given the name "Yahweh"), but even that bit of recognition now seemed meaningless.

Ofttimes, he felt nostalgic for that state of mind that had made his own mild tendencies toward sin somehow more naughty and daring, when he believed that there would be—if what he had been taught by his mother and the priests was true—a final reck-oning, to be undertaken in the great chamber of heavenly judg-ments. This was a prospect that had only slightly perturbed him, for, at his worst, his sins, most enthusiastically pursued in Europe, were of a carnal, perhaps idiosyncratic nature, involving brothel women. And his only other moral lapses could be called sins of envy, such as when he heard the music of Ravel or Stravinsky and felt himself merely a petty writer of little formulaic operettas and tunes—no matter how much physical comfort and money those compositions had brought to him.

For the most part, in those days when he first returned to Habana, he looked forward to his reunion with Rita Valladares, the singer for whom he had originally composed "Rosas Puras" nearly twenty years before.

She and the song were inseparable in his mind. When he thought about Rita Valladares that melody came instantly to mind, and, conversely, hearing that song, he imagined that he would turn around to find Rita standing behind him. But his feelings about "Rosas Puras" went beyond his past love for that woman, for it was the song that changed his life and brought him sudden fame, uprooting him from his tranquil existence in Habana. From that composition sprung his sojourn in Europe and many tours, operettas and ballets that were performed in the concert halls of Italy and France. That melody not only evoked the feelings he had for Rita Valladares, but, as well, the many eight-course meals he consumed in the restaurant of the Ritz Hotel and certain other indulgences, among them a passion for long-legged women in red garters. And, yes, he would remember, it also brought back the harassments and eventual incarceration in a camp, by those Nazis in occupied Paris, who, whatever his protests and his sometimes righteous ways, took him, a Catholic with a crucifix hanging around his neck, for a Jew.

LITTLE

MEMORIES

"Firmiter Profi Temur Hic Hoc Misterium Fidel"

("We firmly believe in the mystery of the faith")

—INSCRIPTION ON THE PORTICO
OF THE CENTRO GALLEGO DE LA HABANA

"My dearest Rita," he thought to write her those years later, as he settled again in his house. "I have been thinking about my childhood lately—and often. It seems that time has gone by so quickly—why is it that one seems to have lived a hundred years in infancy, only to see the passage of every moment, as one gets older, rushing for-ward, one day folding into the other? I can remember being so conscious as a child of how long a single hour took to pass; I can remember sitting before my father's Swiss mantel clock and waiting endlessly for the minute hand to move, or of sitting before the piano and practicing my scales for hours at a time and feeling afterward that I had been on a long, long journey, and yet the remainder of the day would stretch on forever. Two hours before dinner, enough time for me and Fernando, may God bless his soul, to head over to the used-book shop off Galiano to look for old American magazines and then to come back and play games on the patio, to hunt down some poor chameleon or salamander, that we would then hold captive in an old bird cage and torment with twigs—the poor creatures. And then we would still have time, to wash and dress for the evening meal, to say a prayer. I can remember being conscious of how slowly the moon rose, that I was quite aware of how the stars filled the sky and took to their paths in such a leisurely manner that I tor-mented myself with the notion that sleep would prevent me from seeing all of them—those nights seemed to last forever, the very recitations of poetry that my father read to us before we retired to our beds, seeming so epic in length. How long could he have read to us, perhaps only an hour, or a half an hour, and yet, the move-ment of those words was such that one's thoughts always had time to slip in between them—and that was even true with music, my dearest, the notes I'd play on the piano as a boy of seven or eight always seemed to have great spaces of silence between them, so lengthy that one could have his little dreams.... And now? What is an hour but something that passes in a flash.... Why I am think-ing of time I cannot say, but now that I am back in Cuba I have been awaiting your return, fascinated by how in that context time once again goes quite slowly...."

A FEW NOTES ON HIS NAME AND FAITH

Of course, it had never occurred to Israel Levis that he would one day get into trouble because of the apparent Jewishness of his name: it was something that had never seemed possible, for there was a part of Levis that would always be, as his family had been for generations, quite irretrievably Catholic. For years, he never doubted the roots of his faith. The family name, Levis, originated with some distant Catalan ancestor, who may or may not have had some Jewish blood, but nothing was made of that, for, going back centuries to postmedieval Spain, as his father once explained, the peasants often derived their names from their masters—and there had been many prosperous Jews living in Spain before the inquisitions of Isabella forced them either to convert, to die or to flee her sacred kingdoms. Judaism had never been a matter of discussion, for in the family tree there had been many priests and nuns—and in the late eighteenth century there had been a monsignor named Sebastiano Levis, whose parish had been in the small town of Mesia, near Santiago de Compostela, that most religious of Spanish cities.

Catholic devotion was so strong in their household that among his first memories in life were of the many hours he spent, as an infant, contemplating the face of Jesus, the great and suffering Son of God—on the crucifix over his mother and father's canopied bed, a grand cross made of oak and bronze that had been in his mother's family for generations. That Jesus was the "King of the Jews" did not matter, for no discussions of the Messiah's ethnic origins ever graced their table. All that the young Levis knew was that he had been given his first name, Israel, after a great-uncle who had been a doctor in Spain, a country where, after all, Isaiahs and Isaacs and Macedonios and Anibals were appropriated for the weight and colorful grandeur they gave to a person.

(As such, it never bothered Levis in later years when strangers mistook him, in his fairness of complexion and the slightly Arab cast to his expression, for an Irishman or, more commonly, a *marrano*—a Jew—or a *polaco; "Bueno, soy católico,"* he would say. In his youth he could never have comprehended that his own last name, Levis, was anything more than a relic from his family's distant Catalan past— for he was a Spaniard, and what Spaniard did not have a descendant somewhere with Jewish or Arab blood? And what difference did that make? he had once naively thought.)

So it was in the year of his birth, 1890, that his mother and father named him Israel—its associations with the Old Testament greatly pleasing them—for all the magic and goodness that life could hold out was contained in that book. He so greatly believed in the Bible—its stories and lessons were the fairy tales of his youth—that he emulated the devotions of Doña Concepción, who could not pass by the parlor table on which their Bible rested without touching her fingertips to its gilded cover, giving it a kiss and making the sign of the cross—"It's for the blessing of God," she would say, and Levis, as a boy imitated her.

Those decades later, as he would pass the lonely hours in his house on Olivares, he would feel a nostalgia for the pleasures that his boyhood imagination afforded him, when just touching that book or turning to one of its pages, even before he could read, brought him in communion with the mysteries of God's history in the world—the gardens of Babylon, the destruction of Sodom and Gomorrah, the great flood, the biblical patriarchs, Jesus and the apostles, and those angels that came down from heaven—some' how flowing out of those pages into him.

Whatever God was, He cared enough for the boy to send his good energies out of that book through his fingers; everywhere he

looked, he felt *His* presence. Not just in that Bible, but in the crucifixes and *santos*—statues of saints—that his mother and father
kept in that house. So certain was he of God's existence that his
own little world—contained by the high walls of that house on
the calle Olivares, with 1890s Habana barking, wailing, whistling
outside—seemed vibrant with evidences of *His* presence.

In the afternoons, when he heard the great acacia tree in their
yard wavering in the breeze, or when the light suddenly shifted, he
was convinced that it had been caused by some heavenly action,
and he moved through the happy hours of his day with the certainty that he was not only blessed to have such a tranquil home,
and a mother and father who loved him, but that he was also being
protected by an angel who safeguarded his body and soul.

Still, there were contradictions to this vision of a good and
loving God. There had been an early tragedy in that household,
for before Levis had come into the world, two older siblings, the
twins Olivia and Leandro, had perished as infants. They had been
his mother's darlings—their sepia-toned images now framed for
eternity, peer out into the world from their tintypes on the parlor
wall. Olivia, a sweet and wide-eyed girl—*la hembra*—succumbed to
malaria at the age of four in 1885, and a few years later the boy,
Leandro, died at six after falling from a high branch of one of the
acacia trees—the cross that weighed most heavily on his mother's
pious shoulders. She regularly said prayers and burned candles for
their souls, and though she was often saddened by their absence,
she always told Israel that "if God called them early, it was
because they were saints."

Such was his mother's love for them that she often reported
seeing their spirits in the middle of the night—Olivia appearing

before her in a blue dress, her hair tied in a white ribbon, holding a bisque doll; Leandro with his handsome and expressive face, in his short pants and Sunday-school jacket and cap, bearing a glow- ing heart in his hand for her as an offering.

"They told me they are happy," she would say matter-of-factly. "They have recently been traveling, in a caravan of angels, to France, I believe." Her eccentric claims were often supported by the family's *mulata* servant, Florencia, who slept in her own room at the far end of the house and also spoke of "seeing" these poor children. But no one else did—not their father, Leocadio; nor their brother Fernando; nor their younger infant sister, Anabella. Still, Israel Levis passed through his days anticipating the twins' sudden appearance. And though they never came to him, to please his mother Israel sometimes told her that he, too, had seen them in their garden, playing happily under a tree, simply so that she would pull him close to her in an embrace.

His appearance

Those deaths made Doña Concepción overly vigilant when it came to the well-being of her other children, especially Israel, who suffered from a slight asthmatic condition—hence he was forbid- den in his infancy to wander far from her sight, or to climb any of their trees, commanded to avoid the rain, and urged to pray and pray to God that He protect him. She rewarded his obedience with a great abundance of food—the heavy and delicious cuisine of the tropics—plates of plantain fritters and yuca, pots of stew and plat- ters of crisped pork, Galician ham, Navarro sausages and Cádiz clams. She fed him so well that Israel did not mind the confinements (for she gave him the illusion of freedom), and he became, for a few years, a smaller version of the ever plump and massive figure that would later be well known in that city.

His face was already round and jowlish. He had blond hair, later to darken—perhaps Sephardic in origin—large ears and a decidedly sharp, ridged nose after his father, or in the manner of a tobacco shop Indian. Still, the warmth and intelligence of his eyes were unavoidable; they were intensely dark and, though of a quite normal size, seemed lost in the expanse of their broad sockets—and yet in those days when he looked at everything with a child's unrelenting curiosity, moving from object to object and face to face quickly, his eyes seemed so minuscule that one expected to hear the rattling of peas in his head, or the seeds in the calabaza gourd.

With a voracious appetite for food, he was always going up and down in weight. He lived for comfort and like most children of his social class, he did not have to go work at an early age. But the advantages that Israel enjoyed did not end with the privileges of his social level; he had also been spoiled by nature. Such was the early manifestation of his future virility that their house maid, Florencia, when bathing him often remarked, "What a wonder!" But he paid little attention to her, unable in his extreme youth to decipher the enchantment of her expression, and in his innocence regarded her delight as nothing more than the outcry of natural affection.

THE BLOSSOMING OF HIS LIFE AS A MUSICIAN: THEIR SALONS, 1895

One rainy afternoon when Israel was but a boy of five (so began the legend regarding the seeds of his musical career), he had been in their parlor watching his father play a few Bach pieces on the piano. As a physician attached to the Hospital de Reina Mercedes and with duties at the Hospital de San Lazaro, a leprosarium, and a private practice that he conducted from their home, Leocadio spent his scant leisure hours at that keyboard honing his skills and finding solace in a ritualistic playing of scales. A reserved man, whose main devotions were to his own family and to God (for men, as he often said, were wretched creatures, prone to inflicting misery and violence upon the world), he sometimes played the organ for a local church, and upon occasion held salons in the family's parlor, doctors and lawyers and city officials with their wives and children turning up on Sunday afternoons to dine and to converse.

Loving literature with nearly the same passion as he loved music, Leocadio had filled that house with books, his favorite works adorning the shelves in his study. There he kept the writings of Cervantes and Quevedo, Montaigne and Rousseau, and such Cuban writers and poets as Gabriel de la Concepción Valdés (or "Plácido," as he was also known), Juan Gualberto Gomez and the much revered José Martí, among many others. And when guests came to the house, such works were often a subject of discourse, poetic sentiments as profuse as the serrations of sunlight that fell against the octagonal-tile halls.

Formal, dignified and with a serious demeanor, Leocadio was a man who did not easily smile, his intelligent and compassionate eyes reflecting the sufferings he as a physician had witnessed over the years.

In those days, the 1890s, during the prelude to the formation of the Cuban republic, there was an abundance of patriotism and politics in the air. The city of Habana itself was in the process of change. The Prado, the main boulevard, was unpaved but lined with rows of royal palm trees and Spanish laurels; church bells pealed every hour; sanitation and toilet facilities, save for that to be found in the houses of the rich, were deplorable. In the 1890s, three hundred brothels, two hundred cafés and dozens of dance halls, as well as scores of fried-food eateries, or *fritas,* operated along the waterfronts. People got around the often muddy roads of the city in single-passenger carts called *volantes* and in larger coaches, *quitrines,* whose wheels were the height of a grown man. In the parks, scattered here and there around the city, municipal bands performed Gluck, Haydn, Domenico Scarlatti, under gazebos constructed of bamboo and crenelated steel. The Malecón drive on the gulf had not yet been built—rather, the sea crashed freely against the rocky shore.

A main port of call for more than three hundred years, the city of Habana (from the name of an Indian chieftain, Habaqua-nex), host to countless travelers and mariners, bustled with the energy of an old European capital, much discourse and a longing for independence from lofty Spain—a goal.

During these gatherings, Leocadio, ever formal in a white linen suit with a stiff-collar English shirt and lace bowtie, offered pieces from the classical music repertoire—Brahms, Bach, Mozart—and songs from Cuban zarzuelas and the music of island composers, like that of Ignacio Cervantes and Manuel Sammuels, as well. Occasionally, the wife of a friend joined him in recital with her especially good voice. Two dozen high-back chairs would be brought into the parlor, shots of rum were poured out, the men smoking cigars and the ladies sitting with their fans, sunlight glaring through the windows. Now and then, he invited literary figures into his household, the spirit and nationalism of José Martí prevailing over these gatherings. Martí was a poet and journalist, living in exile in New York, whose tracts and poems were read aloud and taken as a source of inspiration. And although Martí, a native of Habana who had grown up on the calle Industria, never visited, his mother often attended. When the music ended, certain individuals might get up before the gathering to recite some famous bit of poetry, a fragment of a novel memorized by heart, a bit of Ovidio in Latin, or in the instance of a professor affiliated with the Academia de Ciencias in Habana, a discourse on why a species of Cuban rodent, a *hutia,* or "silent dog," lacked vocal chords.

Hosting those occasions, his father, a man known for his measured manners—he was neither glib nor prone to quick pronouncements, except when it came to matters of discipline, medicine and religion—took great pleasure in his performances and liked to think that had his life turned out differently he might have been a musician.

In his own quiet way, Leocadio was a patriot and deeply believed in the cause of Cuban independence from Spain, even if he himself had first come to Cuba as a young medical officer in the Spanish army corps in 1872. But he had fallen in love with the climate, the affability of its people, and in the late 1870s with a pretty naval captain's daughter named Concepción Murillo Sanchez, whom he had met one Sunday morning on the steps of the church of Espíritu Santo. Their romance went beyond the attractions of youth—or near youth, for he was already past thirty and she an "old maid" at twenty-four—but in their mutual devotions to the passions of Christ they embarked on the course of a devout and sound family life, in a manner befitting such a pious Catholic couple.

During these salons, in the course of his toasts, it happened that Doctor Leocadio Levis always acknowledged his two masters: *"¡Para la patria y Dios!"* ("For God and country!") he would say, and everyone joined in, as this was a time when God still lingered in the world and when even a man of science like Leocadio Levis believed greatly in the moral virtues that religion brought into life. Whether the doctor believed in such matters like the soul or the punishments of Hell and the rewards of Heaven, like his wife, seemed irrelevant: rather, he was a man who trusted in the old traditions of Catholicism and its rituals—prayer and worship being conduits to the very worthwhile contemplations of the mysteries surrounding them. And above all, Leocadio, a man of order, fastidious and precise in his little ways, believed in the necessity of a system, superstitious or not, that appreciated the differences between right and wrong, even when he saw that unprincipled men sometimes flourished, that very good men, loving of their families and pious to their bones, collapsed into heaps of sagging corrupted flesh from leprosy, or that even the most pure of children succumbed to myriad diseases at the drop of the hat, as his own daughter had. He was the kind of man who traveled over the countryside, and if he encountered a poor soul at the brink of starvation, he thought nothing of giving his food away— "There will always be more for us." He hated the injustices of life in Cuba under the Spaniards, even if he had not long ago claimed himself a Spaniard.

Nevertheless, when he raised a toast to God and country he meant it. That was a time when every man, woman and child who passed through the doors of their house carried some religious object with them—a rosary, a crucifix, a scapular, a pendant of the Holy Mother, a ring bearing the image of a cross. And when the Levis, also imbued with their Catholic identities, bid their friends farewell, they did so fully satisfied that the values of friendship, culture, patriotism and religion had been splendidly observed.

THAT AFTERNOON IN 1895 WHEN HE HAD GRASPED AT INVISIBLE BELLS

One rainy afternoon, as his father serenely played Bach, Israel, standing behind him, studied the movement of Leocadio's stately hands over the keyboard, the symmetry of the notes that he pro-duced creating an atmosphere in which bells seemed to be ringing here and there in the air, tones dropping and rising in so fluid a fashion that before the child's eyes there formed a most comforting and invisible structure, like the room of a palace, its ceiling sup-ported by alabaster columns, its walls covered in velvet, and even the very wood of the floors, like the cedars of Lebanon, vibrating with an ageless harmony.

Shortly he found himself wanting to enter into that magical realm; though he was but a child of five, and knew nothing about the keys of G or E♭, nor of what the black hieroglyphics of his father's music books meant, his soul separated from the plump and amiable body that was its carrier, drifting into that palace room and grasping the bells as they passed him by, Israel happily float-ing inside a wondrous and supernatural place, as if through the soft folds of God's own heavenly cloak.

Such was his desire to imitate his father that his brows creased in concentration, and with a remarkable grasp of the process, he memorized his father's fluid movements over the keys. And even though he had heard his father, and other pianists, performing different pieces during those salons, it was as if he was experiencing something vitally new—like seeing bloodred wine in a glass for the first time, or the sunset colorations on the skin of a mango, or noticed how marble tears fell along the gaunt cheekbones of the downcast Jesus in church—life filled with so many remarkable things, and the music of Bach suddenly a part of it.

And just like that: when his father finished the piece and turned to his son, saying, "Bach was a genius, yes?" the boy nestled beside him and placed his fingers upon the blessed ivories, reproducing, without error, two full measures of what his father had just played, and though there was an unavoidable awkwardness to the child's movements, his touch was delicate and his grasp of the phrasing complete.

In that instance, this display of precocious talent so impressed and delighted Leocadio that this guarded man called his wife into the parlor, and instructing his son to play again, declared happily: "Can you see—¡qué maravilloso!" ("How wonderful!") And Doctor Levis broke out into the broadest smile and then added, more seriously: "Tomorrow, when I return from the hospital at four, we will sit together by this piano and we will see if this is something that you really can do, or if it is an illusion."

But as he retired to his study, where he often spent his evenings examining the slides of human blood and butterfly wings under a microscope, he was heard to say to his wife and their maid Florencia, "You see? Are not the surprises of God many?"

HIS EARLY TRAINING AND A FIRST RECITAL

Daily the doctor made time for his son's instruction, and in that glorious epoch of becoming, which, in memory, seemed to have lasted for more than two hundred years—such did the moments of his early youth move ever so languidly forward—Israel's life became one with his devotion to music; in those days when he was neither praying nor eating nor roaming among the flame blossoms and palm bushes of their back garden, he spent his hours by the piano, diligently practicing the scales that his father had written out for him, the reading of which he quickly mastered. Soon he was playing the gavottes and fugues that Bach had affec-tionately composed for his wife Anna Magdalena, and within a year he was performing several of Bach's more complicated pieces with such self-assuredness and maturity that it was not long before Doctor Levis came to the conclusion that the boy would greatly benefit from more-formal training. Thus he contacted the well-known piano teacher Hugo Van de Meer, a professor of music who taught at his own makeshift conservatory in an old mansion on Virtudes. This goateed Dutchman, who years earlier had journeyed to the island out of curiosity and then made Habana his home, took on the tutelage of the doctor's son three afternoons a week.

He received these lessons in a high-ceilinged room in Van de Meer's second-floor study, the interior of the building with its great and decrepit halls and hanging chandeliers and its neoclassi-cal appointments so reminiscent of the sunny palazzi that Levis would visit years later in Italy. His trips to the conservatory, in the company of Florencia, away from the confines of their house and into the center of the city, he would remember fondly. Habana was filled with so much life—street vendors, beautiful women, soldiers and priests—and when he climbed the stairways of the conservatory itself, he could hear so many other students of vary-ing ages, practicing their violins, trumpets, pianos, voices—of bari-tones and tenors and sopranos ululating; it seemed as if he had entered into a realm, where he, as a boy of "considerable gifts" and a delicate nature, felt naturally at home. Though Van de Meer was a sometimes demanding teacher, presiding over these sessions with such an attentiveness to the execution of proper technique and the repetition of scales that no child, even Levis, could ever enjoy, the future composer nevertheless relished those sumptuous dreams that music allowed him to inhabit. And though the joints of his plump hands sometimes ached and he often cried out for his mother and father, there would be a time in his life when Levis, looking back, would most remember his little moments of triumph, when he had satisfied the worldly Dutchman, when his teacher's mask of authority collapsed and he simply smiled, nodding approv-ingly and saying, "Bien hecho" ("Well done").

Whatever his struggles, the rigors of such training produced in Israel an early virtuosity, and in late 1897 he gave his first pub-lic performance during one of his father's salons. "It is my plea-sure," the good doctor said to that gathering, "to present my son Israel, in a rendition of Wolfgang Mozart's Rondo alla Turca."

By that time, Israel was already quite a portly child, and in his own linen suit, with a looped cravat, which his mother had knot-ted for him, he nearly cut the figure of a man. He was in the habit back then of parting his hair in the middle so that his brilliantined head glared in the midafternoon light, as he quickly bowed before the gathering in such a demure way as to make many laugh; then stuttering out a few words, he sat down before the piano. Though nervousness would always attend his public performances, once he laid his fingers upon the keyboard, the first notes he played managed to shut out the rest of the world: "Concentration is everything," Van de Meer had often told him. "Let God move you," his father had said. *"Dios te has dado un gran talento"* ("You have a God-given gift"), his mother had often said.

With these words in mind, he overcame his child's timidity.

Once again he entered into the invisible bell-ridden room that he had first imagined while hearing his father play Bach, a serene place, removed from this world, closer to the genius of God, that heavenly presence whom he prayed to every morning and at night flowing through him. Though he was already playing in an accom-plished manner, humility prevented him from believing that he himself could have been the source of such pleasing sounds.

Of course, he knew that the many hours he spent practicing made a difference—Israel supposed that anyone, given the proper training, could execute a piece, but being so young and at heart lazy in so many other ways, he was simply amazed by his own proficiency. Lifted away from that parlor, nothing else existed but the keyboard and its lovely notes, and though he was too young to understand what would happen to him, during those spells of pure and isolated concentration—akin to meditation—years later, he would come to conceive the act of making music as something of a mystical experience, for with the world put off, with no other context to define them, musicians were left to face the deity alone.

When he finished the piece, he turned to the gathering, his

largish ears brimming red, for he felt as if he had been on a long journey to another world, and he bowed. They applauded him: women, grandmothers and middle-aged wives, nodding approvingly; the men, so much wrapped up in their worldly affairs, but with a bent for high culture, striding forward to offer him their hands, to rap his back. And his own father and mother, beaming with pride, were no less pleased.

Precociously adept at the piano, Israel Levis was soon performing in other salons and parties around the city. Often attending concerts at the Teátro Tacon and the Albisu, which featured such renowned pianists as José Manuel Jiménez and Tomás Martín, he began to acquire certain affectations—pulling a carefully folded velvet cloth from his pocket to dust the piano bench or chair, or a handkerchief to occasionally wipe the sweat off his perspiring and fleshy brow. And though his younger sister, Anabella, was only five years old when he had commenced upon his life as an informal recitalist, Israel was so enamored of her natural charms and prettiness that, for these gatherings, he enlisted her to turn the pages of the sheet music that were set before him, raising his brows as a cue and nodding; Anabella, a vision of loveliness in a blue dress and with a barrette in her curly dark hair, assiduously attending to the pages and partaking of the rapturous applause that often greeted those "precious" children.

In those days, Israel acquired something of a quite professional demeanor and a modicum of ambition, entering and winning medals in various juvenile-category competitions, such as those sponsored by his school and by different cultural societies of the city. To his mother and father's delight he accumulated a number of first- and second-place distinctions for performance. So agreeable was his playing that it seemed a matter of destiny that he become a serious musician and composer, and not a medical student, like his brother, Fernando.

CHURCHES, 1899

Then, too, he was of such a maturity and so prone to a religious devotion that with his father's approval, Israel, at the tender age of nine, began to play the organ in the churches of Espíritu Santo, La Reina de la Merced, and Nuestra Señora del Pilar in La Habana, and shortly, he began to lead their juvenile choirs, such was his mastery and love for sacred music. Spending so many happy hours under the vaulted ceilings of naves, with the strong presence of Christ and God the Father and the Holy Spirit ("Three but One"—"Tres pero uno"—being the name of a piano piece he would later write about those days), he truly believed that if the world were to end in an instant, he would be lifted directly up into the heart of that divinity.

In those churches, the sight of so much statuary and the scent of incense and candles brought him into an intimate communion with those saints and holy figures who were posed here and there on globes and pedestals and marble niches, their hands held out to him, their expressions so compassionate and loving that he considered his work—the playing of Bach on those church organs and of devotedly leading children's choirs in chorales—a humble offering to the glorious presence that had made everything in existence.

HE'D
WRITTEN OUT
THE MELODY

IT HAS BEEN SAID THAT when Israel Levis wrote his most famous song, *"Rosas Puras,"* in 1928, he was standing by the counter of a street-corner luncheonette, in old Habana, sipping coffee and eating with delight a caramelized pastry; that the melodious cry of a passing flower seller on the street so inspired him that he quickly wrote the tune out on a paper napkin, its notes coming spontaneously to him, as if from Heaven. Another version has it that Levis, in a state of profound disillusionment over the political situation in Cuba (for he had been a member of the Grupo Minorista, which was not favored by the Machado government), had been preparing to leave his beloved Habana for Paris as an exile. Or, as rumors went, that "El Maestro," of an "artistic disposition," was in love with a man and that he could no longer take the repressive atmosphere of life in that city or the shame of his desires; that he had spent many an hour in his house on the calle Olivares composing *"Rosas Puras"* as an anthem of nostalgia; that he had nearly wept during the process of its conception. But the most accepted lore has it that Levis composed this song while dining with his lyricist Manny Cortez in the Campana Bar, famous for its croquettes, a theatrical hangout on the intersection of Virtudes and Consulado streets and that he had written it quickly, in a matter of twenty passionate minutes.

What is certain is that *"Rosas Puras"* was brought into this world long ago, its composer pulling that simple melody out of the balmy October air of Habana, and though he first sat down before the piano to play that piece, at eight-thirty in the evening, after the moon had risen over the east and the stars had begun their timid orbits across the sky, he could not have imagined that this little piece of music would not only outlast him, but that it would seep through time, like a ghost, and reach innumerable hearts and souls.

In any event, this famous song was first recorded by the singer Rita Valladares, whose presence in his life had evidently been another source of Levis's joy—and longing.

WHEN HE WROTE THE MELODY

He was thirty-eight years old, corpulent, tall, beset with a heavily jowled, Catalan-Gallego face. Never one to rush around, he, in the languidness of his movements, always gave the impression that he had just awakened from sleep. Moderation was not in his heart. Well known for the quantities of food and brandy he could consume at a single sitting, he was the subject of something of a myth that came about because of a few candid remarks uttered by the *celestinas* of the city's brothels: that he was as virile as his waistline was expansive. Nothing like the suave dandies who were a fixture at the Habana Yacht Club and who wooed the ladies at high-society dances and the bars of the tourist hotels, Levis could nevertheless effortlessly command the attention of a room; not just because of his physical immensity, for he often towered over others, nor because he moved through the world in a cloud of kindly emanations, for he had friends everywhere, but because he exuded such creative—and thereby virile—energies that his presence was always preceded by a wave of recognition. He was unmistakably rotund and could be easily picked out a block or two away. He found the sidewalks annoyingly narrow, especially in the older quarters of the city, so much so that he would have to step down off the curb and gingerly navigate the traffic-heavy streets.

His eyes were warm and not yet capable of expressing the horror and disillusionments of his later life; eyes so kind that small children and babies were always reaching out to touch him while he caressed their faces with his enormous hands, tenderly; his thick and wavy hair combed back was a pleasure to feel.

On many a day he supposed that if he lost seventy pounds a more angular, sharper face would emerge—somewhere under the fleshiness of his facial skin were the high cheekbones of his late father whose classically Spanish features had blessed the countenance of his older brother Fernando.

Although he was the son and brother of doctors, whenever he felt any symptoms of illness, he went to church, prayed and then resorted to "natural" cures. For a special purification of the body, he sometimes took the saltwater baths of the Campos Eliseos, by the sea, or if he experienced indigestion he might enter a pharmacy for a bromide. Occasionally, if he suffered from a stiff back or a killing shoulder from his labors by the piano, he resorted to the herbal remedies of a Chinese apothecary, or relaxed his muscles through an especially heavy bout of drinking, or he visited a *santera* in her *botánica* for a cleansing with incense and burning tobacco leaves.

Otherwise Levis, ever engaged by both superstition and the formality of his Catholic faith, left the state of his health to the "fates," for as he often thought, what did medical treatments really matter when one comes and goes in this world according to the whims of God, anyway?

His sister Anabella

Often, as he walked along the streets of Habana, when he saw young couples strolling hand in hand, he reflected upon the sad fate that befell his younger sister, Anabella, who had not lived to experience many of life's pleasures. His page-turner, who he loved very much, had died at the age of twelve in 1907 from a massive infection of the kidneys, which had eluded her father's diligent treatments. Even more than twenty years later Israel Levis remembered how fiercely troubled he, as a seventeen-year-old, had been over his younger sister's illness.

Before she had fallen ill, she had loved to sing popular songs and to linger in the kitchen helping the cook, or to follow Israel out onto their back patio, the garden blooming around them, as he studied a piece of music, his sister regarding him lovingly and waiting on his every whim. In those days all he ever thought about was how permanent and everlasting their mutual love seemed to be—the outside world be damned—for they were insep' arable and felicitous in their musical collaborations: Israel per' forming here and there in the city; Anabella, in a flowery dress, a radiant and loving angel by his side. It was a pity that she had come running into the parlor one day after school to cry upon his shoulder, frightened by the sight of her own blood-ridden urine, not from menstruation, but from uremia.

"*Hermano,* hold me," she had said to him, the loveliness of her vibrant eyes giving way to sadness and fear. With the apprehen' sion that Anabella was journeying to a destination from which she would not return, he maintained a vigil by her bedside for months as she, bloated and septic, wasted away. Sometimes when she seemed most in pain he had felt like screaming, could not eat, and restlessly prowled the hall. Or he sat before his piano banging out chords and scales so loudly as to drown out her moaning. Or he played a magical passage by Beethoven, escaping into the sylvan' and castle-dotted lands of middle Europe in another cen' tury. (On the other hand, piano pieces by Ignacio Cervantes trans' ported him into the drawing rooms of plantation-life Cuba, circa 1870s.) One day, on his way back from the conservatory, he saw his father on the street outside their house, speaking to the morti' cian Orfeo Malone, and he knew what had happened. With his stomach a tangle of knots, he rushed quickly to her side, pushing open the door to her room as his older brother told him, "*Hermanito,* don't!" Doña Concepción was sitting silently beside her daughter's bed; Anabella, with her powdered face, a bouquet of withered roses clasped in her hands upon her lap, dead; his mother trembling and fixing him with an anguished gaze that asked, "Why have I lost three of my children?" Beside his sister's bed, set upon a small table, a pitcher of water, and a crucifix; a mantilla had been left draped over the back of a wicker plantation chair—all stillness in that room. At the same time, there was much sunlight streaming in through the shuttered windows: that light, in patterns of undulating eighth and sixteenth notes, spreading across the Spanish-tile floors, against the faded yellow walls, and streaming over Anabella in repose, so "lively" was that light as it were, so permanent seeming, that for a moment Israel believed that his sister would be awakened by that solar music and arise to the day, like an angel.

He believed in many things. A member of the Theosophical Society of Habana, on the calle of San Ignacio, he found the society's teachings compatible with his own feelings that "something beyond the physical eye is there." Raised with the apparitions of saints and angels and of Jesus, brimming with light, that came to him, a good Catholic child, in his dreams, he, as an adult, heartily believed in the supernatural. Not only did he have a fondness for priests and pious people, but had come to admire those local practitioners of "sympathetic magic" and spells who were known as *santeros*. As a matter of nocturnal habit, he liked to roam various neighborhoods in the city of Habana and its outskirts in the countryside, observing the rituals of the various cults—of Santería, Abacúa, Mayombé—wherein animals were sacrificed, feathers and bones and seashells were strewn over the ground, drums were beaten, and dancers, chanting and circling bonfires, communed with their ancient African gods. Often on those excursions he witnessed the performance of minor miracles—or acts that seemed as such—priests and priestesses curing chronic headaches and cases of impotence with a dousing of water, encouraging fertility in a woman, or bringing about love, with potions, the passing of hands over an ailing part of the body, a supposed cure.

Nearly medieval in his Catholic beliefs, Levis was convinced that Heaven, Purgatory and Hell may well have existed, these "places" translating in his mind as "Joy, Sadness and Loneliness" (or, musically speaking, as the keys of G major, A minor, and E♭ minor, 7th).

So great was his belief in those other realms that he once had a dream in which he found himself traveling by carriage with his late father and his brother over the Cuban countryside, the carriage passing through Heaven, Purgatory and, most vividly, Hell. As his father pulled on the reins, Israel saw an entire valley going up in flames, the fires rising higher than the highest royal palms, the earth smoldering, smoke everywhere, and flaring columns of fire scorching the sky.

He already had a reputation as being slightly eccentric, religiously speaking, and could not rationally explain certain of his beliefs to his most doubtful friends; for example, the notion of souls in transit, as per the teachings of Madame Blavatsky, with reincarnation at its center. How was it, he would ask, that he sometimes had vivid dreams of meeting Johann Sebastian Bach, of finding himself in seventeenth-century Germany, in a church, watching the great choirmaster conduct a chorale? And of trembling with excitement over the prospect of shaking this solemn man's hand. Or what of his dreams about being a black slave in Cuba, circa 1820, running across a field in the attempt to escape a cruel plantation owner, his ankles, bruised and cut by shackles, the dream so intense that he would wake in the morning to his legs throbbing in pain? Who could explain that? He would pour more drinks and shrug his shoulders, lifting his right palm upward, in a circular motion: "Who can say?"

Surely, his exposure to the African culture, as it existed in Cuba, may have planted the thought of having once been a slave, but what of the German he heard being spoken in his dreams, that language which he had heard sung in lieder but did not particularly take pains to understand?

"Why shouldn't we return to achieve the perfection that will lead our souls to heaven?" he sometimes asked his doubting friends.

And ghosts: In this regard his mother's influence was strong. He was so curious about these spirits that he occasionally went to the Cementerio Colón to wander among the tombs and mausoleums, sensing, he would swear, an intimation of the souls resting there. Inclined to stand perfectly still in the center of that marble necropolis, famed for its gaudy and opulent "birthday cake" tombs and mausoleums, the carved images of angels and saints around him, he often lingered before the entranceway to a gated crypt, taking in its dank scents of moss and gravesoil as if Lazarus might suddenly emerge, the spirit exuding calm and peace.

For the most part, Levis thought that he was living under the protection of an angel, or the six spirits of the dead that he'd imag-ined presided over the dense vegetation of his family's garden and that escaped as vapors from the ground, in the early mornings.

ISRAEL LEVIS AND WOMEN

In those days his first passion in life was his music; women—even those he most secretly cherished—existed mainly as tantaliz-ing reminders that he, for all his musical facility and professional-ism, was an amateur when it came to matters of love.

Evenhanded and respectful of others, particularly women, and so grateful for what gifts that God had given him, as his mother had told him time and time again, he never really lamented his soli-tary bachelor's state; as he saw it, the niceties of dining and drink and the pleasures of the brothel were enough—most of the time.

Eating and drinking to excess, he did so as a kind of compen-sation for the fact that he had no woman, besides his mother (and Santa María, if you like) in his life; the celestinas—who merrily sat-isfied this corpulent but kindly man, and who always made him feel good about his rather impressive masculinity—these women, often young and uneducated (except in the use of their bodies and tongues) did not count. And while the ordinary women of his acquaintance found him, in his courtly nature, a man of abundant charms, his presence never seemed to induce in their hearts the kind of romantic fervor and passion that he often had wanted, nor were they able to draw much emotion from his heart.

Resigned to the fact that in all likelihood he would never have

his own family, Levis found solace in the small ecstasies of creativity and public acclaim—the sound of applause in a crowded
theater, suspending time and transporting him, in his own mind, to
some grand, if fleeting, place of glorious abstract pleasures. He
was proud of the way he earned his livelihood—especially when
he'd turn on his crystal radio set and happen to hear one of his
own compositions played over the air, or when he walked in the
park and the municipal orchestra performed his own "Gloria por
La Patria," and most satisfyingly, when he overheard a young man,
strolling with a girlfriend along the Malecón or the Paseo de
Prado whistling one of his melodies.

Wary of romantic involvements, he had never been married, had
no children, and while he often thought that he would one day
bring himself to an amenable state of mind for such an enterprise,
he almost preferred the inspiration that his longings and loneliness for women brought to him. He supposed that, had he a different, less moralistic character—if that crucifix around his neck
meant nothing to him—he might have used his position as a more
or less well-known composer and director of various orchestras
to his advantage when it came to the ladies. But he remained
polite, self-effacing and generous, never expecting anything from a
woman other than a little gratitude, a smile.

Besides, he was one of those Cubans whose greatest love was
for his pious mother. Levis was his mother's protector, her provider, her companion to church and in prayer, her dear son, who
always affected a deferential manner around her.

She was, after all, his first muse and a widow.

A LITTLE PIECE OF HIS LIFE AT HOME IN HIS HOUSE ON OLIVARES WITH HIS MOTHER

Each morning he would rouse himself from his bed, retreat into the bathroom, gargle with salted water, brush his teeth with baking soda, take a shower, dress and then join his dear and beloved mother for breakfast by their back patio table. He always treated her tenderly and, looming over her, for she was a small woman, planted a kiss upon her cheek, saying, *"Un besito para mi mamá buena"* ("A little kiss for my sweet mother"), and she would laugh and grasp the lobe of his right ear, saying, *"Gracias, mi hijito bebé"* (Thank you, my little baby son), even though he was well into middle age at the time and would have crushed any cradle.

They would sit under the heavy fronds of a mango tree, their maid, Florencia, bringing out trays of his favorite repast: three fried eggs with chorizos and bread, sliced papayas and mangoes (from their own trees), lots of strong coffee. And then, if Doña Concepción was in a good mood and had slept well the night before, no solemn thoughts possessing her, she might men-tion that she would be joining several of her female companions for an afternoon excursion to a movie (*"Ese señor, Buster Keaton, ¡es fantástico!"*) or that she was going off with one of her friends to look at dresses in the shops along O'Reilly, some new French fashion that she had seen in a magazine having caught her eye.

She would ask him for money—as he supported her in those days.

"Cómo no," he'd say, pulling from his pocket a twenty-peso note.

Or, if he was not too busy, or intent on finishing a piece of music, he would accompany her out—for they were often seen walking together through the streets of La Habana—to look in shop windows and to light candles or to take confession in church, and when her heart was sad, to roam among the tombs and monuments of the Cementerio Colón, where she would place fresh bouquets of flowers upon the graves of her late husband and sweet children, weeping.

There was something else: Though dead for nearly ten years, Leocadio lingered in that house on Olivares. If the life of Israel Levis could have been staged as a zarzuela, the good doctor's ghost would have wandered through the rooms of their home, in a faint aureole of light, and only Doña Concepción would have seen him.

He had died in the year 1919, during a journey on horseback through the Sierra Maestra mountains when something had startled his mount and he was thrown from his saddle, breaking his neck. When several *campesinos* found him lying on the ground near a stream, with a blue butterfly still fluttering in a net, they brought his body down by mule to the city of Holguín and packed it in ice. The composer himself had been in the midst of rehearsals for a zarzuela, *La Reina Isabel,* when he heard the sad news. Interrupting his work, he journeyed by rail to Santiago, where his brother Fernando lived and had a medical practice. The two traveled together to claim the body and to bring it back to La Habana for a High Mass and proper Catholic burial.

Israel's was the face—flushed, eyes sad—and trembling hands that greeted visitors and family members to the house. It was he

who, with Fernando and members of the staff of his father's hospital, carried the weight of the coffin upon his shoulders.

The good elder doctor was of such importance as to be
acclaimed in an American book as a member of *One Hundred
Prominent Cubans* (Harvard University Press, 1907), and his funeral
procession to the cemetery drew a crowd of several hundred
mourners, including president of the republic Menocal and other
dignitaries, and many of the poor whom Doctor Leocadio Levis had
treated out of charity. Life, as Israel knew it, had changed forever.

Deeply shocked and saddened by the loss of that warm and
loving man, Israel had the consolation of knowing that at least his
father had lived to see the flowering of his musical career, for over
the years Leocadio had proudly attended every zarzuela for which
his son had composed music and nearly every one of his salons
and recitals, and the doctor was quick to brag about the medals in
composition and performance that Israel Levis had been given
along the way.

"My son, you are one of the glories of my life," he had said.

The composer had privately wept, especially in the late hours
of the night when the world seemed a quiet place, and he would
set his fingers upon his piano keyboard and, sounding a single
note to begin a Bach prelude, recall seeing his father's face as he
lay in an open casket, and with the finality of his death the very
thought *This is the last time I will touch his flesh* colliding with all the
sadness—or call it a nagging and agonizing suspicion—that his
father would never hear Bach again or open his eyes to a single
ray of sunlight, or that he himself would never gaze into the
warmth and intelligence of his father's expression.

He had the comfort of knowing that his father was a quite

religious man, who had lived well, but at heart Israel suspected that he had no belief in the afterlife, even if his father had possessed enough of a mystical bent as to say, one morning, for no particular reason at all, "When my day comes to leave this world, I imagine that it will be a curious thing."

And not a day has passed when I have not thought about him.

"Do you remember, my son, how by this time of the morning your papá would be leaving for the hospital?" Doña Concepción would say during breakfast. "Remember how your papá, may God rest his soul, was always dressed to perfection, not a stitch out of place? Remember how he would take his exercises just before breakfast—he was very fit my boy, not fat like you at all."

"How could I ever forget, Mamá?"

And sometimes just the mention of his late father was sufficient to sustain her through the day, but if she had a sad dream the night before, a more problematic situation would evolve—Doña Concepción, coming to tears easily, and seeming, in that early morning light, so frail and vulnerable that the composer would be hard put to leave her side.

"Come and sit with me while I work on some things in my study," he'd say. Or, he would hold her hand in the warmth of his own, his large palm dwarfing her's, and kiss her knuckles tenderly. "Oh, Mamá, you know that we all love you very much; you have nothing to be sad about." Even if his mother did not join him in his study, as she did not want to intrude upon the thoughts of her "genius" son, he made it his practice, as he would sit before the piano, to call out to her—"Mamá, where are you?" Or, "Mamá, are you fine?" And she'd answer, *"Aquí"*—"I'm here"—from a room deep in the house.

After her husband's passing, she had spent a year, in black, without venturing from their house, save for attending Masses, and lived in so thorough a silence that for a long time Israel knew of her presence mainly through the ruffling of her dress skirts, the opening of a jar, a sigh.

On those sad days she had seemed barely able to answer him.

"Are you hungry, Mamá?" he'd ask.

"Are you ready for church?"

"Do you like this piece of music?"

A silence even followed her into church, where she sat through the services without even bothering with the responses and prayers, as if she no longer cared. Sitting beside her, he noticed the slightest movement of her lips, nothing more, as if her very life had been drawn from her, or, as if she were decidedly questioning the reality of the God who had failed her.

Then she entered another phase, engendered by a dream, in which one morning she announced: "My son, the idea has come to me that perhaps your father was a Jew. And that is why God has been acting so cruelly to us." Then: "We must make up for this with our prayers."

"Let us pray," she would say, again and again.

On yet another morning, Doña Concepción reported that in the middle of the previous night, as she had been wandering through the house, she saw Leocadio sitting in his study, examining slides through a microscope.

"He was so real, my son, I could barely breathe," she told him. "He told me to take a look through his microscope." Peering through the eyepiece, she saw, in the center of a glass slide, a con- figuration of crystals, burning with light, which she took for the Holy Ghost. And this had greatly boosted her spirits, for she con- fessed: "My son, to tell you the truth, for a time I had lost my faith in God. But I can see now that he has taken your papá to his heart. He is in peace and waiting for me."

It was not long before Israel began to see a change in the voracity of her religious beliefs: ever more small statues of the Holy Mother, and crucifixes appearing everywhere in the house, Doña Concepción, with a rosary in hand, praying continually, and often greeting her son with a few dabs from a vial of holy water, which she applied to his forehead. And waiting—so it seemed to her son—for her day of salvation to come.

Though he was of the opinion that his father's death, above all others, had affected her reasoning, he never neglected her. He always brought her along to his Habana concerts, sometimes trav- eled to nearby towns with her by his side, his *"muñeca"* (or "doll"), as he called her, keeping after him. Even so, Israel hoped that she would remarry, for she had aged well, and in fact seemed much younger than her years, her skin as smooth and unlined as a young woman's. To that end he often brought prospective suitors—pro- fessors and pharmacists and bankers, of a quite "mature" age, who were widowers or who had never married before—into the house, or invited her out to social events, but to no avail.

In the meantime, she intimated in little ways that Israel Levis was at the center of her life, and no matter how often he made the gentle suggestion that she might be happier staying with his brother Fernando and his family in Santiago, his mother, who had lived in that house in Vedado for more than forty years, was not at all inclined to move away, no matter how much she loved her other son.

"I will live here until the day I die," she often said, for she could not imagine being apart from those emanations that remained of her late husband, ever present there.

It was not that he never left his mother's side—in his absence she often presided over the household, tormenting Florencia with her inordinate insistence on cleanliness and chastity. (Or on "good" days she would sing a lullaby and sew and dispense advice to the maid about matters of religion or love.) Taking great pains to assure that Doña Concepción would not be lonely in his absence, Levis would ask his composer and musician friends to visit her during his journeys away. And he enrolled her in various societies that hosted balls and parties, which she never attended. Her one constant visitor, on Tuesday afternoons, was the local priest Father Celsus, with whom she often prayed (for her husband had met his fatal accident on a Tuesday). Occasionally one of her sisters came by with her children to visit, but mainly she spent her hours conceiving her life as an unending vigil.

TERESA VILLÓN

Certainly there had been women he might have married had he been able to bring himself to an agreeable state of mind: Once, when he was just twenty years old and already monumentally fat, a figure whose shadow fell as wide as a church's along the cobblestone street, he found himself in the company of a fellow music student from the conservatory, Teresa Villón, who had been foisted upon him by his mother. She was a young singer of a delicate and frail nature, whom he had often accompanied on piano at recitals, and who, in her docile manner, plain looks and near invisibility, struck his mother as the kind of girl she could order about and keep closely in her control, as she wanted a daughter-in-law that would never abandon her or persuade her husband to leave his home, as had her older son's wife, Gloria. Up to that point Israel had pursued a few flirtations with other female music students but nothing had come of these, as he was mainly interested in four things at that stage of his life—music, food, God and the occasional sexual pleasure—and found courtship both tedious and time consuming, the necessities of polite banter with a woman, in the presence of a chaperone (usually a broomstick-wielding grandmother), on the chance that a romance might be pursued in the future, so aggravating Israel Levis that it became his usual policy to extricate himself from such situations by quickly overstepping the bounds of gentlemanly behavior. (And doing so with a sad and puzzled expression upon his face.)

But the waiflike and thin Teresa Villón seemed, in her apparent absence of personality, to have thoroughly enchanted his mother, who, meeting Teresa at a recital, quickly invited her over to the house on a Sunday afternoon. During this visit Israel and Teresa sat next to each other in high-back chairs in the parlor, so that they might become better acquainted, Doña Concepción and Teresa's mother watching them. Although Levis and Teresa had gotten along well during their recitals, the notion of this arranged romance absolutely terrified them, mainly because, in just about every conceivable way, they were opposites—Levis voracious in his wish to consume the pleasures of this world and to fill it with music, while Teresa, in her placid indifference to life, seemed more like a graveyard spirit than a woman to him. She seemed so delicate that when the young composer happened to fantasize, however fleetingly, what it would be like to make love to her, he imagined the mating rituals of a mastodon and a kitten—in other words, a physical impossibility.

Appreciating her voice—she was a fine bel canto singer—he worked hard to overlook the plainness of her appearance, for he was, deep down, a *caballero*—a chivalrous gentleman.

Still this could go only so far. Even though they spent that first Sunday, and several others after it, agreeably enough, they really did not have much to say to each other, this would-be couple often sighing and only speaking when addressed by Concepción, who would make supercilious inquiries along the lines of: "Perhaps you two youngsters might care to discuss which operas you like most." Or: "Teresa, my son likes to eat, a lot, which is a good thing because I am sure you are an excellent cook, aren't you?" Then: "Perhaps, you could discuss with us your approach to one of my son's favorite dishes, paella."

Not that they didn't like each other, but even listless Teresa was already in love with somebody else, and Israel himself, in accommodating his mother, only seemed to come to life whenever Teresa's older brother Miguel, a dentist, came by to join them for lunch: Levis's heart rate quickening over the man's beauty and suave manner, a confusing reaction, especially back then, in 1910.

LEVIS AND HIS BROTHER FERNANDO

That he and his older brother Doctor Fernando Levis, joined by common blood, were so different in outlooks, especially when it came to women, was a matter of disposition, seemingly formed in the womb, for Fernando had an uncluttered and direct view of life: marriage, children, profession and the sound management of one's personal affairs. He lived in a large house in Santiago with his wife and young infant, Victor, and though he sometimes came to Habana to attend symposiums and to visit with his younger brother and mother, he was so busy in his practice and with his own minor political ambitions that he tended to have little leisure time. Somehow, Fernando, so loose and freewheeling in his youth (yet studious at the same time), and who had always tried to encourage Israel's participation in the more ordinary pleasures of life, had become a most serious man, a figure of such composure and dignity that Israel had come to feel, at times, that he no longer knew him.

As a young man, when Fernando tried to encourage him to get out into the world, mainly to dances, Israel had remained demure. Even in his youth he had never liked to dance, not the rumba, not the conga (though another side of him, when drinking holiday rum, always wanted to enjoy the carnival festivities and parties at the local social clubs of the city). The young ladies of Habana, well-bred but fun-loving, and, in fact, searching for future husbands, were both intrigued and puzzled by the formality with which the doctor's son carried himself and by his solemn ways. While it was perfectly natural to dance—the other young men, among them Fernando himself, madly in love with Gloria López, who would become his wife, took every opportunity for courtship, exalting in the merriment and veiled sexuality of those *fiestas*—Israel was content to sit off to the side, watching the proceedings around him. Of course, now and then he made his way out to the dance floor, but in his portly youth he was so self-conscious about his size that when he joined the crowd to rumba he had the impression that his head was as large as a house. Inevitably his older brother cajoled him into dancing with one of the young women, and he performed as best as he could manage, never truly enjoying himself, so much did he, for various reasons, feel apart from the others.

Despite his indifference to these events, he was never impolite to anyone and in his way he was friendly. But he was already so prone to introspection that it was hard for anyone, even the loveliest of young women, to draw him out. Invariably, he would leave those festivities alone, walking home through the Chinese lantern–lit central *placita,* by the church, past the telegraph office and the bakery, to the family's house, half-hidden in the closure of massive, heavy-boughed trees, in through the garden door. There he often encountered his father working late into the night or he entered the house to an absolute silence, would suddenly feel overcome by a state of expectation, as if on that particular evening something remarkable, as the abrupt appearance of spirits, might happen. Nothing ever did. Solitary as a monk, he would retire to his room and read by the light of a kerosene lamp into the early morning hours, so many odd thoughts coming to him.

Still, they enjoyed the occasions when they saw each other— the artist and the doctor, who had taken different paths in life, joined by their love and their mutually agreeable memories of their father, whom they had loved very much, and the tacit agreements they had come to about their mother. Even when his older brother had offered to take their mother in—and in this regard he was sincere—Israel, long a creature of habit, accustomed to their weekly outings to church and dedicated to her well-being, like a good Cuban son, was in any event, a bachelor (though that was not strictly the case—he was wed to his music), and he felt it morally correct that he remain with his mother, looking after her— even though she never seemed to appreciate the numerous compromises he had made regarding their life together.

His study, 1928

As long as he could compose, in relative peace, he would remain content. After all, once he stepped into his study—with its doors that opened to a garden—that was life enough for him. Habana was his universe and, in those days, he considered himself already widely traveled and well-lived.

By then he'd been to Europe four times, acquiring along the way a certain measure of sophistication—or say, a dollop of worldliness, even if he was always happiest in his own home. His earliest and most memorable journey, made with his family before the First World War, on what was then called the "Grand Tour," had lasted six weeks. His visits to the major cities of Europe left a strong impression upon him and he cherished, aside from so many encounters with good wines and food, certain photographs of his very proper family—his father and mother and his brother, all formally attired, posing before the Arch of Titus in the Roman Forum, and, among many other places of note, on the steps of the

Vatican itself. (Later he had watched his mother, a wisp in a dress, so religious and devout, weeping before the papal altar.) And yes, there had been that photograph taken in front of the Arc de Triomphe in beautiful Paris (later, "hellish Paris").

With a fondness for objects—anything that would commemorate his friendships and accomplishments—he had collected not only various scores (composers Ravel, Fauré, Respighi dominating) but numerous mementos from those travels: a bronze gondola paperweight from Venice, a marble nineteenth-century *Eros* shooting an arrow that he'd found in a bric-a-brac shop in Arles, a Moorish tile from Seville. Even though his instrument was the piano, he returned from Spain with a flamenco guitar that he kept propped up on a bundle of pillows on a couch in the study.

Indifferent to order, he allowed his study to become a clutter of sheet music, scores, items of clothing, wilting flowers and newspapers. This kind of minor disarray was somehow pleasing to Levis, for he took pleasure in having a plentitude of things. During his walks through the city, he found himself compulsively spending money on whatever objects struck him as potential sources of inspiration: Chinese lanterns, neoclassical bric-a-brac, rare old Spanish fans (from one of his favorite shops on calle Obispo 119— Carranza's Fan & Curio Store) wooden birds and gilded cages, and many instruments that gave his parlor and study the air of a bazaar. Add to this many books, medals and awards from his competitions (first prize in the "younger category" for a zarzuela composition at the World Exposition in Havana of 1913 among them) and many religious objects, along with, in a secret drawer, certain sepia-toned photographs that he'd purchased in a brothel, with so many other things, that one has an inkling of just how Levis's nearly carnivorous desire to absorb life itself was unbounded, his sources of inspiration many.

It should be noted that he had acquired, by way of a Jesuit education, some knowledge of Latin, a spattering of French, and a few phrases in English that might come in handy durings his dealings with American patrons. He was somewhat aware of world history—acutely knowledgeable about the history of Cuba—and he was something of a writer, often reviewing performances for newspapers.

Often, on his evenings alone he would pass the time contentedly, listening to acetate recordings of Caruso or Beethoven on a crank-driven Victrola, or simply drinking himself to sleep.

THE DAY THE SONG WAS WRITTEN

One late autumn morning in 1928, Israel Levis, having slept poorly the past several nights, found himself standing outside the window of an oculist's shop on Obispo, a mock giant eye hanging over him. As he peered in, he was momentarily fixated upon a pair of gold wire-rim bifocals that lay glowing in the sunlight amid a display of dark spectacles, monocles and mother-of-pearl-handle magnifying glasses, for lately, especially at night, he had been experiencing minor difficulties reading both the entablature of music and books. When he would sit in his study before his piano to review the progress of his own compositions, which he would meticulously lay out in dark pencil on staff paper (later to be copied in ink), and find that the notes tended to blur and dance about, his kindly eyes often grew bleary as he tried to keep track of them. (This condition had its felicitous effects, however, for one evening, while working on a piece of incidental music that he was writing for the radio station CMQ, a bit of a mundane habanera with a tango feel, his misreading of certain notes pro-duced, he believed, a better phrasing than his original.) This bleariness of sight was at its worst after he'd spent long hours at his labors, or had come back from a festive evening spent with friends here and there in the city, or had found himself particu-larly exhausted by worries over the sad political situation in Cuba, then under the control of dictator Gerardo Machado.

Though Levis often suffered from strained vision and his eyes had become decidedly compromised, he had done nothing about the condition; the very idea of wearing glasses seemed an assault upon his vanity and his belief that his creativity would keep him forever young. ("I do not feel differently now than when I was a child, a little hung over perhaps, and heavier from so many brandies, but inside I feel the same," he said to himself each morning.) He believed that his body was but a receptacle for his creative soul, a *volante* of flesh and bones, often wheezing, always hungry for the pleasures of this life. (If he were an animal, he thought, he would have been an ox, who'd grazed too long but whose very grunts were mellifluous and inspiring.) And while he knew that any feeling of immortality was an illusion, no matter how the process of composition seemed to lift him out of time, he could care less about his physical condi-tion; he had not exercised a single hour of his life, nor passed by any doctor's office with any compulsion to go in.

Despite consultations with a local healer, the bothersome con-dition of his eyes had worsened and was even reaching into his sleep. Just the very night before, as he rested in bed with his shuttered window open, for he liked feeling the fresh air on his face and hearing the birds singing happily in the morning, he saw through the mesh of mosquito netting a burning yellow star—the planets Venus or Jupiter, perhaps?—that had appeared to hover over the silhouette of an acacia tree on his rear patio, and his astigmatism, or his dreamlike state, had made the star vibrate wildly, as if in intimate communication. Levis, a superstitious sort, had wondered if some special message—what he could not say—was being conveyed to him out of the mystery of the beautiful sky, that great and inviting expanse which his religious mother had called the "cloak of God."

As he stood before that window perusing the variety of filigreed eyeglass frames and the oculist himself (a Lebanese fellow who wore a fez and a glisten-buttoned guayabera) gestured toward him cheerfully to come in, Levis became aware of passersby whose reflections he could make out in the shop window: a procession of sidewalk vendors, lottery ticket sellers, dapperly attired gentlemen and certain ladies, often walking in pairs; and on the street of a wood-frame beer truck, noisy with rattling bottles, a Model T, a horse and carriage, still in use, rolling by on the cobblestones. And he could just make out the facades of buildings across the way, half in sunlight and half in shadows, with their dashes of neoclassical or rococo flourishes, pink and yellow and blue pilaster walls and doric column arcades, Spanish-tile foyers and myriad signs (he could have been in Madrid or Rome at that instant), a dry-goods shop, its entranceway cluttered with crates of *narangina* and beer bottles (¡*Cerveza Tropical!*).

Through that blurry peripheral maze, he saw the unmistakable Rita Valladares, a rose in her hair, rushing along the sidewalk to some rehearsal or on her way to the ferry to see her mother in Guanabacoa, and he instantly turned and delightedly called out after her, whistling the first three notes of one of his tunes, *"Oh wistful flower,"* which Rita herself had sung at the Teátro Martí a few years before, during a production of his own zarzuela *La Vida de María-Elena.*

She stopped and breathlessly cried, "Ay, Don Israel!"

In that moment, Levis had tried to remain calm and unperturbed by her presence, as he had certain unfulfilled romantic delusions about Valladares. But the very sight of her lithe and curvaceous body, ever-quivering in her silken tassel-hemmed dress of a vaguely oriental design, filled him with such a rush of blood and such thoughts of affection that the composer's face flushed and the pupils of his eyes dilated.

She was an octaroon: that is, like so many Cubans, one-eighth black, due to a distant ancestor (though she would always be thought of as a *"mulata"*); her skin the color of curled cinnamon bark, and she had a quite graceful cast to her face; her eyes, startlingly blue, like forget-me-nots, emanating a tenderness and warmth that tormented him. Stricken, he thanked God that she could not read his mind, because frequently, during the past several years, when his more pleasurable thoughts were not about music or food, they often involved Rita, with whom, he supposed, he had always been in love. Had she been able to read his mind on certain nights during her performances in cabarets or in the theater she would have found that Levis, despite his flawed devotion to piety, often grew aroused at the sight of her, as she stood under the spotlight, her body barely hidden by her clothes, and that he often undressed Valladares in his sleep. She would have known that when he sat by a table, across from her, on those nights out to those cheap dockside cafés, or fritas, with a group of musician and composer friends, and he held forth about some light comedic lyric opera that he was writing, and she happened to look upon him with kindness (or what he saw as kindness, for what would such a young beauty have to do with a gargantuan loner like himself?), he daydreamed about resting naked beside her in his bed; that his right hand nearly trembled at the very thought of what it would be like to touch her (he had always been inordinately fond about the shapeliness of her but-tocks, and in his little dreams he rested his palm upon the small of her back and leveled his long middle finger into the darker, damp alignments of her nether region); that, most simply, he often wanted to sit beside her, but was so timid, and "gentlemanly," so bent on maintaining an image of propriety that he pretended to ignore her, wishing, at the same time, that he were a different kind of man.

He might have confessed that in years past, if he had gone to the racetrack at Oriental Park and saw Rita, ever splendid in some blue ensemble and elegant in a cloche hat, sitting on the veranda of the Jockey Club beside an English lord or marquis—those men who were always sending her flowers and passing her notes writ-ten in often tragic Spanish after her shows—he felt a certain out-rage and such jealousy that he would be lost to the races for the rest of the day. Sometimes he envied the attraction she held over men—why he could not say—or if he had been on his way to the Hotel Inglaterra, for a drink with a friend, and had taken a certain route, through the gallery that had once been called the Paseo Isabel, and encountered her standing before a flower stall, with a handsome man, picking out bouquets of gardenias and moss roses, he found himself stepping aside to appraise the character of her companion, reading the fellow's motivations and wondering, if at some hour of that day he might lead her off to some assignation, seducing her. The very thought of a stranger bedding his beloved was so unpalatable to the composer that he would quickly duck into a bar for a few drinks to calm his nerves, so much did he worship her from afar. Or that when he promenaded along the Prado at night, taking the air, amid the crowds, the tips of their cigarettes and cigars glaring like fireflies, the murmur of voices around him, the distant sound of music coming from some plaza, swallows darting through the air, he found himself hoping that he would come across Valladares, alone.

The greatest irony of it all, as his dear friend and sometime lyricist Manny Cortez had pointed out, was that it was obvious to everyone that Rita Valladares always softened around him—had she not often raced after Levis if she saw him on a street? Or always asked if she could visit him in his house, under the pretenses of singing some operatic arias for him? (*You always refused didn't you?* the composer recalled, years later, as he roamed the rooms of his house on Olivares.)

HIS AFFECTION FOR RITA

That was all true, Levis would say, but he was too much of a gentleman to impose his presence upon her, for whenever he thought about Rita, he believed that if she cared for him at all, it was for the avuncular role he had played in her life. Not so many years had passed since that day in 1918 when he had first heard her singing in the choir of the church of Espíritu Santo and offered to put her in the chorus of his zarzuela *La Bella Negra*. The composer was twelve years her senior and had been so taken by the nascent riches of her well-timbered voice, as well as her striking beauty and figure—*"bien formada"*—that he could not restrain his enthusiasm for her. She was sixteen years old then, and the job he offered her had come during a particularly difficult time of her youth, just after her father, a pharmacist, had recently died in a street tram accident, and Levis, with a soft heart, had taken it upon himself to oversee the direction of her promising career. She was not only a fine singer, but was already something of a natural pianist. He had introduced Rita to the finest piano teachers in the city, among them the now elderly Hugo Van de Meer, with whom he himself had once studied, and had watched her, bursting with talents, excel as both a singer and a classical pianist.

And when it came to her life as an onstage performer and their later collaborations, he had always "written" lyric roles that were suited to her voice. By the time Rita had reached her maturity and had become a part of the Cuban music scene, performing in both classical and popular venues—playing Beethoven on a Friday evening and singing with a *charanga* band on Saturday—he was constantly (but reservedly) by her side.

Privately lascivious (for he was a habitué of the brothels), publicly righteous, he was at heart a moralistic fellow. Even during those years when he had first taken Valladares under his wing, spending many an hour in her company, often alone, he had not once acted upon his desires. He could never forget the utter pain that lingered in her expression in those years after her father had died, and reckoned, rightly, that any intimation of affection she felt for him had to do with her father's absence from her life. And because of this he refused to take improper advantage of that circumstance.

Along the way, he tried to act as a religious adviser of sorts, extolling the virtues of God and the good deeds of Christ as a model. He gave her a crucifix as a memento one *Navidad* and urged her to attend Mass and not to be taken in by the superficial allurements of the performer's life, in a city bustling with clubs and cabarets. He gave her this advice in a country where Catholicism was but the hub of a spiral of more superstitiously prone religions, and by Israel's lights not taken seriously enough. By these actions, he'd hoped to win a measure of affection from her, though it was unnecessary, for she often described Levis as the kindest man she had ever known.

He had been on hand for her first radio performances, which were broadcast on Habana station PWX in 1925. He had accompanied her into the makeshift recording studios in the Horter Building on the calle Obispo, #7, which had been set up for one-month stints by the Victor and Columbia labels, who had shipped their equipment down from New York for those sessions, the temporary studios later to be dismantled and removed. And when she needed songs to record, Levis delighted in writing new pieces for her, among them *"La Vida Sabrosa," "Canto Cubano"* and *"Te Espero."* Often they performed together at different venues in the city of Habana, and the provinces—Camagüey, Cienfuegos, Santiago—concerts of Cuban song, presented in the company of other composers, who each took his turn at the piano while she sang. He had watched her flourish as a performer, had witnessed the transformation of a pretty wildflower into a lavish rose. Eating his meals with much gusto, he sometimes grasped a thin and unadorned spoon and thought of the earlier, more demure Rita, with her schoolgirl innocence and simple blue dresses; as he ladled stew from a pot, or picked apart a piece of *lechón* with an ornately detailed fork, he thought about how Rita Valladares had, over time, dispensed with her more humble attire and appeared in the latest fashions—*moda alta*—from Paris, which the shopkeepers of Habana begged her to wear, with feather turbans and silk gowns, her lustrous shoulders bare, a vision of such magnificence that the audience shouted, whistled and applauded her beauty and style the moment she stepped on stage.

She was so popular among the best composers of the city— Jorge Anckerman, Sindo Garay, Eliseo Grenet, Ernesto Lecuona and Israel Levis himself—that it seemed inconceivable to Levis that she had once been available to him. Even before she had begun to find her measure of fame, she was a constant object of romantic attentions. So many musicians and composers were impressed by her talent, her beauty and her good nature that she could have eas-ily had her choice of songwriters and men. Her reputation for bringing life into even the most solemn compositions was so great that songwriters were constantly seeking her out. For his part Levis, feeling some responsibility for her emergence, never coveted her talents or demanded from her any preferential treatment.

Though her head was always turned by the glances of hand-some men, especially in Habana, she lived with the gloom of some-one who believed that she had missed a true opportunity for love. In her case it was with the composer of "*Rosas Puras,*" Israel Levis himself, who, ever gentlemanly, to her disbelief, had always been too timidly disposed around her.

Yet for every pang of desire that he felt for Rita, there was always some handsome fellow walking along to turn his head on the street, a man with clear green eyes and a certain petulance that he found beguiling, or a man so thoroughly masculine as to throw him into a reverie of questions—Where is he going? Is he a tender soul? What does he do for amusements?—his eyes darting quickly to the side for a glance, a fleeting look at a passing object of adulation.

In any event, their love was an impossibility, for in 1922 she married a banker, Alfonso Ortegas with whom she later had two children, and although Levis accepted the situation and blamed his own timidity around her, he could not restrain his more amorous fantasies about Rita. In fact, Rita Valladares married Alfonso at a tender age, mainly, it was thought, for the security that a banker's income would provide. He was handsome and affectionate surely, though somewhat rigid in his proclivities, and so contrary to the creative spirit and disapproving of her performing career that she often privately despaired. Rita, loving the life and the buoyant personalities of show-biz folk, always found that she had to repress her fun-loving side around him, and because of that, her marriage to Alfonso remained one of the great romantic mysteries of Habana.

Often, before Valladares entered into her first marriage, she had seemed particularly affectionate with Levis, and in times when she was struck by some sadness, as when she would feel the loss of her father and longed for comfort, she cried on his shoulder, the composer barely able to manage more than a few reassuring words, terrified of overstepping the bounds of proper gentlemanly behavior.

As a man who kept his notions of piety separate from his lusts, Levis held her in such reverence that his more lascivious thoughts about her made him feel ashamed of himself. Even when she would tell him, "Don Israel, you know that I owe you so much," he always told her, "Forget about me, it's God who gave you your talents." And God gave her that body, which tormented him and worked him into such a state in the middle of the night that he would resort to the tawdry manipulations of self-release, his seed wasted, the majesty of his virility a secret which he wished to share with Valladares. "If only I were different," he always thought.

There had been an evening in 1922, after the premiere of his zarzuela *La Perla de La Habana* at the Teátro Encanto a few weeks before her impending marriage to Alfonso, and the company had gone out to a dance hall and were all very drunk (drinking heavily in elation over the good reception for their production). Around midnight he and Valladares had stepped onto the veranda to get some fresh air and to watch the stars, and because she was feeling the intimations of panic, for she was reluctant to marry Alfonso, an urgent need to dispense with the formality of their relations came over her.

In the years she had known him, though she had often noticed the way he sometimes looked at her, with hunger, he had not once dispensed with his avuncular manner around Valladares, no matter how tender and affectionate her expression, no matter how her blue eyes flared with joy at the sight of him. She was wearing a flowery dress that night with pearl buttons and a camisole under-neath, and as she stood near him, she was nearly overcome with the desire to open the top of her dress, to rest his hand upon her breasts, and she had wanted to wrap her arms around him—no easy task—and to find within the voluminous expanses of his white linen trousers that male animal, which, as she had imagined and, as rumor had it, was a marvel, and then to plead with Levis, "Please save me from this matrimony."

No doubt about it, she would have given herself to him that night, if he had so wanted, but when Valladares nestled closely to him, he stepped away. She had not loosened the pearl buttons of her dress and taken his right hand to her breast; her taut brown nipples had not swollen with his touch.

"Don Israel, can you not feel the affection I have for you?"

And what had he answered?

"But child, you are confused," he told her. And then had he really said: "You know I'm a religious man, and really, my child, you should not let the rum go to your head." And if she remem' bered correctly, she had laughed, and asked quizzically: "Are you joking?" And when he told her that he was sincere, she then said: "But you like women, don't you?"

"I do."

"Then why don't you feel the love I have for you?"

He had looked at her compassionately, tenderly as he always had, that expression conveying a nearly priestly reserve, and yet he began to perspire, and his face flushed red. Then he told her, "Really, my child, I don't want to complicate your plans in life."

For all that, she was about to place his hand upon her heart, and declaim, as if in a lover's bolero, the depths of her love for him, but a baritone named Victor Valencia called out from the doorway—"Rita, we need you for a song!"—and she turned away from the composer, disappearing into the hall, to take the stage, Levis remaining outside, under the stillness of stars, lighting a Suarez Murias cigar, and feeling foolish:

Why was it, that I could not for the life of me look into a mirror and see a woman there beside me, and why not Rita?

Now, six years later, on that afternoon in 1928, when the com-poser found himself standing before Valladares, in front of the oculist's shop, he, in his courtly manner, doffed his black-brimmed cane hat and bowed before her, asking: "Ah, Rita, where are you going in such a hurry?"

"Oh, Don Israel, I'm in a state of hysteria," she said. "The day after tomorrow I'm sailing to New York." She was breathless. "I have an engagement at the Roxy Theater there, and then I begin a tour."

"Ah New York," he said. "I have been to New York, a very great city, yes?" Then: "But why are you so anxious?"

"I'm worried because I have to make some recordings for the Victor company, but I've got nothing new to offer them." Then: "Don Israel, have you any songs I can take with me?"

He gave this matter some thought and told her, in his boyish manner: "Don't be worried, my dear Rita. I will write something for you this very afternoon. And because you are wearing a rose in your hair, I will use that as my inspiration." Then: "I promise that I will have something beautiful for you to sing. If you like, I will be waiting for you at the entranceway of the Campoamor at nine, tonight."

"Yes?"

"With complete certainty."

"You are a saint," and happily she planted a kiss upon his face, then disappeared into the shadows of a market arcade, toward Neptuno, as Levis watched her.

Parting company from Rita, Levis went to his favorite barber-shop, cheery with light, a place where he often thought about music. It was just after twelve, and while Levis always walked in as an ordinary man of flesh and blood, greeting the others and instructing Sergio to administer his usual trim and shave, he always seemed adrift in some other realm; with his head tilted back, eyes closed, as he sat in the barber's chair, he seemed to instantly enter the throes of creation, a private place, as if there were no other world than what existed within the intimacy of his thoughts. His barber was used to this, for that had been his manner since childhood, when Levis was something of a timid and humble prodigy and knew it, his whole being imbued with the sense that he had been given by God a special purpose. And because he had been coming to that barbershop for many years, he felt so much at ease that, with a cigar burning in one hand, he often tapped out the time scans of songs with the other, often humming, in the midst of such little daydreams, a tune.

As he clipped a few of Levis's errant nostril hairs, Sergio noticed that the composer was humming a melody and asked: "Is that a song you're inventing?"

"It might well be a song, the notes are always coming to me."

"As it should be," his barber noted.

"I get many good ideas coming here," he told Sergio. "Today I have a little project of some importance. It is good for me to come here and think, for I must quickly execute this idea."

"That is good, Don Israel."

His face covered with a froth of cream, Levis, thinking of a song for Rita Valladares, began to consider some notes that had been floating around in his musical head for days, a melody that he picked out from the chirpings and trilling of birds sounding merrily from the high branches of a Spanish laurel in Parque Central one evening at dusk, the flow of notes he'd determined were in the key of E♭—from numerous observations, he'd concluded that this was the key most avarial creatures found pleasing.

Finding it impossible to separate Rita from the beauty of flowers as he considered so many possible melodies, he saw himself sitting on a bench in the park with Valladares; a thinner, more handsome version of himself, some ten years younger. She was leaning her head against Levis's shoulder, and, smelling sweetly from a Parisian perfume, she had rested her right hand upon his knee, and sighing as Levis adamantly whispered, "Rita, I love you very much," and she, touching his face, repeated: "It is the same for me." And in those moments, she unbuttoned her blouse and allowed his hand to rest upon her breast, her nipple growing taut between his index and forefingers. Despite his timid manner, there emerged a slight grin, a curling in the corner of his full lips that bespoke of his sexuality—but he never forced himself on women, not even Valladares, whom, in his fantasies, often satisfied him, screaming with pleasure in his bed.

For their part, the trees, lined in rows along a receding green—for one could see the harbor in the distance—rustled in the breeze, and from their trunks came the music of sonorous violins; and the birds were as flutes; and the very flowers—the beds of roses and chrysanthemums around them, the bougainvillea lilting over the walls—sounded as bells.

To the Campana

No sooner had Sergio whipped off his apron than did Levis hurry off to the Campana Bar to meet his best friend, Manny Cortez, his longtime lyricist, for their usual lunch and drinks. That bar, famous for its delicious croquettes, was a congenial place in which to pass a few hours; a cool and intimate room on a second floor with shuttered windows that looked out onto the street, and because it was situated a few doors down from a concert hall, other composers of the day—from Eliseo Grenet to Horacio Monteagudo, fellow masters of the *danzón* and rumba—often gathered there; Levis walking in and greeting his friends with slaps on the back and offers of some freshly purchased "tobaccos," a half dozen Suarez Murias in his pocket.

In the Campana he might encounter the formidable composer Gonzalo Roig, bespectacled and intense, and they might discuss the genius of Bach, whom Levis considered a "divinely inspired" composer, or dissect the piano compositions of Claude Debussy, which Levis found overbearing, while Roig did not. Who was the greater composer, Bach or Mozart? What were the prevailing opinions about Stravinsky or Ravel? What of that "jazz" they had started to hear in the big hotel ballrooms? Or they argued about opera—Rossini versus Puccini versus Verdi or Donizetti. And did anybody have tickets for the Italian opera company's performance of *Aïda* at the Teátro Nacional that night?

THAT HE BECAME A COMPOSER

That he became a composer was the natural outcome of his love for music and his own patriotic feelings about Cuba. He had been raised with zarzuelas and *contradanzas*—the older traditional forms of music derived from Spain—and with the bel canto of Donizetti and Rossini, but he was most acutely aware of the music that came directly out of the Cuban spirit: that which the *guaracheros*, or "country musicians," played in the social clubs and back alleys of the city, and the older form of the habanera, which had flourished with songs like the Spaniard Sebastian Yradier's "*La Paloma,*" written in 1860, or Eduardo Sánchez de Fuentes's "*Tú,*" composed in the early 1890s, flashes of music that one heard in salons and played on parlor pianos everywhere. (Listen to the famous habanera of Bizet's *Carmen* and you are hearing snatches of an older Cuban song called "*El Arreglito,*" and with that you are transported to a parlor on a street just off the Parque Maceo, where men in long-tailed topcoats are leading their rustle-skirted women in a circle, the scent of candle wax, perfume and tobacco around them; Levis at the piano, a mantel clock ticking far more slowly than it would today.)

There was also the continual presence of guitar music in his life—and why not?—for it was part of Cuba's history. The guitar, convenient to the mariners, who had been coming to the island for centuries (for what other instruments would a sailor take on a ship with him beside a horn pipe or accordion?), had found its way early into the countryside, songs of various origins—mainly Spanish but also French and English adapted by slaves and slave owners, by troubadours and minstrels, and enlivened by the addition of African rhythms and intonations—were made into their own. Even a famous Cuban melody like *"Guajira Guantanamera,"* which would be formally adapted to the words of José Martí in 1928 (the same year in which Levis composed *"Rosas Puras"*), had been around for several hundred years and was thought to have first come from a Portuguese folk ballad.

People who lived on plantations broke the solitude and silence of their evenings with music. Lonely, begrieved slaves took up guitars and drums, and eventually created the rumba—a dance of few closely held (chain-bound) steps—that "low class" music finding its way into the dance halls and salons of the bigger cities like Santiago and Habana, alienating the ever proper Spaniards, and inspiring the island composers.

What Levis experienced in his youth, during the dawn of the Cuban republic, was a calling. A gifted pianist, he had studied composition and harmony as a young man with the teachers José Mauri and Ignacio Tellería, dedicating himself to the mastery of every form and finding ways to express through music Cuba's emerging national soul. He quickly "Cubanized" the Spanish zarzuela, wrote numerous habaneras piano pieces and songs that utilized *guajiro* airs, and became a part of the modern repertoire.

Mainly he tried to capture those feelings that filled the hearts of Cubans in their most intimate moments.

Fragments of his own music, that had once played on a rinky-dink piano or a scratchy Edison cylinder, would always come back to him, the simple melodies of many a song he had written in his youth echoing in the halls of his house on Olivares those years later, songs with titles like: *"Los Chinitos Gorditos"* ("The Fat Chinamen"); *"¿Por Qué Ríes Tanto?"* ("Why Do You Laugh So Much?"); *"Recuerdos Felices"* ("Happy Recollections"); *"Cortesana Linda"* ("Beautiful Courtesan"); *"La Virgen de La Caridad"* ("The Virgin of Charity"); *"El Zapatero"* ("The Shoemaker"); *"Danzones de Amor"* ("Love Dances"); *"Las Tres Hermanas Bellas"* ("Three Beautiful Sisters"); *"Mensaje de Felicidad"* ("A Message of Happiness"); *"Somos Guajiros"* ("We're Country Boys"); *"Serenata Habanera"* ("Havana Serenade"); *"Mangos y Papayas"* ("Mangoes and Papayas"); *"Mis Cubanas Lindas"* ("My Pretty Cuban Ladies"); *"Voy a Habana Para Casarme"* ("I'm Coming to Havana to Get Married"); *"Ilusiones"* ("Illusions"); *"Sueños de un Chaval"* ("Dreams of a Gallant Youth"); *"Caballero de Santiago"* ("The Gentleman from Santiago")—among so many others, more than three hundred in all.

Back then, he always carried a leather valise in which he kept a sheaf of staffed music paper and pencils, as he did not know when the muses would come to him. Perfume excited his imagination and so did the other scents in the air—of coffee, beer, of horses and manure and of blood and sawdust from the butcher shops, somehow mixing with the sweeter scents of flowers and eucalyptus and of the thick-rooted acacias, ceibas and slender lemon trees from the gardens that people kept in the inner courtyards of their houses. Often he wrote in the park amid the royal palms and little gardens, enjoying the sight of passersby, or he got ideas while walking along the harbor, or while looking out over the recently built Malecón seawalls by night. Or he went into the movie

houses, where, in his youth, he had earned money as an accompa-
nist to silent films (his most recent favorite films including those of
Charlie Chaplin and *"El Gordo y El Flaco")*. Everywhere he went,
whether to the offices of the Municipal Conservatory on Galiano
or into the vast interior of the Catedral de la Virgen María de la
Concepción (Habana Cathedral), with its massive columns and its
porphyry-domed grand altar, where he would often sit and think
about the passions of God and of songs, Levis heard a kind of
music.

The *tick tack* rapping of the shoemaker's hammer, brooms
sweeping dust out of darkened entranceways, the cries of children
playing in the gutter, the singsong chants of vendors selling newspapers, coffee, lottery tickets and roasted peanuts—*"¡Maní!"*—
others ringing bells and selling shots of *aguardiente* and bottles of
medicinal items with names like "Neptune's Cure" to protect
against malaria, for half of the city slept under mosquito netting at
night. He heard music in the sonorous tinkle of water-splashed
fountains, in the *clip clop* of horse hooves, in the clanging of
church bells, in the straining voices of *divines* preaching in the *placitas* on Sunday mornings. And in churches, like Jesús María, or
Nuestra Señora del Pilar, or Espíritu Santo, which he frequently
visited, for the stony saints and images of the suffering Jesus
inspired him, the latter two being the churches, where, in fact, he
had gotten his musical start as a child prodigy of nine playing the
organ (and receiving the grace of God) during services.

Although he was already known by then as a composer of
popular entertainments for the cabarets and theaters of the city,
symphonic poems, overtures, string trios and versions of his songs
had once circulated everywhere in the form of piano rolls and

occasional recordings, he had also written religious works, a requiem, a Stabat Mater, and several Ave Marías, à la the great J. S. Bach and Esteban Salas, in which he took the deepest pride.

Most simply, he would thank God for bringing him into the world in which such a magicality like music existed.

Of course, he most often wrote his music at home, in the large and airy room that had been his late father's study, open to a garden, where the jonquils and sunflowers inspired him. He had a grand piano, a Steinway, which he had purchased in 1920 during a journey to New York, where he and Fernando had availed themselves of the cultural resources of that city, visiting within ten days its opera houses (where he heard Caruso) and burlesque halls, music shops and museums like the Metropolitan—Levis, at thirty, still a relatively young man and quite impressionable, so stunned by the alabaster winged genies of the palace of the King Ashurnasirpal on that museum's second floor that he composed in their honor a ragtime-sounding tune, a *divertimiento* with an exotic minor motif that he'd never published but played for the amusement of his friends during evening and Sunday-afternoon salons.

That was a time when he used to walk the streets of Habana, in his cane, flat-top, black-brim hat, as if he were the mayor of the city, greeting the actresses, singers, fellow composers and musicians in his life, and stopping off here and there to savor a cup of coffee or a brandy. He would wear a white linen suit, suspenders, a crisp (if bewilderedly stretched) stiff-collar cotton shirt and a crimson bowtie, and though he would stand out in any crowd, given his stature, he seemed very much a more or less typical Cuban gentleman of that epoch. And he smelled of strong cologne and tobacco, for he could not begin his days without a cigar, nor compose, conduct or practice his piano scales without those aromatic tubes burning beside him.

He did not walk down the street with just a billfold in his jacket pocket, a cameo watch bearing a photo of his mother and father hanging off a chain, a few pesetas in his trousers and a *pañuelo* (or "handkerchief"), but with an imaginary orchestra of some thirty-two pieces following him around—a dozen trumpets blaring, drums beating, *babalaos* dancing in squares, *troveros* ("troubadours") performing in the *placitas* of the city, symphonies, such as he wished to compose, resounding in his head.

Back then he was well liked, as much for his talent as his congeniality. Good natured ("if a little sad," as he often thought himself), he was helpful to his fellow musicians and always delighted when he encountered a person of genuine talent. And while he could be tremendously complimentary to his fellow composers, Levis often expressed disdain for the charlatans who pretended they were composers; whenever he saw a composer of ordinary talents behaving arrogantly—especially those of the thinner, far more handsome breed, for he felt that his own corporality was an expression of the depths of his own gift—he was often moved to write the occasional scathing review, to ignore the man when he entered a room. Nevertheless these were the little flaws of a person who otherwise had been generous to his fellow composers, and truly loving of the adherents to that world—the opera singers and actors and actresses and musicians whose industry and wondrous energies delighted him.

Occasionally, if he found himself standing outside a house and happened to hear a laundress or maid singing in a particularly beautiful voice, he would take the trouble to knock on the door or to call into a window, simply to offer a kindly suggestion, saying, "You're much too gifted to waste your singing on a sheet. Why don't you see a friend of mine over at the Teátro Martí—he's look-ing for some singers to fill a chorus for a zarzuela." And he would offer himself as a reference, tip his hat and then move on. Or if Levis, craning his head upward so that the jowls of his fleshly face vanished, heard a student or a more accomplished musician prac-ticing at the piano, he would stand outside listening, sometimes for an hour, and if he was deeply moved, he would make that musician's acquaintance. He had no restraint in that regard. In 1903, when he was thirteen years old, he had put together a *danzón* orchestra, simply by walking around Habana. Hearing a violin or a coronet or a bass coming out of an edifice window, he would knock on the door and ask the musician if he would care to play in his *conjunto;* and while he was often turned down, the opti-mism expressed by this young and plump *caballero,* ever formal in a white linen suit, was such that within a few days he had orga-nized his little band, Levis playing the piano and conducting musi-cians twice his age, who regarded him, even in his tender youth, as a *maestro.*

Possessing a fondness for children, for the fineness of their features, the minuteness of their little hands, and their unbounded energy, he saw them as the future of Cuba; hence, he often helped in the formation of children's choirs, mostly for churches, and sat as a judge in many juvenile competitions; and for these children, many of them from poor families, he always purchased toys—wooden horses and rubber balls.

The evenings would find him joining up with friends. They'd

head over to one of the city's parks for a band concert, or make their way to a private residence for a salon, where all kinds of artists would take their turns before the gathering. A magician displaying sleight-of-hand tricks, a schoolteacher reciting a patriotic poem by José Martí; actors declaiming scenes from popular plays; singers and instrumentalists, one after the other, until someone urged Levis to get up out of his creaking, ever-too-narrow high-back chair to play the piano—often something new that he had been working on . . .

"My dear friends, a piano interlude which I will call, '*The Song of October*,' in your honor," he might say.

HIS FRIEND AND LYRICIST MANNY CORTEZ

He tried many things; for example, setting *The Raven—El Cuervo*—by Edgar Allan Poe, to music, with a translation by Manny Cortez, a poet of small renown who was also a journalist for the English-language *Habana Gazette* and other newspapers. It was presented in the fall of 1922 at the Palau auditorium. They had been friends since 1918 and had first met while attending a salon in the house of Jorge Anckermann, composer of the well-known bolero "*Yo Quisiera,*" and although the music was good, once a local university professor had launched into a discourse about the *Conquest of New Spain* by Bernal Díaz, each had gravitated again and again to a back room to drink and had regaled one another with bawdy stories, and because this Cortez was a pensive, handsome and funny sort of man, Levis had decided to take him along to a favorite brothel, a memorable night.

In any event, Cortez had made a professional mission to translate as much of Poe into Spanish and had persuaded Levis to write the music for *The Raven*. This work was written in the style of German lieder, solemn and deep, with much tremelo; an actor in a crow costume crossing the stage at certain moments and intoning, "*Nunca Más*," or "Nevermore."

It was performed three times, to a tepid reception, but Manny, a devotee of Poe, had been greatly pleased.

Poe was one of Cortez's idols, and consequently his own lyric musings sometimes possessed a rather supernatural or macabre feel, and his very physical presence seemed affected by his inti- mate verbal contact with the late poet's sometimes bizarre mind. So while Israel Levis, who'd never passed up a meal or a glass of brandy, had the air of someone who had rested quite luxuriously the night before, poor Cortez moved through the world like a haunted aesthetic, his face drawn, with shadows, like patches of a moonless night, under his eyes. And he had a nearly penitential bearing, and so ironic a view of life, as if everyone, regardless of good fortune, was ultimately doomed—all things of this world of such a fleeting nature that little, perhaps save for "art," mattered.

Without admitting it, there was a part of Levis that saw in Cortez the composer's hidden self—the Levis plagued by the nag- ging suspicion that his own religiosity and his sense of a God in the world, despite so many evidences to the contrary—*or lack of evidences*—were just pipe dreams. Feeling a revulsion—a gloom over these sentiments—Israel had always made it a private mis- sion to persuade Cortez, over drinks, during visits to the brothels, in the after hours spent by harborside cafés, that there was a God and that religion, and particularly Catholicism, was a good thing— as if, in that process, he would persuade himself. They tottered along the edge of a pier in Habana harbor—sharks, Portuguese men-of-war, sea turtles and luminous medusas (gorgonean octopii) floating underneath the beautiful moonlit water, the stars imperiously jewel-like in the heavens; the prettiness of the world (in certain moments) filled Levis with such utter appreciation for his very existence that he would nearly throttle the weaving Cortez and declare: "Don't you see, my friend, the glory and grandeur of *El Señor!*" to which Cortez would respond: "It's simply cosmetic," and laugh. "All that proves nothing, my friend."

And yet Cortez—whose official stance: "I am an atheist by calling, a romantic despite myself"—deeply appreciated the composer's good heart and found Levis's sunnier and yet quite serious disposition a comfort, for if the world was being ruined by evil men, at least there were some counterbalances that brought out the good (in Levis's case, music) and subsumed the bad.

And while his own life would end in a way that seemed to underscore his belief that "nothing was there," Cortez had an oddly calming effect on Levis. When the hurricane of 1926 swept across the island, and the Pascuali warehouse in the neighborhood of Luyano was devastated, hundreds upon hundreds of piano rolls of the composer's music—mainly *danzones* and habaneras that he had kept there in storage—were carried out of their bins and scattered over the ground in pieces, or were turned into pulp. In the aftermath, with Manny Cortez by his side, Levis arrived at the ruins of the warehouse by horse and carriage, the roads muddy and often unpassable. Along the way, trees were strewn everywhere, animals floated on their backs in newly created ponds and streams, a fetid stench filled the air. The destruction that had overwhelmed the shanties of the poor, who lived in cane-walled, thatch-roofed houses and were left to beg by the roadside, had made that journey a heartbreaking affair; but worse was his discovery that the *ciclón* had eliminated, within a matter of a few hours, much of nearly twenty years of his work.

He would always remember arriving at the site of the warehouse, which had once been as long and as high as an American barn, and picking through the debris with a cane—pulp and more pulp everywhere. They were quite a pair—Levis, stately and immense, lumbrous in his movements, and Cortez, thin as a branch, navigating the site nimbly. Levis could barely speak except to say, when he encountered the distraught Pascuali, "I can't believe this."

Most heartbreaking was the loss of original music. Levis had never been too well organized and had made it his habit to give Pascuali the original sheets of his compositions without having bothered to make copies of his own. These would have been used by a compositor who would transfer those notes onto a piano roll maker, which resembled a Linotype machine. Pascuali had kept Levis's originals neatly stored in wide leather portfolios in a special room beside his office, but the room and its contents no longer existed. And along with those originals, Levis had also lost certain fragments of works in progress that he'd abandoned or put aside for one reason or another, several zarzuelas and operettas that he had never completed but had hoped to return to, works that were now gone forever, save for a few snatches of melody that he either remembered or had kept in notebooks at home in his study.

As he picked through the debris, ever so sadly, for he

lamented not only the loss of his work but, as well, that of many of his fellow composers, he found himself thinking that this was as painful as anything he had ever known—save perhaps for the death of his father some years before, or the loneliness he some-times felt. Nothing could be salvaged, but what he would fondly remember was how Cortez had, at one moment, simply taken hold of his left elbow and squeezing it, said, "*Bueno, caballero,* this is a pity, but don't forget, my friend, you are a genius, and much more music will flow from your pen."

Behind that Levis felt a great disappointment over how the good Lord had allowed this destruction of his work—probably, he reasoned, because of his sometimes arrogant attitude about his "God given" talents. Perhaps he had overstepped some boundary in assuming a connection to God. Though he said nothing of this to Cortez, he secretly thought: "*I* am but a humble servant to You." And: "I will be more levelheaded in my thoughts, and a bet-ter person, I promise you that, Lord." And yet, the loss of such works was really nothing compared to the sufferings and deaths experienced by so many others—for thousands died in that hurri-cane.

As Manny Cortez had put it, "At least we are alive and well." Then: "Let's have a drink back in the city." And more specifically: "Let's go over to see if Miranda's"—a brothel—"is open and per-haps we can forget our little troubles."

And so, among his collaborators, Manny Cortez was his favorite—not only because he had dashed off, upon request, the lyrics to many a song, and the librettos of zarzuelas like *Los Amores de Beatriz* (*The Loves of Beatriz*) and *El Conde Llega a Habana* (*The Count Comes to Habana*), but because he was a good drinking companion, a family man with his own wife and children, and committed to social change; a journalist (blackballed by Machado) who seemed to fear nothing, not in this nor any other world.

He had once said to Levis, a few days before he died: "I love seeing the world through your eyes—the good man in the sky. . . . I will drink to that. And I truly hope you are right, my friend—and not so much for myself but for all those who deserve justice, and against those to whom justice should be served—I hope there is a Heaven for you and me; I would personally like to make the acquaintance of Edgar Allan Poe, and I would relish a vulture feeding on the liver of our dictator. To that, I will drink, my friend. Here's to your little dreams about our world, coming true."

But mainly, because he cherished the company of his friends and loved to observe the world as it passed by, Levis also went to cafés and bars to compose or to finish his work. Even the tedious process of copying out music went more pleasantly when he could pursue those little indulgences, of food and drink and conversation, which he considered a fuel for his creative mind. It should be noted that Levis had already composed some twenty different zarzuelas, or light operas, for local Habana theater companies, many a lyric one-act comedy, a few serious concert pieces for piano, and perhaps a hundred songs that in the United States would have fallen into the category of "Tin Pan Alley"—jaunty parlor tunes, *danzones* and habaneras—most of which had been replicated on piano rolls, only to be lost. From this output, along with his other capacities as sometime music teacher and conductor for various symphonic institutions, he made a living.

THEIR MUSIC

And always, there was at issue, among the composers who gathered in the Campana Bar, the notion of liberating Cuban music from the lingering influences of Spain and Europe. As such island composers like José Mauri, Jaime Prats, Amadeo Roldán and Israel Levis, among many others, took enormous pride in those inventions that incorporated Taino and African melodies, the rhythms of the blacks, and many different kinds of percussive instruments— from jawbones to cowbells to the claves (the tika-tika-sticks)— elements which characterized the much disparaged but fiery "native" music. It was a music that for many years had been looked down upon by the island's Spanish ruling class and by those more conservative and lofty criollos who were sympathetic to and benefiting from their rule, a class of slave and plantation owners whose racial prejudices were strong and whose contradanzas and sevillanas were tame and predictable. Because they identified such African-influenced music with the revolutionary movements of the nineteenth century, the Spaniards had often enacted laws to ban its public performance; and yet, fecund as the dense tropic woods, the music flourished and spread everywhere.

It took form in the voices of laundresses and cane workers who sang their Yoruban melodies aloud to pass the day, or to mourn the death of a loved one to murder or war; it was played on bottles and pots and through whistles, empty crates and on coconut and conch shells. It emulated the rivers, the wind through the treetops, the laughter of the birds, the cackle of roosters. It rattled like chains, and bled like a slaughtered animal. It was played by trios, by small drum and brass bands, by larger orchestras with trumpets and violins and flutes. Its rhythms confounded, its vocals were chantlike and emphatic, its drumming wild. It was a mystical, heart-wrenching music, part love song, prayer, and shout of despair that floated through the cultural landscape of Cuba like a rickety masted caravel on a stormy, windswept sea.

Levis's generation, whose antecedents were to be found in composers like the great José White and Ignacio Cervantes, was living through an explosion of this "native influenced" music, a boom that, it was supposed, dated back to postindependence Cuba of 1910, when the rambunctious *son*—a form of *guajiro* dance music—with its mixture of Spanish and slave melodies and rhythms, first made its way to Habana from Oriente province in the east. For someone as well trained as Levis, the "true declaration of musical independence," as he had once written in a column for *El Diario de la Marina,* was of the first importance to any serious Cuban composer.

The musical scene of Habana in 1928 was tremendously vital—despite governmental indifference to "native" (therefore "insurrectionist") arts—with classical institutions like the Habana philharmonic and Habana symphony (la Filarmonica y Sinfonia de La Habana), with opera and zarzuela companies putting on regular productions in the Martí and Nacional theaters; there was, as well, a profusion of country bands performing everywhere—in the bars and clubs and *placitas* of every neighborhood—this African music not only inviting official opposition, but influencing a whole generation of Cuban composers who absorbed those melodies and rhythms and made them their own. Coming as they did from so small and uniquely minded a nation, they felt they had much that was new (but ancient) to give to the world. In their discourses they had a sense of mission: to give the rumba and *son* symphonic and operatic form—at least that was the case for Levis.

Often he had thought that his life would go a certain way, that he would live perfectly content in that house on Olivares, and Cuba, emerging into the twentieth century, would, in political terms, straighten itself out, and he would grow old, a serene and revered composer, a *soltero* who would have his moments of happiness and fame—perhaps to open one day his own school of music, like the Conservatorio Peyrellade, or to preside over a theater that would present progressive works, without the impediments of government interference. His pride in Cuba was such that when he gazed at the florid colorations of the sunset as it spread over the Prado, the sun a gold Eucharist host dropping into the sea, he was filled with so many feelings of religiosity and nationalist pride that, indeed, he believed that though there were many other wondrous places in the world, he would never leave Cuba for good, as had so many of his friends.

Though his livelihood was most respectfully earned through the dispersion of the classics and his knowledge of that technique, he most enjoyed the performances of his own *danzones* and *son* that he had written for orchestras, arrangements of which he would later enliven with the spatterings of jazz that he had picked up here and there in his travels to New Orleans and to the clubs in Habana, arrangements of jazz which he'd enthusiastically copied from many an American pianist who passed through that city, fellows whose cakewalk and piano rag techniques he studied carefully.

Dropped 7ths, augmented 13ths, and flowing runs—he learned these styles to the point that when he sat down before the piano, his fingers flew energetically over the keys as if he'd been playing in a Bourbon Street bar for years and years.

His own compositions, while documenting the influences of African music, also paid homage to Cuba's other musical roots. He had actually composed the music for a short review entitled "A History of the Cuban Bolero," which premiered in 1916 at the Teátro Albisu. In essence, as he was writing the music for this piece, with spoken narrative and featuring his adaptation of prominent Cuban boleros, he hoped to convey the development of the bolero, a music of sad lamentations that originated with the troubadour tradition; songs of romance, coming out of Spain, were often sung loudly, for tradition had it that a suitor declared his melodious love to a woman awaiting him on a balcony. But in Cuba, where the houses often had large first-floor windows that opened to the street, these remonstrances could be sung more quietly, hence the intimacy of the Cuban bolero. And in a physically beautiful country of a quite temperate climate, which had its share of war and natural disasters, longing and lament informed the lyrics and the very tone of those works.

MUSIC AND POLITICS

These gentlemen spoke of politics in a whisper for they were living in the midst of the Machado dictatorship. Gerardo Machado was a short, stocky and grim-faced man who by 1928 had become infamous for bribe taking and murder. Elected president of Cuba in 1925, Machado had begun his stewardship of the government promisingly, for during his first year in office he had initiated the construction of a national highway across the island, had pledged to modernize the electrical systems of Habana, and had begun to successfully attract more substantial American investments to Cuba. Unfortunately, along the way, while lining his pockets with money, he had become indifferent to the principles of freedom. By 1928 there were already stories to be told—of bombings, of student dissenters imprisoned, of rioters shot, of kidnappings, torture and murder. (As early as 1925 he had crushed a railroad workers strike in Camagüey, killing thirty labor leaders.)

Called the "Father of Misery" and "second Nero," he was a megalomaniac who lived opulently, named boulevards after himself and traveled around Habana in a thirty-thousand-dollar armored car, with a hired army of gunmen to protect him. He spent a fortune to finish the construction of the magnificent Capitolio (or Capitol Building which he based on the one in Washington, D.C.) and yet surrounded it with machine-gun posts.

Despising intellectuals and artists he had closed down the university in Habana for a year in 1927 and was active in suppressing the free press, for talk of a revolution was in the air. With his secret police everywhere, he threw many of the island's journalists and intellectuals into prison, or sent them into exile. He jailed, without trial, chemists, professors, congressmen, striking sugar cane workers. Intolerant of free expression, he threatened to close down any newspaper that carried items critical of the government and made it a practice to have his agents confiscate from the newsstands of Habana any editions of foreign publications like the New York Times, the Herald Tribune, the New Republic, Common Sense, Time, Plain Talk, Collier's, Reader's Digest—any that might report the truth about his regime.

Over time the editors of *El Heraldo Comercial, Karakato, El Día, Bohemia, Política Cómica, La Estampa, Unión Nacionalista, La Semana, La Campana, La Voz del Maestro, La Voz del Pueblo, Siboney, El Sol, La Voz de la Razón,* and *Havana-American News* would be either jailed, exiled or murdered.

By the end of his reign he would pass a decree stating that no more than three persons could gather in a public place, a control that he could enforce on the streets but could not succeed with in the dance halls, where the ebullience of Cuban social life was impossible to suppress.

In his efforts to destroy Cuba's unions he sent his agents out to infiltrate nearly every labor and professional organization—the bar association, the federations of doctors, dentists, pharmacists, the society of engineers, and the academies of science and history. Even the theaters and music halls of the country were not exempt from harassment, for representatives of Machado's Unión Federativa Nacional Obrera, approached the owners of the music halls demanding representation, so as to better oversee the content of staged productions.

In 1927 Israel and Manny had marched with protest groups at the university; squads of military officers beat back the crowds and sprayed them down with fire hoses. Israel marched with them, however fearfully, putting up a good front. He did not know he was being watched, that he was placidly getting himself into trouble, signing petitions and letters against the government.

With a force of secret police dispersed throughout the city to monitor and suppress any murmurings of dissent, even the most veiled criticism of the regime—as found in the lyrics of a song—often landed the composer and lyricist in jail, if not worse.

For someone like Levis, the son of a doctor, who came of age with the dawn of the republic, whose youth was spent in the company of men ever impassioned by the notion of true liberty, the current situation was a thorn in his idealistic, more serious side. In his creativity he was detached enough from the immediate realities of the day to ignore the risks he was taking in signing so many petitions and letters of protest and proclamations against the government. Without intending to he had aligned himself with certain movements, notably the Grupo Minorista, a group that, in proclaiming an affinity with the island's African past, called for a change in racial policies and a "new society," with which the government did not agree. He had many friends who had joined the movement of "veterans and patriots" that opposed the government, and counted both anarchists and communists among his drinking mates.

For all of that, he had been barely aware of just how much his younger peers in the arts—journalists, writers, poets, painters and such—truly despised the government. If he supported such an anti-Machado stance, he did so partly out of idealism but also with the satisfaction of knowing that he might please such friends as Manny Cortez, who was like a second brother to him.

And because he was friends with other known anti-government intellectuals and artists, among them the black poet Nicolás Guillén and the essayist Alejo Carpentier, who had left for France, and the songwriter Eliseo Grenet, composer of "El Lamento Cubano," who would go into exile in Spain, he was, without being aware of it, under the scrutiny of the police.

He had gotten used to a certain level of apprehension during those times, of the sensation of being followed. One day, when he suspected that he was being tracked by a secret agent in the guise of a postal worker, he roamed through the neighborhoods of Habana purposely wasting his and the man's time—and he did so wondering if, indeed, he was being followed for reasons that were political.

But even Levis could not escape the censorship. When he had mounted a zarzuela called *La Bella Negra* a few years before, set during the slave uprisings of 1868, its plot, about a once kindly master who falls in love with a beautiful slave whom he con-demns to the gallows after the revolt—"With joy, for there will be another!"—the production was closed down after its only perfor-mance, for the role of the slave master was interpreted as a veiled portrait of Machado himself. Both Levis and Manny Cortez were picked up on the street and hurried off to the central jailhouse, where they were left to ponder their fates for the night—"*Esto es una barbaridad*" ("This is a travesty"), the composer found himself repeating, after having to relieve himself in a pot.

No torture, however, no execution, but a warning from a rather belligerent and self-amused sergeant who told them they could be jailed for "unpatriotic sentiments," a threat that Levis preferred to ignore, even when Manny Cortez, himself, decided to pursue the secret publication of anti-Machadoist pamphlets.

These circumstances, like so many other things in life, would surely pass, Levis thought, and although those current conditions might lead one like Levis to despair—for did not all artists seek to escape the idiocy that ruined the pleasantries of existence?—these composers all took solace in their fraternity, Levis a familiar and welcome figure among them.

They were my brothers, were they not?

Now, when Levis saw Manny Cortez, no such notions about politics occurred to him, and he said, his head filled with notions of pleasing Rita: "*Necesito la letra para una canción que voy a inventar para Rita Valladares, ahora mismo, y de pronto*" ("I need some lyrics for a song I'm going to write now for Rita Valladares, and quickly").

Accustomed to the sudden demands that his prolific friend often placed upon him, Manny simply shrugged and asked, "And what is the nature of this song?"

"Let's order some food and drinks, and I will tell you, shortly."

But first the croquettes and the brandy, a glass of which, along with his cigars, he savored every morning before setting out from the quietude of his late father's house into the world. In those days, Levis was so facile in his composition that he could chew his croquette with one hand and set down the notes onto paper with the other, whistling, to the amusement and admiration (perhaps envy) of his harder-working friends, those charming melodies that seemed to have come spontaneously out of the smoke blue air. Not infrequently he had composed the tunes beforehand, but he would look off into a corner of the room as if suddenly inspired (a way of showing off, because he liked to give the appearance of genius). Often heard in that bar came the phrase "*El Gordo* is at it again!" followed by friendly laughter, and he would nod at his fellow composers, shrugging as if to say, "What can I do if the muses come to me?" He worked quite hard—too hard—on his more serious pieces, derivative of the Europeans, he would have to frankly confess, whose somber tones and formal tonalities bored him. But in the case of *"Rosas Puras"* he had truly conceived and rendered the body and chorus of that rumba in a blessedly short amount of time. He conceived it as a call-and-response song, a pregón-rumba: a pretty flower seller (Rita Valladares) in a Habana arcade behind a cart; a lively, vivacious soul, of a fine figure and a flirtatious man-ner, wooing male passersby with the promise of love, as embodied by the purity of the roses. He told Manny Cortez about this notion and wrote out the notes, quickly, in twenty minutes—E♭, Rita's lovely eyes; F, her fulsome lips; F♯, her delicate cheek; G, her pearly teeth; A♭, her tongue, plump, moist, set back in a laugh; B♭, her brow; C, her shapely breasts; B♭, her compact rump—then whis-tling the tune, he said to Manny: "Now find your inspiration, man! Think of a red rose in Rita Valladares's hair, and see what you come up with!"

Poor Cortez required the better part of that afternoon to improvise its lyrics, his finest line, which greatly pleased Levis: *"La rosa pura siempre se dura, como el amor, en nuestros corazones"* ("The purest rose will always last, like the love in our hearts").

AT 9 P.M.

Levis, a little tipsily, ambled back to his house to sit before his piano and put the finishing touches on the song. Finding its melody and chords adequate, he carefully wrote out a fair copy of the music and lyrics (in black ink and in beautiful script); then, because he was eager to please Valladares, he had a few more brandies, to calm his nerves. He passed the time playing Bach, then applied a translucent polish to his two-tone shoes. Then he made his way over to the Teátro Campoamor, where he had agreed to meet with Valladares at nine that night. He had rolled the sheet up and tied it with a red ribbon, into which he slipped a rose, from his own garden. Of course, she thanked him—"¡Eres divino!" she had said—and pecked him on the cheek. He stood by as she quickly looked over the music and sang a few bars. "Oh, Don Israel, this is so wonderful!"

Whenever he was in Rita's company, he fought off gloom, for he had not realized, until it was too late, how much he cherished her. And now she was married, which was why he blushed when she gave him another kiss and stepped away from her. And then she left him. He remained under an arcade, making much of his own foolishness and timidity, berating himself, and giving little thought to that song.

THEN MIDNIGHT, IN HIS FAVORITE BROTHEL

Later, he decided to visit his favorite brothel, which was on a side street off Zulueta, near the grand Arsenal of Habana by the harbor. Standing on a narrow, poorly lit sidewalk before a high wooden bolted door, he knocked, rapping three times. A slide panel opened, eyes peered out. Entering, he followed the stoop-backed woman he knew as Paula down a tiled hallway into a par-lor; a young woman, smoking a cigarette that dangled from her lips, was sitting behind a piano, playing the melody of a Gershwin tune. The room itself, which opened to a patio, was crowded—

American and French sailors, businessmen, many Cuban fellows lounging about small tables, drinking, each with a woman by his side. The proprietress, an older Spaniard of faded beauty, wearing a mantilla and a comb in her hair, greeted Levis and snapped her fingers at the bartender, who poured him a Carlos Quinto brandy.

"Don Israel," she said. "Perhaps you will play for us later?"

He always did:

"This is a piece I wrote for the World Exposition of 1913," he might say to the frowsy harlots. Or, "Here is something from my zarzuela *Las Palomas de Vera Cruz.*" Or, again and again, on suc-ceeding occasions in many another brothel, such as he would find in Paris, he would begin to play the piece that would become most identified with his oeuvre, *"Rosas Puras,"* that most Cuban of songs.

"Yes, of course," he told the proprietress. Then: "Anyone new here?"

Such was the kindness of his heart that the composer often chose the most ordinary-looking of women, but that evening he settled upon a *celestina* named Dahlia, who could not have been more than sixteen. He followed her down a hallway, where there were many doors, into a room that in its spare furnishings—a bed, a chair, a pan of water and candles—was reminiscent of a convent chamber. She was wearing a plain, pink floral-pattern dress, slip-pers; in the lamplight, her supple body seemed to float inside her garment, the unmistakable triangle of her pubic mound, lushly dark and giving off a sweet warmth, not two feet away from him, for she wore nothing underneath but a pair of garters. When he just con-tinued to stand, motionless before her, she, in a matter-of-fact, nearly sisterly manner, said to him (or nearly said, for his memory was elusive), "But my, you're a strange bird." Then: *"Mírame aquí."* And she lifted the hem of her dress, up over her navel. "Is this not something you want?"

He admitted that he did.

Disliking the whole business of removing his clothes, for the sight of his own enormous stomach filled him with melancholy, he sat in a chair, with his trousers and undergarment pulled down to his ankles, his shirt covering his upper torso, and the *celestina,* Dahlia, kneeling before him, laughed, not just because he comported himself in a courtly fashion, nor because he was so tender, but because he had the look of a man delirious in his imaginings— "What are you thinking, *hombre,* come on!" she cried.

In the meantime, Mother Nature had taken over, and Dahlia churned and pulled at him, as if withdrawing from the earth a great root; a glow (in memory) was generated by this body part. Soon she removed from her thigh a red garter, which upon his request, she wrapped around his sex and commenced to perform the act of oral love, grasping his "magnificent instrument" with both her hands, her cheeks expanding and compressing in her movements—in fact, given the massiveness of his body, the plumpness of his stomach, as he sat in a chair, and the remarkable length, curvature and thickness of his virility, she seemed as if she were playing some great and fleshy bass saxophone.

He was nearly embarrassed by his thoughts in those moments, for Rita Valladares was very much on his mind, and while the *celestina* attended agreeably to her duties, and the composer idly fondled the livid tip of her right breast, he felt the despair of his inward loneliness. He was thinking about Valladares.

That night he pretended that Dahlia was Rita, and by and by, he found his moment of release. Then he finished a second brandy, and with a lingering desire, he began to touch her, here and there; he had been pleased greatly by the fullness of her breasts, and he had laid the palm of his hand on her navel, and then, kneeling before her in supplication, had pressed the right side of his face, against the dampness of her pubic mound, intently listening, he would swear, to the dim flow of a forest stream; and the scent of her, like flowers after a meadow rain, and of dampened clay red earth, such as one would find in Cienfuegos, intrigued him, as if this young girl had within her the fecundity of the world itself, as if from her skin, so smooth to the touch, could not only sprout laurel sprigs and branches and roots, but would give forth, as if at the creation, the skies and waters and stars (the tears of God) of this Earth.

Then he entered her, a sacred act. In the slowness of time that exists with that kind of experience and sensation, the world was reduced, in those moments, to a primal state that Levis relished, for it made him forget so many things. Dahlia's mouth, her dense tongue, her frantic hips, her ingratiating cries of obeisance, her laughter, the sweat of her back, the pliancy of her limbs, the eternal seeming softness of her womb, the honey taste of her nipples, defined the very parameters of that room, his sensations of her surrounding him, as if he had not simply mounted her, but as if she were above him, to his side, in every direction—like his notion of God, *if there is a God.* Though he, ever so lumbrous, went at her like a courteous brute, and seemed, indeed, to be panting and shaking in ecstasy, what most intrigued him was the absolute primitiveness of the act—as if he were a Neanderthal—and then he thought how marvelous it seemed that the human body had not changed at all in a hundred thousand years, that this bodily ritual had been cherished by countless generations of men.

As he always did, he later performed a bit of Chopin on the brothel piano—but the truth was that, aside from the delights of his carnal dalliance, what he most enjoyed that evening came later: a platter of paella, dense with shrimp, mussels and chunks of chorizo, that he, after leaving the brothel, devoured on the patio of a little restaurant overlooking the harbor, the stars reflecting like green diamonds on the water, Levis, savoring his food and taking in the night sky with great concentration, and wondering if he would again see the yellow star, as if that, too, would serve as inspiration for a song.

WITH RITA

IN NEW YORK:

A POSTCARD, 1928

"Cuando cantan encantan"

(When women chant they enchant)

—MIGUEL CERVANTES

The music of a string quartet by Jo-
hannes Brahms followed the composer
around that morning in 1928, when he had
gone off to Habana harbor to wish Rita
Valladares good luck on her journey to
New York. It had been one of those clear
days, of a pleasantly mild temperature in
the low seventies, with a breeze blowing
off the water, the sky so blue that one
thought of the Mediterranean and of how
life seemed as if it would last forever. That
morning he delighted in the clarity of the
shimmering blue sky, which somehow
made him feel youthful, and by how, despite the clamor of the streets, the sounding of ship's horns, he continued to hear

the sonorous music of Brahms, for earlier as he sat by his breakfast table he had passed his time studying one of that master's
scores. Once he had read the notations, he actually began to hear
the music.

Even as he approached Rita and her husband, Alfonso Ortegas, it seemed as if a string quartet followed him to the very spot
where he stood on the dock before the gangplank to the vapor
"Cristóbal Colón." It was as if these musicians had set chairs
down near them performing, the inescapably dulcet strains of
Brahms emanating from an invisible ensemble of violins, viola and
cello.

She looked remarkably beautiful and mysterious, under a white
hat and veil—like a Persian concubine, he thought (and more, for
there was a part of him so gentlemanly that his ears flushed red, as
standing before her he recalled the indelicate fantasies that came to
his mind when he would think about Rita). He presented her with a
box of French chocolates—little cherry-filled bonbons that he'd purchased the afternoon before in a shop inside the Hotel Inglaterra.
"These are for you, my dear young lady," he said, even while her
solemn husband—unhappily acquiescing to this journey (so the
composer thought), mainly to keep an eye on her in New York, for
she liked men very much—sanguinely regarded Israel with the kind
of expression that seemed to say (as he saw it), *This fellow is a fruit,
no doubt about it.*

One could not blame Ortegas for this opinion. Before leaving
his house, Levis had poured on the cologne and stuck a carnation
in his lapel, and, in those moments, seemed more an emanation
from a perfume counter than a man. The softness of his handshake
did not help the image, nor did his finely manicured fingernails,

which his mother attended to with a pair of small scissors and a file each Friday morning of the week, and as such, in his zealous attention to what he considered a gentlemanly grooming, he tended to give a suspect or misleading impression.

Mr. Ortegas said to Levis: "Thank you, Don Israel, we always appreciate your little gifts," but he had not seemed to mean it and had given the composer an amused up-and-down. Levis nodded, civilly, secretly thinking: "If you saw my sex organ, friend, you would probably faint or throw yourself in front of a tram."

In any event, as the ship's horn sounded, as the cello and violin and viola inside Levis's head (and swirling about him, among the passengers and porters and seamen all) moved into a *divertimiento*, Rita Valladares, up on her tippy toes, had given the composer a kiss.

"Thank you, thank you, my dear Israel, for that beautiful song. I can't wait to perform it."

"I hope my score is adequate—if I'd had more time I could have done more with it...."

But she told him: "No, the score for piano and voice will be enough, and it is beautiful." And then she embraced him, and thanking him again, hurried off to board the ship. He had waited another half hour, waving up at her as she leaned over the railing, along with so many others. He stood there, with the music of Brahms—not "*Rosas Puras*"—resonating in his head, and without the slightest idea of how that little song would so change his life.

Then he went back home to experiment with an idea he had for a ballet, and a few hours later he went off to the Campana Bar, as usual, to join up with some of his chums.

NEW YORK CITY

Once Rita and her husband arrived in New York, not five days after the composer first brought "Rosas Puras" into the world, they were put up in the Plaza Hotel by the Schubert Organization, and Valladares began her preparations for making her upcoming performance at the Roxy Theater a success. As such she spent the first week in long rehearsals with a ten-piece band, fellows she'd never worked with before; a few of them, reassuringly, were Cuban, but the rest consisted of Broadway show musicians, many of them veterans of the Ziegfeld Follies, whose grasp of the Cuban charts had been at first so disheartening that she nearly fell into a state of despair and came down, as she often did in times of stress, with a case of bad nerves. Her stomach was such a disaster that she threw up once in the morning, once in the afternoon—a bileless vomit, frothy like simmering water, and so enervating that during rehearsals she would often have to sit down for fear of falling. So tense was she about presenting a starlet image that she could barely bring herself to eat anything but soda crackers and jam.

She was both pleased—and intimidated—by the wave of publicity that preceded her engagement in New York. For weeks her image had appeared on posters, newspaper ads and on sandwich boards carried by forlorn men along the autumnal streets of the show district of Broadway and Seventh Avenue, wherein a sultry and scantily clad Rita was billed as the "Queen of Tropical Swoon" and "The Greatest Female Singer from Cuba!" Though she considered such hyperbole necessary to the brisk sale of tickets (for her costume in such advertisements showed Rita in tinseled shorts and a gold silk brassiere over which was draped a gauzy gown—so that she almost resembled a stripper), she found that persona a source of irritation, for she regarded herself as a serious pianist, a good composer (thanks to the many hours she had spent in the company of her dear friend Israel Levis) and a singer of true operatic range.

Her own compositions—"Cuban Prelude," "Three Piano Pieces from Habana," "Concerto in F"—she sometimes performed in Cuba, and to some acclaim, but she was always sheepish about playing such works around *El Maestro,* even though he always approved of them. *"Chiquita,"* he would tenderly say, "you have a gift beyond gifts," and she would tremble with delight.

Even the program she planned had been a subject of dispute with the Schuberts, who had blanched at her insistence that the show be divided into two equal segments—a classical recital, followed by a more lively program of Cuban song and dance music, which at that time was just first being heard in America. In the process of negotiations, when her manager in Habana pleaded with her to dispense with such hardheaded nonsense, she had threatened to cancel the show. But it had been such a long-sought engagement that in the end she compromised; the classical portion of her recital would be abbreviated, and this the Schuberts agreed to.

In any event, gone were the days when she could present herself as an unknown, an innocent and petite girl from a humble family in Habana whose talents, mellifluous voice and startling delivery always surprised her audiences. Long gone were the days when a simple dress was sufficient to the occasion, whether singing a Donizetti aria for her professors and fellow students at the conservatory, or performing with a charanga band before a crowd of farmers in the square of a crossroads town in Las Villas province.

Now she had the pressures of blossoming stardom to live up to.

ON THE NIGHT WHEN SHE PREMIERED *"ROSAS PURAS"* BEFORE AN AMERICAN AUDIENCE, SHE THOUGHT ABOUT HER MARRIAGE AND LOVE, OCTOBER 30, 1928

Sitting before her dressing-room mirror backstage in the Roxy Theater, with the house manager rapping on the door every so often, and with her husband in a pinstripe suit, sitting gloomily in a corner, his hand folded over his lap, checking his watch or cracking his knuckles, his expression conveying a disapproval of her show biz life, as if at any moment he would say, "Really, Rita, do you think this life is worth it?" Just having him there threw her stomach into knots, and she would feel like heading off into the bathroom to purge herself (a ritual that she would observe before nearly every performance over the years). With all that, she had to fix her mascara, apply the ruby lipstick, douse her lovely *mulata* face with a translucent lotion, powder her underarms and fight off the little terrors: eruptions of sweat on her brow, a tightening of her gut and that general sense that she was being too closely observed by her husband—who, as of late, she had begun to consider a hindrance to the enjoyment and progress of her career.

A MOMENTARY DIGRESSION ABOUT AN UNREALIZED DESIRE REGARDING THE COMPOSER AND RITA VALLADARES

That they had come to that point surprised her: In the days when she first fell in love with him, Alfonso Ortegas had never shown any tendency toward jealousy or excessive control. When they met, some seven scant years before, in 1921, after one of her performances at the Sociedad Pro-Arte Musical de La Habana, he had been a consummate gentleman, attentive and gallant, as if he were a throwback to some other time. (In that way, he reminded Rita of the composer himself.) What did she know of life then? She married him for innumerable reasons, most of which did not now seem valid. He made a good livelihood as a banker for Chase Manhattan in Habana, and she, desirous of a life in the arts, ever so precarious in Cuba, had wanted to ensure herself and her widowed mother some measure of financial security. She was eighteen years old when he proposed to her back in 1922, and although she had her doubts, she agreed to marry Alfonso. He was a good husband in some ways, but so demanding in his desires to control her, personally and professionally, that she often lamented the "sanctity" of their marriage. Amused by the constant attentions of men, especially in Habana, she lived with the gloom of someone who believed that she had missed a true opportunity for love: in her case with the composer of "Rosas Puras," Israel Levis himself, who, to her disappointment, had always been too timidly inclined around her.

If only the composer had shown any interest, she would have gladly married him, instead, even if he was a bit plump and a little older—and a little too pious—but not once had he properly understood her feelings for him. Somehow, in the manner of their ways together, they had fallen into a pattern that blinded the composer to certain possibilities. Though tender and affectionate in his demeanor around Valladares, he never allowed things to progress. There were nights when she would have gone to bed with him, if he had so wanted, nights when she became bitterly

angry over the composer's seeming indifference to her affectionate manner.

"In another existence, were it not for music, I might have
become a priest"; then he amended this: "Or a priest composer,
like Esteban Salas!" he once said to her.

Valladares was so perplexed by the composer's coolness
around her that she, feeling unsettled and wanting (for the sake of
her mother) a home and family for herself, allowed Alfonso into
her life, even when she had looked up to Levis. But she had never
been certain about why Levis always avoided her attentions. On
the one hand, he was one of those "artistic" sorts, so dedicated to
his calling that he seemed above the fray of normal human pursuits—priestly in his devotion, a bachelor whose impregnable
demeanor could not be changed. But not once did she believe—or
care to believe—that his romantic disinterest in her had to do with
an aversion to women. Had their not been times, she would swear,
when, in her presence, she felt his sexual *"poder"*—his strength?
And had she not once sat upon his lap beside a piano for a group
photograph that was taken in the parlor of the house of Eduardo
Sanchez de Fuentes, in 1924, and felt this enormous and fleshly
heat growing rigid and stately under the weight of her shapely bottom? (Because she had been wearing a simple cotton dress, with
only a few layers of cloth and silken undergarment to mediate
between his penis and the sexual heart of her body, the poor man
could not control the movement of a shaft whose width and fan-
tastic length abruptly impinged upon the spacious sanctity of her
buttocks and so spoke to her naughty side that she could not resist
a little bit of a wriggle. Right then his face and ears burned red, like
a child's, and, all at once, she felt his hand tighten around her arm,

which he had been holding, heard a sigh, then a whisper—
"*Perdóname*" ("Excuse me"). So upset was he by this lapse of self-
control that he had been solemn and quiet around her afterward—
as if he had brought shame upon himself: if only she sat on his lap
long ago, she would have happily explored the fleshly greatness of
a timid man, whose kindness and talents she had already found so
inviting.)

But what could she have been thinking? Her first motive had
always been to make Israel Levis jealous, to draw him more closely
toward her. Was he not the father of her career? Was he not in
her company often enough to know that they would have made a
good matrimony? Did they not console each other over the cold-
ness of death, visiting the cemetery together, where she would
place flowers on her father's grave; had she ever failed to express
pure joy at the sight of him? Had they not collaborated often?
Would she not have taken care of him? Had he not often called
her, with great affection, "My little nightingale"?

She did not understand what had happened—or did *not* happen—between them. His gentleness, the way he loomed over her
protectively, leading her safely through difficult times, had filled
her with such gratitude that she would have done anything for
him. That his creative power made her tremble was something he
could not have known. Nor about certain dreams that she sometimes had about him, not just erotic but also mystical dreams, the
two of them walking hand-in-hand on the water of Habana harbor, Levis lifting her out of a chair in the parlor of his house and
carrying her into his bedroom where she would undo his trousers
to uncover for herself that which would set her eyes aglow, as if
she found a cache of jewels. . . . Levis approaching her in the form

of a bull, whose back she rode across a field, her body teeming with pleasure. . . .

Somehow, on a certain late Sunday afternoon in 1922, for weddings were often held toward the end of the day in Cuba, she found herself standing before a church altar facing a priest, Alfonso beside her, about to receive the sacred vows. And even then, when she turned around to quickly glance at the composer, who, dressed in white from head to toe, demurely nodded his approval, she wished that he had stood up and carried her out of that church, off to his house on Olivares and to his bed (his mother's presence somewhere in that house, notwithstanding).

Instead, he sat quietly. . . . *Why my love, why?* she asked herself plaintively a thousand times.

There had been the wedding celebration, in a social club, where her dear friend, Israel Levis, got very drunk, to the point that he fell over a banquet table and four men had to take him out onto the veranda for some air. She caught sight of him, half dead to the world, waving to friends; when she rushed to his side she wondered why had he seemed in so agitated a state of pain.

That night when she first experienced the physical love of a husband and a wife, she had so many misgivings that she estab-lished in her husband's mind a pattern of sexual responsiveness that lacked promise; her husband, that good man of fastidious habits, handsome and lean, and with a paterfamilias alert to its duties, could have been a bristle-haired tarantula, such was her reluctance to give of herself to him.

Nevertheless, two children came about from this union, and with them arrived an immeasurable joy as to make her life, with certain comforts, quite tolerable: a house on Industria, a maid, the company of her mother, the babies crying, her music—piano scales and rehearsals in a back room, tours. Did she love the banker? Yes, she would tell herself. Did she love the composer more? Possibly— but she could not bear the weight of that question. And why was it that her husband now seemed so afflicted with gloom and impa- tience over her life as a performer, when she had made it a condi- tion of their marriage, for music and the adulation of her public were also her loves?

They argued often, passed days without speaking, then recon- ciled.

Contradictory rumors about them ran rampant in Habana: that she often fell ill and took to her bed for days out of sadness about her marriage; that he was so loving of her that he would not let her out of his sight; that he smothered her with so much atten- tion that she, while loving him, felt that she would go mad. There was no truth to the rumor that he sometimes beat her, nor that she, in her married state, sometimes went off with other men to spite him. Nor that she and Maestro Levis met secretly, not to have a drink or to rehearse, but to fall back on the love that both had passed up.

The truth was that she told her husband not to interfere with her business.

So he reluctantly allowed her the tours, the concerts in the provinces, put up with her occasional nightly performances at cabarets and theaters and her excursions out with her musician friends. He liked Ernesto Lecuona very much—a gentleman. But Israel Levis—he felt a certain discomfort when he came over to visit, mainly because Rita softened so around that man. Privately, he referred to the composer as "that strange chubby fellow you seem to like," and he fiercely objected to her suggestion that they ask Levis to stand as their first son Alejandro's godfather.

Along the way, in her absence, he spent his days in the bank's office contemplating, rather jealously, the effect that Rita, in her more flamboyant state, had on men, who were always sending her flowers and passing her notes after her performances. The poor fellow suffered, even when, at that time, he had no grounds for thinking that she might, in certain situations, pursue the attentions of another man.

That night, as she made herself up before her dressing-room mirror, her husband's face was a collaboration of shadows and of contorted, jaded features that said: *One day you will learn to obey me, and you will understand that I only mean well.*

His disapproval of her professional life so contributed to her anxiety that when it was time for her to dress for the stage, she would send him out of the room. She always brought a stage trunk with her: fresh underwear, long stockings, formal gowns and the more revealing costumes. And she wore a girdle, the first thing she would put on. There was always a moment when she stood naked in her dressing room, looking at her reflection in the mirror, and she would say to herself: *Rita, get those bad thoughts out of your head.* A certain sadness that Israel Levis, whom she loved, would, in all likelihood, never see the loveliness of her naked body; that he would never know the touch of her skin, against his own.

Later, as she walked out onto the stage of the Roxy Theater, Valladares was wearing a formal gown, a glistening tiara on her head. Bowing, she sat before a grand piano, beginning her program with a recital of classical pieces by Bartók, Dvořák and Manuel de Falla; and then works from the modern repertoire of Cuban composers Amadeo Roldán, Alejandro Caturla, Ignacio Cervantes and the well-known Ernesto Lecuona, who had been a student with her at the conservatory in Habana. The audience, a mixed crowd of middle-class and affluent New Yorkers, many *hispanos* among them, politely and admiringly applauded her virtuosity, for she was a gifted musician with a light touch and a refined technique; and yet the men in the audience were mainly awaiting the sultry Rita Valladares whose starlet image had been displayed on posters along the rainy streets of midtown Manhattan for days.

An interval of some twenty-five minutes passed (a film short by Chaplin was shown); she slipped out of her formal gown, fitting herself into an outfit that most proper Cuban women would consider scandalous. She had no time to throw up, as she would have liked. The curtains were raised again. Her band was onstage and, followed by a spotlight, Rita Valladares came out dancing to a conga rhythm. Bejeweled and plumed, with pearls in her hair, she wore a somewhat diaphanous costume of saffron and magenta silk, and as she moved her lithe and voluptuous body, the hooting and clapping audience followed her motion as if she were a living flame.

In quick succession she performed a sequence of Cuban danzones and boleros, among them *"Te Odio," "Ay, Mamá Inéz"* and *"Canto Siboney,"* the joyfulness of her delivery and the bell-tone clarity of her voice living up to the title "Queen of Tropical Swoon," as she was referred to in the Cuban press.

It was on that night that she first presented that newly born song *"Rosas Puras"* to an American audience. This she quietly introduced in English, as "a little rumba especially written for me by a dear friend, El Maestro Israel Levis, in Habana." And from the first bars that most Cuban of songs communicated the intentions of its portly, lovestricken but extremely reserved composer (for he had written it especially for Rita); its playful and nearly childish melody—so simple was it in its phrasing—conveying those very images of Cuban life and spirit that Americans then believed in: Habana on a balmy afternoon, perfume, sunlight and birds, beautiful women and courtly men (like Levis himself) tipping their hats, enamored or on the verge of love, and all to a jaunty *tika tika tike—tiktik* rhythm, a caravel of delight.

For that tune, she wheeled out a cart filled with roses and, clutching several blossoms to her breast, coquettishly sang:

> *Rosas puras de Habana*
> *Bellas y fragantes*
> *Dulces y tiernas*
> *Estrellas de mi tierra cubana*
> *Espejos de tu amor. . . ."*

> ("Pure roses of Habana
> Beautiful and fragrant
> So sweetly tender
> Stars of my Cuban soil
> Mirrors of your love. . . .")

It was a song for courtship, whose doubleentendre lyrics brought whistles from the certain members of the audience—the Cubans calling out, *"¡Vaya Chiquita!";* a song for whorehouses at three in the morning, for cafés at dusk, along the harborside, a quiv ering crimson sunlight spreading over the water; a song embodying the emotions of a man, stunned by the apparition of a shapely and pretty woman, to whom he says, with his not so innocent call, *"¿Puedo, señorita?"* ("Can I, miss?") ... *"¿Dime, puedo?"* ("Tell me, can I?") ... *"¿Comprar estas flores de amor?"* ("Can I buy those flowers of love?"). Rita Valladares tossing, at song's end, roses into the audience, many of them flung lovingly back at her feet, Rita bowing regally like a queen.

In that audience had been Walter Winchell, whose column would mention the famous personalities in attendance—composer George Gershwin ("taking notes"); Al Jolson ("with a carnation in his lapel"); and the actress Claire Windsor ("swooning with delight")—summing it all up with: *"For a finale, that dark Cuban dame brought down the house with a great tune, 'Rosas Puras.' "*

Afterward Jolson went backstage to introduce himself, inviting Rita and her husband over to the Biltmore Hotel for a few drinks so that they might get better acquainted. Previous stays in New York, where she once studied music, had given Rita an ability in English, but her husband (who would have preferred that she stay home in Habana with their two infant children) knew no more than a few phrases in English and detested those nights out in the company of Americans, like the Schuberts, with whom they had once torturously dined.

Passing his time in silence, Alfonso found the necessity of having to rely upon Rita's translations perturbing and taxing.

However, drinking Manhattans with Al Jolson, who drew a round of applause just by entering the crowded Biltmore bar, should have been a more joyful experience, but around her husband Rita felt much restrained. In the security of their home, he could be serene, tranquil, but in public settings, particularly around artists, he had always been uncomfortable, and for that reason alone, her marriage to Alfonso was something that she now often regretted.

She was thinking about this even as Jolson was peppering her with questions: "You ever do a Broadway review?" "I got a new show on the boards; it's called *Wonder Bar.* Ya interested?"

"And that song—'Rosas-something'—you said a pal of yours wrote it? How about asking him if we could use it in my show?"

She nodded and smiled and told Jolson: "I will speak to him when I get back to Habana."

Then they had more drinks and Jolson graced the room with a rendition of "The Sheik of Araby," and then more drinks were poured, and while Rita would have been delighted to spend the next few hours in the company of Jolson, greeting actors and musicians, and reveling in the frenetic energies of the jazz age, at quarter past one her husband wearily told her: *"Rita, vamos, ahora mismo"* ("We're leaving right now"). Then: "I can't take another minute of this nonsense."

Jolson was crestfallen at their departure, but he understood the necessities of rest, for she had another week of shows at the Roxy Theater. In his expansive fashion, Jolson gave Valladares a hug, rapped Alfonso on the back and as they left, called out after Rita, saying: "Don't forget about me—you got my card, don't cha?" And then to the room: "Ladies and gents, you're seeing a future star."

She was elated; her husband a little annoyed.

It had been raining that evening and the streets were slick with streaks of light, the reflections of buildings distending in a wash of colors.

They caught a taxi to the Plaza Hotel.

The Empire State Building did not yet exist, a trolley line ran down Fifth Avenue.

The moon floated over the south end of Central Park, sadly blinking.

LATER THAT OCTOBER, 1928, A POSTCARD TO CUBA

Though Valladares had come to New York for a weeklong engagement at the Roxy Theater and would then commence a brief tour in the northeast, she had also arrived in the city to make some new recordings for the Victor company. In that regard, her theatrical run turned out to be good preparation for the recording of "Rosas Puras." By the time Valladares made it into the studio, down on Lafayette Street, Rita, despite a lonely and enervating half hour stuck in an elevator on the way up to the twelfth floor, was so well acquainted with the song that the business of record-ing it with a seven-piece band went smoothly enough.

The producer, Silvio Fuentes, the head of Victor's "Caribbean Wing," in his perpetual quest for new recordings for the South American and Caribbean markets, was so pleased by her rendi-tion that he told Rita, "We'll have this out within the month. *Tú verás* (You'll see)."

That same afternoon, she sat on a bench in Central Park, along Fifty-ninth Street, and with sparrows circling her feet, she wrote out a postcard to the song's composer. In it, she addressed Israel as *"Mi querido gordito bueno,"* or "My dear sweet fatty":

I am here in New York, missing Habana and all my friends. But
I have made the recording of "Rosas," and it came out especially

well. The feeling is that we will have a great deal of success with it. Anyway, I am off to Boston the day after tomorrow—I hope it is not too cold there. Take care of yourself. I send you my tender affections.

And she signed it *"La Chiquita Rita,"* wondering if the note might have seemed too forward in tone.

It was a Friday in late October of 1928 when she posted the card from a corner mailbox; a mailman picked it up and transported it to the Thirty-third Street U.S. Post Office station; another courier placed it in a heavy burlap sack marked HAVANA, CUBA, and that sack traveled by mail train to Miami, then by boat to Habana harbor. It took a week, but by and by, a local mail carrier, Pablo, was walking along the pavement on calle Olivares when he came to the front patio gate of the composer's residence; as on innumerable occasions, he lifted the gate latch and followed a short path under a heavy-branched acacia and past a little garden full of chrysanthemums and roses, then he tapped on the door. He could hear a few notes being played on a piano, followed by several chords, from a room deep inside that house, and birds chirping, the buzz of insects around him, too; then the composer calling out: *"¡Aquí!"*

Shortly, Israel Levis himself, jowl-faced, a little harried and rumpled—for he tended to wear the same white linen trousers and bowtie and suspenders (a "lucky outfit") each day of his beloved toils—towering in his immensity over the mail carrier and saying: "Ah, Pablito! What do you have for me?"

The mail carrier handed him a small bundle of items: a few letters addressed from Spain; a letter from a Cuban in Chicago; a copy of *National Geographic* magazine, which he subscribed to; and the postcard from Rita (bearing on one side an image of the Statue of Liberty), which he had not at first noticed. But, as Levis had a natural inclination toward friendliness, he asked the mail carrier: "Would you like a coffee?" Then: *"¿O un traguito, eh?"* ("A little drink"), to which the mail carrier answered: "A drink would be good, my right heel is killing me."

Inviting Pablo into his kitchen, the composer poured him a full glass of rum, and even as the mail carrier seemed a little nervous, perhaps anxious to resume his route, Israel also filled a glass with rum for himself, and then said: "Come with me, my friend," and he led the carrier down a hallway, into a back room, to his study, its doors opening to a courtyard and garden. It happened that Israel had been working on a new piece for the piano, using Cuban folk airs, à la Lecuona and Heitor Villa-Lobos, the great Brazilian composer, and had been tinkering with the modalities of Yoruban chant. And because he loved company to break the solitude of his hours, he sat the carrier down on a little *sofá* and with a slight but benevolent madness in his eyes, he began to play what he had of the piece he called "Kubanakan," grunting, humming along, puffing at a cigar and touching from time to time a crucifix that hung around his neck, dangling against his great belly, whenever he breathed in and out.

"This may be for a little ballet," he said. "This would be the first movement."

The carrier had been in that study before, and yet he was always a bit intimidated by the learned atmosphere of that room, for high shelves filled with all kinds of books rose on the walls, and there were evidences of knowledge that the mail carrier could only imagine: books on nature and ornithology, and medicine, reams of articles, music reviews and commentaries that the composer had written for the Habana newspapers, and stacks of annotated sheet music. His eyes closed, the carrier nodded appreciatively as Levis played the first portion of his composition, and when he was done, the composer said, "*Mira,* you're a man of taste, what do you think? Is it too esoteric for the average person?" And when Pablo told him, "No, no Señor," he so delighted the composer that Israel fetched the bottle and refilled the mail carrier's glass, saying: "Then you must listen to more."

An hour later perhaps, Israel Levis led the watery-eyed but happy mail carrier out to the street so that he might resume his route, and he did so sadly, as he liked the carrier's quiet manner, his gold-toothed smile and guileless eyes—trusting in his opinion, above all, as he was an exemplar of the "ordinary man." He could have spent the afternoon with him, drinking and playing different pieces—and the carrier would have stayed, for it was not every day that the composer, with his own little fame in Habana, did that kind of thing. But, as Levis thought, work was work, and he did not want the fellow to lose his job. Yet, feeling that it would be useless to attempt further composition, as he had consumed four glasses of rum and could only write well under the influence of three, Levis planned to take a nap, resting for his excursions out into the city later in the evening.

He was feeling rather good when he finally came across Rita's postcard from New York, rereading her salutation a half dozen times, and greatly touched, in a perhaps overly sentimental way, by the line: "we will have a great deal of success with it." The single word "we" throwing him into such a state of pure affection for the singer that he found himself thinking the unthinkable: that were he of a different age and character, he might once have told Valladares: "*Rita, sabes que te quiero mucho*" ("Rita, you know that I love you deeply"). But she had long since married, and in that area of his life the composer had always been timid beyond timid, and at thirty-eight years of age and very plump, he could not imagine that so elegant and talented a young beauty could have ever had similar emotions for such a *viejito* like him.

So as he always did, he took his own feelings for Valladares and fashioned them to suit the avuncular tenor of his ways of self-restraint and the deepest respect for her person, despite the erotic mischief that always lingered in his heart when he was around her—for, in many ways, Valladares would forever remain a child to his foolish, foolish heart.

ANOTHER MORNING, 1947

My dearest "Chiquita." It's as if you are the only person that I have in the world to confide in, the last link to my youth and to the good times. Anyone looking at me now only feels pity. I know of it, firsthand. . . . Do you know that just last week I was presented with a special citation at the Gallego Society for a lifetime of "furthering the cause of Cuban music," as they called it. The director of the Teatro Martí, Eliseo Martínez, read a very nice elegy (I would call it an "elegy"), and though it was filled with the usual praises (usually what you would hear at a funeral), I could not feel a single thing. I got up, rather reluctantly, and made a few remarks— "I am, of course, indebted to my supporters and friends here in my beloved Habana, and I must express my gratitude to the government of Grau San Martín for its assistance. . . ." I began, and then I can hardly recall what I said, only that at times I could barely lift my head to face the audience. I'd perhaps had too many drinks beforehand—as I would have preferred to stay at home, for what did honors mean to me now? And what had they expected of me to say, anyway? . . .

It is true that in my life I have managed to compose a few "entertainments," the kinds of songs that the cumbacheros make much of in the dance halls; and, of course, you must know that I am especially speaking of the song I had written for you on that day long ago. But what does any song really mean, in the end, to the world, but a few moments of amusement, while the greater machinery of life grinds down so many people— among them, this old fellow. . . . What, for example, is a song next to the event of the birth of a single human being? That I never had any children hurts me so now. Can you imagine what would have happened had I the courage to do something so monumental, instead of wasting so many of my years with my so-called lofty pursuits? Nor have I ever told you how many hours I have spent imagining what life would have been with you by my side. . . . That I secretly hated myself?

Remember the photograph of me as a baby that hangs on the wall of my study? You were always delighted by it—"My God, but you were a sweet child," you'd say. I was six months old—and sitting, yes, dear Rita, on a cushion surrounded by roses—can you imagine that? When I look at that purely innocent face, with the large, expressive, warm eyes, I think of the disaster that I am now, and I become fearful of my thoughts, dear Rita, for I cannot bear, on some of these days, the idea of dying alone. . . .

RETRACING

HIS STEPS TO

PARIS

He was forty years old on the day in
1930 when it occurred to him that he, in
all likelihood, would turn out to be one of
those fellows who would be his mother's
companion unto her death, and though
Levis accepted this duty, he often found
himself in a cantankerous disposition
around her. While Doña Concepción cod-
dled him—shampooing his hair, manicuring
his hands and cooking special treats as the
mood suited her—she quite expected that
he wait on her in return. And so, when
they were at home, and he was not at
work before the piano, she ordered him
about. He would take her walking in the
parks of the city, to the cinema, off to the
cemetery to visit his father's and siblings'

graves, and not once on these excursions did she ask him about his life. She spoke about herself, her prayers to God, her dreams and the small diversions by which she amused herself. He would take her to the big department stores and to the dress shops along Neptuno, spending hours in a chair while she ordered the clerks about, criticizing the fabrics and designs. Often she chastised him over his sudden lapse of attention to her if a beautiful woman happened to pass along the street, saying, "What would you want, my son, with a woman like that, anyway?"

And although he nodded like a gentleman and kept his less kindly thoughts to himself, there were times when he would have liked to have shipped her off to his older brother's house in Santiago—for good.

He had been only once really angry with his mother, when she seemed to take an active disliking to Rita—why he could not say, jealousy perhaps—but in the days before Rita's first marriage, in 1922, when she would come over to the house to perform a song, or to hear a new composition, his widowed mother, who previously had been so warmly disposed toward Rita, began to treat her differently. Suddenly the pretty girl was too dark skinned, too presumptuous, even when Rita had always been polite and respectful of the older woman. It was his mother's failing, he would tell himself years later, to see how he might have greatly benefited from the company of so vivacious and vital a young woman.

One Wednesday those years before, when Rita came by, Doña Concepción treated her as if she had never been to the house before. His mother had been nothing less than cordial and charming, taking Rita by the hand and roving through the rooms of that house, as if escorting her through a museum: "This was once my late husband's examination room and study. This is where my son Israel now writes his music. Sometimes when I am not sleeping well, and the house is quiet, and my boy is out doing whatever the young people do, I can sense my husband's spirit in his room."

For her part, Rita had seemed to enjoy the visit, even if the composer, so remote, so charming, so often feigning indifference to her presence, seemed a nervous wreck, patting his brow with a handkerchief. And though he did not say a word afterward, as he walked her out to catch a streetcar, he felt a great gloom. It seemed that his mother did not want to share him with anyone else, not even the wondrous Rita Valladares, who surely would have been a good and attentive daughter-in-law.

"I have spoken to your father," she told him that evening. "And while I don't really mind that girl at all, your father seems to have his doubts. And I must concur with this my son, you must be careful and ask yourself, What does she have to offer me?"

As a result, Israel Levis, in his acceptance of the situation, seemed destined for a kind of perennial bachelorhood, as he could not conceive of violating the sanctity of that place with the introduction of another female presence—*One is enough,* he often thought.

Still, there was little he would not do for her—as he knew her pain was great and saw that his mother had been given by God a life of mourning and solitude. He treated her gently, deferentially, ever so careful as to assure her that he was her loving son. If he traveled outside of Habana without her, she had always said to him, "I want you to come back safe and sound so that you will be with me the day I die." But, of course, he thought, she would probably outlive him; he found the situation claustrophobic, even if it seemed to outsiders as something noble, earnest. Sometimes he laughed, for somehow, in his devotions to his mother and to his life in music, he had turned around to find himself one of those *solteros* who had forgone a more normal life because of sacrifices. But they kept out of each other's way; that is, Levis always man-aged to find his little escapes, largely through composition and brandy; he was not so far gone like one of the men he had heard about who literally shared his mother's bed each night; and yet sometimes, when his professional duties required travel, he felt such a pure exhilaration about leaving his familial situation that he was often in a celebratory mood—nearly floating through the world, as if the prospect of freedom had liberated his body from gravity—a short-lived revelry: doused by a hidden wishfulness that she vanish from his life forever, the prospect of solitude, in a world lived without her, despite the difficulties, at once rankling and frightening to him.

Yet he remained dutiful. He would take her to fortune-tellers and astrologists, search the flea markets and shops of the city for religious relics and pieces of jewelry to adorn her. Powerless before the fact that she was preparing for the next life, even if she was in good health, he, feeling a deep compassion for her, had turned around one day to find himself in the midst of a perpetual wait—for what, he did not know.

Rita's Stardom

By that time, Rita Valladares had, in fact, become a star. It happened that the Spanish-language recording of *"Rosas Puras"* had become a remarkable success: the first twenty thousand copies of its initial November 1928 pressing sold briskly in shops and department stores all over the Caribbean; within the new year, fifty thousand more had been sold. In the fall of 1929, just before the American stock market crash, record sales had reached more than six hundred thousand, her rendition attaining a great popularity in Europe, then beginning its fascination with what was being called "music from the tropics." Israel Levis himself had been quite pleased by Rita's recording and was delighted to dis-cover that bands in the big hotels of Habana were beginning to play his composition in their shows, treating it with the reverence accorded to a standard. He began to hear it on the radio, humbly making nothing much of it, other than he had managed to quickly write a more or less fetching tune.

When Levis walked with Valladares in public, people were always calling out "Hey Chiquita!" and stopping to chat with her—just a smile, a few words from her lips, making people happy (for it was an otherwise gruesome time in Cuba, the depression had hit the island and the dictator Machado still remained in power). A fixture on the radio and in constant demand, she had even made a name for herself in the United States, as part of a musical review with Al Jolson that made a cross-country tour, in early 1930. She danced, played the piano and sang *"Rosas Puras"* and other Cuban songs on a schedule that found her both exhausted and missing the *dulzura*—the "sweetness"—of her life at home, and the warmth of her people in Cuba.

She had liked New York, disliked Detroit; San Francisco had been an enchantment. In May 1930, she filmed her first musical short, alongside Jolson, a five-minute film shot on a soundstage and directed

by Busby Berkeley. The long hours under the hot lamps, in combination with a case of influenza that had nearly paralyzed her vocal
chords, left her quite ill, though one could not tell from the infectious
joy of the finished product, which Levis would see himself on an
August night in the Neptuno Cinema. In a clingy, somewhat revealing dress—one could make out the distinctive shapeliness of her
breasts—she appeared behind a florist's cart on a Habana street corner, singing, her hips asway as she hawked roses to handsome
passersby. Each of the roses, through the magic of the cutting room,
in the blink of an eye turned into a long-legged and voluptuous dancer
in a scarlet red bathing suit with petal skirts. Such was her absolute
ease on camera that it was impossible to guess that her throat was
raw and inflamed and aching—despite the painkillers administered to
her—that in the narrow bathroom of her dressing room she had vom-
ited blood and in those moments had become so inordinately home-
sick for Cuba and the company of her children and friends like Israel
Levis that she would soon quit the tour. She made this decision after
she had collapsed on stage during a show in the beautiful but "bru-
tally cold" city of Cleveland, in a place called Ohio.

During that tour Rita had often written Levis, the tone of her
correspondences becoming, over time, more world-weary. She
always spoke of missing her two children but rarely mentioned
her banker husband. Always she sent Israel her love. He cherished these postcards and letters, written out in her careful,
diminutive script, and always looked forward to seeing Rita upon
her return to the city. If he'd owned a telephone he might have
called her every day; he was forever delighted to run into her, to
visit Rita, however briefly, at her house on the calle Industria. He
made his visits as would an uncle, always bringing along toys for

her two children, pastries and bottles of port. He smoked cigars, made small talk with her more or less tolerant husband Alfonso, and sometimes entertained them at the piano. (Actually, Levis had been kind to her husband, though he envied the man's good looks and his fortune at having married Valladares. He genuinely wished them happiness, and yet, after being in their presence, he invariably left their house feeling vaguely depressed.) And always there came the moment, when readying to leave and standing before Rita, he would blush when she leaned close to him to plant a kiss on his cheek.

He had long since resigned himself to the fact that there was nothing between them, other than a quite amicable, professional relationship; and yet, sometimes, in his mother's company, as he would kneel before Doña Concepción, as she sat in a wicker chair, rubbing the soles of her feet after a long stroll through the city, he would think about Rita. That he still longed for her startled him; even if he had never married and sometimes felt himself in the throes of some penitential test of character, he cursed his inability to have acted upon his desires around Rita, hated that he had come to think of her as "his little sister."

Occasionally the composer would go on walks with Rita, often in the company of her children, for her two sons liked him and his soft and genteel emotionality. Around Levis she always seemed to leave the weariness of her professional life behind and regained her buoyancy and ebullience. In fact, whenever she and the composer were together, a change came over the very atmosphere of light between them, as if a million threads flared out from their perfume- and cologne-sweet bodies, connecting one to the other. And yet what always made their time together most difficult was their mutual sense that each had sidestepped the other, as if they should not have been husband and wife.

Really, Israel, who were you fooling?

On one of their excursions, as they sat alone by a bench in the Parque Central—it was the summer of 1930—Valladares abruptly began to weep.

"My child, my child," he had said. "What is it?"

"Ay," she had cried. "I am absolutely at my wit's end with Alfonso. He is many things, Don Israel—he is a good provider, a fine husband, but my God, he is a bore. I am bored, Don Israel," she continued. "I am twenty-eight years old and feel like a grand-mother! And I don't know what it is; if it is the work—which I love—or the aggravations of life with that man. He looks at me like I am his pet, a little hound, and heaven forbid if he allows me a moment's peace at home. He can't bear the idea that I am devoted to my profession. In public he is tolerant with me, but at home, we do nothing but argue about it. Even my own mother had come to notice my unhappiness. . . ." Then: *"Don Israel, eres un sabio—"* ("You are wise—") "tell me what I should do?"

"Well, you are his wife, and were married in a church. What can anyone do in such a circumstance but wait for God's hand to intervene." Then he added: "I do not know what else to tell you."

She turned and looked directly into his eyes: "Is what I'm telling you so unclear, Don Israel, that you can answer me in that way? Is it really that unclear?"

In the romantically dim recesses of his mind, it dawned on Israel Levis that his *"Chiquita"* had invited his intercession, and though he most nearly took hold of her hands and pulled her close, he could not imagine that she would have wanted him to do so. Swiftly, he assumed the older brother's mantle, that of teacher and protector. Even when he would later roam half drunk through the streets of Habana, feeling the fool, he decided to take the "moral" road, and told her: "If you would like me to, I can speak to your husband on your behalf."

And that made her laugh: "Oh, Don Israel, even though you are something of a genius when it comes to music, there are many, many things that you don't understand." Then, as abruptly as her tears had come, she shot up from the bench and left him to ponder the uncertainties of his judgments when it came to being a man.

A MOMENTARY ENCHANTMENT

The very spring that Levis's clouded mind failed to see what should have been clear about his life with Rita, he had made the acquaintance of the Spanish poet Federico García Lorca. Famed in Cuba for his "Gypsy Ballads," Lorca had arrived in Habana in March 1930, to deliver a series of lectures on literature at the Principal de la Comedia Theater. His invitation to Cuba had come from Fernando Ortíz, noted musicologist, president of the Hispano-Cuban Institution and a longtime friend of Israel's. Upon meeting the poet at a reception in the Hotel La Unión, Levis was dazzled by Lorca's erudition and otherworldliness, his dandy-esque attire and absolute delight with Cuban music, notably the *sones* of Oriente province, many of which he seemed to know by heart. In the three months that the handsome Lorca spent in Cuba, mainly in Habana, Levis must have seen the poet a dozen times, attending both his public lectures and the impromptu readings he would give at literary gatherings held in private houses, notably at the Loynaz family mansion in Vedado, not far from Levis's home. During those days of their acquaintance, Levis came to the conclusion that the great poet was, in a very subtle way, effeminate in nature, his· wounded and soulful eyes so piercing that Levis would feel his heart racing with his glance. *That was something else I never understood and because of those feelings such men sometimes frightened me.* Yet he enjoyed Lorca's company. Quick to strum a guitar and sing, to drink, dance and improvise a line or two of poetry, Lorca was an odd combination of free spirit and troubled soul, for like Poe and Martí, he seemed obsessed with his own mortality (a preoccupation that, with religion and love, Levis determined, constituted one of the fuels of the creative mind). He had been by Lorca's side for a concert at the Bach Society, had accompanied Lorca, Fernando Ortíz and a young poet named José Lezama Lima to the bawdy and surreal vaudeville-style shows at the Alhambra, had visited the poet in his hotel suite where before a group of admiring students Lorca, dressed in his nightclothes and sitting up in bed, recited a poem he had written about Cuban music called *"Son"* and then a portion of something he was in the process of writing, called "Ode to Walt Whitman"—that late afternoon, of spellbound titillation, the last time Levis had seen his eccentric and deeply gifted Spanish friend.

RITA WENT OFF TO PARIS, 1930

Later, that autumn, God "intervened" and Rita, seeking to escape her husband, went off to Europe, traveling to Paris. She had joined a Cuban review under the direction of Sindo Garay, composer and impresario, and had made her debut, to much acclaim, at the Palace Boulevards Music Hall, singing Grenet's "¡Ay! Mamá Inés" and Levis's "Rosas Puras," the most popular of the songs. The Parisians, eternally in search of "le chic" and already smitten by Josephine Baker, heartily welcomed the new Cuban diva. In fact, they were so obsessed by the sexual allure of cocoa-colored skin that it soon became a fashion, among Parisian women, to pluck their eyebrows and to artificially darken themselves with dye-filled pomades (a precursor, it might be ventured, to their later obsession with the "tan"), Rita becoming an object of adulation and much sought after by the club owners and promoters of that city.

She wrote Levis: "My dear Gordito, you must come and join the party!"

That same autumn she spent three months in Paris, and in that time a rumor came back to Habana: Apparently, Rita Valladares had made the acquaintance of a French actor, with whom she had fallen in love. They had met in the Ritz Hotel and it was said that they were seen everywhere together, that Rita seemed especially happy in those days—far happier than she had been around her own husband.

This rumor, conveyed to Levis in a Habana bar, struck him as a myth—That does not sound like Rita, he told himself—but Rita's husband took it quite to heart. Having remained in Habana with their children during her tour, Alfonso went off to Paris to bring her back. One night, when Alfonso confronted Rita with this allegation of infidelity, demanding that she return with him to Cuba, they fell into a violent argument. He had so badly beaten her that she could not return to the stage for a week, the rumbera Urbana Troche taking her place in the show. Whether this accusation of infidelity was true or not, the beating had left bruises all over her body. With her eyes open to the mistake of her marriage—and the fragility of love—she vowed never again to share her bed with Alfonso.

Another soul might have responded differently, pursuing the restoration of their romance, but Alfonso, having many obligations, returned to Habana without her, sent the children off to their grandmother in Mariano and shut himself in his house for a week, inconsolable and quite angry.

It was not long before, poor Alfonso, of a temperament that would have been called "sanguine" in the twelfth century, lost his mind, if only for a moment, but in that moment he happened to be quite drunk, and—just like that—while teetering on the edge of the Antonio Maceo pier, he decided, in a kind of mad vengeance, to throw himself into the water, the eternal-seeming moonlight sweeping across the bay.

HIS OLD ROLE RESUMED, DECEMBER 1931

Levis had been by her side with her two children during the whole business of the funeral, the man interred in the Cementerio Colón not one hundred paces from the obelisk that would one day mark Levis's home, near a bush of sun-burst flowers and an avenue of mausoleums. She was so bereft that she blamed herself for his demise—"If only I had been more reasonable," she told Levis. "I don't know what got into my head."

They were walking along the Avenida Maceo on the Malecón when Levis could not resist asking her: "Was there . . . somebody else?"

"Oh, Israel, *por Dios,* how can you ask me such a thing?"

He did not answer, but then she said: "There was somebody

who was my companion at times in Paris, but it never went beyond companionship. Certainly, I would have told you so."

He had listened, wondering if Valladares could have been concealing the truth from him; he preferred to believe her, though her resignation to the fate of her late husband startled him, for soon enough she spoke of only two things: her children and an eventual return to Paris.

"I am going back because life is freer there," she told him. "And this time I will be taking my mother and children along. Conditions here are not pleasant for me. . . . My late husband's family hates me, simply because of a piece of gossip to which there was no truth."

She was dressed in black when they entered the church of Espíritu Santo together, Levis telling her: "Come, and let us pray. It will make you feel better." Afterward he gave her a rosary whose crucifix bore the bone chip of a saint, said to be Judas, which he found in an antique shop. He escorted her home and lingered briefly in her front salon, watching her two boys playing with a few kittens on the floor. She had sighed and he, not knowing what to do, had simply given her an embrace, as if to squeeze out the demons of her grief. He would remember that a police siren sounded outside on the street, that he heard pops of gunfire in the distance, and that he, feeling cowardly, could not find within himself the resolve to become her suitor—the fact that she was now a widow spoke to his formal side, and he found himself thinking it appropriate that he respect the period of her mourning—it would be a year, nonetheless, before he could entertain such an enterprise. But why should she, with her mounting fame, show any interest in him? He would remember that the situation made him feel akin to a vulture about to feed upon the carrion of the fallen. After all, wasn't she in a fragile state of mind? And how could he take advantage of the situation without betraying their friendship? No, he would respectfully keep his distance from her, as he always had, and wait for the appropriate moment to pursue a romance.

He'd even consulted an astrologist—it had been his misfortune to have been born on a summer day, August 24, cusp of Leo and Virgo, so that the planetary and stellar influences upon his own actions were often nebulous, open to various and confusing interpretations, and, like the composer himself, indecisive when it came to matters of love.

Instead, he continued the ordinary course of his days, regarding Rita Valladares and her recent tragedy from the safe distance of his more or less solitary life at home. There he could savor the joys of his creative endeavors, then wallow in his agitation over his loneliness; there he could exhilarate in the familiar pleasures of his life with his mother, shuddering with the joy of a child whenever she would wash his hair, or feeling a simple soaked-with-brandy contentment while sitting with her out on the back patio during an evening of lovely, temperate weather, then torment himself over his feelings of entrapment. Mainly he wanted to be left alone and yet suffered when he thought about Rita, the man damning himself for his lack of resolve and romantic independence.

POLITICS AND MANNY CORTEZ, 1931

The early 1930s were an especially brutal time for the arts in Cuba, and Levis found himself working in an even greater solitude, as many of his musician and composer friends had departed for either the United States or for civilized, genteel Europe. (Some musicians, hearing of the lynching of Negroes in the American South, would never step foot in the States.) They'd left partly out of a search for lucre, partly because of the political situation in Cuba— not the Cuba that American tourists were flocking to, not the Habana of palm-enshrouded courtyards and brothels, plush hotels, rooftop garden restaurants, and swimming pools, of the "sultry" women in the latest French fashions with mantillas slung over their shoulders, nor of the night clubs and the cheap but good cigars and rum, but the Habana of the secret police, of murders, kidnappings and mutilations.

It seemed that nearly every other day he heard about yet another friend who had vanished without a trace or had been sent to prison. Though he gave money to help friends leave the coun-try—and was well aware of his own weariness with life in Cuba— he lived with the illusion that the ever-growing list of crimes com-mitted by the dictator Machado and the intensifying oppression and mockery of the arts would pass, in time. Still, many a morning found him down by the harbor to see these friends off, Levis waiting on the dock until the ship vanished on the horizon, and then sadly making his way to one bar or another for an early drink. Sitting in the Campana Bar, he often had a letter or post-card from a friend in Europe or the States stashed in his jacket pocket, his old crowd, it seemed, bit by bit, leaving him behind.

Often he entertained the sad notion of leaving Cuba himself, but it seemed to him as something that only a more adventurous, less homebound soul would do.

Even when he received offers to go on an extended tour, he

lived with the terrible misapprehension that his dear mother would somehow perish from a wilting of spirit if he were to leave her, and he thought, foolishly, all those years, that he could not sever his ties to her. He made an exception to his rule about travel only for the briefest tours (one of them to Spain in 1929, to appear at the exposition in Seville), but mainly to Mexico, and principally to perform in the city of Mérida, filled with many Cubans, or to New Orleans, where he had been enthralled by the jazz of the American Negro musicians. Or if Rita Valladares happened to be giving a concert in one of the provinces and wanted Israel Levis to accompany her on the piano, he always tore himself away, even as she, in the thrall of stardom, seemed to be changing and given over to something that she had not possessed before—vanity.

A favorite photograph from that time, circa 1930–31, is set on his dresser and shows Levis posed with friends along the Paseo del Prado in Cienfuegos. Now bespectacled, he is wearing a black-brim, flat cane hat, a rumpled suit, and sits with a folded raincoat and a pile of music scores upon his lap. Beside him, to his right, Rita, buoyant in a feathered hat and flowery dress, coquettish in high heels, beaming for the camera; to his left, the jaunty and ever smiling Ernesto Lecuona, in a dark suit and top hat, worn at a rascally angle. The others, as he would remember (*and how hard it is to remember such names and faces*) the journalist Guillermo de Cárdenas, the composer Eduardo Sánchez de Fuentes, that handsome man dressed entirely in white, and a fellow musician named Eusebio Delfín... *such dear and beautiful friends.*

As a creature of habit, he remained by his mother's side, their weekly rituals of attending Mass together on Sundays somehow reassuring to the composer, for while contemplating the timeless-ness in which the symbols of Christianity dwelled, he found it impossible to believe that good would not prevail over the world. In the midst of prayers, or while hearing an Ave Maria and while gazing with pure devotion at an image of Christ on the cross, His eyes compassionate and ever loving, he believed that the greater power of God would preside and solve the little disagreements of man. (He imagined a great and lordly figure seated before a key-board with a feather quill in hand, changing certain notes within the *pentagrama* of his score, fixing this and that and patiently awaiting a favorable melody to emerge.)

But those were troubled times. The poor and destitute were everywhere, and so many of his friends had been arrested or deported that uncertainty entered into even his most private thoughts. So disagreeable was that atmosphere to the creative spirit that not even the beauty of the city could assuage his aching soul. He had other worries—not so much about his own dear mother, but for his friend Manny Cortez, who seemed to be getting more deeply involved with anti-government activity. Beyond the printing and distribution of anti-Machado pamphlets, he had become active in arms smuggling from Florida. Where once he could depend on Manny to accompany him to the brothels, his friend seemed now to have far less time for such "nonsense." He disappeared for days at a time, going off to other towns around Cuba for secret meetings. And whenever he and Levis got together, instead of speaking about poetry or music, Cortez now tried to draw the composer more deeply into the cause of overthrowing Machado.

Levis's answer, which always angered Cortez: "My dear friend, haven't I done enough? And what can I do but compose my music?"

The years when he was willing to write letters against the government or sign petitions and proclamations had passed, as far as Levis was concerned, as the situation had become too dangerous, especially if he wanted to stay in Cuba.

"You cannot continue to live in your dreams," Cortez told him. "You cannot live with the delusion that the world can be changed through a piece of music."

The composer's answer was this: "Manny, you know that I do what I can in my own way. I give you money, do I not? And have not some of our works together, by their very Cuban nature, done much to further the cause of Cuba for the Cubans?"

"Yes, but things will not change just by wishing them away."

They were such good friends that Levis and Cortez could not part ways, but, little by little, they seemed to grow more distant from each other, a sadness coming over Levis as he would stand before the door to a brothel at ten at night, rapping against the wood, waiting quietly alone.

A NOTE ON THAT "SWEET ENTERTAINMENT"

Though *"Rosas Puras"* had been something of a trifle for its composer, when it was rerecorded in 1931 for the American market by the Paul Whiteman Orchestra, this version with English lyrics by one Marion Moonlight and sung again by Rita Valladares, quickly swept the United States and brought him, at five-cents-per-copy royalty, a fair amount of money.

As *Variety* would put it, "That mirthful and infectiously rhyth-
mic composition 'Pretty Roses' brings into our dance halls a welcome change from the foxtrot and Charleston. This rumba is a
godsend, and we should tip our hats to the Cuban composer,
Israel Levis, who wrote it."

Even when Levis, who had much more serious aspirations (and
often despaired over the limitations of his creative imagination), fan-
cied it as nothing more than a sweet entertainment that he had
knocked out for Rita Valladares, *"Rosas Puras"* became his signature
tune, the piece that would be remembered by future generations,
long after his more serious works—operettas, zarzuelas, piano con-
certos and symphonies—were swept away and forgotten.

In that future, which he could never have imagined, whenever
a director of a theater production or of an atmospherically
charged film set somewhere in the Caribbean wanted a familiar
theme, he relied upon that composition. The portly composer himself would be featured in a 1932 RKO short, filmed in a Mexico
City studio, leading his own orchestra in a rendition of that
song—big silver palm trees and a glittering half-moon behind him,
a beautiful and shapely singer clutching a bouquet of roses against
her breast and seductively singing, *"Rosas / Rositas puras / Se
venden las rosas más bellas en Habana"* ("Roses / Pure little roses /
The most beautiful roses in Havana for sale!").

It would crop up in several Spanish films—*La Bella de Madrid*,
(1932) and *Pa Habana Me Voy* (1933)—and Fred Astaire had tap-
danced, gyrated and twirled to *"Rosas Puras"* in the 1935 MGM
film short *Rhumba Crazy*.

Over the following years, that most Cuban of *canciones,* so
popular that it was something of an unofficial national anthem,

much like *"Guajira Guantanamera,"* would play nightly, all over the world, at dance parties, during weddings, in numerous nightclubs and cabarets, from Buenos Aires to Helsinki, the fourteen notes of its first beatific measures cropping up in the midst of jam ses- sions at two in the morning—the melody of the song something that every musician seemed to have learned. No Latin-style band excluded *"Rosas Puras"* from its repertoire—it was so much a mother's milk for musicians that it seemed to transcend time itself.

And he would have been amused that different versions of *"Rosas Puras"* could be piled up in stacks and fill a living room. Louis Armstrong recorded it in 1932 as "Pretty Roses," as did the Don Aziapu Orchestra, the Tommy Dorsey Big Band, the Xavier Cugat Orchestra, among many others. Desi Arnaz, Bing Crosby, Mel Tormé, Peggy Lee and Ella Fitzgerald, Julio Iglesias and Celia Cruz—all would make their versions. In the jazz world, Bill Evans, among so many other players, would extend the simple phrases of *"Rosas Puras"* into a thirteen-minute meditation on chordalities; there would be versions by Charlie Parker and John Coltrane, too, and Theolonius Monk, working that melody into one of his purposefully casual improvisations.

WITH GEORGE GERSHWIN

Even George Gershwin himself, visiting Habana in 1930, had been deeply impressed (not only by the brothels and women of that city) with the composition; so stricken was he with the infec- tious rhythms and joyous melodies of that song that he had sought out the composer. Levis met with Gershwin in the dining room of the Hotel Inglaterra, on the west side of the Prado, facing the park, and there, with Manny Cortez acting as translator, the two men, their mutual love for melody in common, had an agreeably pleasant meal and talked over the differences of form between the American stage musical and the Cuban zarzuela, of which Levis was a master. Oddly it was the deliciousness of their food that Levis would most remember. He ordered an entire roasted chicken, its skin nicely braised, with rosemary potatoes and a salad, the kind of fare that served the palette of the American clientele who often stayed in the Inglaterra. Mr. Gershwin ordered filet mignon (with french-fried potatoes and onions), which, to Levis's despair, he barely touched ("Tell your friend, Señor Levis," he said to Manny, "that I've got to watch my waist-line—*mi cintura*"). Even when he had finished off his chicken, leaving only a carcass and the slightest residue of salad oil on his plate, Levis could not help himself from looking enviously at those tender and succulent morsels that lay largely untouched under Gershwin's fork and knife, for, in those moments of small desires, a kind of sadness having to do with the missed opportunities for love in his life came over him, and he, his mouth watering, was half-tempted to finish his fellow composer's meal. That night they set out to visit various clubs, theaters and brothels together, and in the end they parted as friends, Gershwin extending to Levis an invitation for another dinner, should he come to New York. Levis returned to his house in Habana to work on a zarzuela based on *"Rosas Puras,"* and Gershwin went north to compose his "Cuban Rhapsody," which owed much to Levis's song itself and something to the other pieces of Cuban music, like Ignacio Piniero's *"Echale Salsa,"* that he heard being played so vividly all over that city.

AN INTERVIEW, ENTITLED, "WITH HUMILITY, THE
CUBAN COMPOSER SPEAKS," FROM THE ENGLISH-
LANGUAGE *HAVANA GAZETTE*, APRIL, 7, 1931:

Q: Señor Levis, which composers do you consider inferior to
yourself today?

A: Few.

Q: Which do you consider superior to yourself?

A: Almost all.

Q: Whom do you prefer, Mozart or Bach?

A: They were both pure and divinely inspired artists, born to
music.

Q: How does hearing American jazz affect you?

A: I like the compositions of Gershwin and the trumpet playing
of Louis Armstrong.... But, if you listen carefully you will
see that "jazz," as it is called, owes a lot to our Cuban music,
especially in the rhythms. One day I will compose my own
piece in the jazz style.... Perhaps I will stage a concert in
New Orleans....

Q: Have you been surprised by the success of your composition
"Pretty Roses"?

A: I am surprised by anything that is not a disaster!

Q: And if Brahms or Bach, whom you are fond of, were to sit by
you today, what would you say to them?

A: I would thank them very much for all the pleasure they have
brought into this world....

IN PARIS

(AND AFTER)

1932, HABANA: THE BEGINNING OF HIS WEARINESS

Though Israel Levis would never be able to pinpoint that moment when he decided to leave Cuba for Europe, this was certain: At around nine-thirty in the evening, January 11, 1932, on a night when Florencia, the maid, was away visiting family and while the composer had been out playing cards with friends in the Campana Bar, two men, well dressed and with "feral eyes," as his mother would put it, descended upon his house on Olivares. As Doña Concepción stood in her doorway, one of these men shoved her aside, and she fell onto the tile floor of the entrance, sustaining a fracture to her right arm. Although she screamed and screamed and later managed to attack them with a broom, they made their way into the master's study, where they conducted a rather hasty search of that premises. From Levis's *escritorio* and a recently purchased black Chinese cabinet in which he kept his works-in-progress they removed his papers and letters, ripped many of his scores to shreds, smashed several lamps, and with a crowd gathering outside (for Doña Concepción had eventually fled to the street, crying out for help), they quickly left. The whole business was over in twenty minutes.

This happened at a time in Cuba when it was not at all unusual for members of the secret police, or the *"porra,"* as they were also known, to raid a household at will, without accountability; when attorneys and unionists, schoolteachers and doctors, were roused from their beds in the middle of the night and thrown into a dank cell deep within the confines of the Atares Castle, without due process of law; when even someone as prominent as Doctor Orfelia Domínguez Navarro, head of the feminist league, could be carried out on a stretcher from her sickbed and sent to jail for months, without being told of her offense. This was the Cuba hidden under a mountain of risqué postcards, of maracas decorated with palm trees, of aromatic cigars, rumba bands, troubadours, handsome singers and spectacular female dancers—the Cuba that the world did not know.

One of his neighbors from across the way later set out that night to the Campana Bar, where he found Levis in the midst of a good poker hand—he was holding a pair of queens, a pair of jacks and an ace—and informed him of what had occurred. And with that the composer's body trembled. He felt such an apprehension crossing his chest that for a few moments he thought that he might be having a heart attack. But a glass of quickly absorbed brandy settled his nerves, and in the company of the composer Luis Casas he hurried home to find a crowd of neighbors milling about on the street outside his home. "What's happened here?" he asked. "The same thing that happened to me, two weeks ago," said one Don Alvarez, a reformist mathematics university professor. "They are doing just whatever they please, whenever they feel like it."

Inside, Israel found Doña Concepción sitting in a high-back chair by their dining table with two of their neighbors, a rosary grasped in her hands, praying rather emphatically to God that *He* send all the evil men of the world to Hell. When she saw her son and cried out, *"¡Nene, abrázame!"*—"My boy, hold me!" Levis did so. Unaccustomed to embracing his mother, he was surprised to find that she was nearly weightless, her bones as delicate as porcelain, her frailness alarming him (she was as frail as he would be years later). Even though she would later carry on—"What has happened to Cuba?" and ask of him directly, "What have you done?" (to which he answered: "Nothing, they are animals, Mamá") and she would repeat again and again, "Thank God, your father is not alive to see such things!"—he was most troubled by the effortlessness with which his creative sanctuary had been violated. For the first time in his life, he had spent the night in his mother and father's bedroom, seated upright in a chair, unable to sleep—nor wanting to—apprehensive.

It had been a night that ran counter to the notion that "life is short," the hours moving so slowly that I would remember it for the dense and weary prognostications that came over me, ever so sadly, from some distant place, deep and dark as the heavens at night, over which I had no control.

Then there was what happened regarding the prospective zarzuela stage production of *Rosas Puras*. He had begun work on this the autumn before; a French promoter by the name of Jacques Auffrey had come to Habana and approached Levis on behalf of Rita Valladares with the proposition of mounting a show at the Opéra Bouffe de Paris based on his widely popular hit. It was an offer that provoked in Israel great interest, for while the idea for such a production had swirled through his mind before—he'd hoped to stage *"Rosas"* at the Teátro Nacional, with Rita in the main role—prospects for a Habana production were remote, as the times were hard, and theaters, under threat of fines or of being shut down, were loathe to engage his services, so effective were the harassments of the government against him.

In fact, by that time, 1931–32, Levis had gotten to a point where his own life in that city had become more difficult than he wanted. It was not so much the censorship of the government—nor that the dictator had closed down newspapers for months at a time, nor that graft and avarice flourished in a country where so many lived destitute and in poverty, nor because of America's control of their economy, nor the betrayal of the republic's idealism by many of its politicians—but rather that gradually, during the years of dictatorship, his associations with the cultural and anti-Machado elite of the city had become a matter of great personal sadness and concern, for so many of them had vanished from the face of the earth.

Then, too, his commissions fell away and he was not allowed to publicly perform in Habana. Partly it was his own fault. In a way Levis, in thinking that he was ultimately above the political fray, had not taken his circumstance seriously enough. With the bemused detachment of an artist who felt secure in his profes-sional reputation, which he was certain would preserve and pro-tect him through even the worst situations, he had become a little careless in the remarks he would make in public.

Given his status as a highly regarded composer in that city for nearly twenty years, Levis frequented many of the private clubs and societies, as a guest performer and lecturer, among them the Havana-American Club on Virtudes and Prado, where he made the acquaintance of journalists from the States. During the bad Machado years, Levis, in the course of his conversations with such journalists, hoped to convey a careful and balanced view of the situation in Cuba, but his general anxiety and liking for booze too often loosened his tongue. On one occasion, in the fall of 1932, after he and a journalist had retired to the club's smoking room for brandies and cigars, Levis held court before a small gath-ering of newspapermen, who were quick to exploit the com-poser's inadvertent candor.

A few of his remarks, which made their way into an October 1932 column by Chester Wright for a left-wing newspaper in the States, the *International Labor News,* went as follows: "The tyranny of Machado has dispersed many of our best artists to all parts of the world. If I have not left my country it is because I still have a faith that, in the end, justice will prevail over injustice and that the beast who calls himself our president will be overthrown." Another comment that was reported in the *New York Herald Tribune,* that same autumn, quoted Israel Levis as saying: "I am always saddened to hear that one of my fellow Cubans has left this country or died. With every violation of creative and per-sonal freedom, Cuba marches one step closer toward barbarism."

As a favor for an old friend, there had been the editorial he wrote for an exile magazine, *Cuba Libre,* published out of Mexico back in 1931, under the heading "When Will the Arts Flourish Again in Cuba?"—an impassioned plea for the reopening of the university in Habana, as well as other schools and cultural institutions, Levis wrote, in part: "A generation of our children are being educated only in violence and murder, and without the beauteous nurturing of the muses' sweet, sirenic songs. That garden, which is youth, will wither under the heel of a dictatorship indifferent to beauty. A culture based on stone and concrete will never last. Long live free thought and expression. . . ."

Then, too, there were the remarks critical of the government that he casually made in the Campana Bar, or in the brothels of the city, or while sitting in the park with a friend—remarks that were, in all likelihood, overheard. And he was also being watched constantly—so many eyes peeking out at him from behind the arcade columns, from behind the market stalls, through a cluster of bushes and prickly stemmed roses as he walked in Crisantemo Gardens. So many eyes around him, as numerous as the notes of a hundred symphonic scores—everywhere.

WRITING THE ZARZUELA

Though he had originally conceived of that aforementioned zarzuela as a way of keeping Rita in Habana, her life had moved on, without him. Strong-willed and glory-prone, Valladares, in her widowhood, had commenced upon a schedule of tours that had taken her throughout Latin America and Europe. And while she kept her house in Habana, she rented a small apartment in Paris in

1931, where she sought to continue her great successes on the stages of France.

Setting out to write the zarzuela with Paris and Rita in mind, Levis had prevailed upon his more and more evasive friend Manny Cortez to write the libretto. They would meet once every few weeks, usually on a Sunday afternoon, either in Levis's or Cortez's house in La Regla, though the latter, near the sea and lovely, was a more distracting place to work, as Cortez's children loved to harass their father with their affections and demands, for in those days, Cortez was often away, pursuing secretive assignations that convened all across the island. On those Sundays, the very thin and ascetic Manny Cortez and "El Gordito," passed the afternoons musing over plot and lyrics, drinking and often pretending that they were not working under duress. Or, more correctly, Manny, with his own presentiments of doom, carried on diligently despite his other worries, offering up new texts every other week, for he wanted the production to be a success so as to provide an income for his family "should anything happen to me."

And because, Levis had often thought, it was a labor that honored an old friendship.

By 1932, in the midst of that new collaboration, Cortez seemed to have taken on an air of stoic acceptance of a certain destiny. Like José Martí, who had foreseen his own death in the weeks that preceded it (he had died riding a white horse during a charge against the Spanish in 1895), Manny Cortez, too, had become resigned to the prospect of martyrdom in the cause of liberty, his eyes heavy with fear and sadness. He had even come to resemble the writer Edgar Allan Poe, a foreboding wistfulness in his expression, a universe of stars falling down invisibly around him.

Nevertheless, Levis relished their hours together. In Cortez's company, he often felt overwhelmed by a desire to caress his dear friend's face, to pat him, as he sometimes did, in his nearly childish way, upon his back, to squeeze his arm to convey his faith that whatever trials Manny (and all of Cuba) was enduring would surely, in time, pass. He prayed for the man, not so much for his physical safety, but that the sadness that hung over him (as it did over all of Cuba) be lifted.

Yet the prospect of mounting a production in Paris seemed such an encouragement to Levis that on an April evening of 1932, when he and Manny Cortez met in the Campana Bar to discuss the completed libretto for *Rosas Puras,* to which the composer was putting his finishing musical touches, they had gotten drunk and talked over the idea of going to Paris together—"Think of the times we can have!" Levis enthusiastically said. And Manny considered it, gratefully, but told Levis: "Of course, I want to—but only when we have passed through this difficult period."

Levis would remember his friend's expression that night, the contortions in his face, down to the tremulous veins that stood out on his head, the livid redness that suddenly consumed him. "I am speaking about the future of Cuba, my dear friend," he told Levis. "And only until we have solved this problem, only then will I be at liberty, again."

"My God," Levis had thought. "He is deadly serious."

Feeling that Manny Cortez had been led too far astray by his convictions, to the point that he blinded himself to opportunity and the value of their friendship, Levis simply nodded and said, softly, "Well, there will be plenty of time ahead of us, Manny. I am sure of that."

"You, my friend, are more of an optimist than me." Then: "*Salud.*"

And they had a few more drinks and left the café just before midnight: Levis made his way back to his house, leather satchel in hand, while Manny went off to catch a ferry home. Parting, they had embraced, the bigger man nearly crushing the smaller man. Later, Levis slept restlessly, and had a disquieting dream about a raven crouching on a skull, its flapping wings and cries of *caw caw* so loud and mocking that he abruptly awoke at three in the morning, half-frightened to death by the darkness, even in that most familiar room. In those same moments, Manny Cortez, having left a certain residence in central Habana, was walking along an arcaded street through a corridor of Moorish columns when a man had approached him, asking for a light. And as Manny was ruffling through his jacket pockets for some matches—he was a Lucky Strikes addict—a second man stepped out behind him from the shadows, placed the muzzle of a snub-nosed .38 caliber revolver to the back of his head and fired off two shots. Dogs began to bark, pigeons and nestlings fled their roosts. Traces of the lyricist's bloodstains were to be found on the paving for weeks.

Manny left behind a wife and two kids—over the years Levis saw to it that they received royalties from that song—but he could never forget how subdued his friend had been whenever he'd visited his house, in those days, and so especially tender with his

family, as if Manny was already aware of what was going to happen to him, his expression, ever so sorrowful and filled with longing every time he left them. And there were occasions as well
when Manny regarded the composer with such a clear reading of
his mind that it startled him: "Don't give too much weight to what
others think, my friend," Manny'd say. "Live as if no one else
matters."

That April of 1932, after his dear friend's funeral, he'd
decided that he had enough.

May 1932

My dearest Rita,

*I am sick to my heart over what has happened here in Cuba.
As you must already know, my dear friend Manny Cortez is
dead. It is assumed that he was assassinated, in the same way
that Mella was shot down in the street in Mexico City. I cannot
tell you how heavily this weighs upon me, and I am thinking now
of joining you, at least for a time in Paris, to think about and
look forward to better things. You know that despite his serious
side, Manny wrote a quite amusing libretto for "Rosas." You
should tell M. Auffrey that I have most of the score done, though
I can't pretend right now that I am not begrieved or sick to my
heart about it. All the same, I think you will find it pleasing. . . .*

*I have also decided to undertake certain engagements in
Latin America and Europe, with an orchestra that I have put
together here in Habana. I've already gotten many offers—and
before I come to Paris, I will be working in Mexico. Can you
imagine that somebody wants to put me in a movie? And there*

are offers from Spain for a tour. . . . I don't really want to go, as I am such a lazy creature of habit, so set in my ways, that the very idea of these changes alarm me, but what else can I do, Chiquita? Lately I haven't been able to even sleep well—I am convinced that my own life might be in danger, but I could care less—I am thinking about my mother—she's had enough grief in her lifetime.

So I will be taking her to Santiago to stay with Fernando. She would be better off there, instead of being cooped up in this house with our maid, Florencia, whom she would surely torment. As for traveling with me in Europe—she is too old and set in her ways for that. Certainly I would not leave her alone without someone in the family to care for her.

Besides, at my ripe old age of forty-two, I think it is time to see something more of the world again. A fortune-teller has con-firmed my feelings, and I have spent many hours in church pray-ing for guidance.

In any event, I will be coming to Paris soon. . . .

Adieu for now, Chiquita.

Your servant,

"Gordito"

HE TOOK HIS MOTHER TO SANTIAGO, JUNE 1932

But it had not been easy for him to persuade his mother, Doña Concepción, that leaving their house on Olivares would be the judicious thing. She had become greatly distressed over the prospect ("Have I not lived here for the past fifty years?"), and yet, though her mind often dwelled in another realm, she was practical enough to see that the times were difficult. She had not forgotten about the incident of the two men, nor was she unaware that her son had been deeply troubled—perhaps frightened—by the death of Manny Cortez. On many a night she had been awakened by the composer's shouts in his sleep, or noticed, as she got up at four in the morning to use the *inodoro,* that he was often pacing restlessly in his study, sighing deeply as if he were having difficulty breathing. So despite the fact that she had, at first, resolutely told her son: "No, I will die in this house, alone, if I have to," his monumental solemnity in those days was such that even she, with all her attachments to that house and her memories, could not withstand his logic. "It would be better for all of us," he said. And she was surprised when he, sitting her down, had added: "Mamá, you know that you are the world to me, but I've reached the point where I must now leave you for a time. You understand that, don't you?"

She was looking down toward a rosary that lay entangled in her hands, and nodded, saying quietly, "Yes."

"But you understand that this will not be forever; we will be together again, one day"—she had looked at him furtively as if thinking *"In heaven?"*—". . . I will come back to see you often, no matter my travels, understand?" Then: "And you know that Fernando and his wife, Gloria, are very happy that you will be coming to live with them?"

"Yes," she said. Then: "But, son, you know that I love you very much."

"Yes, Mamá."

"I will feel sad, nene."

"Yes, Mamá. So will I."

Once they'd come to this resolution, several days were spent in the preparation of their departure to Santiago; two large trunks were packed with her favored clothing and possessions, and though this was planned as a temporary change, to last perhaps for a few years—as Levis could not imagine living away from Habana for long—neither mother nor composer son could have known that they would never live under the same roof again, as they once used to, that an epoch in his life had ended.

The train out of Habana took ten hours to reach Santiago, and shortly thereafter his mother, Doña Concepción, became a some-times quiet, sometimes tyrannical fixture in the household of Doctor Fernando Levis, while her son, Israel, composer of "Rosas Puras," began to experience the surprisingly invigorating airs of various freedoms.

A ship to Mexico across the gulf, a ship from Mexico to Europe, to Marseilles, or to Vigo, or up to New York, trumpets blaring, the sun burning red over the horizon . . . a man of immense size leaning over the railing, whistling a tune, composing in his head, searching for mermaids and the unseen wonders of this existence.

It would take Levis another year to
find himself in Paris, presiding over the
production of the zarzuela *Rosas Puras.*
During those intervening months, between mid-1932 and mid-1933, he put
together a formidable band of Cuban
musicians, whom he named the Habana
Melody Orchestra, traveled far and wide
as both a pianist of the classical repertoire
and as the conductor of that aforementioned band, playing jazz ("the music of the
times") and Cuban *danzones* and rumbas
("the music of his passions"). The heavier
his schedule, the better, as he wanted to
lose himself in his work.

Some months would find him in Europe, others would have him doubling
back to the Americas. In the midst of such

journeys, he managed an excursion to the United States. On a trip to Manhattan in early 1933, at the invitation of George Gershwin, he had given a solo performance of his music at Carnegie Hall, to much acclaim, appeared on a NBC radio show (*Night of the Classics*), and participated at a benefit in the Plaza Hotel for the New York Society for the Blind, leading an orchestra of pickup musicians, several of whom had played alongside Rita Valladares. He had taken long walks in downtown Manhattan, the scale of the city, with its towering skyscrapers, provoking in him a kind of vertigo. And though he loved the diversity of the people there, and the sense that the world had poured through its port, he found that he preferred the quietude of Europe. Even when there was much money to be made in New York City, as so many had told him—Rita Valladares, his friend Don Aziapu (who much liked *"Rosas Puras"*), George Gershwin—he found the maddening and rather noisy life of that city too frantic for his taste.

He saw, however, that the city could be reasonably pleasant: One evening during his stay—in that city where José Martí had once lived—he attended a large dinner party given by that tall and darkly handsome composer Mr. Gershwin at his penthouse apart- ment on Riverside Drive, Levis passing the evening drinking cock- tails and looking out at grand views of the blazing river at dusk, (his head abuzz with musings about the English language), his host taking his place behind a piano and entertaining his guests for hours. Levis himself sat down to perform some of his more deco- rative, distinctively "Cuban" pieces, the guests applauding and the American composer toasting his Cuban counterpart: "To a long friendship!"

A lovely evening, of course, and a salubrious toast, for each was passing into the indefinable future—Gershwin knowing nothing of the disease that would take his life in four scant years, nor Levis of what awaited him in Europe.

On these rigorous, not particularly profitable tours—for the composer of *"Rosas Puras"* paid his musicians well, Levis and his orchestra were as much in demand as his songs. Having put together his Habana Melody Orchestra with classically trained musicians versatile enough to play in any style, he traveled, his trunk filled with various charts, many of them of Levis's own compositions that, from time to time, he revamped according to the way his own tastes were changing. He liked the music of Duke Ellington, very much, and included certain of his compositions in his shows; mainly, however, he used jazz voicings in his arrangements of Cuban song, or leavened the jazz with a bit of Cuban melody. (One of his show pieces was a version of "St. Louis Blues," which Levis had liked for its simplicity, and into which he worked parts of *"Rosas Puras,"* presenting it with a strong claves rhythm section.)

Along the way, Levis, ever reticent privately, learned to play the role of the confident and beaming, aloofly serene conductor on stage. Though he was neither handsome nor given over to choreographed stage theatrics, he managed to throw in some dance steps, to raise his arms dramatically at certain moments, bowing gracefully to applause. He often appeared in a dapper topcoat and tails, a silk vest and silver bowtie, cutting an elegant figure that he played down before his musicians ("It is a disguise").

And his audiences seemed delighted by what might be described as his essentially soulful, and, therefore, comforting, presence.

During those months, he performed so often that the specifics of his tours and the individuals he encountered would become a haze of names and places, for he had no particular fondness for life on the road and had, in those days—given his many long-ings (for Cuba, for Rita, for the departed, and God)—taken more heavily to that great eraser of the mind, drink, in the form of brandy, whiskey and wine.

SPAIN

In the later part of 1932 and into 1933, well before the Civil War of 1936–39, he often traveled in Spain and throughout its provinces, appearing with his orchestra in the cities of Madrid, Barcelona, Seville and San Sebastián. It seemed that every Spaniard wanted to hear his version of *"Rosa Puras."* Such was that song's popularity that his appearances were always sold out. Receiving a very special adulation in Spain, he was fêted at banquets and even invited to perform in the grand ballroom of El Escorial. In Madrid he met the blind composer Joaquin Rodrigo and thought him remarkable; in Cuba he had known the blind pianist and orches-tra leader Frank Emilio Flynn and marveled how such men could move through life triumphantly under such conditions. He made various recordings in Madrid for the Gramofono label, among them *"Babylon Rumba," "Pensamiento Cubano"* and his own instrumental version of *"Rosas Puras,"* which sold well despite the fact that two dozen other versions had already been recorded by then by differ-ent orchestras and singers in Spain. Such was that song's many incarnations that he could have lived well off his Spanish royalties alone.

And the zarzuelas he'd composed over the years in Habana

proved also quite popular in Spain, where his only rivals in popularity, in terms of compositions, were his fellow Cubans Eliseo
Grenet and Ernesto Lecuona. Levis's *The Loves of Beatriz, La Bella
Negra* and *La Reina Isabel* were frequently revived, his music
lauded for its lyrical and picaresque qualities. They were a
Cuban's version of light opera but with spoken dialogue to bridge
the arias, and much influenced by the great Italian bel canto composers. Floating on a cloud of his accomplishment and reputation,
for onstage feelings of godliness came over him, he savored the
amenities of his life on those tours: taking the occasional woman
to his hotel room, eating two or three meals in the course of a single evening, swilling Carlos Quinto brandy into the early-morning
hours. He often drank until the cobblestones of those narrow
Spanish streets carried him along as if he were walking on water,
the very buildings with their wrought-iron balconies glowing so
protectively in the moonlight that he believed himself immortal
and impervious to harm.

As a concertizer and the conductor of his own orchestra, he
also traveled to England, Italy, Portugal and Austria, the doors of
Europe opening to him. His European journeys so delighted him
that he often composed little classical pieces to commemorate
these places. Hence, in Italy he wrote *"Un Giardino Romano"* ("A
Roman Garden"), *"L'aria Napolitana"* ("A Neopolitan Air"), *"Una
Camminata nel Foro"* ("A Walk in the Forum"). Then, a symphonic
tone poem, after Respighi, that he entitled, simply, *Sicily.* He and
his orchestra performed on Italian radio, gave concerts in Turin
and Milan, attended La Scala, he appeared as a pianist at the
Accademia di Santa Cecilia in Rome, and met Mussolini at the
Palazzo Venezia, in 1933, where both the Cuban national anthem,

"*La Bayamesa*," and the fascist anthem, "*La Giovinezza*," were played one after the other at the reception. (A comment that Levis had made to a journalist from *La Tribuna* along the lines that Italy "seems more beautiful and better run now than from what I can remember" had pleased Mussolini, who, as it happened, had counted "*Rosas Puras*" among his favored songs at the time.)

I had a wonderful audience with the Pope himself. This was, of course, arranged by the government, a private audience in the Pauline Chapel, which is up the stairs, to the right of the Vatican Palace, and though this Pope Pius was a severe-looking man, he was very kindly disposed toward me; I had him sign two Bibles, one for myself, of course, and one for my mother. I couldn't wait to give it to her. . . .

In the north, he and his orchestra visited the cities of Stockholm and Göteborg, enchanting the straitlaced Swedes with the very music, raucous and lyrical, that they would come to love. (Two of his musicians ended up eventually marrying Swedes.) There was Vienna, austere and elegant—she always moved him. But there were the cities that he did not care for: he had no taste for Berlin nor for Munich, despite their loveliness. At the time of his visit to Germany, in the early spring of 1933, a few months after Hindenburg's appointment of Adolf Hitler as chancellor of the Reich, he and a few of his musicians were walking along a street in Munich near the Odeon Theater after an evening performance when they came across a group of about a dozen young Germans, each dressed in a matching gray quasi-military uniform, attacking two men as they were leaving a restaurant. Their shouts of "*Juden!*" perplexed the Cubans, who had tried to intercede. Levis and a violinist, Rogelio Díaz, and a trumpet player, Vincente De Léon, had crossed the street as the attackers, shouting and cursing in German, kicked and punched the fallen men. The musicians themselves were also assaulted; Levis, who had never as much laid his gentle hands on another man in violence, found himself kicking and punching these assailants with blind abandon. And he was suddenly astounded to discover that he could easily knock a man unconscious. This happened as he tried to pull one of the beleaguered men up from the sidewalk and his elbow inadver-tently crashed into the temple of a gangly German youth, just as he was lunging forward to stop him. But that was the height of their success. Though this group quickly dispersed—the restau-rant owner called the police—Rogelio Díaz suffered a sprained wrist on his right hand and De Léon had a broken rib. Levis him-self, held in place by two of these attackers, was punched so hard in the stomach that he had doubled over, vomiting.

Later, as they caught a taxi to their hotel, Levis asked his musicians, "Did we really leave Cuba for this?"

Then, too, there were the "Germany for the Germans" rallies in bonfire-lit squares, the agitated crowds, the marchers, the burn-ing books—an atmosphere that left Levis greatly distressed.

On the other hand, there was the evening in Frankfurt at the Frankfurter Hof when Levis had been so tense, so agitated and depressed and filled with longings for Cuba—the Cuba he had so idealized in his music—that he prevailed upon the concierge to send a woman up to his room. He did not speak much German, but it was not necessary, for she knew a few words in English, as did he. And it was in that language that they communicated. She was perhaps a quite experienced prostitute, businesslike in her manner, but with a pretty and broad Nordic face, blond hair and a monumental corporality. Everything about her, from the setting of her jaw and mouth, to the width of her hips, to the gargantuan proportion of her breasts, to the heaviness of her limbs and the thickness of her bones, made her the largest, if not fattest, woman Levis had ever seen naked. She was perhaps six feet tall and with farmer's hands that could have been a man's, so lengthy and large knuckled were her fingers. Nevertheless, whatever her own immensity, or the range of her experiences—mainly he supposed with the bowler and derby-hatted businessmen who did com-merce in that industrial city—she had not yet encountered a "phys-icality" as well developed as the composer's.

Coquettish and demure—even frightened of mounting him at first—for that is what he, lazily inclined, that night preferred—once he'd introduced himself into the recesses of her massive body, she proceeded, with a volcanic heat, the weight of her comely flesh and great strength of her limbs to so further excite Levis, that his already ample sexual proportions increased, as with the welling of a symphony, and she started to scream as if she would burst apart. And even then, he calmed her.

"*Por favor, fräulein,* more slowly," he said.

She was so touched by his gentleness and concern that the satisfaction of that man, in the setting of that pitiless world, became her mission. This woman remained with the composer in that room, drinking and copulating with him, until the church

bells began to toll and they began to hear the thrashing of street
sweepers' brooms coming from the gutter below—it had been a
Saturday—one of the few better memories he would have of his
sojourns in Germany.

June 1933

My dearest Rita,

What can I say about Austria and Germany? These are
places where the people and their attitudes about life seem so different from our own. They are completely enamored of a certain
kind of regimentation. Everything is clean, of course, in ways
that our street sweepers in Habana could never imagine; the toi-
lets are spotless, and I have often wondered if one could eat off
the floors in some of those places that I've been to. Only in the
beer gardens have I seen things getting out of hand, for then the
people who frequent these places seem to relax and drive themselves to such a point of abandon, singing, making loud jokes and
so many rude noises that you wonder if this behavior is a matter
of class or education, or simply the other side of the coin, for so
many of these people, particularly those attached to the cultural
institutions and so forth, are quite urbane, what one would
expect from men of higher learning and breeding.

It is hard to explain, but the Germans seem a volatile and
paradoxical people, at once both civilized and barbaric. I cannot
say that I enjoy performing in their concert halls. Even when they
have tended to receive my music warmly, I always feel a little
startled when I look out and see so many in the audience dressed
in military uniforms, and with expressions that seem to me, mi
Chiquita, so cold that I can only identify it with the worst inten-

tions. *They wear red armbands with a crisscross symbol in a cir-*
cle of white called a swastika—and, my God, although it seems a
harmless affectation, I feel quite uncomfortable just being near
the men who wear them. I suppose they remind me of our corrupt
police back in Habana. I can't tell you how happy I am to be
leaving this country. . . .

These words are being written at a late hour of the night—
just a few lines to let you know that "Gordito" is thinking about
you. If you care to respond, I will be in London, next week at the
Claridge's Hotel, and soon enough I will be coming to Paris.
Con besitos,
I.L.

THE ENCHANTMENT OF PARIS—SPRING, 1933

Of course, the Habana Melody Orchestra came to play in
Paris, occasionally heading the bill at the Le Grand Duc and
Bricktop's in Montmartre, but Levis had also come to Paris to
pursue the production of *Rosas Puras,* at the Opéra Bouffe—and
to be near Rita Valladares.

He had not seen her in nearly a year when they were reunited.
Installed in a suite in Le Grand Hôtel by the French promoter
Auffrey, Levis had waited for Rita in its cavernous lobby during a
rainy afternoon and had paced anxiously about—*for she was an*
hour late—peering out beyond the continual parade of guests and
bellhops and waiters who seemed to swarm across its Florentine
marble floors and up its carpeted second empire stairways, and
under the light of great hanging chandeliers—*a posh and very proper*
hotel—checking its high arched entranceways for Rita, his Chi-

quita, his "nightingale." He had planned an evening out for them and already had a notion, firmly in his mind, that his many misgivings about life and the solitude he often felt might flutter away if he dismissed his own awkwardness and timidity and confessed his most deeply felt emotions to her. He rehearsed what he might say: "*Rita, we go back a very long way and although you know that we have always behaved in a certain manner together, so much time has passed, and our lives have been disturbed by so much uncertainty that it would be a marvel for us to pursue our mutual love...*" No. "*Rita, as you know, I have always been so tremendously fond of and dedicated to you, and although I know that you think of me as you might an older brother, there is something I have to tell you regarding the feelings in my heart, and that is that I will always be someone who you will be able to depend upon, even if I am not the most exciting or romantic man...*" No. "*Rita, I have come to the juncture in my life when I have begun to feel such an emptiness that even music cannot fill it, and, it is for that reason that—*" No! "*...My dearest Rita, when I look at you I am not just filled with admiration for your talents and gifts, but I firmly believe that you and I, joined in a mutual enterprise of love...*" No...

He was observing a couple—a flapper in a silk toque hat and her quite stately, well-coiffed husband, who had the most beautiful blue eyes—when he abandoned this little sequence of mental phrases, thinking that if it were a piece of music, the notes would have sounded all the same. He began to disparage not only his lack of romantic finesse, his inability to find those words that would properly convey his deepest sentiments, and quite frankly, had so intently continued to follow the movements of the handsome man across the lobby that he was largely unaware of the *tack-tack-tacking* of Rita's high heels on the floor. In a velvet dress and feathered cap, Rita appeared nearly simultaneously behind him, slapping Levis on the back and saying, with a laugh, "Ay, Don Israel, don't you recognize me?"

A great gloom came over him—even as he felt a certain happiness at seeing her—for instantly he realized that it was his way to prefer those adorations of Rita that he had made from a safe distance. Nothing had changed about him at all in the past year, his timidity following him even there, to the city of love, Paris.

By the time of Levis's arrival in Paris, the French had become fanatics for all things "tropical." The music of Heitor Villa-Lobos, the murals and paintings of Diego Rivera, Clemente Orozco and Wilfredo Lam, redolent of the mysterious powers of the African, of the savage, the primitive. And this passion extended to a mania for the orchestras and singers from Cuba, who, with American jazz musicians, had taken over the nightlife of that city.

There were many Cubans already living there, not just Rita Valladares, who had gone to work its club and theater circuit (and to sing in Levis's planned stage production), but so many others, the exiled and the free-spirited alike. An influx of Cubans—who had come to Paris for study or to escape the political situation in Cuba, or to make some money, or who had been on vacation and had decided to stay—had been taking place for some time by then.

One of the first Cubans to settle there had been the pianist Oscar Cello, in 1927, who opened his own club, "La Cueva," or "the Cave," in Montmartre; and the rumberos Julio Ricardo and Carmenita Ortíz had begun to put on many a performance at the Palace Boulevards Music Hall in 1928. Groups like the Sexteto

Habanero and the Lecuona Cuban Boys were playing regularly in Paris, Monte Carlo and the French Riviera, while old friends, like the musicians Ignacio Piniero, Agustín Gutierrez, Panchito Chevrolet, Bienvenido León and Armando Orifiche, among so many others, were appearing in French clubs and beginning to record for French labels.

Israel had arrived in a Paris that, musically speaking, possessed two souls. There was the Paris of frenetic American Negro jazz, of Dixieland and blues, its smoke-filled clubs hosting musicians who faithfully covered the tunes of Fats Waller, Duke Ellington and Louis Armstrong. It was the Paris of the great gypsy guitarist Django Rheinhart who, in emulating the expansive and free-wheeling American style, worked toward his own Europeanized version of the blues and speakeasy jazz. And then there was the wildly beautiful and erotic music of the "tropical clubs," where people flocked to dance the rumba and conga, and to watch barely clad women in transparent blouses and silken knickers shimmying suggestively across a fake palm tree–laden stage. It was the Paris in which even the lowliest Cuban musicians earned a good wage and mounted the stage in lavish, ruffle-sleeve, bell-studded guarachero shirts and tight spangled trousers, their costumes created by the finest high-fashion designers, like the famous Zenelle of the Casino de Paris. These musicians played melodies and rhythms that the Parisians (and most of Europe) had never heard before. They played a music that charmed the imagination and made the sexual juices flow; a music whose danceable rhythms and catchy melodies exuded both the unbridled energies of youth and the darker passions of love. In that Paris compositions like Lecuona's *"Siboney,"* Grenet's *"Conga*

Dans La Nuit" and Anckermann's *"Flor de Yumurí"* were part of many a band's reportoire. It did not matter how often these kinds of songs were performed—the Parisians clamored for more.

In Paris Levis began to wear a cape and a large felt hat, with a feather in its brim. Along the way he made the acquaintance of many Cuban homosexuals, who seemed to be everywhere, and re-veled in the free-booting atmosphere of that city. It amazed Levis that these men, however effeminate, could go wherever they pleased without castigation, such as they would have encountered back in Habana. He felt oddly comfortable around them, enjoying their company and the air of freedom their manner and behavior conveyed.

That he would remain there, however, for the next decade, long after the fall of Machado in August 1933, had, in part, to do with the allurements of the artistic ambience and elegance of that city. With its gardens, its intimate scale and architectural splen-dor, Paris in the 1930s was at once a more cultured and pleasur-able place than Habana, and while Levis had much enjoyed certain cities in Spain, like Seville and Barcelona, the atmosphere of Paris seemed free of social restraints and of the fascist elements that in those years were, at any rate, on the rise in Spain and elsewhere in Europe (when he traveled in Germany with his orchestra he always left his black musicians behind). And while the Spaniards were most enamored of his zarzuelas, Parisians were far more enchanted by the dance steps that his music generated. And he loved their enthusiasm for Cuban music and his life among them as a minor celebrity.

It was in Paris where he would give a recital at the Sala Gaveau for Maurice Ravel and José Iturbi, and at the Sala Pleyel, he played some of his compositions on a program with Igor Stravinsky. He became friends with Ravel, Stravinsky, Nadia Boulanger, and made the passing acquaintance of popular entertainers like Noël Coward, Maurice Chevalier and Charlie Chaplin. He met Picasso, who made a pencil sketch of him, met an old friend of Lorca's, Salvador Dalí—*an odd bird.* Even Jack Johnson, former heavyweight champion of the world, who in those days led a jazz band, once asked Levis to become his musical director.

And everywhere he looked there were princes and princesses, counts, viscounts, and dukes—among them, many an impostor.

WITH RITA IN PARIS, LATE 1933

Settling into his work for the production of *Rosas Puras,* he saw Rita often.

They would meet for drinks in the lobby of the Grand Hôtel and walk the streets of Paris like happy tourists, navigating the labyrinthian passageways of certain neighborhoods, like Montparnasse, which fascinated him, as if he were inside a dream. In Paris, where she was nearly as popular as Josephine Baker, with whom she sometimes appeared, Rita was often recognized on the streets—French men stopping her on the chance that she might entertain their attentions.

"Ay, Don Israel, you are such a refreshing change from those shallow and handsome French men," she would say.

In her company he savored the good food, the international cuisine of the restaurants, Levis eating his way through the delicacies of that city. They'd sit in the Café La Sirena, on the boulevard Saint-Michel in the Latin Quarter, watching passersby, much taken by the high fashion, "le chic" and elegance of the people, especially the women.

They'd take long strolls along the rue de Seine, crossing the Pont des Arts, Levis eating sausages on the boulevard de Sébastopol. They haunted the Marais Jewish ghetto, picnicked in the Montsouris park. They ambled along the Place de la Concorde. They went to the ballet and opera together and visited the bookshops along the rue de Verneuil. They ate fried potatoes in the Faubourg du Saint-Denis, floated like phantoms among the willow trees of the parks of that city in the fog, went to the Louvre, wandered idly in the Jardin du Luxembourg, listened to the organ grinders along the rue Danton. Paris, beautiful, even on rainy days.

Occasionally we'd take rail trips down to Nice, to Cap d'Antibes and picnic on wine and cheese by the sea, in verdant fields where buzzed capricious honey-drunk bees.

He'd remember these places, not so much by their names, but for the constant light and buoyancy he felt in his heart when in Rita's company, even if others seeing them must have wondered about their relationship. He walked alongside her nodding at her every word. She seemed young and vital; he, avuncular and protective. If he had wanted to tell her that it was perhaps the time for a man like himself to get serious about marriage and his own future, he never did so. They never spoke about love, despite an ambience that led couples into the shadows under the bridges of the Seine for agitated copulations, their moans of pleasure rising into the night.

Rather, their conversations were about musical engagements, the dinner party at so-and-so's place, the terrible food at the Gigolo café.

On gloomy and chilled days, I would think about Manny Cortez and fall into long periods of silence; in such moments, the existence of death at all seemed an outrageously unfair consequence of life.

Even when Rita, feeling tenderly toward him, placed his hand into the suppleness of her white leather gloves, he could not escape his feelings of self-restraint. This was his fault, or "nature's," for all Levis's good intentions, there was something so innately pent up inside him that, though he'd resolved to confess his true feelings, he could not say a word, as if his vocal chords had been silenced, like that of the *hutia,* the silent dog of Cuba.

HIS SECRET LIFE

The funny thing was that, as he would remember, in her company he remained a quite pious fellow: "Make sure that you and your boys get to church on Sundays, because even if people make fun of religion, both you and I know that to have God in one's life is a good thing."

"Of course, Don Israel."

"And don't forget that if you cannot take the boys to Mass, just call me and I will turn up at your door to get them."

They usually parted company long before midnight, Rita, ever preoccupied with her children, rushing back home, and Levis, feeling at liberty, availing himself of the more decadent possibilities of that city. His evenings without her found Levis in one or other of the many Habana-style clubs—the Cabaret Lido, La Cueva, the Palermo, the Melody Bar—either listening to other Cuban bands or performing himself. Late into those nights he would explore the darker recesses of the city. He went to opium dens, sex clubs, pornographic theatrical shows and gambling houses in which naked women worked as croupiers, not so unlike the bawdier side of his beloved Habana. He went to pink-walled, orange-lit nightspots where rose mists sprayed through the air and where the women, with their tight lamé dresses, blue ostrich-feather cloche hats and Theda Bara eyes were in the habit of dampening the back of their ears with both perfume and dabs of tantalizing scent from their own vaginas. And upon occasion, he had been absolutely stunned by the beauty of certain men, like the actor and music aficionado Ramon Novarro, a Mexican famous for playing Ben-Hur in a Hollywood film. (Of course, he pretended that he felt nothing at all.) He saw many strange things. In one establishment, where a strict dress code was observed (evening attire only, please) Levis entered a plushly carpeted room, its walls bare save for wooden wheels to which men were chained by their hands and feet; a woman or a man would perform the act of oral love upon the chained individual, and then, as the bound man approached the moment of climax, the woman would spin the wheel around, as if it were a roulette game in a casino—*really, the strangest thing to have seen.* He went to a parlor in which there would begin at midnight a parade of fifty young and quite beautiful women, who would enter the ballroom of an old palace, wearing only a single gemstone in their navels. He visited establishments where the women dressed like men and where the men wore lipstick and covered their faces with white powder. And in these places he was often confronted with the inevitable question, posed by one man or another who had noticed his boyish interest ("strictly curious," was what Levis thought) in men, who would ask: "Are you searching for a companion?"

"No, thank you," he would politely say.

Often, he was elated by his feelings of independence.

For his own taste, he preferred the more traditional sort of places, like the "One and Two" brothel, taking his fill. He also practiced his piety, attending Mass each Sunday, ever devoutly, in the Cathedral of Notre Dame.

MAY 1934, PARIS, BEFORE THE OPENING
OF *ROSAS PURAS*

Rita, too, apparently had a "secret life."

One afternoon, a few months before *Rosas Puras* was to open at the Palace, as they were sitting in a café over a bottle of wine, Rita said: "There is something I have to tell you, my dear friend."

"Yes."

"Do you remember once asking me, during the years I first came to Paris, in 1928, if there was 'someone' in my life?"

"Yes."

"Well there wasn't then. But there is someone now. His name is José Murillo. He is a Spaniard, a fine tenor, and someone who has caught my attention."

"I see."

"And I have asked him to join us today, so that you can meet him." Then, joyfully: "He is a wonderful man!"

Levis seemed a little low, slumping in his seat, finishing his wine quickly, then snapping his fingers at the waiter for another bottle.

"I am happy to hear this, Rita," he said.

"You will like him, *es muy simpático*." Then: "I am hoping that he can sing the role of Rodolfo, in *Rosas. . . .*"

"Ah?"

And, as if out of a scene in a zarzuela, within a few moments a tall and striking-looking man approached them, a fellow impeccably dressed in a three-piece suit and so self-contained and proper that nary a stitch nor hair on his head seemed out of place. With his hair brilliant in the sunlight and with so intense an expression, he could have been a cousin to the lofty Cuban chess champion, J. R. Capablanca, or of the handsome George Gershwin. Levis, a gentleman of course, stood up to greet him, and once the introductions had been made, the composer had rather liked the man's response. For when Levis had said, "I am honored to meet you," José Murillo had emphatically declared, "No, it is my honor to meet so great a composer."

And he turned out to be an affable, quite pleasant fellow, attentive to Rita, and incidentally so handsome that women would take a second look at him as they passed by.

"You must travel to Cuba some day," Levis said to him.

"We are planning to."

He was studying voice in Paris, had known certain of Levis's compositions, had heard *"Rosas Puras"* so many times that he, without realizing it, whistled the melody as they sat there. And he had often gazed into Rita's eyes with the intensity of someone who had an intimate knowledge of her.

The composer called out again for the waiter.

Then Rita announced: "Now that we are all friends, we can go around together." Clutching Murillo's arm, holding him as if he were a prize from heaven, she beamed happily. "My boys love José," she told the composer.

Later, when they had left him, Levis remained in the café drinking wine until dusk, and then he reasoned it was a good time to switch to a fine grade of Napoleon brandy, for there was some-thing about the drinking of such a liquor that created the false but reassuring impression of more time passing than actually had, a few hours in the waning day, shifting like a continent of moments, so grandly, that weeks or even months could have passed. His last memory of that evening was of devouring a roasted pheasant with fried potatoes in a bistro near the Bastille, then of sitting on a metal bench along the railings of the Pont des Arts and daydream-ing as he watched the lamp-lit reflections on the river, quivering like his thoughts.

A melody entered into my mind then, something that seemed to drift out of some cavernous domain of minor notes, inspired by Cuba, perhaps it was my memory of the sea and the star's traces, the very long distances I had traveled, a piece of music that would be played quietly on a piano and meditatively, one of the more compelling sequences of notes to have occurred to me in a very long time . . . though by the morning I would not remember it.

And, yes, he would remember his late-night visit to the bor-dello where the women dressed like Carmelite nuns, of a room lit with blue votive candles, of a scapular removed and raised up over a winged bonnet, of the good sister, unfastening a cloth belt, of felt buttons coming undone in the front of her habit, of the white cloth parting and the most succulent and supple breasts springing out into the world, before his eyes.

ROSAS PURAS, JUNE 1934

Of course, his greatest success in Paris had come when he pre-miered the show based on *"Rosas Puras,"* with the libretto written by Manny Cortez (now dead, like so many others, and roaming in an afterlife, Levis sometimes thought, so much like the haunted rooms in the poems of E. A. Poe, sarcophagi and mortuary slabs stretching endlessly into a world of lightless places). In Paris in June of 1934—a year and two months after Manny had been murdered—that show opened with the shadows of that pointless death and the rise of European fascism looming over it.

Rosas Puras consisted of two acts and a simple plot: Esmeralda, a poor flower seller in Habana, circa 1925, sells a bouquet of roses to a handsome man, Rodolfo, a high-society, Habana Yacht Club type on a quest for love; but the women he seeks to win are vain and selfish, and he falls into the habit of seeking Esmeralda's guidance in matters of the heart. A strong mutual attraction ensues between them. He is falling in love with her, but she comes from a family so poor that he cannot take his feelings seriously. Over time, between scenes played out on a tennis court and at a ball held in the vast salon of a wealthy industrialist's house, Rodolfo begins to realize that he should seek out a more simple and affectionate kind of woman, like Esmeralda. But by then, his engagement to one Olga has been announced, and he, a man of honor if not good judgment, chooses to convey this news to Esmeralda. He tells her that he will not be returning to buy roses from her again, but when they look into each other's eyes, they realize they have fallen in love. As they part they sing about the cruelty of life, that they had not met in a more auspicious time.

The second act opens in the salon of a mansion where Rodolfo and his new wife are suddenly given news of a financial reversal: Rodolfo learns that a family investment has gone badly, that the family wealth is lost, and when he reveals this to his new wife, she, disbelieving him, accuses Rodolfo of trickery and deception. In the meantime, Esmeralda meets a witch and asks if love is in her future and learns that "her true love will come back to her." Rodolfo, desperate to restore the family's fortune, learns of a man selling an old treasure map and buys it with the last of his money, but his wife, a greedy and distrusting soul, steals the map and sets out on a boat to an island off the coast of Cuba, where she and her crew are caught in a storm and drown.

Poor but free, with his "eyes open to the truth of his foolish ways," Rodolfo returns to the flower vendor's stand, tells Esmeralda his story and confesses that he had been blind to true love. Just as he joins Esmeralda at the stand selling flowers, he is informed by a family lawyer that his estate has been restored. With that he proposes marriage and she accepts. Swept up in a carnival celebration, they sing of their mutual love and of the promise of the future, under a rainfall of flowers.

The program for this show was as follows:

Rosas Puras

Zarzuela comique en deux actes
Oeuvre original de Israel Levis et Manuel Cortez
Donnée en première au Théâtre Opéra Bouffe à Paris, le 17 juin 1934

LISTE DE PERSONNAGES

Rita Valladares	"Esmeralda, vendeuse de fleurs"
José Murillo	"Rodolfo Montez, un célibataire riche"
Mercedes Blanca	"La fiancée méchante, Olga"
	"La autre fiancée"
Matilde Rossy	"La Sorcière"
	"La Dame Montez"

Grand Orchestre et Choer sous la direction de Maestro Israel Levis

Acte Premier

1. Ouverture
2. *"Rosas Puras"*: Rita Valladares et Choer
3. *"Canción de soltero"*: José Murillo
4. *"Duo de Esmeralda y Rodolfo: El destino"* Acte 1 (1 part): Rita Valladares et José Murillo
5. *"¿Qué es una flor, qué es una mujer?"*: Rita Valladares
6. *"Duo de Rodolfo y Olga: La vida buena"*: José Murillo et Mercedes Blanca
7. *"Rumba de La Habana"*: Rita Valladares et Choer
8. *"Canción de un baile"*: Choer

Acte Deux

1. *"Canción de amargas revelaciones"*: Rita Valladares
2. *"Duo de una pareja desencantada"*: José Murillo et Mercedes Blanca
3. *"Besos y deseos"*: Rita Valladares
4. *"Lamento de un hombre abandonado"*: José Murillo

5. *"La Bruja graciosa"*: Matilde Rossy avec Rita Valladares
6. *"Baile de la tormenta"*
7. *"Rumba de funerales y fiestas"*: José Murillo
8. *"Tenemos un amor precioso"*: Rita Valladares et José Murillo
9. *"Canción de matrimonio"*: Choer
10. *"Rosas Puras"* (reprise): Rita Valladares et Choer (finale)

The show was a success. Levis, at the head of the orchestra, would take his bows with the final curtain, an impressive and massive figure in a long-tailed coat that could be seen easily from even the highest tier. *Le Monde* and other Parisian papers were laudatory of this grand entertainment. It was so popular that it would run for nearly two years—and for a large part of that time with Rita in the flower girl role—the houses were consistently full.

Conducting most of the performances during that show's first months, Levis suffered stoically through those more intimate scenes of love between Rita and Murillo, the composer's heart twisting into knots with the final and lingering stage kisses in the final act, knowing well the passion enacted upon the stage was being carried out in the bedroom of Rita's apartment on the Left Bank, for Murillo had moved in with her. And when she and Levis made their outings around the city, usually on a Sunday afternoon, she had begun, with the tremulous excitement of a schoolgirl, to speak about the prospect of matrimony with this Murillo—perhaps a life with him in Madrid or a return to Habana.

Powerless to change a thing, Levis could only wish her the best. In a way, he loved Rita so much that he did not mind stepping aside.

As if I would have ever done anything different.

HIS JOURNEYS BACK TO CUBA AND OTHER TRAVELS, 1934–1936

He was always busy. Though he had chosen to make Paris his European base once *Rosas Puras* opened successfully, after a few months, he abandoned his conductor's duties of that orchestra, grew restless and began to tour again. He went to Mexico, via Habana, in late 1934, performing on a bill with Augustín Lara. In Buenos Aires, he appeared at the Hotel Miramar with Carlos Gardel, whose famous tangos were an influence upon and result of the very music that had been coming out of Cuba for years (the tango being a descendant of the habanera.) He returned to Europe, wrote film scores in Spain; back in Paris he began to compose the music for another theater piece, *Les Follies Cubaines.*

His friends were many, acquaintances so widespread that he could hardly keep track of them. He sent postcards for his casual correspondence—and with a small knack for self-caricature, always drew a cartoon of himself underneath his signature, a round-headed, bespectacled gentleman, with an amused expression.

In fact, he and Rita most enjoyed each other's letters, which never broached the missed opportunity of their love. Among her multitudinous skills, aside from being able to turn every man's head whenever she entered a room, aside from singing and dancing so well that she often brought crowds to their feet, she was something of a watercolorist, a passion that she had picked up during her conservatory days in Habana. She gave Levis her drawings, which he treasured. In another life she might have been a painter

or a sidewalk artist in Habana—or Paris—such were her render-
ings so pleasing and full, like her voice.

He kept everything relating to Rita—the playbills and an-
nouncements of the shows they had participated in; copies of
the sheet music of *Rosas Puras* on which Rita, in a plummed tur-
ban and silk dress, appeared inside a wreath of roses; every little
photograph of them, taken here and there in Habana and in Paris,
left out on the tables of his suite, simply so that he would think
of her.

LEVIS AND THE PROSPECT OF LOVE

He was not so far gone with his little disappointments about
Rita that he closed himself off to others. Rather, he remained a
pupil from that school of man, more or less accepting of his own
solitary existence and sometimes ventured out. His love, or call it
"strong compulsion," toward Rita, was the exception to his normal rule, for most women, while pleasing him with their soft ways
and manners, could not begin to sway him from his path.

Men, in fact, continued to interest him, though that was a line
that he would never cross.

Sometimes he thought about having children, especially as he
approached fifty.

There were moments—when he entered into the physiological
depths of his soul and envisioned the vast archives of talent that
lingered in his very seed—when the fact that he had no children
seemed a waste of something that had been God-given, and he
wondered if in some way he were failing God.

And yet, religiously thinking, he also reasoned that had he

become a priest—even a composer-monk, albeit one who loved his creature comforts—there would have been no question about his solitary ways. Still, there were times when he saw Rita's children and felt a longing for his own. Even when he watched bratty Parisian children tormenting their mothers on the greens, there was a part of him that went wanting, nearly envying them, for though these children were sometimes devils, he reasoned that if he had a child to raise he would do so in the Cuban way, with authority, affection and a fear of God.

On the other hand, why should he bother?

Surely, he had left himself open to introductions, to possible love affairs. The number of parties he attended in those years in Paris, hosted by his Cuban friends, was such that he always found himself making new acquaintances. During his shows there were always young actresses, dancers and singers, often from the poorest families, who would make themselves available to him if he so wanted. But, ethically speaking, in the same way that he had always been well mannered around women in Habana, he could not bring himself to take improper advantage. Sometimes he was overly attracted to the innocence and freshness of youth—a young singer, an actress or dancer in a show, seeking his guidance. In these situations he rarely diverted from exercising good judgment and moral rectitude, for he did not want to become part of the wicked world that would surely destroy their purer spirits. Hence, as he always did in Habana, he tried to help young aspirants out with lessons, or recommendations, and jobs. Even when he felt sick to his heart to see such women manipulated by other men, he kept his misgivings to himself, as he did not care for anything that violated the sanctity of his mental energies.

As for going out with women, he often felt himself too busy for such "nonsense," and there was a part of him that could not imagine closing the door entirely on his devotion to Rita—the unattainable—which suited him fine.

Instead, he preferred the "professional" ladies, some of whom he took on as his mistresses; that is to say, on Sunday afternoons, a certain woman would come to his suite and they would go to bed, and then set out to some event together, often clubs—he liked L'Aiglon on the Champs-Elysées, Maxim's, Club Paradise—where he treated such women with utter gentility, often making gifts of strings of pearls, perfume and cash. Living in the Grand Hôtel, he found himself a part of that fraternity of gentleman, often older, distinguished and quite rich (much displaced royalty in those parts), whom he would encounter in the elevators and lobby, these silver-haired men with their coat and tails, Bismarck mustaches and professorial goatees, sitting with their ladies and speaking in soft tones, oblivious to the possibility of criticism or discovery.

Once or twice he paid the rent on a small flat or atelier in which they might stay, visiting them as he pleased during the late afternoon when he'd finished with his composing chores. He had no room for emotions beyond the niceties of temporary infatuations and admiration for their loveliness. Timid about revealing the portliness of his ample body (or for that matter his inner thoughts), he nevertheless lived for the exaltation that often came into a woman's eyes when, in the throes of arousal, his sex had achieved its full and stately majesty.

He wanted nothing more—just enough admiration to fuel his creative mind—and why could he not do so, with whomever he so pleased?

In terms of sexual acts, the composer was rather conservative, though in those Paris years he had developed a fascination with the rear ends of these ladies. As they'd rest on their bellies in bed, he'd approach them from behind, spread open their plump thighs, finding the confluence of a crimson or mauve slash and the corona of curling dark pubic hairs, with the round and shapely buttocks such a pure joy that he would sometimes kiss, lick and otherwise smother himself in that well of lovely female scent and heat for hours at a time. He was open-minded enough to accommodate certain whims. Though he found caudal sex redundant and unsanitary, he occasionally complied, simply because the woman had requested it (though he could not comprehend why they seemed to enjoy it so). But he only felt offended if a woman, in the midst of an orgasm, happened to cry out, "Oh God, oh God!" or made some such religious allusion, for in those moments, he felt that a Holy rule had been violated, and then, feeling ashamed by the situation, he would abruptly lose his carnal interest.

He did not give much thought to these women, never dwelled on the possibility of taking up with a woman as part of a *pareja*—a "couple." He was always good company on outings with friends, though if the decent and quite well-bred ladies he met posed any potential threat to his lifestyle with even the slightest intimations of devotion, he'd vanish, hiding out for weeks at a time, never calling or pursuing them in any way.

He did, however, feel startled that he would find himself the subject of a searing, inquisitive gaze from certain young men who he'd encounter as they walked haughtily across the lobby of the Grand Hôtel. *It was as if they knew some deeply hidden part of my thoughts.*

PHOTOGRAPHS

Photographs of Levis from this period—aside from the usual touristic snatches of the composer as he stood posed in a topcoat before such landmarks as the Eiffel Tower or Arc de Triomphe—often portrayed him sitting behind a piano. Despite his size, the refinement of his long-fingered and quite delicate hands, and the placid concentration of his expression—and the way the light played upon his fair complexion—gave the impression of a man far removed from the concerns of the flesh.

Certainly one would not picture him in a brothel, taking hold of a harlot's hair as she practiced her arts upon him; nor would anyone imagine him even thinking about the act of oral love with a man. Even when he was privately enthralled by the fantasy of "showing off" his spectacular member to another man, he maintained to himself that he would always play the role of the man. While such thoughts disturbed him, he considered them the result of too much work, too many hours alone.

His comforts in Paris and the demands for his services were so great that his temporary stay in the city of light became more and more prolonged. He discovered a second life there—as a concertizer, performing in auditoriums and theaters here and there in Europe, as a symphonic composer and conductor, as the presenter of his own zarzuelas and lyric comedies.

During his latter days in 1947, the composer often wished he had been more decisive about his life, certainly in matters of love. As he often told his assistant, Antonio: "When the day comes when you are truly stricken by a pang of desire in your heart, give in to it, as you will not know when it will come again."

The young man was polishing a pair of shoes, and puzzled by the composer's remark, for from his youthful point of view, Levis had lived a full life. Yet the older man's sadness touched him, and his silence through the days was, in a way, unnerving. Levis spent long periods of time looking in the mirror, and sometimes he stood before the piano in his study, as if he would momentarily sit down and attempt to compose again. But at best, he would play with one hand, while standing, a scale, or a phrase out of Bach. How he got through his days was such a tremendous mystery to Antonio, who wondered if old age would bring the same despair to him in the future, and with it, the slow movements, the pained expres-sions, the melancholic gazes.

By day, the composer often liked to sit under the shade of a bottle palm tree in his back patio, among the blossoms, thinking. At night he watched the stars with the intensity of someone reading a book. And sometimes the composer stood before his father's old apothecary cabinet, at the far end of a hall, a high oak affair filled with porcelain and glass jars, each marked with pencil labels; certainly he knew what to take for headaches. Certainly he must have known what to take to end his own life, if he so wanted.

(*Oh for a little bi-chlorite of mercury,* he had sometimes thought.)

"Maestro Levis, can I get you a drink?"

"No! Leave me alone, young man!"

His success: Paris, 1936—1937

His professional life flourished. In Paris he wrote his well-liked
Cinq Melodies, a *pastorale*, a *serenata*. And working with a French
librettist he had a second great success, after *Rosas Puras*, with a
musical called *C'est Moi*, which ran through 1936—37. That he was
more well known and venerated in Europe than in Cuba quite
appealed to him; that he had come to know and socialize with some
of the grander composers had given him the impression that he was
also of the first rank. He composed constantly and considered Paris
a succor to his soul. When he was not traveling around Europe—as
a pianist, or leading his own orchestra—he remained in his hotel
room to work. Everywhere he went, even when he performed
Bartók or Bach or Debussy, or his own more serious compositions,
there came that part of the program when he would have to give his
audiences a taste of his most famous composition, for he had put
together a quite concertized version of that song, whose melody
floated through many a crescendo and wavering tremolo.

*Little known to the world, and not even to Rita Valladares, was that
I had quite a good singing voice, and could have sung professionally, perhaps, but my singing voice, like my inward most feelings, was something I
kept between myself and God.*

By this time, Levis had begun to realize just how popular that
song had become, for no matter where he went in Europe, if he
turned on the radio he was bound to hear it. Often he heard Rita's
version, though there were others. In Paris it was played as frequently as Josephine Baker's *"J'ai deux amours, mon pays et Paris,"*
along with those popular tunes by Piaf and Chevalier.

He had, by then, heard numerous times how the success of "Rosas Puras" had opened the world's ear to Cuban music. To be sure, there had been some interest in Cuban music prior to its composition, with catchy tunes like "Tú" and "Mamá Inés" having become popular standards, but such was the widespread renown of his composition that by then even beer-garden bands in cities like pretty Düsseldorf were performing it.

"Maestro Levis, you have changed everything for us," he was often told by his fellow Cuban musicians, and he accepted such kind words with humility and gratitude.

By 1936 shiploads of fine and long-legged *mulata* dancers were coming to Europe from Cuba—to France, to Italy, to Germany; with them came singers and many a band—that music was every-where—and his own fame increased. (Even the Nazis seemed to like that music. According to Israel's friend Ernesto Lecuona, who often played Berlin with his band, the Lecuona Cuban Boys, Adolf Hitler himself, master of the Third Reich, whose favorite movie star was Gary Cooper, was said to have secretly attended several of their performances, in disguise; and because Lecuona performed his own arrangement of "Rosas Puras" during his con-certs, it could be said, much to Levis's later bemusement, that Hitler was familiar with—and possibly liked—that winsome tune.) So frequently was Levis introduced and applauded as he sat in a Paris club that he came to expect it, and felt a near disappointment if for some reason he had not been noticed. On certain occasions, movie stars like Johnny Weismuller, Gary Cooper and Marlene Dietrich drew attention away from him, and while he did not mind it, at times, he eventually developed the disease that comes with fame—even a composer's fame—a desire to be noticed.

One night at the Club Eve, he happened to glimpse a quite familiar-seeming man with the most craggy and solemn face at the next table, the man sipping one martini after the other—and emanating in Levis's opinion an air of expectation. Once he realized this man's identity, Levis notified the waiter, and shortly the band-leader announced his name from the stage: "Ladies and gentlemen, in our audience, sitting before me at the second table, we have none other than the distinguished film comedian Buster Keaton."

And with his ears brimming red, Keaton stood up and bowed. Soon after, Levis fell into conversation with him. Keaton could speak some French; Levis was quite fluent in that language by this time and knew just enough English to qualify certain of their exchanges. Levis asked Keaton if he knew Stan Laurel and Oliver Hardy, the film comedians who played *"El Gordo y El Flaco"* in Hollywood—actors who, in their close friendship and childish ways, enchanted him (to live in a world where a man could share his bed with another with impunity, like Laurel and Hardy, who slept together in long nightshirts and pointed nightcaps). Keaton answered that he did, noting that he sometimes played golf with the "fat one," that they were quite nice fellows and most private in nature, which pleased Levis.

Passing the time, however briefly, with an actor whose films had much entertained Levis back in Habana was but one of many such brushes with the famous. Gary Cooper, he would remember, was a gentleman. The writer Hemingway was a bit bombastic, but generous about buying people drinks—he liked that. Still, what he most enjoyed was the company of the musicians, those Cuban fellows, many of whom he had known or heard of back in Habana and encountered again at parties and clubs in that city. Along the way he had developed quite a taste for watching the chorus girls, with their diaphanous gowns, their fulsome, dark-tipped breasts. Ever the gentleman, he restrained himself from pursuing them, although once backstage at the Opéra Bouffe (so he seemed to remember) after a party, he allowed himself the swift and shallow pleasure of love, taken while he sat in a chair, with a young dancer named Mireya, or Mariela—he could not remember). It seemed that she had convinced herself that seducing the portly composer would be a boon to her prospects for work in Paris. Encountering him in the theater, after a few moments of conversation, she led him down a dark corridor to a private place, where she commenced to caress him through his trousers. What most startled him was the absolute liquidity of her pubic mound, for in her act of seduction, she had opened her robe and placed his fingers into the damp groove in the center of her silken frilly panties. How could he have turned away from that?

Such was the benefit of the illusion of fame.

AND YET HIS HEAD WAS ALWAYS TURNING TOWARD MEN . . .

In the back of his mind, during these unseemly and impulsively taken copulations, and in the course of his days, spent mainly working in his suite in the Grand Hôtel and while walking along the boulevards of that city, he sometimes wondered, then checked in place, his occasional attractions to men. He was most taken by classically handsome men, not so much for any attraction to the flesh, but for an almost artistic appreciation of the beautiful. Yes, it was true that he had felt unnerved by the handsome Italian

Beniamino Gigli, back in Habana, had experienced moments of such affection for friends like Manny Cortez, but generally when he considered the mechanics of such momentary infatuations, he concocted the theory that the physical feelings that a man might have for another man was, in a way, a form of sexual narcissism, and he dismissed it as vanity.

Then why did I have those recurring dreams about long-necked swans, of caressing their downy feathers, the curvature and length of their guttural flank pleasing me? Or of fellating myself, my appendage, made of marble, and as long as a cowboy's lasso?

And yet he spent many a day quite aware (entranced) of the presence of those men whose proclivities led them to the embrace of other men, and he was often impressed by the tranquillity of their expressions, their happiness, for they seemed to know just who and what they were.

His speculations sometimes followed him into church, where he dwelled upon the sexual nature of Christ himself and of the saints. Though the statues of these sacred personages, with their cloaks and folds of stone and marble and wood, were but the ide-alized representations of what each may or may not have been, Levis, in the midst of prayer, sometimes imagined the bodies therein, and he had sometimes been startled by his perception of Christ as a man: of Jesus waking in the morning, on a mat of straw, the ground hard beneath him, with a nocturnal erection; Jesus Christ craving water and food; Jesus, very much a man, crouching down in a field to relieve himself; Jesus Christ stung by a hornet, or experiencing a single headache. Why was it that when he contemplated the sad and transcendent face of that man, he felt an anger toward God? How could anyone truly believe

that God—whatever He is—would so defile the spiritual perfection, the mystery of the divine, by taking on the aspect of a man?
Would that not be a demotion? And would He not already know
everything about "man," down to the most secret of thoughts, like
those of Levis himself, as he wondered what it would have been
like to have been in the presence of the man who was Christ,
wanting to hold him—and why was that a sin?

Such odd thoughts came to him in Paris, the city of love.

LETTERS FROM CUBA

A creature of habit, the composer had adjusted to life in the
Grand Hôtel. Ordering his meals from the kitchen and attended to
by a solemn valet named Pierre, he enjoyed these amenities, as it
allowed him more time to compose. He was so dedicated to his
artistic routine that his strong ties to Cuba and his house in
Habana became more and more remote; the notion of Cuba itself,
like his love for Rita Valladares, entered into a phase of vague
longings, and nostalgia.

Twice monthly he received a letter from his brother, and these
usually conveyed good or ordinary news.

"I know you are set in your ways brother," Fernando would
write, "and very busy, but don't forget that you have family here.
That you are missed very much."

And he missed his family, missed Cuba itself. In fact, the number
of mornings in which he arose and his blurry eyes and hungover
brain mistook the interior of his hotel suite in Paris for that of his

bedroom in Habana were innumerable. When his head filled with the most lovely memories of the little pleasures of the life that he seemed to have left behind, his sadness was great. Thank God he had other Cuban friends in that city, like Rita, with whom he could enjoy himself. Still, he might have gone back to Cuba and his house in Habana were it not for the very sad dreams that came to him from time to time, when he envisioned the corpse of his dear friend Manny Cortez laying stretched out on a Habana street with two bullets through his head, and like a character out of an Edgar Allan Poe story, he would come back from the dead and cry out mournfully to Levis, "It was life on this godforsaken island that did this to me," Levis waking with his heart beating so rapidly that he would have to calm himself with a strong drink. And there were times when he dreamed that he had returned to Habana and that everywhere he went, whether walking along the back alleys or docks of that city, he saw a man or a woman who provoked a great erotic urge in him, the composer grinding his pelvis with powerful movements and long thrusts into his mat-tress, those fantasies of possible and illicit loves shattered, his excitements postponed, when he realized that in these very same dreams his dear beloved mother, Doña Concepción, was some-where nearby, lurking and ever prepared to call out to him, "What are you doing with yourself, son? Have you no shame?"

But it was not as if Israel Levis had never returned to Cuba in those years. He had gone back to Habana for a week in December of 1934, some five months after his zarzuela *Rosas Puras* had opened triumphantly in Paris, and fifteen months after a violent general strike, in the August of 1933, had brought about the fall of Machado. (Levis and several Cuban friends had been sitting in a Paris movie house sipping shots of brandy when a Pathé newsreel about riots in the Cuban cities of Habana and Santiago emblazoned the screen; footage of the insurrectionists burning and ransacking houses of the rich, attacking government buildings—the Presidential Palace itself had been looted, its furniture piled out on the street and set ablaze—and facing off, bloodily, against the army in what would be later called the "Revolution of 1933" had moved Levis and his friends deeply. And when they were to later learn that Machado had fled to Miami, many of the Cubans who lived in Paris took to the streets and cafés of that city in celebration.) On this visit to Habana Israel Levis participated in a well-received concert honoring the music of Ignacio Cervantes at the Teátro Nacional, but his busy schedule did not allow him the time for even a short excursion to Santiago, an oversight that deeply offended and hurt his mother.

On that brief trip to Habana he drank too much. Aside from castigating himself for having failed to visit with his family and the odd feelings that came over him when he was alone in his house on Olivares, he was distressed that some things about life in that city had not at all improved since his departure in 1932, even with Machado deposed. During strolls through Habana he was brought to grief by what he saw around him, as if his friend Manny Cortez (dear Manny) had died for naught: children, bellies bloated, laying in the gutters, naked; peasants begging for food and money on every corner; the destitute stretched out on park benches and in darkened doorways; so many filthy and diseased persons roaming aimlessly through certain neighborhoods that he could have been walking the streets of leprotic Calcutta. And there was something else: though Machado's despotic reign was over (the man, syphilitic, insane and quite rich, living in exile in Miami), there remained in place in Habana the somewhat depressing evidences of police and military rule, a lingering atmosphere of corruption and a new government founded upon an army coup.

He had also returned to Cuba in 1936 and 1938, to attend to business, to visit with his beloved family in Santiago, and, mainly, to reassure his mother that he had not forgotten her. Since his original departure for Europe, the very separation that his mother could never have imagined—("Ay, my good son may be a little odd, but I know he would never leave me")—Levis had written her weekly, informing Doña Concepción of his every movement. From time to time, he, a generous soul, sent her gifts from Europe— parcels of fashionable accessories, silk scarves and hats, perfumes and elaborately decorated music boxes. And as much as he felt elated to have escaped into a somewhat different life, he also had days when the sight of an elderly woman walking slowly, perhaps painfully, down the street, filled him with such feelings of concern for his mother's health and well-being that he would rush back to his hotel, fearful that some bad news about her, conveyed from Cuba by cable, would be awaiting him.

She, in turn, wrote to remind her son about the candles she lit each day for him, that she prayed to God for his health and creativity, and that, despite the company of Fernando and his family, she sometimes had to cry herself to sleep, so much did she miss him.

"*I am happy here, my son,*" her letters used to tell me. "*But you have never understood how deeply I've always loved you. Otherwise, you would have never left.*"

Reunited in Santiago for a few weeks at a time, Israel and his mother resumed their old life, taking constitutionals, going to the movies and attending Mass together, Levis embracing her, holding her close, trying to instill his love, even as she, often irascible and moody, remained incapable of forgiving him for having left her at all.

During these visits to the city of his birth, Levis could not help but to think how Habana, "Paris of the Caribbean," seemed so staid and ordinary when compared to the great city in France. By then he had begun to prefer the openly libertine atmosphere of Paris to the more conservative ways of Habana. Enjoying the music, the food and the women of the City of Light, he had concluded in a letter to his friend Ernesto Lecuona, "*As much as I miss my Habana, all this is not so bad.*" Having become accustomed to the utter elegances of Parisian life, he began to take a different view of his own country, as a backward, socially static place. He began to feel himself "Parisian." Not that he would ever pursue a different manner of life sexually—he was too set in his ways—but perhaps, somewhere in the back of his mind, the options available to him in that French city were justification and comfort enough for him to have moved so far away.

Who could have foreseen the love that would enter his life—with a woman—or the presence of the Germans?

PARIS, 1938—WITH THE SPIRITUALISTS

Still, what he once had in Habana he replicated in Paris, down to a membership in the Theosophical Society, whose belief in "transmuting souls" (through an afterlife that was apparently as busy as the Paris underground during rush hour) fascinated him. He attended lectures at the society, off the rue de Verlaine, and believing in fortune-tellers, he had his palm read, the prognostications, when favorable, pleasing him: "You will live long and well." And: "Love will enter into your life."

It was in Paris that he made the discovery of Tibetan Buddhism, which was quite popular there at the time (all things unscientific, intuitive, primitive were), thanks to the writings of Madame Blavatsky and the lectures of men who claimed to have traveled to that forbidden land of the Himalayas and uncovered its secrets. He had no interest in becoming a Buddhist himself but often found the world of its aspirants fascinating, certainly amusing. While attending various cocktail parties, he would find that people had begun to collect many an artifact from Tibet—a chalice, a prayer book, a bowl made of a portion of a human skull, prayer flags dangling from the rims of ornate bird cages or used as scarves. And statues of Buddha. In many a home of the sophisticated for whom Christianity was dead, the impenetrable and myriad teachings of Tibetan Buddhism held a greater appeal than did the more straightforward, moral platitudes of the Church. He mingled with people who spoke of reincarnation dreams and attended séances where he, out of curiosity, attempted to contact his dead father, the late Doctor Leocadio Levis.

During the dozen or so such meetings over those years, he had only once been in the presence of a "guide" who had come close to tracking down his father's spirit. "Why do I see a man holding a butterfly net?" one spiritist said, and Levis had left feeling deeply impressed (for Leocadio had been holding a net at the time of his death) but warily so, for not even this spiritist, who by way of a parlor trick had produced in a glass bowl a lumpy waxlike manifestation of "ectoplasmic" matter, could tell him the simple fact that his father had been a physician.

Nevertheless, he went to these gatherings with the expectation that sooner or later some proof—real proof that human beings lived in a multidimensional world—would come along. Believing strongly that he had, above all men, been privy to the inner workings of the divine and its manifestations in this existence, he attended these affairs with a feeling that some great truth would be revealed to him. He liked these spiritist gatherings, for in their trappings of burning incense and candles, of flower-covered altars, they reminded him of the Afro-Cuban religions that he had often come into contact with as a youth.

For the most part, they all believed in the soul, and even though Levis considered himself a somewhat superstitiously prone Catholic, for whom, in many ways, one's relationship with God—that mystery—was not so complicated, he much enjoyed those little communities of somewhat slightly eccentric people.

SARAH RUBENSTEIN, 1938

At a Tibetan Buddhist gathering in 1938, in the cavernous living room of a certain Henri Moreau, a banker and devotee of Blavatsky, Levis made the acquaintance of a young widow, a teacher of dance named Sarah Rubenstein, whose delicate and austere manner and curiosity about religion appealed to him. She was Jewish, of commendable beauty, thin and elegant, with long, jet-black hair, a wistful spoon-shaped face and eyes that were intensely dark and seemed wiser than her years. In fact, during a consultation with one of the "teachers," she had been described as an "old soul," a designation that had also been assigned to Levis; that is, "a person of remarkable spiritual depths due to the development of the soul during past and virtuous lives."

This was "*un pedazo de miércoles,*" or "complete nonsense," as far as Levis was concerned, particularly about himself, even if he found this declaration humorous, vaguely pleasing and appealing to his vanity.

But the moment the composer first laid eyes on Sarah, he had the unmistakable impression that he already knew her. And when they had looked at each other across a crowded room in a parlor filled with people chanting a Tibetan prayer, Levis, who rarely smiled easily, beamed radiantly at her as if she were a kindly life-long friend.

Later, when they met over glasses of champagne and caviar, his reaction to her turned out to be one of the greater surprises of his life. He felt no timidity, no tendency toward withdrawal around her. He was so taken by her appearance, as if she were a queen from the time of Solomon, that he did not once think about Rita Valladares in her company. When he had first looked at her, for reasons he could not understand, he was reminded of a water-color from the Orientalist school he had once seen in a Paris gallery, of a feast in a harem, and he imposed this memory upon Sarah. Even though she had been dressed modestly in a white ruf-fle-sleeved blouse and long dark skirt, he saw her half-naked upon a pile of silken pillows, himself as some long-bearded Persian or Hebrew Lord, about to take his pleasures with her. Moreover, when he looked at her, he had an instant impression of what she would be like in bed, and when he glanced at her body, he had such a strong sense of her erotic power that he could have been kneeling before her, his head nestled against the softness of her belly. Something about the brilliant jet-blackness of her mane flew quickly into the heart of his sexual speculations about her, as if she were standing without a stitch of clothing before him, and his ears flushed red.

So strong was his desire to put his hand between her legs that he quickly finished a glass of champagne and had another.

Amused by this towering mass of courtly behavior, for he had bowed gallantly before her, Sarah Rubenstein, who must have foreseen, in the way of "old souls," their immediate future, took hold of Levis's hand and, looking deeply into his eyes, as if reading something there, told him, in French: "My goodness, but you are a powerful and spirited man."

At first they agreed to attend those meetings together, then to go out afterward to a restaurant, where, between the mutual explications of their lives, he often spoke of his religious feelings. They concluded that though they came from different faiths—she was of a nonpracticing Jewish family, and he a Cuban Catholic—they each had the glorious sense that "something else" was there.

" 'God' is an overused word that has lost its meaning," she said one night. "The Cabalists believe it is unthinkable to give any name to God and I agree. Whatever it is, this God remains a mystery, through which, each of us, in our way, passes.... But it is very real, and exists outside of time.... Is not that the case?"

"As a Catholic I believe in God," he told her. "And I believe in the soul.... I am convinced that we are nourished from without.... When I write my little compositions and they turn out beautifully, I cannot believe that they just come from the brain, but rather from the soul—how else could that be?" Then: "Sometimes, when I am walking along the street, and I am in a crowd of passersby, I am nearly moved to tears, by the presence of so many souls. Of course, I can't see them, but I feel them. Most are good— I think, with all the best intentions toward the world—but, some are so wicked that if I walk into a room and I sense a certain blackness around me, I instantly leave. . . . I know it isn't logical, but that is something that I have experienced often. . . . Does this make sense to you?"

"Yes," she told him. "But it goes beyond that. When you and I met, I knew that our souls had already been involved in some other place and time. And even if that is not true—for how would we know—I find the thought most satisfying just the same."

Such speculations, however pleasing to the composer, were overshadowed by the pure affection he began to feel for her. It was not only that she was unusual in her sense of the world—like him she believed that souls were everywhere around them—but that he had felt a certain tranquillity in her company.

She was about thirty and lived in a small flat on the boulevard de Strasbourg, in the eleventh arrondissement, one of the Jewish quarters of that city, with her three-year-old daughter, Paulette. Sarah taught at a *lycée,* and on the weekends the composer would dispense with his usual morning labors and take them out on full-day outings—to the city parks, to toy shops, to museums. He lived lavishly if well beyond his means, but had enough money to "help" her with her expenses.

At forty-eight, he wondered what feelings could be coming over him—for her presence of being (her soulfullness) had somehow begun to occupy a portion of his heart that had long been shut off. Suddenly, he felt himself distracted from the ambitions that had defined him; suddenly, he was in no hurry to write a new concerto or chamber piece and the prospect of booking two weeks at the Lido or of flying to Stockholm and overseeing a Swedish-language production of *Rosas Puras* loomed as an annoying disruption that would keep him from his new and recent love.

In those days, the importance of Rita, who had figured so greatly to that point in his life, diminished. Though she remained in Paris, so much of her time was spent away, on international tours— back to Cuba and the Caribbean, and to make films in Mexico— that he had long since grown accustomed to her absences. And just six months, before she had gone to Monte Carlo with Señor Murillo to concertize, when, on the spur of the moment, and inspired by an excess of champagne and the fairy-tale ambience of that petite principality, she abruptly decided to marry him. (Levis had not been on hand for that ceremony, and when he heard about their wedding, after the fact, he felt deeply hurt, as if he were an uncle excluded from his favorite niece's nuptials.)

Having settled in Paris because of Rita as well as the other Cubans who were there, he owed his livelihood to the song "Rosas Puras" and to the whirlwind of attention and demand surrounding it, but until he met Sarah Rubenstein, he had begun to feel cheated by life. Despite his good intentions toward the world and the many pleasures he experienced in that city, he felt the sharp solitude of a man, in late middle age, who becomes slowly aware that he will most likely face the rest of his life alone, that he had reached an unchanging plateau of existence, that his days would unfold one like the other, that he would die without anyone by his side, weeping.

But Sarah Rubenstein had changed that; a clock was reversed. Through her, Levis reentered the realm of youth with renewed vigor, for in her presence, his soul felt at rest. During those afternoons when she would turn up at his suite in the Grand Hôtel, or when her daughter Paulette had been sent down to Provence to stay with her grandparents and they passed their nights together in her bedroom, which smelled deliciously of a bakery below, he experienced a physical love that fed upon itself, each copulation followed by another, and then another, to the point that their bodies entwined in such a way that they were neither male nor female, but skin upon skin, two souls awash in a froth of sweat and perfume and bodily aromas.

Long accustomed to the congenial, sometimes affectionate, often detached love of the bordellos, he was shocked, at his ripe old age, by this discovery of intimacy.

With a mere glance, or by the very touch of her hand, she could provoke the greatest ardor in him; a woman of culture so proper and measured and "spiritual" in her ways, she had only to lift the hem of her skirt while she adjusted her stocking, and he would forget the importance of his position in life, his serious demeanor, his timidity, and throw her onto the bed or sofa, and with agitated quickness, fall upon her. And her mastery of the sexual act itself was something that he had never encountered before, not even among the most experienced harlots, for whom expediency was everything. She not only found pleasure in accommodating his appendage, but she knew how to keep him inside of her for torturously long periods of time, of arresting his movements in such a way that the interior of her body would burn like a small furnace. Experiencing her own pleasure she gave the composer such extreme physical joy that he sometimes thought he could die peace-fully in her arms, without a regret in his life.

The change in him became apparent to everyone who knew the maestro. He was missed at the bordellos, to the point that he received telephone calls from the madams inquiring as to whether he was ill. He began to turn up at parties and dinners with Sarah, brought her along to his shows, was seen walking in the parks with her and Paulette, and seemed not only "happy"—a term he would never have applied to himself before—but younger and in better health. He even took them out on a canoe for a row on the River Marne, Levis, unaccustomed to exercising, huffing and puff-ing at the oars, his head streaming with sweat. Though he still smoked his Habanas incessantly, he had cut back on drink—in her company he hardly drank at all—and the pleasures of food, while ever bountiful in Paris, seemed less tempting, for he wanted to lose some weight, and he did manage to drop enough pounds to appear more youthful, even nearly handsome.

By and by, her name crept into his letters to Cuba. He was cautious, however. At his age it was embarrassing to mention what might be interpreted as a frivolous autumnal love, and so he would speak of a "new acquaintance" with whom he was getting agreeably along—"una encantadora," he called her. From the outside looking in, to his friends who knew him well, it seemed that he was in the midst of an "arrangement" between an older man and a younger woman, quite common in those days, but he, childless, had taken Sarah and her daughter to heart. He began to think about marrying her, of having a child by her, and often they spoke of this prospect and of traveling together to Cuba, but only to visit, because France was now their home.

And sometimes, he inadvertently fell into the habit of giving her a familiar nickname, *"Mi Chiquita Francesa"*—"It means 'Dear Little French One' in Spanish," he told her.

HER BROTHER GEORGES AND ZOLA'S *GERMINAL*, 1939

He also made the acquaintance of her younger brother, Georges, a schoolteacher in a small town near Paris. He was a joyful, ever-curious, intellectual sort, a great reader of books, and it was he who had proposed the novel *Germinal* to Levis as a good subject for an opera. He spoke so enthusiastically about this book—"Imagine an opera about a miner's labor strike of the nineteenth century! A story about the joys and sufferings of the common Frenchman, as seen through the eyes of a young idealist, Etienne Lantier!"

"Have you a copy of this novel?" Levis had asked.

"Yes, I will bring it to you."

The composer liked the young man's manners and the cheerfulness of his disposition—he was the kind of fellow who always wore a blazer and a checkered vest, his black hair crisply cut, his blue eyes seemed to give off light, as if lit from behind. He'd run up the street to greet them with arms outspread, his cheeks bursting with health, so much of a jaunty energy about him, that Levis, in his presence, felt enlivened, and never considered it a burden when Georges came along on their excursions around Paris. He was the kind of fellow who smiled if he happened to catch his sister giving the composer a quick public kiss, the type to wink at his sister over the obvious pleasure that the composer took in his meals. Attending various shows in their company, Georges easily fell in love with one or the other of the chorus girls, and he was so handsome and earnest that writing notes and wrangling his way backstage, he often succeeded in dating these girls. Carefree in his life, he was nevertheless quite serious about literature.

Liking him, Levis accepted the grand task of turning *Germinal* into an opera, even when he himself had found the novel interminably long and could not finish the book.

"Georges, you take care of the libretto for this opera and I will write the music. It will be a masterwork, of the first order, I promise you that!"

Even when there was something about Georges that made the composer feel a genuine delight and enthusiasm about their planned collaboration, Levis, with so many other projects to keep him busy, could only dedicate a few hours every other day to this work. Each week Georges would drop off a fresh section of the libretto at the front desk of the Grand Hôtel or meet briefly with Levis over drinks in the lounge to discuss ideas for scenes and arias. Given Georges's inexperience when it came to such a monumental task, Levis had to contend with the inexactitude and wildness of the writing, but, deeply touched by the young man's enthusiasm, he did not mind the extra work and took it upon himself to cull from these often overly long manuscripts those lines that might best be set to music. Truly fond of Georges, for in his love of literature he reminded Levis of Manny Cortez, the composer had only praise for the young man's efforts. "This is truly magnificent!" "*C'est bon!*" "You are a genius in the making!"

Later, in his study, Levis would have to contend with the headaches of setting these words to music. Sitting before the piano, he utilized a method that played upon the sound and movements of the vowels of this novice's work. His notion was to write a more modernistic piece than he had ever attempted before, something along the lines of Messiaen, with his mystical orches- trations, and with the jocular movements of a Stravinsky. Mainly he set out on this happy chore, brimming with hopefulness—not just about accomplishing a serious piece that would draw atten- tion to his great strengths as a composer (he was tired of writing *danzones,* boleros and rumbas, which is what half the singers in the world seemed to want from him in those days, including his dear Rita Valladares)—but for the direction that his life had unex- pectedly taken. So every so often, some long sections of *Germinal* would appear in Levis's mailbox at the Grand Hôtel.

Now it seemed that he had a little family to look after.

WITH RITA AND HER HUSBAND IN A CAFÉ, 1939

For reasons he did not quite understand, he was quite sheep- ish about disclosing this love, late in his life, to Rita. By then Valladares, world famous, with her two homes—one in Paris, the other in Habana—spent her time divided, when not traveling, between the two. Her life was so busy that Levis had seen little of her in the last years of the thirties. And their reunions, always cordial, seemed ever so brief. When doting on her, his expression in her presence always revealed a wistfulness of spirit, as if he wished things had turned out differently.

One day in 1939, he met Rita at a café and told her that he thought he might be in love. He was so awkward in his presenta- tion that she might have wondered if, at long last, the maestro would divulge that he was in love with a man (for what other rea- son would he have been so timid around her all those years?). But when he told her—"There is someone who is my companion, a young woman named Sarita"—she could not have been more pleased and eagerly awaited the chance to meet this woman, this wonder, *"una maravilla"*—who had so moved her dear friend.

It was his misfortune, however, that when they did meet, at a bistro on the rue de Verlaine, that her husband, the singer José Murillo, whose presence in Rita's life had once tortured Levis so, could not keep his eyes off of Sarah. It was unfortunate that they met just when Rita was facing up to her awareness of her husband's infidelities. And though it was not Sarah's fault, Rita later disappointed Levis with her appraisal: "She is very nice," she told him. "And attractive for so plain-looking a woman."

That moment of poor diplomacy, whether from jealousy or bitterness over her second failing marriage, had hurt the composer deeply. "I only wanted your blessing, not your opinion," he told her tersely on another occasion, but that was as close to a rift between Levis and Rita that had ever existed, and their friendship was of such importance to her that Rita Valladares not only wrote the composer a note of apology, but forthwith resolved to treat Sarah Rubenstein with the utmost kindness.

He was so much in the center of this dream of his newly discovered passion and love that he hardly considered the prospect of returning to Cuba. He fell into a new routine and Sarah Rubenstein was a part of it. He resumed a strict work schedule, writing his music from ten in the morning until two in the afternoon, followed by lunch and then a constitutional after that. And if he were conducting or performing in one of the clubs, Levis spent his evenings painfully away from Sarah. But he always had time for the bars and cafés of the city where he met with the artistic or intellectual community.

In those years, of the late 1930s, when surrealism was in the air, discussions of art were most prevalent. He heard about Dada, about futurism, came into contact with those practitioners of hylaen, acmeist and vorticist artistic philosophies. Not prone to experimentation, and somewhat rigid in his aesthetic, he had all the same tried a new method to his composition. In choosing a key for a modernist score, he would roll dice, and assigning a note value to each number, write these out in the sequence with which they appeared. In that way he hoped to produce something akin to a "cubist" music, but was met with little success. This cubist method, however, led him to create pieces that, while using Cuban modalities, were layered like montages. These played upon the ear of the listener in the way that memory played upon the mind, or as in a swirl of singing voices in a dream.

Speaking of memory: In Paris so much of his past began to return to him for no good reason at all. Memories of his house in Habana, when he was a child, along with snatches of visual recollections—of his sister and brother and of his father, especially his father—produced in him the desire to write, contrary to modernist concerns, a very sweet and nostalgic music. In that period when he flirted with dreams of joining the avant-garde he also produced such pieces like "El Habanero," "Las Floritas del Campo" and "Canción de la Virgen de Caridad." He could not help it: for despite his life in Paris, Habana was not far from his heart.

THE GERMANS AND "ROSAS"

In those days, happy in his routines and appreciative of the artistic and personal freedom that he felt in Paris, he hardly paid attention to or took seriously the murmurings that had begun to arise about Hitler's Germany. Though he had never liked touring in that country, for he considered the food awful, he had always been well received, and although he sometimes found the German towns and cities where he performed quite elegant but cold in spirit, he nevertheless felt an admiration for a country that had given the world Bach and Wagner, among others. Still he felt discomforted by the militaristic presence of the "brown shirts," particularly of the youth who would maraud through the streets, flailing torches and beating drums, in an atmosphere that he found akin to what he had known in Machado's Habana.

And he had not forgotten the incident in Munich.

Though his famous song had once been often performed in Germany, and played over its radio, he was aware that it had vanished from the airwaves after 1936. Officially, a "purer Aryan" music (as part of the movement of the *Kampfbund für deutsche Kultur,* or "fighting front for Germanic culture") was to be pursued in the clubs and halls of that country. Though the Nazis advocated this change as an official policy, individual club owners still served up whatever kind of music that their drunken, whorechasing clientele desired, so there were still a few Cuban bands to be found working in Germany.

By 1939 Paris began to see a new influx of musicians—American jazz players and Cubans, mainly white—who had worked the clubs of Germany, from Berlin to Cologne, some finding work and others heading home.

Levis was so comfortably disposed by his life that as the Germans began their conquest of Europe, he made hardly anything of it all. Finding politics distasteful, he could care less about communism and the social democratic movements. He preferred to dwell upon the more genteel realms of music: which operas would be coming to Paris; new works by Stravinsky or Satie or Poulenc; the religious depths of the compositions of Fauré—now there was a devout nineteenth-century Catholic whose requiem was a wonder beyond wonders.

And what of those fanciful American films that one saw from time to time?

And how could one feel uncomfortable in the city that played host to Charlie Chaplin and Gary Cooper?

That he knew many artists who had decided to leave France in the late 1930s seemed not to bother him at all.

Once the aggressions began in Poland and Czechoslovakia, the consensus among most people was that even if the Germans had designs on the French, there was nothing to worry about, for did not France have the largest standing army in Europe?

Lost in his own work and replenished by love, he did not once feel personally threatened, and in any event, by then he had no intentions of leaving Paris, or France, for the *encantadora* Sarah Rubenstein had become a part of his life.

LEVIS AND
THE GERMANS

Shrill violins and dissonant piano keys. No sweet bolero intonations, no darkly enticing tangos, not a high-stepping rumba, not a single sultry female voice, nor the compelling timbre of a lustrous baritone, but a music equivalent to police and air-raid sirens, whistles and the stomping of boots, a music ever so distant from any good human feeling; just black notes floating off a score like ravens and crows, caw cawing violently into the darkness of an endless night. . . .

It had been after the first weeks of May 1940 that the lilting songs of Edith Piaf over the radio were interrupted in midplay and reports that the Germans were advancing toward France began to air, the armies of a certain General von Kuchler having massed along the Dutch frontiers and heading south through Belgium. The French awaited them, poised stiffly behind the massive concrete fortifications of the Maginot Line, a defense built after the First World War, which the sly Germans, in time, simply bypassed, their divisions outflanking the French, who, with nary a shot fired, quickly capitulated; French Marshal Pétain eventually pursued armistice and by the first weeks of June, the Germans prepared to enter Paris in triumph.

. . .

Even Israel Levis could not help but notice the general panic that began to overtake the city in the second week of June 1940: while the composer maintained his daily regimen before the piano, a cigar burning in an ashtray beside him, a decanter of brandy ever at the ready, many people of Paris fled. The boulevards of Saint-Michel and Saint-Germain had become a jam of cars, trucks, horse-drawn wagons; and along those thoroughfares and throughout the city swarms of men and women were out on the streets, pushing their goods and possessions along on handcarts and baby carriages, the freest flight, in that glut of traffic, coming to those who rode their bicycles, baggage mounted precariously on racks or strapped to their aching bodies. People left their apartment houses and piled their luggage on the curbs, trying to hitch rides, or simply dumped their possessions on the pavements and undertook the slow pro- cession out of the city by foot—empty luggage, shoes, dresses, hats, and mirrors, dolls, undergarments, strewn everywhere. In that sec- ond week of June 1940, all shops and offices closed; the Metro stopped running. There were riots in the train stations. Children who had been separated from their parents wandered lost through the streets and back alleys of the city, and the radio stations of Paris went off the air—all this in a matter of a few days.

The religious pleaded with God—a High Mass was held in the Cathedral of Notre-Dame, and in a solemn procession of bishops, priests and the faithful, the small, silver, jewel-covered caskets holding the relics of Saint Genevieve and Saint Louis were carried aloft on canopied litters through the streets, a great outpouring of psalms and prayers rising to the indifferent placidness that was assumed to be Heaven.

And during that time the only concession that the Maestro made to this disheartening course of events was to cut short his work one morning and go to the bank. Although there had been a sudden reduction of staff in the Grand Hôtel, things went on as they normally did—a maid still arrived in the mornings to clean his suite, breakfast and other meals could be ordered from room service, porters still polished the marble floors, and if the usual bell-boy had not turned up with his food, there was the harried manager, Monsieur Henri to deliver the trays, apologizing for the disruption of services; by eleven in the morning, a pianist had begun to play, as usual, in the lobby.

Though the hotel staff and many of the guests had taken flight, or tried to, Levis himself was not disposed to rushing—the only part of his body that ever moved quickly, in those days, did so in the company of Sarah Rubenstein. Speaking to her by telephone a few days before, on the evening of June 12, just as the news of the impending German advance toward the city was becoming common knowledge, he had promised to bring her some money, for she wanted to take her daughter south to her family.

"Surely, you must know what the Germans have been doing with the Jews," she had told him.

Hearing such rumors, he'd thought (or preferred to think) they were exaggerations.

Nevertheless, he promised to help her. There was a man with an automobile who had agreed to drive her south, for a very large sum of money—two thousand francs—and though Levis's face had at first flushed at the amount, he agreed, for there was very little the composer would not do for her.

Languidly, he had dressed, as he never ventured from his hotel suite without a proper suit, a shirt and tie, and a vest (which he'd button tightly, as it gave the illusion that he was thinner). He soon found himself in his place in the very long cue along the rue Dauphine, outside his bank, to withdraw, with his account book and passport in hand, as much money as would be allowed. He waited an hour, in the heat, amid a crowd of panicked, foul-mooded Parisians, only to be told that there was a five-thousand-franc limit to withdrawals, and even then he had to sign numerous papers—for officials were doing everything in their power to prevent a run on the banks. Levis did not worry; much of the income he had made during the past ten years he sent to his older brother in Santiago, and, at that time, he was under the impression that if he were not rich, at least he was comfortably well off.

Later, as Levis made his way over to the eleventh arrondissement, he walked through largely deserted streets. Occasionally he saw some gendarmes, some beggars, a gypsy family carting their goods away, or teenagers and college-age students traveling about gaily in packs, as if nothing unusual were happening at all. As he climbed the stairway to Sarah's flat—many of the apartments had been abandoned, and eyes peered out from darkened hallways at him through narrowly opened doors—he wondered if he should accompany Sarah on her journey; surely the Germans would not remain in Paris long. But then, his own rigidities and devotion to his work, his loyalty to the pattern of his days, prevailed, and though he loved her (or thought he loved her), he chose to remain behind.

After all, even when much of the city had closed down, the

music establishments—and, for that matter, the bordellos—remained open and continued to do a lively business among those
who'd wanted to lose themselves in the pleasures of music and
love, or who chose to ignore what was happening—like Levis
himself. In fact, he was looking forward to a weekly jazz session
with some American musicians at the Club Eve that coming
Wednesday night, looked forward to the fine-tuning of a piano
concerto he had been working on.

He was prepared to endure a temporary separation from
Sarah but not at all prepared for the emotions that gripped him
when she opened the door and he caught sight of her packed bags
on her living-room floor, as if she were going away forever. For a
moment, the light that beamed in through her windows was reminiscent of Habana, taking him back to his youth, and he'd wished
to God that he had met her in the Habana of 1922. She seemed
nervous but organized. She gave him a kiss on both his cheeks, a
slip of paper with her parents' address, took the money—he gave
her four thousand francs—and told him, "I will be leaving at six,
we haven't much time."

Her daughter, Paulette, was then five years old and wearing a
pretty blue dress. She was sitting in her little room playing with
several of her bisque-headed dolls, one of which the composer
had given her that past Christmas, and when he approached her
doorway, he pulled from his pocket a handful of peppermint candies, which she had always liked, and which he would purchase in
a candy shop not far from the hotel. Though he usually spoke
with her in French, he always called her by her Spanish nickname,
"La Niñita Paulita," and with the clump of candies in hand, he
balled up his enormous fists and asked her to chose: she picked

the left, tapping his knuckles, and squealed with delight, because she had chosen correctly; she did not know that whenever they played this game, he always had candies waiting in both hands.

Then her mother had said, "Now thank Mr. Levis," and the child did, with a kiss, and he beamed, tousling her hair.

"Now you be a good girl. Your mama and Mr. Levis are going into my room to talk."

Practical-minded, Sarah locked her door and closed the curtains into that room. She sat Levis on her bed, and quickly she undressed and rested her naked body on the bed, legs spread wide. Slowly he undressed, off with his tie and shirt, down with the suspenders; his trousers he carefully folded and left on a chair.

"*Ay, Mi Chiquita Francesa,*" he said, looking at her.

"Come here, my love," she told him sweetly. And she began to fondle and kiss him, even while he'd kept those shorts on—she liked to pull and bend him around—and on that late afternoon, she was so effective that, in memory, he would recall the largest and most agitated erection of his life. He had thought that if there could be a moment to remember in an enfeebled old age, then that was it (to speak of the physical); but then, at the same time, it seemed all so sad, because in her adamancy, it suddenly dawned upon the composer that she was behaving as if there would be no tomorrow awaiting them. And so between the physical exertions, he treated her most tenderly and nearly wept, even as she shuddered from the force of his weight and thrusts, the joining of their incongruously different bodies, for he must have outweighed her by more than a hundred pounds.

Later, as they rested in bed, side by side, he lay his head on her breast and asked, "Of course we will see each other again, won't we?"

"Of course, we will my love," she had told him.

They fell into the little dream outside of time that occurs among lovers, drifting, as it were, across a sea of tranquil emotions, on the caravel that was their bed. Then, as if she wanted a remembrance, she took him into her mouth; prudishly bound, he always withdrew before the moment of his release, but that day, she refused to allow him to, holding him steadfastly.

Then it was over, and he settled into the shame and gloom of feeling that in abandoning her he had abandoned himself. They dressed—only an hour had passed—and when they opened the door, Paulette was still in her room, playing with her dolls. To further commemorate this moment, she broke open a bottle of fine champagne that she had been saving for a special occasion. She poured drinks and made a toast, "To my dear and sweet composer. May God bless and protect us both." And then she kissed him, with a nip of her tongue, and laughed. "My God, but you're always so timid!"

He had brought her a gift, a black-beaded rosary that he had picked up in one of the shops outside the Cathedral of Notre-Dame.

"I know this is not your style, but keep it and think of me." Then: "And you know, it can't hurt, can it?"

When the driver arrived (a gruff fellow), Levis helped carry their luggage down the stairs: two suitcases, two wound-straw bags—such as one would take to the market, filled with food and toys. It was approaching dusk, just past seven, and even though Sarita paid the man his two thousand francs right then and there, he wanted more.

"Another thousand or I go nowhere." Then he qualified his remark: "The German Luftwaffe have been strafing the *routes nationales* out from the city."

Having loaded her things into the automobile, an old Packard sedan, they said their farewells. She had huddled privately with Levis and placed his hand upon her breast—and kissed him again, on both his cheeks—"*Au revoir,* my dear man," she said. "I will see you again, and soon, when all this clears up."

IN HIS HOTEL

It should be mentioned that when the composer later returned to his hotel, he commenced upon a great drinking binge. Though he was prone more often than not to head out with some friends for supper, around eight, he had decided to remain in his suite and to order up his meal. He had sat before his piano, working through and examining the polytonalities of a work by Darius Milhaud, when a cart of food was delivered to his room; a bottle of a good sauvignon, a bowl of beef bouillon, and a quite nice, crisply baked duck à l'orange, with pomme frites and a salad. He was so nervous that he hardly enjoyed the meal, concentrating upon the wine, which he quickly finished and then followed up by one, and then two and three glasses of brandy.

By this time, Rita Valladares had been away from Paris for some two months, having returned to Cuba, from which she undertook a tour of the States and later work in Mexico on a film. Levis sorely regretted her absence from Paris. The last time he had seen her, they had taken to the stage of the Melody Bar, and as was often the case in their impromptu late-night performances, he accompanied her on a rendition of his song *"Rosas Puras,"* which, of course, had its usual pleasing effect upon the audience, who applauded them wildly. It was the kind of performance, so often repeated over the years, that sent Levis aloft into a timeless place, driven perhaps by a nostalgia for Cuba and youth, Rita Valladares, in her strapless, heart-clutching scarlet dress, an embodiment of that past, *una testiga*, a "witness," to his earlier life, for which, in those moments, Levis had felt much gratitude. It was as if, when Rita sang, nothing else existed.

The incantatory powers that Rita still held over him contin-ued to amaze the composer, and he had come to the realization that it was possible to be in love with more than one woman at a time. Behind such a thought, the lingering influence of his mother, the female from whose side he had not easily parted.... Of course, when he saw Rita off, on an afternoon a few months before, he had not felt the overwhelming loneliness of old, for Sarah would be awaiting him. And yet, now that Sarah had left Paris, such was his apprehension that even his music could not comfort him.

That night he thought that he would have telephoned Rita, were she still in that city; instead, he sat down to write her a letter:

My dearest Rita,

Your old friend, Maestro Levis, is drunk—emborachado— and why not? You have probably heard, along with the rest of the world, about what has been going on here in Paris. The Germans are at the city gates—can you imagine that? And the people here have been running for their lives, and yet, your dear old gordito has stayed behind. I haven't been too much affected—when I look

*out my window, out over the square, the city looks the same to
me.... All those buildings, the many streets, the River Seine
itself, seem as majestic as ever and beyond violation. I swear that I
think the city is a living thing, like a powerful giant of some kind
that would stand up to anyone or anything—of course, I am
drunk and know that this is a little fairy tale. But if I am drunk,
it's because my dear Sarita has left the city to join her family in
the south, and I am alone now. And of course, when I am alone I
am always compelled to think about you—I know I have never
been able to put my thoughts into good order, but Rita, I must ask
you why, in these moments, am I so filled with longings? Am I dis-
loyal, am I frivolous, am I..."*

He stopped there, never mailing it.

"ALL THIS . . ."

"All this" continued, however. At five-thirty the next morning, on June 14, the troops of von Kuchler's army entered Paris
by the Porte de la Villette, marching in two separate columns
toward the Eiffel Tower and the Arc de Triomphe. Suddenly officers from the German high command were pouring into the best
hotels, among them the extravagantly appointed Hôtel de Crillon,
where General von Studnitz, the first commandant of Paris, had
taken up residence.

And they took rooms in the Grand Hôtel, where Levis began
to hear the click-clacking of stud-heeled boots in the hallways.

Badly hungover, Levis could not work and so he left the hotel
and joined the crowds lining the Champs-Elysées to watch the

unending stream of German troops with their golden eagle-headed standards and Nazi banners, goose-stepping along that boulevard. What could he do but get drunk again? Soon he found himself sitting in the bar of the Hôtel Alsace wishing it were the Campana Bar in Habana. Later, he went over to La Cueva, where many of his Cuban musician friends had gathered, the promise of continuing to live in that city now so dispiriting that everyone, save Levis, seemed to be planning to go back home.

"*Bueno,*" he had said. "We will see."

That week he had gone to the cinema, where a Fred Astaire film was showing (not *Rhumba Crazy* but *Shall We Dance?*), and happened to see a newsreel, which the Germans had slipped into circulation, of Hitler, at the signing of the armistice, in the Compiègne forest, stomping his boots in a dance of mad joy ("I am grateful to fate," Hitler was quoted as saying). Leaving the theater in a state of gloom Levis made his way back to the hotel, where he found a note from Georges Rubenstein awaiting him at the desk: *"My sister is in Lavelanet with the family, safe and sound, and she sends her regards. She will be back in Paris soon."*

Then, in larger, more emphatic letters: *"I will be getting more pages for our great opera to you soon!—Georges."*

Such news lightened the composer's heart, and he returned to his labors, in his sun-filled hotel room, spending most of his days before the piano. The normalcy of his routines, the daily business of eating and washing and smoking and heading out on his constitutionals, or, later, to nightclubs, restored his confidence that life would get back to normal. And, for a time, in many ways, it did. Save for the presence of so many young and handsome and quite polite German soldiers, in their black-and-gray, high-collared uniforms, who were suddenly everywhere, and the many swastika flags and banners that now hung displayed on building facades and public monuments, the city seemed the same.

Those citizens who had remained in Paris resumed their nor- mal occupations: shops reopened; the scents of fresh candy and of chocolates, of perfumey necks, filled the air; the schools and transit systems went back into operation. Across the square from the high- arched entranceways to the Grand Hôtel, the opera reopened and Parisians and Germans alike flocked to its performances.

THE SUMMER OF 1940

But within a few months, during his walks through the city, he began to notice the occasional German bookstore, a new restau- rant boasting a German menu; and with the Germans heading out to the clubs at night, for drinks and entertainment and women, the musicians of the city were obliged to work popular German tunes into their repertoire. Suddenly it was a quite different Paris. When he went to a favorite club to hear his friend Maurice Chevalier perform, he was amazed by the joviality of his largely German audience—relaxed, amicable, hooting and whistling—perhaps from the joy of their success and their prospects for total victory in Europe. And in La Cueva, where he used to hear so many Cuban musicians and where he had often performed himself, he was pleased to see that, at the very least, a few other Cubans like him- self had remained behind, though they were now playing more tra- ditional Germanic fare—waltzes and serenades and ever-popular American tunes—for crowded rooms of exuberant Parisians and their German counterparts.

HE MET HELMUT KNOCHEN

On one of those evenings, that late July, he had performed as a solo pianist at a reception held for the German high command at the Spanish embassy, where, upon Ambassador Felix de Lequerica's request, he played a program of Brahms, Bach and Mozart, the guests of honor with their iron crosses and gray-blue military tunics ever officious and polite. Later, after his program, as Levis was crossing the room, he was paid a compliment by the head of the Gestapo Sonderkommando, General Helmut Knochen. A quite tall, sartorial, professorial sort, he had approached Levis and said in quite perfect Castillian *"Señor Levis, creo yo que usted es un pianista muy capaz,"* or ("Mr. Levis, I believe you are a very talented pianist"). Then: "I have heard you in Vienna, some years ago."

And that was all, for the General was an important man, with many others to speak to, and in fact, so civil and refined in his manner that Levis, who considered himself a good judge of character, had left the embassy convinced that as much as he had little use for the Germans, at least their commanders seemed to be men of culture and good taste.

THE RETURN OF SARAH TO PARIS AND A SURPRISE— FALL, 1940

That fall, when Sarah Rubenstein finally returned to Paris to resume her position as a teacher of ballet at the *lycée,* their romance continued as well as could be expected under the circumstances, and they took up their usual routines. But just as their life together began to proceed more or less as it had before, the Germans published a document, the "First Ordinance," which called for the city-wide registration of Jews. Ostensibly, this was for the sake of a census of Jews, the term defined by "all who belong or used to belong to the Jewish religion, or who have more than two grand-parents who are Jewish."

Jewish shopkeepers were instructed to put signs in their win-dows that said: "ENTREPRISE JUIVE," and all Jews were ordered to report to and register with the prefecture of police by the middle of the month.

All this struck the composer as the work of bureaucrats, and he truly felt Sarah's humiliation at having to submit to that process. Yet for all that, their own love seemed hardly affected. Certainly he had not expected to come back to the Grand Hôtel one evening to find in his mailbox a notice from the prefecture of police inquir-ing why he, M. Israel Levis, had not yet registered as a Jew.

Had Cuba not officially declared war on Germany in 1940, then Levis might have been able to prevail upon the government of Fulgencio Batista to afford him some diplomatic protection. Had he not been publicly quoted in papers like *Le Monde* that he had been a supporter of the Loyalist causes during the Spanish Civil War then the Spanish embassy might have intervened more ener-getically on his behalf. An attaché at the Spanish embassy, Señor Ramos, recognizing him as a famed composer and fond of his music, promised to help Levis to Spain, but this Spaniard moved slowly and nothing came of it.

"The Germans do as they please," Levis had been told.

Had he not been asked to leave his Cuban passport "for reasons of inspection" with the prefecture of police, then he might have left the country—but not without Sarah. So disturbed was Levis by the situation that he retained a lawyer to state his case before the offi-cials of the *police aux questions juives,* his claim being that "he was not nor had ever been a Jew, nor a professor of that faith."

He had hoped that a legal distinction, exempting him from the mounting restrictions imposed upon the Jews in the past months— the observance of a curfew that would not permit him to leave his hotel after eight at night, a ban from going to many public places by day—might allow him to help Sarah, Paulette and Georges, should the necessity arise.

At the hearing, a German lawyer, in looking over his papers, had smiled and said to him: "Surely with a name like Israel Levis, you cannot deny that you are a Jew?"

"But I am a Cuban, a citizen of Cuba, and a Catholic. I wear the cross. And I have attended Sunday Mass for years without fail."

"And you have received the Host?"

"Upon occasion." Then: "I have written to the Catholic League of Habana . . . to verify my claims."

The same lawyer then asked him: "Are you circumcised?"

It happened that with his birth his father, Doctor Leocadio Levis, had thought such a minor operation a preventative against the possibility of cradle-borne infections.

"Yes," the composer admitted.

"Then surely that in itself is a proof, isn't it?"

"My father was a doctor who took it upon himself, for rea-sons of health."

The police were amused—how could any man with a name like Israel Levis be anything but a Jew, no matter what his protests?

"Really, now," the lawyer had said to him. "You have wasted enough of our time, Monsieur Levis."

As he was issued a Jewish identity card, Levis became acutely aware of how deadly serious these men were about such designa-tions. He had felt offended at first: Had he ever, in his life, been particularly aware of the Jews who'd lived in Habana, mainly cloth sellers and tailors? Had he ever thought of the composer Jorge Ankermann, in whose own home he met his dearest of friends, Manny Cortez, as anything other than a Cuban? And what were the synagogues of that city, three in all, to him other than evi-dences that the citizens of Cuba came from many cultures? Who were these men to harass him, or anyone else for simply *being?* And what if he were a Jew? Whose business was it, anyway?

Suddenly his thousands of hours of prayer as a Catholic seemed to mean very little. How could they pass judgment on him, a man who had spent countless days in creative endeavors, bring-ing good rather than bad into the world, a man who had lived his life quietly, who enjoyed his drinks and meals, and who once upon a time wrote a most famous tune while eating the croquettes of a bar in Habana? Who were these men, with their shining leather holsters, high jackboots and airs of superiority, to intervene in any-one's life, let alone that of a Catholic Cuban who happened to be living in Paris?

"Hatred" was not a word Levis would have used in reference to anyone, but he found himself brimming with that negative emo-tion in their presence.

I wished to God that He show His hand, but, of course, that did not happen.

Life was funny: shortly before noon, he entered that room on the rue de Téhéran as a Cuban Catholic, and left it an hour later as a "foreign Jew" living in Paris.

Of course, these were not things that he cared to remember. The composer, long since taking on a certain detachment from those events that were the prelude to the newer Levis—the sometimes foul-mooded and quite sad older gentleman—moving ever slowly through the rooms of his house on Olivares, those years later in 1947, and wondering, "What is the point of this continuing exis-tence?" He often passed his time in the garden, snapping orders at his maid, awaiting the return of Antonio from his outings in the city, or to see his nephew, whom he loved very much. And there was Rita Valladares—due to come home from her tours in a week or so, Levis spending so much time before the mirror appraising the face that had aged so, and wondering if he would really be happy to see her again, for in a way, he was afraid that she would be repelled by the disillusionments in his soul, for were not Cubans, even elderly Cubans, supposed to be content? To look upon the world without music in his heart so deeply troubled him that sometimes he just rested on a cot, closed his eyes and began to disenchantedly dream.

PARIS, 1940–1941

Officially considered a Jew, Levis resigned himself to the penalties of that designation. Though he could not roam the city as he used to at night, nor perform in clubs—in any event, he had long since disbanded his orchestra—he always made arrangements to see Sarah on certain afternoons, their lovemaking frantic, care-less, for he would have been delighted, at this point, if she were to have a child.

Though he took solace in his routines, he often felt himself a prisoner in that posh hotel, comfortable, but a prisoner all the same, especially at night. He wrote letters to Cuba, asking for assistance in the clarification of his identity, but received none in return; who could say if his mail was being intercepted?

The last letter he received in late 1940 had been from Rita Valladares, in Habana, with news that she was planning to divorce Murillo, that she did not have plans of returning to Europe while the war was going on—and certainly not Paris.

"Why are you staying there, mi querido?" *she had asked.*

Within the first six months of the German occupation, so many of his Cuban friends had left the city, for the neutrality of Spain or to go back to Cuba, that he began to feel largely alone. Among his other non-Cuban acquaintances and friends, he found that few continued to regard him with the same openness as before, as if consorting with a Jew would bring about the wrath of the authorities—a second round of discrimination, such as he had known during the later years in Machado's Habana. ("Really, my friend, you must surely know that all this business about an Aryan race is nonsense. Surely you cannot believe that these people are sane, or that they will be here for long," he would say.) Worse still was that the hotel management had cut off the tele-phone lines in his suite, as per an official ordinance, so that Levis had to depend upon the telephone booths in the lobby to make any calls, but even then, a German soldier was soon posted nearby to prevent any Jews from using the hotel's public tele-phones.

He could, in any event, continue with the work of *Germinal,* the manuscript growing in size. And he had started to compose a ballet on *Apollo and Daphne,* partly because of a dream.

(*In the countryside of Cuba, circa 1902, outside the city of Holguín, I had witnessed, during a journey with my father, the phenomenon of a woman turning into an acacia tree.*)

He worked by his piano, smoked and drank. With a small Spanish-English dictionary in hand, he listened to the BBC World Service broadcasts on the radio.

1942: THE YELLOW STAR

With the city emptied of its Cubans, Levis now lived with an even greater isolation. While many of his fellow guests at the Grand Hôtel, longtime residents and transients alike, had been courteous, the presence of the Germans there left him continually on edge: they were serene surely, self-confident, but just riding an elevator with one of them was often an ordeal; they looked one over, head to toe, and did not look into one's eyes with kindness, but as if scrutinizing one's thoughts.

More than a year and a half had passed since the occupation of Paris began and then came the time when a new ordinance, the eighth, was announced, and Jews were required to wear a yellow cloth star on their clothes: *Had that been the sign once seen in the sky in a dream, years before?* In those days, he carried a Wauters and Sons cloth Jewish star on which had been stitched the word JUIF, which he had bought in a special consignment shop and could be pinned to his coat or jacket lapel. He would not put it on until he'd left the hotel, otherwise keeping this cloth symbol neatly folded in his pocket. At first it had not bothered him. On the streets of Paris many people who were not Jewish, mainly young students, had taken to wearing the yellow star as a kind of pro-test; but after a time, though he was not a Jew, he could not help but to notice the derision in certain Parisian eyes—expression of mockery, or disdain, of superiority.

On the day before Sarah's thirty-second birthday, in mid-May of 1942, Levis had been standing before an antiques shop's win-dow, not far from the Champs-Elysées, his kindly eyes caught by an emerald necklace. And although the price seemed quite high, he had not at all hesitated about it, for he had been habitually gen-erous to her, helping her with money and always buying her gifts—such acts endemic among those practitioners of what might or might not have been an "arrangement" in the eyes of the world. But when he stepped inside, making an inquiry about that lovely green-gemmed necklace in the window, the female shopkeeper seemed to bristle at his presence and curtly pointed out a sign that said: NO JEWS IN THESE PREMISES ALLOWED.

He had found it funny and had nearly explained—*But I am not what you think I am*—when he had decided upon another tact.

"Madame," he said most politely. "I can put this piece of cloth in my pocket if it will make you feel better."

Unamused by his words, she had told him, with a look of absolute condemnation, "Jews do not deserve such beautiful things." Then: "You will please leave, *Monsieur,* or I will call the police."

He stood there in that shop for a few moments, stunned both by the absurdity of her stance and the way his spirits had been brought so low. Then, though not one given over to such language, he told her: "Madame, may you keep your necklace and burn in hell."

And she had shouted after him as he left: "*Burn?* I am not the one who will be burning in hell!"

Such incidents made me weary-hearted. I had hoped, over my lifetime, that music and the noble motivations of the artist would shut out the bad of the world. What was it that I once told Manny Cortez, years before, as we were sitting in the Campana Bar: "You and I have had the very good fortunes of finding ourselves in artistic professions. Let's toast to music and poetry!" And he had raised his glass and added: "And to hell with those who don't love what we do!"

No matter where he went, to bars or cafés, clubs or theaters, he adopted the attitude that few were to be trusted, for even among the French there were many persons sympathetically disposed to Hitler's plans for a "greater unified Europe" under the leadership of the reich.

He could speak to no one about his concerns, not even his favorite waiters at the Club Eve where he had been known for his robust appetite and large tips, for now even they seemed to regard him with suspicion.

Aside from Sarah, he had no one in Paris to confide in.

Like so many others, he had bided his time, waiting for the situation to pass. He had attended meetings at the Theosophical Society and visited spiritualists—a diversion that gave him, and

Sarah, a certain feeling of normalcy, each taking solace in séances and in the other worlds that, in those days, seemed preferable to their own. He could not go to Mass wearing the star; he was turned away. He took walks with her, drank his wine and brandy, ate good meals, but only in "designated" restaurants. Museums were forbidden, and because of the curfew, they often spent their evenings together in her flat.

It was on those evenings, resting by her side, that he began to feel as if he had entered into the midst of a very bad dream, for Sarah, in her Jewishness, had begun to offend him—as if she were in some way responsible for his circumstances. He never whispered a word of this to her, keeping it all within himself, but she would know that things were not well, for he would maintain great periods of silence and had begun to lose interest in physical love, the moods quickly passing nonetheless, and the composer reclaiming his affable manner, even when he had begun to regret his continued life in Paris.

Throughout this time, there was such a semblance of normalcy in that city for someone like Levis, ever dreaming, to hope for a good outcome. They still went to parties and dinners, in private homes, and though much of the bohemian population in that city had wisely departed for other parts—Portugal, England, Spain and Switzerland—there were enough artists and composers about (Picasso among them, some of them Jews) to further complete the illusion that art and artistry would prevail over all. The French cinema still produced films, and one could find a theater showing the occasional Chaplin, or Laurel and Hardy short to lighten the heart. And the sidewalk cafés were jammed with Parisians, and with the many, many Germans who had come to regard Paris, that

jewel of Hitler's conquest, as a great resort city, a delightful vacation spot to visit. Hounds still lifted their hind legs to baptize the
curbs, musicians still performed on the streets. People got married,
babies were born and Christened—life, for most Parisians, went
on, as before.

THE FINISHED LIBRETTO OF *GERMINAL*, JULY 1942

Levis himself had washed his hands of the politics around him,
leaving that for the young, the impassioned. From time to time
he had been aware that both Sarah and Georges seemed overly
resentful of the Germans—how could they not, with so many stories about what the Germans had been doing to the Jews in Poland
and in Germany. Sometimes when he turned up at Sarah's flat, he
felt that there was something quite private and hidden going on
between Georges and his sister. He would approach Sarah's door,
with a box of chocolates or a bouquet of flowers in hand, to find
that when he'd knocked he'd have to wait; there would be a bustle
of activity within. Inside there would be another young man in
their company, boxes filled with pamphlets, stacked in a corner. He
never asked about them; it was accepted that he knew.

Instead, he came in and played with Paulette and always asked
Georges about the progress of *Germinal,* the subject that, in those
days, formed the context of their friendship.

"It's coming along."

"Well, I am not going to ask you questions about what you're
otherwise doing with yourself these days, Georges. But whatever
it is, please be careful."

In time the composer's unstated suspicions that Georges was

participating in an underground organization was, in fact, verified by Sarah when, on another day, she told Levis: "My dear brother, Georges, is the editor of a resistance newsletter—it just has war news, but it's against the law, as you know, and I am half-frightened to death that he sometimes brings them here to keep."

Whatever the young man was up to, he maintained a regular routine of delivering installments of *Germinal* to Levis, leaving portions of his manuscript in Sarah's flat or dropping them off at the front desk of the Grand Hôtel. Now and then they met, every few weeks, as Levis had done with Manny Cortez in Cuba, and while Georges seemed indifferent to the dangers of his youthful activities, Levis worried that so "beautiful" a young man might have overstepped the bounds of prudent self-preservation, for the Germans were everywhere and had their informers.

Inevitably, Georges dropped out of sight, and Levis assumed that it was the end of their collaboration. Months went by when he did not see Georges at all. But then, every so often, Sarah would have a bit of new manuscript that Georges had left with her for Levis, so that gradually, over the course of five months, the libretto, if not the music, approached completion. He saw Georges only once again in late June of 1942. Having finished the libretto, Georges, then hiding out, could not resist the pleasure of handing the remaining pages to Levis himself.

Sarah had conveyed their meeting place—along the flowery paths of the Bois de Boulogne.

"You see, I've finished this work, as I promised you, Maestro," he had said, smiling. Proud of keeping his word, the young man had added, ever so cheerfully: "I hope you like it. Etienne finally triumphs!" Then: "I will not be around much from now on . . . I've joined the resistance."

"My God, you are joking, yes?"

"Not at all."

Levis should have known, however. There was something tremendously familiar in his eyes—conviction—such as he had seen with Manny Cortez, back in the days of Machado, a thou-sand years before.

But what could he say?

The composer told him, "Well, thank you, my friend. I will fin-ish this music, and one day, we will attend the premiere of *Germinal* together."

Then they had parted, with great embraces, Georges heading back into his world of youth and hope, and Levis to his hotel.

KING KONG

He would also remember the year of 1942 for its moments of promise and despair. For whatever his reasons, Knochen, upon Levis's request, had decided to allow the composer certain liber-ties, mainly to perform around the city, principally at German functions. At half of these events the general was present and ever admiring of the composer's talents as a pianist. He never said a word to Levis but sometimes gave him a nod of approving recogni-tion. This in itself seemed to afford Levis a certain protection and standing among the Nazis, and he found that he could keep his job as an occasional conductor of the Symphonic Wing of the Paris Opera.

On those nights, as he would face the audience in a crowded gilt-ceilinged hall filled with officers and their families, members of Paris society and officials of the Vichy government, he had come to feel like the massive, befuddled creature he had once seen in an American film, *King Kong.* With baton in hand, in the midst of a Beethoven symphony, he wished he could take on the dimensions of that creature and tear through the hall, tossing the Germans from their seats, charge out into the streets and head instantly over to the Gestapo headquarters on the avenue Foch, or to the prefecture of police, opposite the Hôtel-Dieu, to pull down their walls. In his fantasies, he would drive the Germans out from that city, out from his life, and from the world itself. Despite the fact that he was now fifty-two years old, such childish thoughts did, indeed, pass through his mind, for what had been taking place in Paris was so contrary to his civilized soul that he began to depend on fantasy as a source of relief, or delusion.

By mid-1942, the Germans had begun to round up the Jews, for the purposes of documentation and "re-Aryanization." At first, large groups of Jewish Parisians were invited to present themselves at police stations for the sake of verifying their identities, only to vanish thereafter. And then the police and German gendarmes began to cordon off certain districts, like the eleventh and twelfth arrondissements, where mostly Jews lived. Residences were raided; people were taken away. Originally their lists only included those in certain professions—doctors, academics, scientists, writers and lawyers—but soon they began hauling everyone off to prisons and detention camps.

Levis had gone to great lengths to protect Sarita and her daughter. Though powerless as a "Jew" himself, he had resorted to bribing certain middle-level officials at the prefecture of police. At first *El Maestro* Levis made it a regular practice to withdraw money from the bank, but as his funds began to dwindle, every-thing of value that he'd owned went to bribes—certain precious rings, watches, several antique clocks for which he'd acquired a taste and spent large amounts to buy; these, brought him time. He had another plan, which was to apply for a certificate of exemp-tion from the authorities, on the grounds that he was not a threat to the occupation, but a cultural asset to the life of Paris. Cer-tainly that he had made the acquaintance of Knochen might be of help. He had heard from his attorney that this exemption would be honored, and afford protection to his "family"—so he had planned, in those days, to marry Sarah Rubenstein.

THINGS DID NOT WORK OUT LIKE THE MELODY OF A SONG

It should be noted that their last session of love took place just after Christmas 1942 and that this act of intimate connection was slow and restrained and languorous, for Sarah Rubenstein had made her own plans that had nothing to do with marriage or certificates of exemption, for she did not believe that it would change anything.

"You understand that I am thinking of my daughter and my parents," she told him one day. "My brother, Georges, has arranged that we go into hiding, and then, through a network, we can leave the country, to Spain." Then: "And you must come with us, dear Israel."

He would remember experiencing a sense of relief at the

idea—for he mainly cared about her safety. But there was something about defying the authorities, even the Germans, that disturbed his sense of propriety. And yet, he had tired of Paris, tired
of wearing a Jewish star, and longed for a return to Cuba. Even
as she had said that, there was a slight brightening of sunlight in
her bedroom, *as if everything would get better*, and though he had his
doubts as to the certainty of their future, Levis told Sarah, "Then
I will go with you."

A few days before they were to leave Paris, Levis packed away
certain of his most prized possessions—manuscript papers, letters
and some photographs—and these he left in the keeping of that
sympathetic but ineffective Spanish attaché, Señor Ramos, who
had met him at his hotel. Other bits of personal belongings he
stored with friends, mainly musicians who had remained, playing in
the clubs. When the day came, he had chosen to wear only the
clothes on his back, as a suitcase would make him conspicuous.

In the light of afternoon, he left the Grand Hôtel with a carnation that he'd picked off a counter display stuck in his lapel, and
soon found himself mingling with crowds on the boulevard. He
took a tram to Sarita's apartment building. The plan was that they
remain there until nightfall, and then, walking along the alleys and
cross streets of the city, make their way to the Porte de Versailles,
where they would catch a bus to a safehouse in the suburb of
Clamart. There they would meet with members of the underground—presumably Georges would be among them—who would
lead them to safety and refuge.

But when Levis stood before her door, knocking, he heard
no answer. Twice over the past few months Jews had been
rounded up and taken away from that district, and yet Sarah,

through his intercession, he believed, had been protected. He had offered bribes, and prayed, had sat before his piano, in communion with the deity, whom he was sure knew his very thoughts. He had a key to her flat and let himself in, finding the rooms much as they had always been, down to the dolls that her little daughter, Paulette, had loved playing with, scattered mess- ily around the floor of her bedroom. He made certain specula- tions about why she was not there. The first—and the one he'd most hoped for—was that there had been a sudden change of plans, which Sarita had no time to disclose to him. But then it occurred to him that she might have been arrested while walk- ing on the street with her daughter. He must have sat on her bed for a half hour, the bed on which they had often made love, without moving, fearing nothing for himself, but lamenting the price of emotional attachments.

So he had been a *soltero,* a "bachelor," living with his mother for many years in Cuba, and though he had never had what one would describe as an exciting life, he had his little pleasures. How was it he asked himself, his stomach in knots, that he was now worrying for the safety and well-being of another?

A MINOR KEY AND THE MONTHS PASSED

Outwardly, he remained the same. Still physically huge and imposing, a little sad of expression, he had begun to feel the pres- sures of that restricted life. Hearing nothing from Sarita, he spent day after day walking the streets of Paris with his eyes open, not just because he lived with the feeling that he was being watched, but because he anticipated that any moment someone would stop to contact him. He reasoned that if Georges and Sarah were at liberty, they would let him somehow learn of their whereabouts.

This did not happen, and he began to wonder if she had ever loved him at all.

That was Levis at this point in his life—disappointed and selfish enough to take the tragic circumstances that were overwhelming many in the world, personally.

THE MAIL

Each day he inquired at the hotel desk for mail. He had sent a letter to Sarah's parents in the south, receiving nothing in return. He had written letters to Cuba. It seemed that he had not received a shred of mail in nearly a year.

His inquiries about Sarah with the same officials of the prefecture who had been so cooperative when it came to accepting his bribes fell upon incredulous ears. Someone told him: "She was probably sent away, and if you don't mind your own business, you will be, too."

Nevertheless, he felt no personal threat—he had, through bribes, received his card of exemption, which was generally issued to members of an organization of Jews who had proved useful to the Germans, the UGIF (*Union générale des israélites de France*). This was his salvation, he thought, and he carried it everywhere with him.

HIS DRINKING

Among his problems was the excessive consumption of alcohol, and every time he drank he prayed to God, his simple faith so

agitated by brandy that he sometimes wept, feeling for the suffering in the world. (As if that would bring about anything good.) He
thought again and again about the sweetness of his childhood, and
how he had once gone into the churches of Habana, dressed like a
proper young gentleman, that he had loved working the foot ped-
als of the organ, with its great and tremulous vibrations, as he
played Bach for the congregation. His mother's face, lowered in
the devotion of prayer, came back to him; his father, Doctor
Leocadio Levis, he could swear had sometimes entered that room
in the Grand Hôtel, his father's serene, no-nonsense presence reg-
istering in the brilliance of the midday light.

Ay, and how I missed Manny Cortez, whose strength I so needed.

Composing in his hotel room—for what else did he have to
do?—he moved into realms of utter sadness. One would not have
identified the music he was then writing with the cheerful passages of "Rosas."

He hated disturbances; someone rapping on his door—a great
interruption. Even if he had not been sitting before the piano, he
would often call out: "I'm at work, leave me alone!" Sometimes he
found himself laughing—"Oh to think that not so long ago I had been
quite happy with my little evenings out in Habana, and look at me
now. . . ." Occasionally he would make note of the date—"May 7,
1943," or "June 2, 1943"—the idea that so much time had effortlessly passed, falling through the recesses of his thoughts, ever so
cavernous, that alcohol had induced in him.

Sometimes he did not leave his suite for days.

The hotel management had become aware of the large quantities of brandy that he'd ordered up from time to time, and although he managed to pay the brunt of his bills, for he was still

occasionally earning money in Paris, he had started to accrue quite a large balance. As a longtime resident, he was treated with fairness, reasonably well, but when he fell off on his payments, he began to receive nicely scripted notes, on very good stationery, from the manager suggesting that he might move into a more modest room until he could catch up with his debts.

This he ignored, like so many other things.

By then he found solace in playing the music of his favorite Cuban composers—Cervantes and Caturla among them—and anyone passing by his suite might hear his piano. On good days, he would play for hours, sipping brandy until the light of Opera Square became the light of heaven and he began to feel a transparency of being, nearly weightless, a pure soul glorying in his music.

Of course, he continued to compose the score of *Germinal,* which was growing to an impractical but timedissolving length.

He drank because he dreaded the solitude and confinement of his evenings. And he dreaded those nights when he would head off to one embassy or the other to perform for the Germans. Usually the embassy staff would send a car to pick him up, treating him courteously, but as soon as he walked into those halls, a certain illness of mind, soul and body came over him. By and by, Levis began to arrive at these engagements drunk, and his performances suffered, the composer fumbling notes, skipping over entire passages of the pieces by Bach and Mozart and Debussy that he had once known well.

On one such evening, at a reception for Marshal Pétain himself, he was stopped in midprogram and escorted away from the piano. He could not remember the specifics, only that he found it quite funny, being rushed out of the hall, lumbrous and wobbly, he laughed, as if he were immune to the troubles of this world.

In those days, I was oblivious, placidly so, to certain facts: that the Germans were, in fact, beginning to lose the war; that the Germans in Paris in wanting to please their masters in Berlin had stepped up their deportations to the camps.

THEN IT HAPPENED, MAY 1943

It was about seven in the evening, on a late spring day in 1943, when someone knocked on his door. He was in the midst of an instrumental passage from *Germinal* in the key of B minor, and though he had stood before the door vehement, "I am at work, please come back later," the visitor knocked again, more insis-tently, a voice firmly announcing, "Open, this is an official matter." He momentarily found himself standing before two gentlemen, members of the Gestapo, in their long black leather coats. Though he had no choice but to let them in, Levis, his card of exemption close at hand, had felt no fear. The card made no difference to these officers, who informed the composer that he was going to be "detained" for reasons of protection of the state against "Jewish terrorists and their sympathizers."

By then, Levis had resigned himself to the unforeseen future that lay before him. He put on his jacket, put out a cigar and swigged the remaining brandy in a glass—his salvation in those days. He was treated almost cordially. Driven in a black sedan to the prefecture, he was questioned about the whereabouts of "Georges and Sarah Rubenstein," who were known to the police as members of the underground. That Sarah was still alive was good news, but that he knew nothing of their whereabouts did not please his interrogators. After some hours, during which he often repeated, "As a citizen of Cuba, I demand my rights," he was locked in a cell for the night and taken from there in the morning to the train station of Bobigny.

HIS LIFE CHANGED

At the station, there was much activity. An enormous crowd of perhaps a thousand Parisians, many of them with suitcases in hand, were being escorted by armed guards into railroad cars. There he happened to recognize in the crowd a certain monsieur, a fellow adherent of the Theosophical Society, a Jacques Levinstein, a painter and a man of wealth, whose large house in the outskirts of Paris, along the rue de Versailles, had, as with so many of those individuals who believed in the emanations of things, been full to the brim with paintings, from Matisse to Picasso, statuary, Chinese porcelains, iconic figures, plaques and a vast collection of antiqui-ties, from which he must have hated to part. He looked the worse for wear, and the very fact that Levinstein had been apprehended at all surprised Levis, because he remembered thinking that in the absolute clutter and disorder of his lodgings, one could well have hidden away forever inside one of its many rooms. Whatever had happened, he, too, had been arrested and now stood among the crowd, in a black bowler, and fine three-piece suit, like a figure out of a Magritte painting, looking rather bewildered, a small suitcase in hand.

Levis, smiling in his courtly manner, had nodded, as if to say, "This, too, will pass."

THE BEAUTIFUL COUNTRYSIDE

And for a time he had the illusion that he was, at the very least, being treated preferentially. Maybe he dreamed this, but while the others were being shoved, pushed, jostled and forcibly jammed en masse into the carriages, he was singled out and escorted to a first-class coach, at the front of the train, a plush seated carriage with polished bronze railings, woven carpets, a bar whose glasses would tinkle with the motion of the locomotive engine. In fact, the velvet-covered seats were so comfortable that he nearly dozed and half-expected a train porter to come through with champagne and caviar. He was most surprised, however, when none other than the stately Knochen himself, and two orderlies, joined him in that car.

Instantly he was told: "Rise in the presence of the *Kommandant!*"

He did so, but Knochen told Levis in Spanish, "You may remain as you were." Then: "Have you been told where you are going?"

"No, sir."

"Usually men in your position are deported to either Auschwitz, Bergen-Belsen or Neuengamme—do you know of these places?"

"No."

"It does not matter, I have arranged that you will be transported to the Weimar Station, to a place near Ettersberg. It's quite lovely there. *Un lugar muy maravilloso.*"

Uncertain as to whether he should thank the general or not, Levis did not say a word. Then Knochen told him: "It's not something that I do for everyone—but I have much enjoyed your musicianship."

And just like that, the general gave a curt nod to his orderlies, and they left the carriage as abruptly as they had come in. Then a whistle blew and the train lurched forward. Alone in the coach, the composer began to believe that perhaps, because of his gifts, he was being taken away to concertize. As the hours passed, he watched the countryside, so lovely that from a purely visual perspective, the war did not seem to exist. He saw great fields of wheat and vineyards, haystacks, and oxen and cows lolling, and felt such an unexpected feeling of appreciation for the beauty of this world that he nearly wept, thinking with great nostalgia about so many things: the sun, the stars at night, the murmuring ocean, hounds, ice cream, a woman's succulent breast, chocolate, the expression on a baby's innocent face, and music—the world brimming with music. He fell into such a reverie that he forgot the immediate danger of his situation, wished the train would stop so that he could get out and wander in a field, among the flowers and butterflies. He took a small measure of comfort by the way the Germans had treated him—certainly everything would be cleared up—and yet it was all an illusion: Halfway along to his destination, in the north of France, the train stopped—and an officer and two soldiers entered the car and ordered him out of his seat, at gunpoint. A troop of German officers then swarmed into the first-class compartment, and Levis was forced into another car—a freight car—where, moments later, he found himself in quite a different situation.

.   .   .

So, he had been mistakenly taken as a Jew, mistakenly arrested and put on a train, mistakenly transferred from a first-class car into another, lightless car, whose air was nearly unbreathable, and where he huddled with fifty other men, women and children, similarly and frightfully bewildered as himself. He reached his destination two days later, and first saw light again at the Weimar Station, in Germany, at noon. Out on the platform, the composer had a few moments to stretch, to luxuriate in the crisp and pure Alpine air, as he, in his now filthy and soiled clothes, was rushed along with the throng and transferred to another train.

Not long after, he arrived at the station of Ettersberg, a medieval town whose surrounding countryside of hills and pine and beech forests was quite beautiful. It had once played host to the likes of Schiller and Goethe—a place of such Alpine loveliness that it had been the source of much poetic inspiration. In its blueness of sky and lush greenery it was much like what the artist Maxfield Parrish captured in his famous prints, a place that seemed the setting of Nordic myth, as far away as the moon from what Levis had once known in Habana. Then, shoved into the back of a truck with many others, he was driven to the entranceway of a grand complex, set in the midst of a beech forest, the rolling slopes of the Ettersberg in the distance. He joined a queue and entered a main gate, its inscription extolling: ARBEIT MACHT FREI ("WORK WILL SET YOU FREE").

If he were a tourist he might have gone into town to visit Goethe's house, or up to the lodge of Ettersberg, where holiday travelers often stayed, sipping whiskey or a snifter of warmed brandy by the fireplace, the setting so serene. Or if he were in Habana he might head off to see Rita Valladares in her house on Industria, or go strolling along the Malecón, and watch the young couples walking hand in hand, the pleasure of feeling the sea mist on his face ever so strong. In those moments, he would have given anything to have wandered into some back alley in Habana, circa 1907, where some rowdy and life-loving *rumberos* had gathered to play their trumpets and drums and dance the evening away. Or to rest back in bed in Paris, to look up at Sarah Rubenstein's face, as she, having mounted him, fell into pieces. Or to sit once again before his piano and play a simple chord.

But, as things stood, he seemed to have indeed entered that place known as Buchenwald, a munitions complex that was not a "death camp," but a place in whose harsh conditions and punitive regimens many perished, anyway. And for the next fourteen months, the maestro did not believe the things he saw, nor the sounds he heard.

THE

LOVELINESS

OF A DREAM

(HABANA, 1947–1953)

CANE IN HAND, WITH
Antonio by his side, Israel Levis was
walking along a street in old Habana, near
the Hotel Regina, on a Saturday afternoon,
when he happened upon a café where a
trio of black musicians were serenading the
tourists as they sat by tables in the open
air, these musicians strumming guitars and
performing with splendid harmonies,
"Rosas Puras." Dressed in white from head
to toe, frail and unassuming, Levis watched
them as they played, their amulets and crucifixes that dangled on golden chains on
their chests awash in light, these musicians, seemingly beyond the troubles of
this world. And as they entertained and
flirted with the tourists—a coterie of
middle-aged women and their husbands,
and younger honeymooning couples sipping daiquiris and rum-spiked iced teas

(and presumably being amorously aroused by the romantic en-chantments of that city)—neither musicians nor their audience were aware that the song's elderly seeming composer (but he was only fifty-seven!), the thin, white-haired fellow with the kindly myopic eyes and wire-rim glasses, was standing under the shade of an awning not ten paces away from them, taking in their perfor-mances with both affection (for that ancient art of song and music) and revulsion over those feelings that sometimes came over him whenever he heard it, no matter how wonderfully performed.

Nor did they know that on some days, when he would think about the events of the past twenty years of his life, the song barely made any inroads on the course of his thoughts—and yet that on other days, when he found himself living in a Godless uni-verse, that very same melody brought the saddest thoughts. Then he would simply seem to be staring off into a distance, as in this moment, even as the Habana street bustled all around him. And Antonio, who by now had begun to know Levis well, shook him, asking, "Don Israel, where are you going?"

He had crossed over to some other place on a bridge of sung words, angelic voices intoning a bewitching melody. . . .

> *Si deseas amor, ven aquí*
> *Tengo rosas puras pa' ti!*
> *No importa si estás cansado de la vida*
> *Si compras estas rosas puras de amor*
> *Te casarás. . . ."*

("If you're craving love, come over here
I have some pretty roses for you

Doesn't matter if you're tired of life
Once you buy these roses of love
You'll soon get married. . . .")

And suddenly it was another Saturday and he is in that place he'd rather forget. He is being escorted out of his barracks to a warehouse, the "Canada," where he is fitted with a formal suit that had been taken from some poor, unfortunate man. He is given a pair of reasonably good shoes and stockings, a pomade for his hair, which has grown back, and though he is well-groomed, given his circumstances, he wishes he could clip, rather than chew down on, his nails. At dusk he is driven out from the camp on the winding roads toward the Ettersberg Inn, which is on a hill overlooking a scenic valley. It is where the Germans host their parties, and he is led in through a kitchen, a battery of cooks preparing the evening's elaborate meal, the aromas of roasting chicken and lamb chops and buttery potatoes, heavy with fat, filling him with nausea. And because he seems unsteady, nearly fainting, he is given a cup of milk and some bread with a piece of sausage on it, then a shot of brandy so that he might have sufficient strength to later perform on the piano. The Germans attend to their reception, with champagne glasses and snifters of brandy in hand, and, later, as he plays, he cannot believe that he is their lounge pianist, and though they are in the same room, with a roaring fireplace and a brilliant chandelier, all of that falls away, and he is on the stage of the Teátro Martí in Habana, circa 1922, where his friends and family and fellow composers and musicians sit in the audience, listening to his little recital with appreciation and good wishes. Then, he thinks about how wondrous it would be to go off at a late hour of the night with these friends for a meal in a harborside café, Habana Bay aglow with the shale light of the moon, a carpet of diamonds and turquoise blossoms stretching from the earth to the sky over the rippling waters. And the image of the moon, risen in the sky, makes him think tenderly about the Communion Host, as it is being raised before the altar. Bach comes to him...the music of Salas—and yet some rather drunk commander disrupts his thoughts—

Everyone knows that the Germans are losing the war, the camp is rife with fear that they will start shooting all the detainees dead, to eliminate their witnesses, but this commander makes a toast, and alludes to their pianist, a "very famous fellow," but refers to him not by his real name, for the Jewishness of "Israel Levis" would seem repulsive to his guests, and instead he calls him "Monsieur Sebastiano of Paris"—and the composer laughs, for it is only a name, and wonders if "only a name" can account for all the suffering that he has seen.

But he does not complain: afterward one of the waiters always slips him a cloth napkin filled with a few ounces of food scraps, and what he does not eat, he takes back with him to his barracks and wishes that he had the power of Jesus to multiply this fare, but he is thanked, anyway, by his emaciated and skeleton-ribbed fellow prisoners, among whom he enjoys a prestige. Some of them are brilliant philosophers and some of them are hoodlums, and it makes him laugh to think that somewhere, over the past fifteen years, they must have heard his most famous tune at least once, if not many times. . . .

"*Rosas Puras*" accompanies him everywhere he goes, like the background music of a film. It plays on a piano, or with a full orchestra. Sometimes, as he looks up at the sky, Fred Astaire comes bounding down a staircase, in top hat and tails, dancing a marvelous and highly stylized rumba to it, beautiful showgirls surround him, swooning and swaying their bodies, and sometimes in the midst of that distant dream which is memory he is watching Rita Valladares from the back stage of a theater—it's Habana or Paris—and she is singing that song better than anyone will ever sing it, and he thinks about how he had knocked the melody out for her, on the eve of her journey to New York, and how that sequence of arranged notes has landed him, by and by, in a place like Buchenwald. But God has spared him, his weekly outings to perform for the Nazis afford him just enough additional nutrition to make it to the next week, and the next after that. Even so, he just wishes he could get that song out of his head, along with the notion that the universe is an indif- ferent place, wishes he did not smell so much ash or see so much humiliation around him. . . . Then he thinks about Sarita Rubenstein and Paulette and Georges, who, like so many others, seem to have disappeared forever, and he is confounded by the apparent absence of God from that place, and tries to cheer himself by remembering the little homilies he had learned as a child: "Blessed are those who are persecuted for righteousness' sake." And: "Whoever will come after me, let him deny himself and take up the cross."

But he takes an even greater solace in his memory of music, recounting scores note by note from heart. Day in and day out he thinks about both Rita Valladares and Sarah Rubenstein, who somehow become interchangeable in his mind, he dreams of a concept that is so much a part of Cuban life—that music is good!— and he clings to that thought tenaciously throughout many of his days until that seems useless and he can barely feel anything at all.

The composer had recalled this while contemplating the performance of *"Rosas Puras"* by a trio of black musicians whose simple instrumentation and good singing he, in his way, found charming.

HABANA, 1947: THE BODY

With some early-morning stomach problems, he had lingered long in the bathroom attending to his necessities. Then he had stood under the shower until the sight of his own sagging naked-ness, his powdery white skin (the numbers he could not wash away), sickened him. So it was no wonder that he had sent his maid into hiding, for, in his worse moods, he would seem to explode at nothing; poor Octavia, quietly sweeping the tile floors or beating the dust out of an old carpet in the yard and humming, accused by the composer of making too much noise—"Why I can't even think in peace!" And even the evidences of Antonio Solar's presence in his house—a pair of two-toned shoes set out in front of his door, a half-filled pack of Lucky Strikes left on the dew-covered patio table—annoyed him, as if the young man were being disrespectful, or taking advantage of the composer's generosity.

"Imagine what his life would be like without me," he would think.

Of course, he was aware that such foul-moodedness was tied up with the discomforts of his advancing years—everything took so much more energy and time—and he could not stand the idea of being so easily fatigued, though he had to admit that neither the brandies he would consume in the morning nor the two or three cigars he would smoke by midday could not have helped. And there were other things, for when he made his way into his study and stood before his piano, the continued silence of those keys,

which he was loathe to touch, bore testament to what he per-
ceived as the evaporation of his talents—or was it symptomatic of
some kind of divine retribution, working bad thoughts into his
mind?

For in thinking of his recent past, he wondered what he had
done in his life to have to come to such a point, where the very
idea of writing yet a single passage of music seemed to invoke a
fear, as if sitting down to play the bass lines to a habanera with
his left hand while improvising a lilting melody with his right
would bring about a horrid consequence.

Hardest on the composer was the way that his body no longer
cooperated with him. It was with tremendous difficulty that he
raised himself out of a chair, a slackening of his muscles, pinching
to his nerves, a failing of strength defeating him. And during his
walks through the city, for his constitutionals, he found the heat
and traffic much more unbearable and fatiguing than what he had
remembered. Only while sitting in a church did rest seem to come
to him, the coolness and quietude of the nave a solace. Still, it had
been hard for Levis to get around; how was it that he, at so young
an age—for he was only fifty-seven—had become just like those
older gentlemen that he had once felt sorry for; how was it that
he found even undressing himself a chore?

*Such little difficulties always reminded me of how my father used to
go out into the interior patio in the mornings to perform the calisthenics
that I had found so amusing as a portly child, my father telling me: "If
you don't start doing this son, you'll regret it one day." It had been enough
for me to cart my bulk around for years—who had I ever harmed, in my
bodily indolence, except for myself?*

HIS LITTLE SECRETS

Another morning and the maestro was sitting in his back patio reading a newspaper and reflecting upon how he did not miss the bordellos (or, at least, that he, at his age, had been freed from the distractions of the flesh). His indifference to his own pleasures was something that he had become accustomed to. But even in his youth, his sexual release had been more of a distraction than a mis-sion in life (not at all like what Manny Cortez used to go through, the poor man, for even when he had a wife and kids back home, he suffered over the sight of every beautiful woman). Back in his early days in Habana, when there was often a line of men waiting their turn in the brothels, the composer almost always tended to shy away, unable to take his place alongside them, even when he, in his physicality, was, perhaps, someone to be envied. The sort of man who saw a crowd and went in the opposite direction, he had never cared for others to know his business. When it came to his sexual release, he was always careful about the setting. How was it that he, in his prissiness had considered the act of love a source of "animal shame," a phrase he recalled his father using in reference to Aristotle's appraisal of man's attitude toward the body's excretory functions; the various releases of the caudal region linked in his mind with the secretions of passion—somehow he had mixed these up—for that "animal shame" had never left him.

Perhaps, because of that, the men he saw in the brothels seemed like animals—bulls, wolves and tortoises, horses and asses—each waiting, hooves stomping, nostrils snorting, for his turn inside, such had been the makeup of their personalities. In the midst of such energies he had always preferred to take a walk, and wait until things calmed down, often until the early hours of the morning, when he could pursue the act more privately.... He would laugh now, knowing how, in certain circumstances one grows accustomed to anything. Where he had once felt annoyed at the inconvenience of nature's call—especially if he were composing—at least he had the amenities of a commode, or, at the very worse, an elephant-footed toilet, which one crouched over, as in certain bars in Habana.

Back in Buchenwald there had been a long, open and fetid trench latrine—the sight of even the most dignified men sick with dysentery emptying their guts in midstride so common an occurrence that after a time nobody cared who was watching, save for me....

That very humiliation was something that, to say the least, had led to his dismissal of the bodily urges. How could anyone think of a woman (or for that matter a man) in such circumstances? (And yet, he had seen his share of chronic masturbators, men standing off in the corner of a crowded barracks, trying to eke out a few moments of pleasure.) No wonder he had become even more careful about his grooming, spending so much time each morning, washing his hands, again and again, before stepping out into the world.

At least he had the solace of knowing that no human being, not even Jesus Christ, had been exempt from such necessities. Not Mozart, nor Beethoven, nor Bach. Every such thought leading him to a contemplation of the grave ... all men ending there, in a heap of bones and flesh, that over time, would resemble compost.

Why oh why God, do such thoughts come to me on so lovely a morning?

HIS MAJESTIC VIRILITY

He had always been dismissive of his sexual power. When he had first become aware of his own massiveness, as an adolescent, he had guarded that like the most secret of secrets, his holy apparatus, so "unspiritual," so "impure," that, for the life of him, he had only known shame and sin when, out of necessity, he hastily purged himself. What a pest his sexual desire had been while he would compose, especially in his twenties. With a life of its own, his member would swell up in his trousers, even as he simply leaned forward to make a correction of a song for a zarzuela. To facilitate the fleshly exercises of his youth, he had often relied upon a favorite sepia-toned "artistic" photograph, circa 1902, of a Cuban girl wearing only a headband of feathers and a beaded belt around her naked waist, bending over a seated sailor, his trousers pulled down to his knees. The young girl held his erect penis as, he supposed, she was about to take the sailor's appendage into her mouth, and yet the detail that most enchanted him was the roundness of her bottom, the strands of electrically charged pubic hair that peeked out from between her comely buttocks. Sometimes he sequestered himself in their bathroom, with its scent of the damp earth that flowed up through its plumbing, relieving that desire, three or four times in a single day, long ago.

Thank God for his discovery of the brothels, even if his copulations would send him to church to confess his fleshly sins. Thank God that he could rejoin life with a cleansed soul and walk alongside his mother, on their way to church, knowing well that if the world were to end in that moment, that he and his mother would rise up to join the throngs of the devoted and saintly.

"Mamá, what happens when we die?" he'd once asked his mother, as a little boy.

"Oh, you rise up one day in Heaven to join all the people who have ever loved you."

"And will there be pianos in Heaven?"

"Anything you want or need will be there, my son."

For years, during his childhood, he had believed in both the res-urrection of the body and of the world in which one had lived—the Habana of his upbringing to be re-created and awaiting him at the end of his life. Over time, he began to believe, as perhaps his father did, that if anything survived, it might be the soul, perhaps to roam the world, memories and affections intact. And for a time, he had allowed the Hinduesque theories of the theosophists to influence his views, the notion of one's soul coming back to inhabit another body enchanting Levis, for at the heart of those teachings was the prospect of survival (and with that the narcissism of identity). But by now, as the composer was sitting in his garden, he had amended his beliefs to the following: either there was nothing awaiting man (the certainty of paradise turned into a doubtful immortality), or, if "souls" existed, as he so wanted to believe, these were pure and identity-less emanations that would be joined to (for want of a bet-ter phrase) the divine light, without memory and context-free—spirit energies without names or nations, without bodies.

And that conclusion depressed him, for he felt a certain ran-cor that God's design of the world was such that both "good" and "bad" men, those innocents who had perished in the war and those who had killed them, would vanish, their souls intact, into the same abstraction into which every man and woman would anonymously pass.

And such thoughts would put him into an even more wistful frame of mind.

This, at about ten in the morning, Habana, 1947.

His nephew

Despite the late and more noble dalliances of his life with Sarah Rubenstein, he considered the book of his carnal curiosities closed, though the tawdriness that he had always much enjoyed in his life, spoke—whispered—a reminder that he had perhaps frittered away the gift of a majestic virility and, possibly, the opportunities for a true love.

But like music, sex and love were matters of the imagination, and the timidity and righteousness of his character had led him to such a state of indecision that he, as he often had thought, may as well have become a priest—he would have probably been better off.

Still, he would catch himself tottering along the brink of too many regrets—once that became a habit, a man was certainly doomed to sadness. Of course, he lamented the fact that he'd had no children (his seed—his "germinal"—wasted), though he found the company of his nephew, Victor Levis, an agreeable substitute. Busy with his medical studies, Victor would come over to see his uncle once or twice a week, and they would go off for lunch or on some other excursion. His nephew, an athletic sort, liked to go swimming at the Habana Yacht club, and when he brought his uncle along, the composer would sit, fully dressed, on a deck chair under the shade of an umbrella, watching his nephew, fine of body and of form, and as handsome as the actor Tyrone Power, swimming his laps, the composer's head turning, from time to time, when a particularly shapely woman walked by in a one- or two-piece bathing suit, or, as of old, quickly appraising the bronzed and well-muscled torsos of young men—what could he do, he was still alive, after all?

And it was very strange—for in one moment, it seemed that he had been in Hell, and the next, in a kind of heaven.

On those excursions, he treated his nephew with the respect and affection with which he had regarded his brother. They never spoke about the composer's experiences during the war, nor did he ever drift into sadness in his presence, for they mainly enjoyed the affable and secure trust of the blood bond. Sometimes he would lighten his nephew's heart with some recollection of his late father—"He was always so studious, like you, but, at the same time, he liked his pleasures. He especially had a way with the ladies and was a very good dancer, much better than me."

Just the utterance of a phrase like that brought his brother's presence back into their lives for a moment, in the form of a smile, a change of light around them.

"Your father, Fernando, was the practical one, and smarter than me—I was good with music, my boy, but when it came to those medical books, I just couldn't see the point of taxing my brain too much." Then: "And while I had no talents for such intellectual labors, your father could have easily been a musician—he was pretty good on the violin and could play a little piano. Who knows, he might have turned out to be a decent composer—you probably have that talent in your blood, too."

No mention of the puzzlement he experienced when he was alone, the sadness that came over him, when roaming through the rooms of his house on Olivares. He missed his family: his father, Doctor Leocadio Levis, poised over a microscope in his study; his

mother, Doña Concepción, whom his nephew knew well, kneeling before Israel as a young man, with a needle and thread in
hand, as she sewed a button back onto his shirt sleeve before a
concert; his younger sister, poor Anabella, breathing softly, her
face aglow with kindness and expectations, as she prepared to
turn a page of his music; and Fernando, so on top of life, studious
and filled with ambition, serenely moving through his days.

"I may be an old man now," he would say to his nephew, "but
when I look at you I am filled with pride, and so happy that you
are with me." Then: *"¿Tú sabes eso, sí?"* ("You know that, yes?").

"Yes, Uncle."

And though he had so many doubts about God, as they'd pass
by a church, the composer could not help but to quickly cross
himself, as was the custom of his mother; nor was he so far gone
with disillusion as to suspend his notion that religion was, at
heart, good, and though he no longer believed in "any of that nonsense," he would say, to honor his mother, "I don't know what
you believe, Victor, but never lose your curiosity about God, for
once that happens, you become dead inside—I have seen what
happens to such men and how they treat others."

Always, there was their parting, the composer saying to his
nephew, each time, "I will see you again, soon, won't I?"

"Yes, Uncle," Then: *"Hasta pronto,"* and off he would go, to his
wondrous future.

ANTONIO

As for feeling that he, in his own way, was helping along the
progress of youth, he could take pride not just in his nephew, but in

Antonio, who seemed to be thriving in that city. He was an eternally hopeful and happy soul, so it seemed to Levis, who had
always looked forward to hearing about the young man's day: "I
was walking along in the park and I met a very nice young woman,"
he would say. Or: "I had a great night, playing the trumpet with
some fellows in an alley near the Club Inferno!" And he surprised
the composer, one evening, when coming home from night school,
he announced: "I think I know what I want to do, Don Israel!"

And the composer had looked up from one of his late father's
books.

"I think I want to become a pharmacist—people will always be
getting sick!" He said this with such utter conviction that Levis
had smiled, saying: "I am happy to hear that, my boy."

SARAH RUBENSTEIN

Now and then he thought about Sarita Rubenstein; that they
had known each other at all now seemed an oddity, a matter of
that time and place, Paris, that business with reincarnation, his
time of "Jewishness," a piece of nonsense that belied the fact of
their mutual loneliness and that deep down he never truly
believed that their love would last. And what would such a young
and vital woman have done with him now, groaning just to get up
out of a chair, and with a mind so indifferent to sex that he would
be hard put to make love, even with her. At least, he knew that
she and her family had survived the war: when he had arrived
back in Paris, in June of 1945, frail and quite sick from his ordeal
(but did I really have anything to complain about, when I was still alive
and so many others were dead?), he had made inquiries about Sarah

Rubenstein, at the Hôtel Lutetia, a registration center for sur-
vivors. There he learned, to his relief, that she and her brother,
Georges, had never been apprehended, nor sent to a camp.

Happily (or unhappily) while he was recuperating in Madrid,
he had received a loving and tender letter from Sarah, who had
eventually tracked him down, reporting the details of what had
happened to her. She had lost her mother and father—they
had been "deported" to Auschwitz—but Sarita and her brother had
made their way to the north of France, thanks to the underground.
("*We were betrayed and had no choice but to leave Paris quickly,*" she
had written.) And she had fallen in love with a farmer, a member
of the resistance, her words falling both sorrowfully and with joy
upon his weak eyes, for in the end, lonely as he felt in the middle
of the day, he had taken heart that she was alive.

And Georges—what had he added to that letter as a post-
script, as if the war had not happened at all?

"*How is* Germinal *coming along?*"

"*My dear boy,*" Israel had written back. "*It is in a trunk, safe and
sound. The day I finish it, you will be the first to know.*"

And Levis had signed it: "*May God bless you.*" Why, he could
not say.

THEN THE DAY CAME WHEN RITA VALLADARES REENTERED HIS LIFE

Thirty-seven days had passed since the composer had returned to Habana that spring of 1947. By then, cynically disposed,
he had endured many a moment when, feeling useless and wasted,
he had (as happened every day of his life for the past three years)
become indifferent to the prospect of going to sleep without wak-

ing again. In his worse moods, he found the rituals of daily life pointless. His was a constant battle between adopting a posture of hopefulness and dejection. Memory, which had been his friend, had become a source of grief—*Another day,* he told himself on some mornings, *And for what?*

How to step forward into the future was something that perplexed him—he had been sapped of his creative energies by his last years in Europe. Buchenwald. He waited interminably for hours at a time, bored and feeling useless, until that point when he would get up from his chair and uncap a bottle of brandy, sipping until he got drunk and a desire to sleep came over him, sometimes retiring to his bed at three in the afternoon.

More visitors, honors, mail and requests for interviews came to the house, but, Levis, as he saw his days unfolding, believed that the pleasures of life were far beyond him. Though he was cheered by how some things never changed—the youthful beauty of his nephew, Victor, and his assistant, Antonio; the lively bustle of central Habana; the loveliness of the sea—Levis had tired of the vehicle that was his body and the thoughts that filled his head. Passing many of his moments alone, he waited for a resolution of the final mystery of life, his own death—perhaps, he thought, by a stroke (for he had suffered two of them in Spain), or by his own hand (the poisons in his father's old apothecary cabinet).

Yet, on another day, as he was sitting by his dining-room table going over some letters, he heard an unmistakable voice in the front entranceway, a rattle of bracelets and anklet jewelry, and he whiffed a lemon-scented perfume, and knew from the brisk clatter of high heels on the tile floors that Rita Valladares had finally come to see him again.

Even though it was a nearly unbearably hot late June day, the air humid and heavy, *"La Chiquita,"* fresh from her travels in Latin America, appeared before him, in a blue-and-white fringed dress and a pillbox hat, so untouched by the forces of nature that she exuded a coolness, as one would find inside the movie houses on Neptuno. Standing by the doorway to his parlor, she ran toward him, startling the composer with her enthusiasm. Flailing her hands about with a theatrical flourish, she cried out: "Israel, *mi vida,* I cannot tell you how happy I am to see you! My God, how much you've improved!"

When she had visited him in the hospital ward in Spain, during the first few months of his stay, he was so ill that he could barely open his eyes. He had thought it a dream, save for the flowers she had left him. Through the haze that was his poor vision, she had seemed to be leaning over him and singing softly a child's lullaby in her inimitable voice, even as she was weeping. He could vaguely remember hearing her say over and over again, "Israel, this is Rita speaking.... You must wake up ... when I count to three you will open your eyes.... One ... two ... three!" And he remembered hearing her beautiful voice echoing lovingly in the deep recesses of his mind. He had glimpsed her standing by his bed and taken her for an angel. Grasping her hand and feeling a great peace, he had not wanted that feeling of protection to go away.

No sooner had he acknowledged her presence, his ears burning red, then did she embrace him, but carefully, as the gargantuan wonder that had been her dear friend Israel was now a frail old man. How long she held him cannot be measured in earthly time. In those moments he left the room that defined his narrow life and found

himself running across a field when he was a boy, as if he were chas-
ing blue birds and swallows across the horizon again, as if he had
backtracked nearly fifty years. Then he passed through innumerable
concert salons, sitting down before a piano, with Rita by his side.
He crossed a hundred stages, a few steps behind Rita, in halls all
over Cuba and in Europe—looked out across a table, in many a
crowded seaside café, at Rita, as she was about to chew on a piece
of crispy plantain fritter or in the midst of a laugh (or looking at him
curiously) a hundred times—his life with Rita, with its infinite
moments, reduced like the converging lines and planes of a cubist
painting, dense with music notes and memories, inside Israel's head.

He found himself on the verge of tears. He found himself, as
he looked her over, saying: "Rita, I can't believe it's really you."

"Yes, of course it's me, my love," she told him. And then,
because he had closed the parlor's shutters to keep out the sun,
she drew them open so that the room was suddenly flooded with
light, declaring: "My God, Israel, is it true that you have become
something of a hermit?"

"No, Rita, I am just a little quiet these days. I much enjoy my
moments of rest."

"Ah, quiet and rest?" and she flailed the air as if swatting at a
fly. "You are too young to talk that way!"

"But Rita . . ."

"Mario Riviera at the conservatory tells me that you are refusing everything, even the easiest commission! But, *chiquito mío,*"
and she stomped her foot. "This is not going to go on, my dear
friend. Not at all! *Hombre,* I need you to write some songs for me—
there are others who are very good songwriters, mind you, but
you, dear Israel, are the best and you cannot refuse me."

"But I am retired my love. I've had it."

"No!" and she stomped her foot again, her anklets tinkling. "Too many times I have let you do what you want to do. I can-not—will not—allow that to happen again. Besides what are you going to do with yourself, anyway, my dear friend, but sit around here in this house doing nothing all day? That would be a crime, you understand?"

He found her ardor and determination amusing—the vivacious persona of the stage had, over the years, apparently taken over her everyday manner.

"Rita Valladares, are you nagging me?"

"Yes," she said happily. "And I will nag you to death."

He felt so invigorated by her presence that he could not resist smiling, and, on his feet, hoisting himself up from his chair, his weight balanced upon his cane—he wrapped *his* arms around her, repeating, *"Ay Rita, ay Rita."*

"Yes, yes, my boy. Where you were once my maestro, I will be yours."

And then she told him where and when she needed him: "First of all, I am giving a special performance at the Presidential Palace for Grau San Martín, in two weeks, so you had better start practicing your piano, for I will not sing with anyone else. If you refuse I will never speak to you again. And there is a new club that's just opened in the city, in the suburbs, La Tropicana, and I am giving a perfor-mance there too—and as you know, Israel, everybody still wants to hear *"Rosas,"* and I cannot think of anyone more suited to lead the orchestra than you, so you better get accustomed to the idea."

"But Rita . . ."

"And I need some new songs—don't forget that, okay, my love?"

And as world-weary and cantankerous as Israel Levis could be, he found himself saying, "Of course, as you know there is very little I wouldn't do for you, Rita."

HIS "HAPPY" OUTCOME

Rita had married for a third time by then, and though she was maintaining a quite busy schedule, with more tours and obligations to perform on the radio in Latin America and in the States, and had endured those burdens that came from being the most popular singer in Cuba, she took much care to bring the composer back into the world. And to a certain extent she succeeded, for from time to time he appeared by her side in the theaters of that city, a much venerated man—and it gave him more life.

One night in the Tropicana, when she took to the stage—dancing about and working the audience—the high point of her performance was her rendition of the song that she had made quite famous.

"Ladies and gentlemen, I am now going to sing a little song that I think you all know very well. Before I begin, I would like to introduce the composer of that most Cuban of *canciones*—ladies and gentlemen, my dear friend, El Maestro Israel Levis."

And she bowed, gesturing toward one of the tables near the front of the stage. A spotlight moved swiftly across the floor of the great open-air, palm-tree-encircled theater, falling upon him. An elderly white-haired gentleman, in the company of a young man, stood up, leaning on a cane, and waved, bowing toward each corner of the audience. As the applause died down, the composer, with some difficulty, slowly mounted the stage where he, in white tails, sat before a grand piano. Before raising his hands to conduct, he looked up at the night sky; a great faded silk scarf of stars—the Milky Way—floated in the darkness above him.

He smiled faintly and blew a kiss toward Valladares, who performed a raucous and lively version of that famous rumba, her penultimate number for that evening.

And there would be this:

Program honoring President Grau San Martín, at the Presidential
Palace, Habana, Cuba, July 20, 1947
At 1 P.M.
Himno Nacional Cubano—conducted by Luis Romero, Director of the
Municipal Band of Habana
Solo for Violin—Fritz Kreisler's "Liebesfreud," performed by
Professor José Molinas, and accompanied on the piano by
La Señora Augustina Molinas
Canciones Cubanas:
"Rosas y Violetas," by José Mauri
"Presentimiento," by Eduardo Sánchez de Fuentes
"Rosas Puras," by Israel Levis, sung by Rita Valladares, with piano
accompaniment by the composer

HABANA, 1951—AN OLD CALLING

He never finished *Germinal*, but during the last few years of his worldly existence, he resumed an old calling. An afternoon came when a very poor woman arrived at his door, with her young daughter, a pretty *mulata* of about seventeen, named Pilar Blanca.

"My daughter has a gift, Maestro," she told him. "Please let her play the piano for you."

"What am I going to do with such people," he had thought. But he could not bring himself to shut the door, and stoically led them into the parlor, where he sat Pilar down before the piano.

"She can only play by ear," the mother told him. "But listen to just how well she plays. She remembers everything from the radio and teaches herself the music on a broken-down piano in a bar near our house."

He sat, cane in hand, waiting. Elegant and nearly aristocratic in her movements, despite the poverty of her dress, she played a fragment from Rachmaninov, a fragment from Ignacio Cervantes, and ended with an entire piece by Lecuona, "Siboney."

She was good—*either you have it or you don't*—but he was puzzled, asking: "She is very talented, but what do you want from me?"

"Maestro, would you teach her? We have no money but I would come here to wash your clothes or cook for you—whatever you want."

A funny thing, since his return to Habana, as more time had gone by, he had begun to have a greater and greater difficulty in refusing to perform any act of kindness, and he told this young girl's mother: "I will do it, but, if you must know, I am not terribly well. I will do what I can."

Then he said: "Now leave me alone, and come back tomorrow at four."

The woman was so thrilled and grateful that she kissed the composer's hand, repeating again and again, *"Eres un santo"* ("You are a saint"). May God bring you a thousand blessings."

. . .

Teaching this young girl to read music and all the theories of harmony and composition that were useful tools to a pianist turned out to be the composer's greatest accomplishment, even better than the writing of that simple song. She brought so much life and youth into that house that it pleased him greatly. Many a day found him at the appointed hour, usually four, waiting impatiently by his front gate, and though she always turned up with a sheaf of music in hand, and in a simple dress and white low-heeled shoes, she may as well have alighted from Heaven on a cloud. The hours they spent together, the composer scolding, cajoling, always ended with a single moment of tenderness, when she, ever quiet, and with a glint of respect and gratitude in her lovely almond eyes, gave him a kiss of thanks. (And she had many reasons for this, for in his kindness, and his weariness over the materials of this life, the composer had never charged her for a single lesson and often gave her pocket change for the bus and a soda. Even when she turned up with a few pesetas to pay the composer, he refused: "What are a few hours in the life of an old man when he is helping a young girl realize her talents?" he'd say. And sometimes he would tell her, "There are some things in the pantry for you to take home to your mother."

Often he could not resist the idea of buying her gifts of candy, or the occasional dress, during his increasingly infrequent strolls through the city.

In that time, he had also become most intrigued by the little friendship she struck up with his assistant, Antonio (who always made sure to find his way into that house when she was just finishing up her lessons), the composer happy to see them making their way off to an ice-cream parlor like two children, or to the park for a "walk," happy to see the masklike expression of this young girl, Pilar Blanca, break up more and more into a *sonrisa* at the sight of him, as if she were seeing the promise of her own future.

A FEW YEARS LATER, AN AUTUMN AFTERNOON

On an autumn afternoon in 1953, one not so different from the day that he wrote *"Rosas Puras,"* the composer was in a good mood, for his student Pilar Blanca had once again arrived for her lesson at the customary hour of four, her musical progress so swift and the refinement and delicacy of her playing such that she, at nineteen now, had been recently accepted into a performance program at the Conservatorio in Habana. And Levis, who doted upon her as he would his own daughter, was delighted to learn that she and Antonio had decided to get married. So to give his blessing, the composer, despite a waning of his bodily strength, had arranged for a party to celebrate these nuptials, and to that end the parlor had been prepared for company and he had invited a number of his friends and musical luminaries in for drinks and food and cake later that evening. The fabulous Rita Valladares herself, who had a fondness for both Antonio and Pilar, was to partake of the festivities, as well as a contingent of Pilar's friends from her *barrio,* the slums of Las Yaguas—poor girls and musicians, toothless relatives who, to his maid's consternation, would soon swarm over that household in the revelry of the feast ("May God spare us headaches," she declared).

Nevertheless, the composer was in good spirits, for the presence of young people somehow made him feel more youthful
himself. And just seeing a smile on Pilar's lips, as delightful as a
beautiful melody, was something he always looked forward to.

Nearly twenty-five years had passed since he had written his most
well-known composition, and yet he was possessed by the impression that only a thin veil separated him from that time, which,
though inaccessible, seemed to surround him. He thought it un-
healthy—a bit mad, in fact—to dwell upon this kind of thing, but
the truth was that memory had become one of his greatest companions. In recent months he had become more nostalgic about his
past and seemed to take an even greater pleasure in those items in
his life that inflamed his memory, as if he knew that he would soon
be taking his leave of this world.

Earlier that same day, he had gone through a closet and discovered, wrapped in felt, the gold and silver medals that had been given
to him, for first and second prizes in music from the Gallego Society
(juvenile category, 1904), a gold medal that he received from the
World Exposition of Habana in 1913 for zarzuela composition, then
another gold medal for performance from the Sociedad Pro-Arte
Musical de La Habana (1917). While foraging about he came across
a few pages of manuscript for the 1922 zarzuela, La Vida de María-
Elena, a piano roll of a song from another zarzuela, La Virgen de las
Aguas. He came across a program from the Palau auditorium for El
Cuervo (translation by Manny Cortez), 1923. A newspaper clip-
ping, from the English-language Havana Journal, mentioning his par-

ticipation in the Exposition of Seville, in 1929, where he had played the piano for King Alfonso XIII and Queen Victoria Eugénie.

He found himself appraising an oil painting of himself, circa 1932, that hung over a mantel, the artist identified as one "J. Es' calante," Levis depicted with the formality of a judge or a profes' sor, thick set in a white linen suit, a cigar in hand, his face heavily jowled and languid, soft eyes peering out and somehow lost in the largeness of his head, his high temples thinning, his brow wide, a man resembling an amalgamation of famous personalities—in him is seen the pallidness and intelligence of a pope, the soulfulness of the guitarist Segovia, and yet somehow, in the broadness of his fea' tures and the mirthful lilt to his mouth, as if he were about to laugh, the gargantuan kindness of Oliver Hardy—*El Gordito*.

What would become of all of this when he was gone? he wondered.

He no longer enjoyed his solitude, a devastating loneliness over' whelming him in the absence of Rita or of Pilar Blanca. Happy as he was about Pilar's successes with her auditions and public per' formances, he wondered if he would lose her to the Conservatory? ("No," she promised him. "I will always come to see you, Mae' stro.") And he wondered whether Rita would continue to come and see him every Sunday afternoon, when she was in Habana. ("You are like family to me, Israel," she told him again and again.) And his nephew, Victor Levis? He had gone off to the United States, to the city of Baltimore and a program in internal medicine at Johns Hopkins. (How he missed the boy.)

THE LOVELINESS OF A DREAM

That afternoon, around four o'clock, Pilar turned up at the maestro's residence for her lesson, ebullient and happy over the prospect of that evening's party. She arrived with Antonio, laden down with a large cake, and as was their practice, she and the com-poser retired to his study, where he took his place near the piano, his eagle-headed cane in hand, a brandy set beside him on a table. She was a formal creature with correct posture and long dark hair that hung down to the small of her back. Quietly, she would draw back her hair, tie it up with a rubber band and turn toward Levis to await his signal to begin. She smiled at him with an awareness that this man had already done much to change her life, for not only had he found her a good used spinet piano on which she could practice at home, but had promised her that she would one day study in Paris, where he still had connections. She smiled, as if to say, *I love you, Maestro, but I dare not say so.* Even she, in her vir-ginal existence, could see that he still had some life left in him, given the way he would steal glances at her when he did not think she would notice. The composer simply staring at her, luxuriating in her beauty and youth.

She was wearing a lovely pink dress and flat-heeled shoes, a rose stuck in her hair, perhaps in emulation of a photograph that Levis kept on his piano of Rita Valladares with a *radiante,* or "Cuban rose," tucked above her right ear. Perhaps Pilar wore the rose because her presence in his life—which brought him so much joy and solace—was also the indirect emanation of a song. And because she knew that there was something about the very sight of a rose that made the composer regard her with greater tender-

ness—and that when she wore a rose in her hair, his eyes sometimes brightened with happiness, or with sadness, as if by looking
at her he was gazing into some great distance at something that he
impossibly longed for.

"What shall I play, Don Israel?"

"A little Bach," he told her. "Please."

He would never know what would happen to her career, never
know that the young girl would one day find herself as a concertizer
and teacher working under the name of Pilar Solar (née Blanca) and
travel the world with her husband, Antonio, ever by her side. For
that matter, he would never know that his own nephew, the future
Doctor Victor Levis, would leave Cuba in the mid-1950s after getting an advanced degree in internal medicine at Johns Hopkins
University, eventually to settle down in New York City, where he
would have a Park Avenue practice; nor that he would spend certain
of his evenings with his American wife and two daughters listening
to recordings of Cuban music, among them his uncle's more famous
compositions, for which he would scour the shops of the city on the
weekends. He listened to this music with both affection and an
exile's sadness in his heart, remembering his uncle with fondness.

Nor would Levis know how Rita Valladares would die, years
later, in 1971, from pneumonia contracted on a tour in Japan—the
chilly breezes of Hokkaido in late September, a resistance to anti-
biotics and a tendency to push herself too hard the causes. Never
know that this dearest friend and great love would eventually
expire in a flower-filled room of a Mexico City Hospital, her sons
and grandchildren, fourth husband and two chihuahuas by her
side, that his name would never be far from her lips, that she
would be crying with tender thoughts about him.

. . .

Pilar always pleased the maestro by playing two of the pieces he himself had first learned as a child, pieces he had used to teach Pilar how to read and navigate the torrential seas of notated music. She played "Prelude and Fugue, Book 2, No. 12 from *The Well-Tempered Clavier*" and then began "Prelude and Fugue, Book 1, No. 2," by J. S. Bach, each executed with facility and finesse.

Listening carefully, he closed his eyes, nodding, keeping time with his cane. In the midst of the second piece, Levis got up from his chair, telling Pilar, "Keep going, *mi vida*, I'm just going to lie down for a few moments." On his way he picked out a rose from a vase and placed it on the piano before her as she continued her lit-tle recital. He was stretching out on a divan in his study, counting out the time and tapping the knuckles of his left hand with his right index finger. Then, in the midst of a reverie, as notes cascaded down around him, just as the composer was experiencing a few moments of contentment that sweetened the more bitter brews of his life, he fell into a dream from which, so it would seem to others, he would not awaken.

That evening, just as the clock was striking the hour of five, he saw his father, Doctor Leocadio Levis, and not Pilar Blanca, sitting before the piano. And his mother, Doña Concepción, just as she was entering the parlor with a tray of food and drinks, and when he blinked and looked again, he noticed how the parlor was filling with guests. Were these people coming to the house in honor of Pilar and Antonio's impending marriage? If so, they were dressed in a quite fanciful and antiquated manner—the men in long-tailed coats, vests and looping neckties, the women with their mantillas, hair combs and fans, suffering greatly under their many-layered dresses—*Hasn't anyone told them how times have changed?* And, joy of joy, he saw Fernando as he had once been years and years before, heading out in all his handsomeness and earnest demeanor to a dancehall, and at the same time he saw his father sitting by his desk examining a bird feather through his microscope, a swarm of butterflies and hummingbirds floating everywhere about him in that room. He found himself in an atmosphere in which bells seemed to be ringing here and there in the air, notes dropping and rising in so fluid a fashion, and he heard the strains of a violin playing the melody of his *"Una Noche de Amor"* and found that he was no longer in the parlor of his house on a quiet autumn afternoon but walking along the Paseo de Prado with his family, circa 1904, the air scented with orange blossoms, magnolias and Arabian jasmine. His father was wearing a pair of wire spectacles and a dark hat, like Sigmund Freud, and his mother, a wide-winged sunhat and a dress whose skirt reached the floor, his brother Fernando beside him and beloved sister Anabella holding his hand and playing as she often did an odd little game of tapping out notes on his palm with a challenge that he guess the notes she was imitating. Those moments of recollection astounded Levis, how vivid and real they seemed to be. He recognized himself as a sixteen-year-old on the stage of the Conservatory, bowing before a clamorous and greatly excited audience, and even as he took his bows, he was sitting down before an organ in the Iglesia de Nuestra Señora de Monserrate, preparing to play a Stabat Mater. No sooner had he pressed the single note of D than he found himself in a Habana movie house, the Rialto, improvising on the piano as images of *The Four Horsemen of the Apocalypse,* starring Rudolph Valentino, flickered onto a canvas screen, and, at the same time, he found himself standing before the high red door to a brothel known as Marina's and, just like that, he was resting back naked, music forming spontaneously in his thoughts, even as his majestic virility was making a young girl of about sixteen, whose skin was as warm as candle wax and was to the touch like honey to the tongue, marvel at his humble and gentlemanly demeanor. And even as he seemed to experience an orgasm that made his eyes tear, he also felt his knees aching from kneeling before the altar in the Iglesia de San Francisco, alongside his mother, who had just finished a good cry over the death of his father, whose face he remembered touching when he was a little boy and he would creep up behind him as he sat before the piano playing the beautiful and timestopping music of Bach (and, of course, that of the wonderful Ignacio Cervantes!). Levis, delighted by his stealth, as if he had planned an ambush, squealing into his father's ear, that wonderful man turning away from the piano and hoisting him up onto his lap, holding him closely. And at the same time, as he saw his father being thrown from a horse, he became aware of walking with his brother and sister across a field of wildflowers in the countryside.

What a sheer joy to see, brilliant against the horizon, a band of pure and silvery dusk laying down under the weight of a thousand dazzling colors, as if the sky was itself going to sleep; and hearing the humming night bells and the evening stars popping up one after the other, letting out with celestial sighs; and he remembered how beautiful it was to look at such a light, when in the perfect faith of childhood one believed that God was not only everywhere but that He was walking beside you, nourishing you with His light and air and water and food, that every creature good or bad was one of His heavenly agents, put in this world to inspire you.

And at the moment of that thought he was a child again playing an E♭ scale for the first time, then elated by the fact that he could suddenly read a piano score. There had been the loveliest instant of first invention when sitting before the piano he created a prayer song for a child's choir, and he remembered how, once upon a time, he had entertained the notion of becoming a simple music teacher in the schools of Habana. He saw himself in that other life, posed in long robes at the head of a juvenile orchestra before whom he was taking a bow. And he suddenly remembered the exact melody he had composed for his first original bolero, *"Lagrimas y Sonrisas,"* which he had written in 1907, just after his sister Anabella had died. But he was also just sitting down to smoke a cigar and drink a brandy, maybe eat some croquettes, in the Campana Bar with his pal Manny Cortez, as they worked on one song or the other, the composer unable to keep himself from leaning forward to embrace his friend of old. How luxurious did those moments seem, with the warmth of Manny's face touching his own, the precious scents of maleness filling his nostrils—of tobacco, of sweat, of a cologne-dappled shirt collar, of virility itself rising from Cortez's whole being, Levis nearly on the verge of tears. *I've missed you, my friend.* And soon they were languishing away again in a brothel, a rickety fan, black blades spinning inside an uneven frame and chirping like cicadas, in its efforts to cool the steaminess of a parlor room, Levis playing the piano and Manny, young and vital again, reciting for the gathering of harlots and louts a bit of Poe (whose spirit inhabited the shadows)—*Those were beautiful nights, were they not?*

Somehow, as Manny leaned forward to pour Levis a drink, the composer could also feel the softness of Sarah Rubenstein's breast touching his lips as she pressed herself into his mouth, her expanded nipple tasting of strawberries and wine, his ears filling with the music of her pleasurable moans, as now they were engaging in four different acts of love simultaneously, Levis straddled by her, Levis entering her from behind, Levis ravishing her from above, and Levis experiencing the depths of her damp and deep center while sitting in a bedroom chair that wobbled precariously, nearly breaking under his massive bulk and making them both laugh. *What we had I cannot say, but I adored you and your daughter very much.* And her little girl, Paulette, came running into his arms, and he planted kisses on her neck and gave her candies, even as he walked along a park near the Eiffel Tower with Georges—Paris and life itself, in those moments, eternally delightful. Surely they would have all stayed together like one happy family, counting the clouds as they passed overhead on spring afternoons, had the world been a little different.

But who could say if he had truly loved her, for his dear Rita was never far from his thoughts, and with that the composer found himself on a bench in the waiting room of a Consolidated Railways of Cuba station in a small crossroads town called Jiguani, in the eastern part of the island, at nine in the morning on a September day in 1927 or so.

In his jacket pocket were three Suarez Murias cigars (but they could have been Coronas or Lopez & Co. or La Escepciónes, as he had once enjoyed them all) and next to him a flask of brandy, from which he frequently sipped, offering a taste of that magical elixir to the contingent of musician and composer friends with whom he had been traveling as part of a review. There were about a dozen of them, and most were lolling, half-asleep on hard benches, their eyes peeking out from under the down-turned brims of their cane hats, waiting for the seven o'clock train that had not yet arrived. The ticket seller could not explain the delay because telegraph lines had been cut in the area, and rumors abounded that a section of tracks along the route to and from Santiago had been pried apart from their beddings by "unionist" agitators; Levis getting up from time to time to see if the train would finally come chugging into the station from the distance.

The odors of cattle and cut grass, of a sugar mill refinery and tobacco leaves drying in the sun, flowed into his nostrils, the tracks trailing off into fields of cane, high bending palms and the incredible blueness of that Cuban sky; Levis turning to tell a composer friend—was it Sindo Garay, José Mauri or Ernesto Lecuona (or one of many others, dozens in all, with whom he had traveled and whose faces floated in and out of that waiting room along with their unforgettable famous melodies?)—that they would have to wait a little longer, *may as well have a drink, my friend, even if it was a little early in the day, yes?* At once he seemed to be looking around for Rita Valladares herself who, with her golden lunar earrings and a flapper's bangle over her brow and frilly blue dress, had stepped outside onto the platform to go over a score with a trumpet player named Mario de la Torriente, and just like that, even as Levis began to smile over the prospect of greeting Rita, he blinked and saw that he was standing on the platform of another train station, Bobigny, in Paris, circa 1943, amid a crowd of beleaguered Jews.

As the Nazi soldiers corralled these poor souls into freight cars, Levis was singled out and escorted to a first-class coach at the front of the train. The velvet-covered seats were so comfortable that he nearly dozed, half-expecting a porter to come through with champagne and caviar. Then, just as his eyes were beginning to close, he looked up to see none other than General Knochen himself, looming over him.

"Have you been told where you are going?" the commandant asked in Spanish. "Usually men in your position are deported to Auschwitz. But I have arranged that you will be transported to the Weimar Station, to a place near Ettersberg. It's quite lovely there. *Un lugar muy maravilloso.*"

A whistle blew and the train lurched forward, the composer watching the countryside through the window, nature so beautiful that the war no longer seemed to exist. Even as Bach continued to ring brilliantly around him in the study of his home, he could see in the fields great stacks of hay, lovely and rounded as breasts, and grain silos so phallically magnificent, the horizon itself with its hills and dipping, shadow-centered meadows, as beautiful as a woman's hips, the sunlight itself flowing as mercury into the aubergine Earth, and he could see in that very same distance, just beyond the meadows, a view of the sea as it appeared along the northwestern coast of Cuba, and he knew that he was somehow heading back to Habana again, to a more peaceful time, long before the horrors had come into the world.

He was carried by that music into a rapturous circumstance, back to that one night out on the veranda of a social club when Rita Valladares gave her heart to him; but this time he, being a courageous and independent man possessed of fortitude, accepted her love. Now they strolled arm in arm through Habana, their own plump little children eating *maní*—"peanuts"—out of paper cones trailing behind them, the two of them, their family, living blissfully forever.

Stars up in the sky, ever so clear, music resounding everywhere.

A piano on every street corner, handsome singers and beautiful female dancers in every alley. Orchestras performing in every park. And processions of religious folk praying and chanting, moving slowly across the city. Of course, it was possible that life, as his old Buddhist friends in Paris would say, was only a dream and that Levis was just capitulating to the ultimate truth in those moments. But in the loveliness of that contentment that seemed to go on forever, he also saw Rita Valladares's face, high up over the buildings and treetops of Habana, looking down over the city from a billboard, filling his heart with both joy and terror: RITA VALLADARES SINGS "ROSAS PURAS."

"Oh Rita. Hold me, my love."

The radio stations of Cuba played his music for days; his funeral procession to the Cementerio Colón, where he would be forever united with his family, drew thousands, among them Rita Valladares, whose photograph, in mourning, appeared in the Habana newspapers.

"I can't believe he's gone," she was quoted as saying. "It had seemed only a few years before, in the 1920s, that we had worked and traveled together, performing in the small towns of Cuba and all through the provinces, at sugar mills and tobacco plantations, a happy time. Wherever we went there was always a group of us to go out late into the night, enjoying ourselves, the maestro always composing new bits of music on the spot or feeling compelled to take his place before the piano in a club or a restaurant or someone's home, even after we had spent the night performing. You know that he was a little on the heavy side and quite tall, so these performances took it out of him, and yet, with his brow covered with sweat, he would always find the strength to play his music. . . . One evening, in the town of Trinidad, we were invited into the salon of a quite wealthy man, and we stayed up all night drinking rum and singing until five in the morning—it was even too much for me—but he was still sitting at the piano and going strong when I could barely keep my eyes open. It was as if he never really wanted to go to sleep, that he could not, deep down, bear to be away from people—nor from the music of Cuba that he loved so dearly. . . ."

In the United States, the NBC radio network broadcast an hour-long tribute to his career that was heard all over the country. Commemorative concerts in Habana and other cities in Cuba were organized, Rita Valladares presiding over most of them. She and many others had wept at his passing.

A

SIMPLE

POSTSCRIPT

How was it that I came to write the music for *"Rosas Puras"*? It is better to speak first about how it is to compose any piece of music. This process begins with the recollection of notes that may have come to you out of the very air—or out of a dream, or even from one's memory of the tone of a voice during a conver-sation; or it begins with the imagining of a lullaby or child's song from youth—a few notes that for some reason have stayed with you, though slightly transformed by what Sigmund Freud calls the unconscious mind. Or you have discerned a certain pattern in the music of birds or hear a unique harmony in the ringing of church bells—these resonate and somehow remain with you when you sit down before the piano, trying to make sense of these sounds in your mind. . . .

I usually get my ideas by hearing them first in my head, and then I whistle the melody or line and therefore bring it out roughly into the world. But sitting down before a piano changes everything, those notes come and you place them in the context of chords, which add harmonies, and in doing so your mind is always changed—and slowly it comes. Something new, some-thing pleasing—that is my hope, anyway.

I can write with lyrics, but I most often prefer to compose the music first and then present this to a clever wordsmith, like my dear friend Manny Cortez—though I always imply the idea. I say, "Manny, this is going to be a song about the trolleys. Or this is music about a girl who sees an apparition of the Virgin." Whatever. That was the case with *"Rosas Puras."* I had a melody that came instantly to me, arranged with the assistance of that unseen and underappreciated inspiration which can only come from God.

　　—From "Interview with a Cuban Composer," *El Diario de la Marina,* June 1932